THE ARIZONA GAME

Georgina Hammick has three grown-up children and lives in Wiltshire. She has published two collections of short stories, *People for Lunch* and *Spoilt*, which are also available in Vintage. *The Arizona Game* was short-listed for the 1996 Whitbread First Novel Award.

D1043497

BY GEORGINA HAMMICK

People for Lunch
Spoilt
The Virago Book of Love and Loss (editor)
The Arizona Game

Georgina Hammick

THE ARIZONA GAME

Published by Vintage 1997

2 4 6 8 10 9 7 5 3 1

Copyright © Georgina Hammick 1996

The right of Georgina Hammick to be identified as the author of this work has been asserted by her in accordance with the Copyright, Designs and Patents Act, 1988

This book is sold subject to the condition that it shall not by way of trade or otherwise, be lent, resold, hired out, or otherwise circulated without the publisher's prior consent in any form of binding or cover other than that in which it is published and without a similar condition including this condition being imposed on the subsequent purchaser

The author wishes to thank the copyright holders for permission to reproduce extracts from the following songs: 'Ragtime Cowboy Joe' © EMI, music by Lewis Muirand Maurice Abrahams, words by Grant Clarke, © 1912 Shawnee Press Inc., USA and Redwood Music Ltd, UK, reproduced by permission of Francis Day and Hunter Ltd; 'Those Magnificent Men in their Flying Machines' © 1965 EMI Catalogue Partnership, EMI Miller Catalogue Inc., USA, worldwide print rights controlled by Warner Bros Publications Inc/IMP Ltd; 'Leaving on a Jet Plane' © 1967 Cherry Lane Music Ltd, administered for the UK and Eire by Harmony Music Ltd

First published in Great Britain by
Chatto & Windus Ltd, 1996

Vintage
Random House, 20 Vauxhall Bridge Road, London SW1V 2SA

Random House Australia (Pty) Limited
20 Alfred Street, Milsons Point, Sydney
New South Wales 2061, Australia

Random House New Zealand Limited
18 Poland Road, Glenfield,
Auckland 10, New Zealand

Random House South Africa (Pty) Limited
Endulini, 5A Jubilee Road, Parktown 2193, South Africa

Random House UK Limited Reg. No. 954009

A CIP catalogue record for this book
is available from the British Library

ISBN 0 09 945731 8

Papers used by Random House UK Ltd are natural, recyclable products made from wood grown in sustainable forests. The manufacturing processes conform to the environmental regulations of the country of origin

Printed and bound in Great Britain by
Cox & Wyman, Reading, Berkshire

For Tom, Kate and Rose

'There's a lot of sadness and madness in our family,' Aunt Hope said. 'I hope you don't catch it.'

I was twelve years old, my aunt was forty-six, and we were sitting at the kitchen table going through a shoe box of old family photographs. I knew, although she hadn't mentioned her, that my aunt was thinking of my mother when she said that; but she also meant their father, my grandfather, Reginald Grissom (whose studio portrait, in First World War army uniform we'd just been looking at), who blew his head off with a double-barrelled 16-bore in his own front hall while his wife ('his third wife, no relation of yours, Hannah') was out shopping. He did not leave a note, but there were unpaid bills on his desk and stacks more, in unopened brown envelopes, in the pigeonholes and drawers of the bureau.

Grandfather's widow had known nothing of their money troubles, Aunt Hope told me, because those were the days when wives weren't expected to worry their pretty little heads about such matters. Like my grandmother, his second wife, before her, she'd not been allowed her own chequebook, let alone to see the monthly statements of her husband's five bank accounts. On Monday mornings at breakfast he'd hand over her housekeeping for the week in cash, caution her to spend it wisely – there'd be no possibility of more if she miscalculated – and, slipping *The Times* under his left arm, hurry away to his underground train. When wife number three needed a winter coat, a hat or a pair of shoes for best, my grandfather would take time out of his lunch hour to lead her to the department store of his choice, where he'd sit on a gilt chair outside the changing rooms, sighing and jabbing the point of his umbrella into the carpet. Aunt Hope said she knew all this because she'd had to accompany her father and stepmother on more than one of these missions. If my step-grandmother found something she liked that my grandfather did not like, he'd refuse to buy it; if she tried on something she was certain didn't suit her but that he approved, then he would. 'Provided the price was right,' Aunt Hope explained.

Then there was Great-Uncle Angus Grissom, my grandfather's elder brother (and better-looking, according to the photographs), who fell out of his office window eight floors up and was impaled on the handsome black railings in the street below. The verdict had been accidental death since there was no proof of his having jumped, his secretary having her back turned at the time. 'But windows are quite hard to fall out of,' my aunt said, 'unless you're very drunk.'

There were drunks in our family too, generations of them, she told me. There were sad people who drank, and people who drank and then became sad. 'No one's exactly sure about alcohol addiction. It's not clear whether it's more the cause of problems or more the result of problems. It's a seamless, circular business, I think.' My aunt took a thoughtful sip of her whisky, first drink of the evening.

But what about ugliness in families? Aunt Hope had said nothing about that. In the shoe box, which had a sticker on the side: 'Style: ladies' court; Type: calf; Shade: tan; Size: 4½', there were curling snapshots of bikers and hikers with wind in their hair; stiff grey-card studio portraits of babies without clothes and bald men with moustaches. There were group photos, taken to mark weddings and christenings, that exposed forced smiles, long faces, crazy laughter. I was on a quest for beauty; I wanted proof that I had a chance of being beautiful myself one day; but photograph after photograph revealed the absurdity of such a hope. If this tribe was anything to go by, my eyes would get smaller year by year, my thighs bigger, my calves chunkier, my back longer, my legs – how? – shorter. By the time I was twenty my nose would be beginning to cast a crooked shadow over my mouth, while at the same time it spread sideways to invade my cheeks. My mouth would not grow; it would tighten first and then fold in on itself. By the time I reached thirty, the pores on my face would be opening into craters and my chin would be cushioned by a second, boneless one. By the time I was forty... No wonder Aunt Hope had never dignified this collection by pasting them into an album! No wonder so many of my prematurely decayed relations took to the bottle or topped themselves!

I placed the photographs I'd been through upside down on the table and sneaked a look at my aunt's profile. The face I knew so well was not beautiful, no, you could not call it that, but it was not ugly, I was relieved to see. (Relieved, because most people thought I took after my aunt in various physical ways.) Aunt Hope's was a sharp, amusing face. She did not look older than her age, I decided. Her brown eyes were not enormous, but they had thick lashes that curled out and then over, like a film star's in a thirties movie. The eyes themselves were unusually bright and when Aunt Hope was happy or intrigued they darted about, as a bird's eyes are said to do. They could be penetrating or mysterious. Very fierce sometimes. (I knew about dead eyes, the ones that never have any expression; Mrs Wanthorpe, our geography teacher, had them.) Also, it was Aunt Hope's face and her brown eyes that Uncle Ber had loved. He used to sing a song about them, an Irish song, he said it was:

> Those brown eyes I love so well
> Those brown eyes I long to see!
> How I long for those brown eyes –
> Strangers they have grown to be.

I'd liked this song when Uncle Ber sang it: the words, which were sad, and the tune, although at the time it had seemed a silly song for him to sing. Aunt Hope was his wife and they lived together – so why should he long for her brown eyes? They could hardly be strangers when they were the first eyes he saw when he woke in the morning.

'Has anyone in our family ever been famous?' I asked Aunt Hope. (If beauty had passed us by, and a sense of style – I was thinking of the limp cardigans and belted gabardines that, the photographs showed, had for years been standard wear for our relations, even for weddings – surely there must be something, or someone, in our history we could be proud of?)

'Not famous exactly, no.' Aunt Hope had found a blue envelope in the box; it contained more photographs, small ones with frilly edges, and she was peering at them, chortling and groaning by turn. 'Here's another of your grandfather. Look, there's me, and there's your mother, and that skinny one is my friend Mariebel who came on holiday with us for some reason I don't remember.'

The snapshot she handed me was brown and had a tear in it. It made me think of the sepia sketch 'Children on the Shore' we had on the wall at the top of the stairs. Here was my suicide-grandfather grinning and kneeling up on the sand, one arm around Aunt Hope and one arm round my mother, both sitting cross-legged and scowling at the sun; here was Aunt Hope's friend Mariebel, her raised arm an out-of-focus smear, about to smash a sandcastle with her spade. The tear, which started at the top left-hand corner, had made a ragged chalk stripe on its glossy surface – sideways first, then down through Aunt Hope's outstanding, frizzly hair; down, down, to the droopy groin of my suicide-grandfather's woollen swimming trunks. I stared at him, at his awful trunks, big nose and toothy grin. I know something you don't know, I told him, and the knowledge made me feel superior and uneasy. You're going to die a gruesome, violent death, I warned him; but the longer I looked at that sunny holiday scene, the harder it was to believe he would. It was such an ordinary face, and the scene itself was ordinary: in the foreground, a ruckled beach towel and the greaseproof leavings of a picnic ('What d'you eat at the seaside?' someone had asked me recently at school, and, when I shook my head, '*Sand*wiches, stupid!'); in the background, dunes and a row of beach huts with bold-striped awnings. There was something bothering about a snapshot's power to freeze the moment with a single click or snap – which a painting, taking hours, if not days or months to paint, could only ever pretend to do. I wanted to know what had happened next, and pictured to myself the sandcastle's collapse; my aunt and mother breaking free from their father's stranglehold and grizzling for ice cream; my suicide-grandfather heaving himself to his feet, dusting the peppery sand from his calves and knees. It was only a step from seeing this to being there. I could smell the sea then, and the seaweed (there were little shiny piles of it strung out in a line in the foreground); I could hear the gulls, crying like babies; I could feel that 1930s sun on my back and shoulders. I could run to the cold repeating frill at the sea's edge, which was not visible in the photograph, and I did so, and the wet-ribbed sand hit my feet hard in the instep. Bypassing the tatty picnic things and the children, squabbling over the spade, I ran the other way, up the beach. My goal this time was the grassy lip of the dunes and a view out over the sea, but the closer I got to it, and the deeper, drier, looser and hotter the sand, the slower my progress until I was almost at a standstill, running on the spot, marking time. I was about to take my clogged sandals off (to hold them by the toes and watch the sand slide and collect in the heels), when Aunt Hope said, 'Guess who this is.'

Who was it? Who? Who was this beautiful person? She had beautiful hair, thick and wavy, loosely piled on top. How were we related? Tell me, Aunt Hope!

I beamed at the photograph and shook my head; I had no idea who she could be. 'I don't know. Tell me.'

'I'll give you a clue. She took the seaside one you've just been looking at.'

Oh. I hadn't thought at all about the photographer, that there had to be one. My grandmother Grissom? But it couldn't be her. She'd died when I was two, but lived for ever in a fancy silver frame on the chest of drawers in Aunt Hope's bedroom. Behind her was the shut iron gate of her Edinburgh terrace, and behind that a hydrangea bush and a bay window. The hydrangea was in flower, so it had to be summertime – except that Granny, hugely fat, was dressed for winter in a strangling fox fur. When I quizzed Aunt Hope about this once, she told me my grandmother had goitre, and 'wore that horrible thing all year round to disguise the swelling'. 'My mother was in her fifties when that photograph was taken,' Aunt Hope had remarked another time. In her fifties? I'd have guessed seventy-five at least.

Aunt Hope saw that I'd given up. 'Well, it's my step-mother,' she said, 'and your mother's stepmother, of course. Your step-grandmother. Irene, my father's third wife, the one I've been telling you about. So no blood relation of yours. Sorry about that.'

I blushed. My aunt had known all along what I'd been searching for in the shoe box! She'd understood exactly what a disappointment the words 'no blood relation' would be. (I was not merely disappointed, I was amazed. I'd formed a picture of my step-grandmother already – a picture of a mouse. Anyone who could have gone along with my grand-father's humiliating behaviour over the housekeeping money and the clothes-buying had to be a mouse.)

'We hated her,' Aunt Hope said without emotion. 'Your mother and I detested her.'

I looked again. There was nothing mouselike about my step-grandmother Irene; on the other hand there was no cruelty in her lovely eyes and mouth that I could see. Then I remembered that everyone hates their stepmothers. There were at least a dozen people in my year at school who had stepmothers and they all hated them.

I wanted to ask: 'Have there been any murderers in our family?' but at this moment her friend Jocelyn put her head round the door. 'It's nearly dark, Hope! Oughtn't we to shut the hens up?' And Aunt Hope rushed away to put her boots on.

After Aunt Hope left the kitchen, I put the photographs back in the shoe box, all of them save the one of my step-grandmother. In my bedroom, in a plaited-straw bread basket, I kept a collection of things that I'd picked up, or that had been given me, over the years: pretty things, shells and tiny, egg-shaped white pebbles, unusual buttons, bits of coloured glass. My beautiful step-grandmother should join these, I decided. 'Irene.' I said her name out loud. 'Good-night, Irene.' I knew the song because in the record cabinet, which Uncle Ber had made for Aunt Hope's forty-second birthday, there were five ten-inch 78s (there had once been many more, but the rest had not survived the journey when we moved to the country) and 'Goodnight, Irene' was one of them. 'Goodnight, Irene, goodnight, Irene, I'll see you in my dreams.' I put the photograph in my pocket. It would have to be buried at the bottom of the bread basket, I realised; but I'd be able to bring it out if I felt like it. When I was alone in my room with the door shut.

I was curious about murderers in the family because I believed I was one – in my heart at least. I was eight years old when I 'killed' my mother. I did it by mistake and it happened like this.

The year is 1968, it's a cold February morning and I'm eating my dinner in the Big Classroom at St Paul's Primary. There are two sittings and this is the second. (The Infants always eat first while the Juniors have to carry on with lessons in Classroom 2. As soon as the meaty gravy smell creeps under the partition wall, our ears become deaf to Miss Blewitt. They're tuned only to our dinner bell, and even when Miss B claps her hands in that dry-skinned, desperate way of hers it's useless – she's lost us for good. We slide

around on our seats, nudge rulers or exercise books accidentally on purpose to the floor and take an age to retrieve them,
bang our desk lids one after another. Lifting our heads, we
pretend to be dogs, sniffing the air with exaggerated, noisy
sniffs. And we speculate out loud: Corned-beef hash, I
reckon! No, mince and mash. Meat pie! Toad-in-the-hole?
Sniff sniff sniff.) I'm eating my dinner, which today is
potatoes, carrots and knuckle bones, bumpy islands in a grey,
fat-glazed sea, and called Irish stew. I'm spooning it in with
my pudding spoon, which is not allowed, adding little pinch-
es of salt because food can never be too salty for me, when
the boy opposite points his knife at my face.

'Hey, you! Hey, Hannah!' he shouts into a sudden silence.
'Why doncha live with yer mum and dad? Tell us then.'

This boy, whose name is Clifford Baines, has been to tea
at my house. He knows I live with my aunt and uncle,
although he did not ask any questions about this arrangement during the visit. He was sweet as a Milky Bar that
afternoon, full of pleases and thank yous and shy, toothless
grins. 'What a nice boy,' Aunt Hope hissed at me, shooing
us – each with a drink-on-a-stick, our post-teatime treat –
into the garden to play. That was three weeks ago. Clifford
has had lots of chances since to ask me privately what he
now asks in public, loudly, for the whole table to hear. I
sense at once that this question has been saved up and planned; that it's artful, designed – but in what way? – to do me
harm. Strangely, no one from school has asked about my
parents and why I don't live with them. Perhaps they assume
that Aunt Hope, who most days is at the school gates at half
past three, is my mother. The few who've been to my house
and met Aunt Hope and Uncle Ber have asked no questions
at all.

Clifford Baines's knife is pointing at my chin; he's staring
at me, as the whole table is, agog for my reply. I concentrate
on the high, enormous window opposite, and the dusty
feathers of pampas grass in the blue jar on its sill; I concentrate on the tattered alphabet frieze beneath the window

14

running the width of the wall. Aa is for Alligator, Bb is for Baboon, Cc is for Centipede, Dd is for ... When I speak, I haven't thought about my answer, the words just come out. 'Because my mum's dead,' I say. 'My mum was ill and she died.'

Royal-blue elbows jab royal-blue ribs, heads twist and lean, and a whisper races from table to table, 'Hannah's mum's dead', urgent and excited, as though this is hot news, a tragedy that has just occurred, this very morning, perhaps.

That was how I killed my mother. At the very moment I did it she was, most likely, sitting in one of the high-backed, pink-and-green uncut moquette chairs with lightwood arms that circled the day room of the Rose Vale Psychiatric Hospital, her hands in her lap, while Nurse Fitzgerald, the kindest and fattest of the nurses at the Rose Vale, encouraged her to eat a forkful of haddock and creamed-potato bake.

Clifford's deviousness backfired on him: my answer gained me star status for two whole days. I might have had it longer if Dennis Pritchard, who had hairy arms aged nine, hadn't tripped in the playground during a game of Prisoner's Base and broken one of his amazing hairy arms in two places.

When people ask me where I was brought up, or lived as a child, or where my roots are, or even where my heart lies (as somebody did ask me once: 'Where does your heart lie, Hannah, geographically speaking?') I say, 'Arizona.' And I may add 'partly' or 'some of the time, anyway'. An answer which is true and untrue.

But Arizona came later, when I was nearly twelve years old and hardly a child. Up till then Aunt Hope, my mother's elder and only sister, her husband, Lieutenant Commander Bertram Eastman, RN (ret.), and I lived in the south coast conurbation, those congeries of ports and naval bases and holiday resorts and twilight-home settlements that start in the south at Poole and eat up the coastline east and north through Southampton, Gosport, Portsmouth, Bognor, Worthing, Brighton, Eastbourne, Bexhill, all the way to, and including, Hastings. How do you tell, can the people who live there tell, where Bournemouth, say, ends and Christchurch begins? Of course I did not think about this then, nor did I know exactly where we fitted into it. Geography, the kind that required us to trace a map of England (the tracing paper invariably slipping or creasing, my pencil stabbing pinprick holes), and to print in the counties and cities before shading coalfields grey and arable land yellow, bored me. From the age of two, when my mother went into the hospital, my world was the semidetached house owned by my uncle and its privet-hedged garden, our cul-de-sac, lined with mountain-ash trees, which, like all the other residential roads in the area, gave onto the thunderous arterial road. My wider world was defined by bus routes – the uphill bus route to school; the one, downhill at first and eventually levelling out, to the shopping centre Aunt Hope and I sprinted round on Saturday mornings; and the one that took us, via the fire station and the police station with two changes, to my mother at the Rose Vale Hospital. In termtime these visits were made on Thursday evenings, after Aunt Hope, who taught at the high school, had finished her marking and after I had finished, or abandoned, my homework. Before leaving for the Rose Vale, Aunt Hope would slip away to the telephone in the hall and have a word with the ward sister. Sometimes, after the call, she'd say, 'Mummy's not too grand today.' When that happened, she would go to the hospital without me or – though this was rare – neither of us went.

One Thursday evening in February, when I was fidgeting at my homework, Aunt Hope, having made her usual telephone call, told me to get my coat on and to hurry, or we'd be late. To put my books away, chop chop.

It was the week I killed my mother, though Aunt Hope knew nothing of this. I'd done it on Monday so my mother had been dead three days now. How could I visit a dead person? I'd been worrying about it all day.

'I can't go, I'm not well.' And I stayed put where I was,

on my chair at the kitchen table. Aunt Hope came over and put a hand under my chin.

'You look all right to me.'

'I'm not. I feel sick.'

'You ate your tea. You ate two fish cakes. You said nothing about feeling sick then.'

'The fish cakes have made me feel sick.' It pained me to tell this lie. Aunt Hope made her own fish cakes, we never had bought ones. They were a mixture of cod and tinned salmon and mashed potato and parsley, and they had a crunchy lid made of flour and egg yolk that was almost black by the time Aunt Hope slid the cakes from the frying pan. I would prise this lid off (it had the look and texture of a knee scab) with my knife and save it till last, it was so delicious.

'You need some fresh air,' Aunt Hope said. 'The walk to the bus will make you feel better.'

'No.'

'No?' Aunt Hope was surprised. I was obedient as a rule. My aunt, who had a quick and frightening temper, was seldom able to find fault with me on that score; it was my lack of interest in schoolwork and in reading – English was her subject – that upset and frustrated her. I was fozy, she often told me, where my lessons were concerned. 'Fozy' was a Scots word, she said, and in its figurative sense meant fat-witted. Aunt Hope and my mother had Scottish blood.

Anxiety at having killed my mother, anxiety about defying Aunt Hope, made me blush and burn until my face was hot as a radish. Aunt Hope placed the flat of her hand against my cheek and then did the same to my forehead. 'I think you may have a temperature,' she said. 'If you're sickening for something you'd better not come. They won't want your bug in the hospital.'

A mixing bowl appeared beside me at the table. I was to go to bed at once, she said, and to take the bowl with me, just in case. She kissed the top of my head. 'Say goodnight to Uncle Ber on your way. I'll come and see you when I get home.'

Uncle Ber was in his workroom when I went to say good-night, at his workbench, under the Anglepoise, whistling tunelessly, working on a balsawood raft. It was a model of the *Kon-Tiki*, he'd explained when he began. He had shown me a book about the expedition that had photographs of the raft at different stages of its construction, and photographs of Thor Heyerdahl and his crew, and of the voyage itself. Uncle Ber's version of the *Kon-Tiki* was a foot long, and he'd been working on it several days. He was making it with the square sail hoisted, and it was this, and the cabin (what to use that would best resemble banana leaves and bamboo plaiting), that was giving him trouble.

'I've had to abandon the idea of canvas for the sail,' Uncle Ber said, 'it was too stiff and unwieldy at this size, so I'm using nylon instead. What d'you think?'

I thought it a pity. Canvas was nicer, the colour – a sort of pale biscuit – and the texture, but I didn't say so. I wanted him to finish the raft. When he did, and if – for it was February – we got a sunny, blue-skied day, we'd launch it on the hexagonal pond at the boundary end of the garden and sail it from Callao, Peru, to Tahiti.

Our pond was always changing identity. One week it was the Indian Ocean, and our craft the *San Gabriel*; the next the Red Sea or the Gulf of Mexico. Any minute now, at Uncle Ber's say-so, it would be the Pacific, an ocean I already knew something of from earlier voyages made by the *Golden Hind* and the *Endeavour*. (It had been late September when, against Uncle Ber's advice and with his arm-folded disapproval, the *Golden Hind* had set sail from the west coast of North America, bound for the Moluccas and, eventually, for home. The sky was overcast, the waters of the Pacific black as treacle, the *Hind*'s progress hampered by sudden, buffeting crosswinds and by eddying shoals of scarlet leaves that had blown off our ancient crab-apple tree. Lying on my stomach in the rough grass surrounding the pond, working with bellows and a walking stick, I'd tried to keep her on course, but it was hopeless. She was caught in a whirlpool; she was spinning and heeling and shipping water. She would have capsized if Uncle Ber hadn't fished her out with a net.

Later we had another try. This time, a mild October afternoon, the tiny breeze that had filled her sails and taken her bobbing out to sea suddenly died, leaving her gently rocking in mid-ocean. I'd wanted to fetch the bellows and set her off again, but Uncle Ber said no. 'Becalmed,' he said, 'peaceful. That's all right, that's what Pacific *means*.')

In preparation for the *Kon-Tiki*'s voyage, Uncle Ber and I had squeezed red clay and straw together to form the Marquesas Islands, planting the islands while the clay was still soft with bright plastic trees we'd bought in the toy shop. Our next task was to make a coral reef for the *Kon-Tiki* to go aground on. When I was seven and old enough to notice, it began to bother me that all the craft Uncle Ber made – the brigs and brigantines, the carracks and clippers, the junks and dhows – were so obviously too big for the seas they sailed. It was the same with the continents and islands, rocks and icebergs, we sent them towards. Didn't it matter that everything was out of scale?

Uncle Ber was amazed when I asked him. Inconsistencies – of scale, materials or anything else – didn't matter a jot, he said; what mattered was one's imagination; and he reminded me of how, when I was four, my favourite toy had been a piece of elm bark I'd picked up on a walk, and how I'd cruised it round Aunt Hope's preserving pan, insisting it was the *QE2* I'd seen on television. The only other thing that mattered was that our vessels should be seaworthy. He had no time for the showy replicas of fully rigged men-of-war and the royal yacht *Britannia* and *Gipsy Moth III*, which cost a bomb in model shops and had 'Not to be placed in water' on their polished display bases. 'What's the point of a boat that won't float?' he'd say. 'Bugger all.'

'You off to bed then?' Uncle Ber nudged me with his elbow. Not wanting to go, I was touching things, picking them up, hovering by his chair. It was a swivel chair with a curved back rail, the sort chief executives in TV soaps swing around in (so they can give the cold shoulder to middle management without warning), though of course I did not know that then. The only office I knew was the cubbyhole, containing files and folders and paper coffee cups and cross Mrs McVitie, at my school. Uncle Ber glanced at his watch. 'Bit early for you, isn't it?'

I was feeling sick, I told him, which was why I hadn't gone with Aunt Hope. Tears sprang to my eyes; they were of self-pity as, I've come to believe, most tears are. I hoped Uncle Ber would say something about my mother. If he would only mention her name I'd be able to confess what I'd done. If I confessed, he would comfort me. (I would lean my head against his smooth tweed back and howl.) Uncle Ber did not mention her, but then – I see now – he never did; just as he never accompanied Aunt Hope and me on the hospital visits; just as he took no notice of my mother when she came to our house.

I hated our visits to the Rose Vale Hospital. Once, when Aunt Hope and I were standing on the step waiting to go in, an old woman had come out and lifted her dress, and done a pee on the step. A huge long pee, standing up. It happened so quickly, we hadn't had time to get out of her way. We were splashed, my new school skirt was splashed. When the woman finished, she smoothed her dress down and smiled at us, a wide smile of toothless gums. A nurse burst out of the door and grabbed her and pulled her into the hall. 'Oh, Mary,' the nurse said, laughing, 'you *are* a naughty girl!'

There was a time when my mother had come home every other weekend and for occasional longer 'holidays', the idea being that if she could manage these she would eventually learn to cope with life outside. But I see now that my mother was already institutionalised, and that any departure from the routine of her muted days and sedated nights terrified her. The view from her hospital window in summer, of yellow conifers and orange roses in a grassed courtyard; the pink, shiny walls and beetroot curtains of her little room; the regular appearance of mild meals and of the medicine and tea trolleys; the vinyl-cushioned tread of the nurses and their uniform plainness and kindness (there were always, on both counts, one or two exceptions); the sweetish oranges and urine smell that hung like cigarette smoke in the corridors – these were the day-to-day certainties that kept my mother, most of the time, from screaming. Yet they filled me with unease so that I longed to be away from the place even as we stood on the step and Aunt Hope pressed the brass-encircled bell.

My mother's visits home, which would begin as well as could be expected – that's to say silently, shakily, anxiously, precariously – would end badly and noisily. On Aunt Hope's instructions my job was that of handmaid to our strange visitor, who seldom spoke and whose rare, jittery smiles were only for herself. Because, even in summer, my mother found our house cold after the Rose Vale, I'd fuss round her chair with rugs and shawls. I'd rearrange cushions, anticipate her desire for tea or lime juice (she would nurse these in her lap but not often drink them); lead her by the hand at mealtimes to her place at the table; tug her, on sunny afternoons, to a bench in the garden. I was to call her Mummy constantly, Aunt Hope said, to remind her who I was; and I did so, though it was hard to see the point: she tolerated my presence and even my organising, but that was all. These were the good times, on Day One, when Aunt Hope and I were working our hardest to make my mother feel safe. By Day Two, after a restless night in an unfamiliar bed, in a room that daylight pierced from an unfamiliar – and therefore wrong, wrong, *wrong*! – direction, her fragility would be palpable. Aunt Hope's creamy scrambled eggs untouched and going cold and solid on her plate, my mother would push the table away and leave the kitchen without a word. 'No, stay where you are, finish your breakfast!' Uncle Ber would command, biffing his newspaper, as I, programmed to shadow her, jumped to my feet. So we'd go on with our breakfast, the atmosphere one of surreal heartiness or taut silence, in which the terrible munching and crunching of toast and the creak of the pendulum clock grew louder and louder until –

Until these sounds were muzzled by another sound, from above our heads: a scream. Or a crash. Or a series of screams or a series of crashes. A series of thuds and bumps and squeals together with a rumbling, as though a heavy armchair with one castor missing was being pushed and dragged over soft carpet and hard floorboards from one side of a room to the other, to end up – wham! – against a door. Loud sobs. Rhythmical soft thumps or thwacks, as though someone was beating a cushion with a walking stick – though why would anyone want to do that? A dry, methodical tearing, as though someone was stripping old wallpaper from a wall. Uncontrollable weeping. Any of these sounds. Some or all of these noises.

Aunt Hope would get up and leave the kitchen then.

Sometimes we got beyond breakfast on Day Two without mishap. But we were wary, watching and waiting. Listening. For the slightest unexpected happening was capable of destroying my mother's frail hold on herself. A telephone or doorbell that rang once too often could do it. A demented bluebottle on a windowsill. Aunt Hope's little terrier, Jemma, barking (at the doorbell or a bluebottle). A radio's sudden blast.

These tantrums were not the manifestations of my mother's illness I dreaded most. No, it was her weeping I could not bear. When she threw herself about in that infantile way; when she slammed her door repeatedly and with such force that the house rocked, or smashed glass and china (on one of those visits home she drove Uncle Ber's old schoolboy cricket bat through every pane in both windows of her bedroom), I could, after the initial fear and shock, distance myself from her. Embarrassment would follow, and shame, but they were for her, and on her behalf, not for me. That a grown-up should behave like that, knowing that I and Aunt Hope and Uncle Ber could hear, and would eventually see, the wreckage she'd caused! How was it possible to have so little pride? For I was convinced my mother did have the power to control herself but that for some reason I knew nothing of had chosen not to use it. Her tantrums were not real, I could tell. They were a game she played, a drama she acted (there was something very theatrical about all her carryings-on), and they required an audience. Even at her most destructive, she never broke anything she really minded about. Plates could be hurled, books torn or trampled, windows smashed, chairs crippled – but it was never her book or her chair that suffered. The two shelves of pottery bears she'd collected as a young girl, which Aunt Hope housed (and dusted and, occasionally, washed), remained intact, whatever else did not. After I'd worked this out I lost respect for my mother. Her hot dramas failed to move me then; they left me cold.

But the weeping and the silent despair, which were her other two modes and moods at home – those were very different. There was nothing theatrical about them. If I've given the idea that breakfasts on Day Two invariably resulted in mayhem, it may be that mayhem prints itself on the memory more easily than chronic sadness does. Or it may be because I cannot bear to think about the silent days, those days when my mother appeared almost paralysed with anguish, her few words muffled, her head sunk on her chest, the hands in her lap too heavy to lift even a handkerchief to her eyes. I would go round the garden in search of strong-scented flowers, roses, pinks, lavender, and hold them up to her and beg her to sniff; but she was lost in her sorrow and incapable of response. 'Who is this child?' she would sometimes ask Aunt Hope in anxious bafflement. 'Who is this little girl?'

I have the impression that it was always raining when my mother's illness took that form; that the house Aunt Hope and I crept around and whispered in (despondency would infect us both in the end) was dark as a December afternoon;

that we were both drenched like my mother's handker-chiefs; that the rain which fell was falling inside the house.

On Day Three my mother would be returned to the Rose Vale.

These journeys were made by taxi, the three of us on the back seat, my mother in the middle between her sister and her daughter. Her bodyguards.

'Well,' Aunt Hope would say, taking my mother's cold hand in hers and chafing it, 'well, Janey, we are going to miss you! Aren't we, Han?'

'Yes.' No. Oh, no!

At the Rose Vale, Matron would be waiting. A quick glance at my mother's swollen eyes and cowed shoulders – or, when she'd been head-banging, at her bruises and abrasions – followed by a dagger look at Aunt Hope.

'I don't know what Dr Medley thinks he's playing at! Putting my patient at risk! Undoing all the good work we're doing here!'

A nurse would be summoned, who would lead my mother away, talking to her soothingly, stopping when my mother stopped, waiting with an arm round her waist until my mother felt able to stumble on again. On the occasions when the patient could not move, her limbs and whole body pet-rified, a collapsible wheelchair would be disentangled from the stack in the hall and snapped into action.

'Wait here a minute, Han.' And I'd sit on my hands on a hard orange chair in the corridor for fifteen minutes at least, swinging my legs, staring at a yellow and blue picture of 'Twelve Sunflowers in a Vase' – a puzzle always: I could never count more than ten – while Aunt Hope and Matron and the ward sister or a staff nurse talked behind a shut door.

When Aunt Hope told my mother, in that hearty way, that we were going to miss her, I always believed it to be a lie. A kind lie, obviously, but a lie. We were not going to miss my mother – how could we? We were going to put her out of our heads as quickly and for as long as possible. We were going to feel relief, to sigh sighs of relief. We were going to laugh. I, if not Aunt Hope, was going to run round the garden at top speed, hooting and letting off steam like a train.

And to begin with, it would seem that I was right and Aunt Hope wrong. On the journey home my aunt and I, side by side on the springy seat of the bus, would release huge satisfying and satisfied sighs – haaah! Or, our mouths shaped in an O, we'd push the air out, as though we were blowing up invisible balloons. Whooooh! When we got home Jemma would bark and leap, and no reason in the world to stop her. Uncle Ber, out of hiding for the first time in three days, would be cheerful in the kitchen with the table laid and potatoes on the boil. All was right and normal in our house. And then it would hit me: there was something missing. No, not something, someone. In every room I entered, in the stuffy, steam-filled kitchen, on the stairs, in the little dark hall, my mother's pathetic absence was more actual than her presence had been a few hours earlier. Before long, reproachful evidence of her brief stay would draw attention to itself. A visit to the bathroom would reveal a phantom toothbrush in the basin (my mother's toothbrushes had to be white, white and no other colour, no one knew why). Moving her bed out from the wall to strip and remake it with clean sheets, one of us would be certain to trip over a crushed slipper or a sodden handkerchief. Hair – long individual hairs and ripped-out hanks and twists – on cushions, pillows and the seats and backs of chairs, spoke of her desperation and of our neglect.

People tend to assume that my son Finch was named after the film actor Peter Finch, and I can see why they do. The surnames of movie stars have often been appropriated by fans as given names for their own offspring. You think of Grant and Wayne and Scott; and someone I know has twins called Costner and Cruise, ten years old. Finch, who knows everything, tells me there's nothing new in this. Herbert, Howard and Sidney became popular as first names, he informed me recently, because they had aristocratic associations, because they were the family names of at least one duke and of several earls and barons. Then there were the hero names, he reminded me – Nelson, for example. Nelson Mandela, for one good example. Mandela being a hero himself, any minute now we could expect playschools and supermarkets to be humming with little Mandelas. 'Any minute now, you wait, someone with the surname Nelson will call their son Mandela,' Finch said.

I said they never would because Mandela Nelson sounded like a girl, it was clearly a girl's name.

'Does Finch sound like a boy?' asked Finch in a mean voice, reaching for the biscuit tin.

I said yes, of course, I'd thought so, otherwise I wouldn't have called him that.

'They don't reckon it is at school, their new name for me

is Bluetit.' Finch bit into a chocolate digestive and closed his little eyes. 'Blue *tit*.'

I thought of all the other hurtful names Finch had been called in his time, in the various schools he'd been to. Fatty, Fatso, Fatface, Fatman, Blubber, Wobble, Piggy, Porky, Lardy Cake, Flab Bag – all the usual, and no doubt lots of others he hadn't told me about. Then there were the names the wits had given him: Skinny (or Skinny Lizzie, or just Lizzie on its own); Olive Oyl, Bony Maronie, Rake, Jack Spratt, Beanpole. Bluetit was bad, and I minded for him, but it didn't seem any worse than some of these.

'Robin's a boy's name,' I said, 'a boy's name that is also a bird's name.'

'I know that. You didn't call me Robin.' With his eyes shut, Finch searched around in the biscuits for another with chocolate on. When he found one he held it up to his snout and sniffed it. Then he took a nibble. Then he inched the biscuit round and nibbled again. And so on. Little nibbles, round and round, carefully maintaining the biscuit's shape as it got smaller. I looked away before the *coup de grâce*. I couldn't bear to go on watching.

My son, who is fifteen now, has two other given names he could use if he wanted instead of Finch, but he doesn't like either. The names are Athridge and Bertram. Finch Athridge Bertram. I called him Athridge to please Jocelyn (it was her name), and I called him Bertram to please Aunt Hope (it also pleased me) and I called him Finch to please myself. We'd had a lot of finches in the garden when I was small, chaffinches, greenfinches, the occasional bullfinch, and I liked watching them on the bird table and trying to work out, from the kitchen window, whether they were really finches or just sparrows. An early love of bird-watching was the reason I gave Aunt Hope for calling my son Finch. But there was another reason, the main one, I didn't tell my aunt. I'd had a lover whose nickname was Finch, a black boy, originally from Kingston, Jamaica, but when I met him from

Brixton, south London. He was tall and handsome, and wore a green beret with a greasy leather trim – an army beret, I imagine it was. He was a Fulham supporter, and on Saturdays would take me to the home matches.

I'd had several black lovers, and I'd hoped to have a black baby or, failing black, a very dark-brown one. But I was seeing other people too, around the time Finch was conceived, pink, grey, white and brown people; and my son, who was purple when he first appeared, and then jaundice yellow for a week, finally settled into a whiter shade of pale.

'FAB,' Aunt Hope said when I'd made my choice of names for my very white baby, 'your son's initials make Fab. The Fab Four.' I was born in 1960 and the first music I was aware of was Beatles music, so Aunt Hope must have thought I'd be amused. 'He'll be known as Fab, you realise,' she said, 'd'you mind? Do you think he'll mind? Do you think you should change his initials round so that he's Abf or Baf or Fba? Well, perhaps not *Fibber*.'

Not knowing for sure who Finch's father was, I gave him my surname, Wickham. And I kept his Christian names (he was baptised) in their original order, largely because I didn't like Aunt Hope doing my thinking for me and telling me what to do. But the sad thing was, and still is, no one to my knowledge has ever called my son Fab. I haven't; Aunt Hope and Jocelyn never did, they always called him Finchy; Diarmid doesn't; and no one has at his schools. Finch can't play games, his girth precludes it, and in any case he's uncoordinated, so his initials never appear on fixtures lists. But they must do on other sorts of lists that go up on notice boards – form lists, duty rosters and what have you. The only story, a terrible story, I've heard about his initials and the impact they've made was when he went to the comprehensive. It was his first day and he was writing his name on his exercise books when a girl looked over his shoulder – I think it was a girl – and said, 'F. A. B. Wickham. Fat-Arsed Baboon, right?'

'Let's get down to work, then. Write your name, Hannah.'

I'm sitting at a table. In front of me is a sheet of lined paper and a thick black pencil. Aunt Hope is leaning over my shoulder. She's printed my name on the paper already, so that I can copy it. I can't write my name unless she does this. I get down to work. Getting down to work means putting my head down, so low my nose almost touches the paper. I grip the pencil.

When I've finished, my printing is not the same as Aunt Hope's. Some of my letters are giants that take up three lines, some dwarfs you can hardly see. Aunt Hope's letters are all the same size.

'Hannah,' Aunt Hope says, reading what I've written with interest, as though my name is a word that's new to her. '*Hannah*. That's excellent. Now, if you can, write your name backwards. Look at the last letter of your name, and write that first, and then the next to last, and so on till you come to the end – or perhaps we should say the beginning.'

I grip my pencil. This is a harder task, clearly. I frown. My tongue shoots out a little way and waggles about. I look hard at the last letter of my name and write it down. H.

It takes some time to write my name backwards, twice as long as it took to write it forwards. When I've finished I put my pencil on the paper and sit back. There. It's done.

'Very good,' Aunt Hope says, 'but you're not looking at it, you haven't looked at it. Look at it now.'

I look at it. It looks all right to me.

'Well?' Aunt Hope says. She sounds impatient.

'Well?' I say. (I'm always parroting Aunt Hope.) 'Well?'

Aunt Hope points her finger at my name on the paper. She points at my forward name first, then the backward one. 'What's the difference between these?' she asks. 'Is there a difference?'

There's quite a lot of difference. I've made some of the letters different sizes. The first 'a' in my forward name is very small. The first 'a' in my backward name is enormous.

It just happened that way. I'm looking to see what other differences there are, when Aunt Hope sighs.

'Oh, dear,' she says to herself, 'the child's a moron; she can't see it. Heaven help us.' To me she says, 'Hannah, look, there *is* no difference; your name is the same, whether you write it backwards or forwards. Look. Not many names, not many words, are like that. When they are it's called a palindrome. P-A-L-I-N-D-R-O-M-E.'

I smile up at Aunt Hope. I am bored now and want to get down. Not down to work but down from the table.

'Hannah,' Aunt Hope says, 'what's your second name?'

Aunt Hope knows what my second name is, and I know what it is, so I don't answer. I just smile and keep on smiling.

'Heaven help us,' Aunt Hope says, looking at the sky, 'the child doesn't even know her second name.'

That's how I remember this early lesson in the palindrome. As I remember it, I was five, the age most children learn to write, if not read. The impression I have is of a five-year-old, with a five-year-old's thoughts and ways. But when, years later, the subject came up, Aunt Hope said I was seven, nearly eight. 'You were a very late starter and developer,' she said, 'and if to you I sounded exasperated, well, I was. I'd spent years trying to teach you to read, and you would not, could not, learn.' Aunt Hope also said that had I been five I would not be able to remember the episode so clearly, if at all.

Aunt Hope's version of the lesson differed from mine in various details (I was not at a table, I was at the child's desk she had had as a girl and still kept in her bedroom). Her ending of it was different too, and the ending was important, she said. Apparently she had written my second name, Eve, down for me and asked me to write it backwards, and I had refused. I'd examined the word and noted the two 'e's either side the 'v' and decided it was a waste of my time to write it backwards. 'It's the same,' I'd said. 'It's one of those P things like Hannah.'

'After that I realised you were not entirely fozy,' Aunt Hope said. 'Not entirely.'

My son Finch learned to read and write when he was three. Nobody taught him; he taught himself, or just picked it up. At six he was reading parts of the newspaper on a daily basis, little paragraphs with stimulating headlines about helicopter crashes and murders. At seven he was reading the leader and the political and business pages, the home news and the foreign news. Aunt Hope thought this wonderful, and that Finch himself was wonderful.

Throughout my life with Aunt Hope I longed to have black or white feelings about her, not both. I wanted to hate or love her and be done with it. I don't suppose I was alone in wanting that; I dare say most of us prefer to make hard and fast decisions if we can, if only because switchbacks and seesaws are so uncomfortable. X is a bitch, we want to be able to say; Y is wonderful in every way.

But I found I couldn't do this with my aunt. And I found that, when I was hating her, my hate didn't affect how I felt about her name (as usually happens when you hate or dislike someone).

I loved the name Hope, which was separate in my mind from the abstract noun and the verb it also was. I liked the look of it on paper, and the sound it made, its huge open 'O'. (Open; Hope – they were the same word, almost.) But my aunt didn't care for her name, which in her school days had provoked such witticisms as 'Abandon Hope ye who enter here,' and 'Hope springs eternal' when she failed to clear the horse in gym. Hope making such a poor showing in the Corinthians 13 trinity was another thing that irked my aunt, even though she was not religious in any orthodox sense. In any case she thought it mischievous to burden girl babies – it almost invariably was girls, had we noticed? – with virtues they might well not turn out to possess. Her fellow triplets in the Corinthians trinity, Faith and Charity, were the most burdensome of these ('Fancy being expected to remove mountains as a matter of course!'); but Patience, Prudence, Grace, Honor, Joy and Felicity were close behind. 'And, of course, it's not just a depressive nowadays who might be less than glad to be Gay. Imagine being at a party, and a stranger greeting you with "Excuse me – am I right in thinking you're Gay? I thought you must be!" ' She made this remark to Jocelyn; and I remember thinking, But you don't go to parties, Aunt Hope. You never do. What are you on about?

I liked some of the names Aunt Hope frowned on. I liked Grace. And I liked Christian, a name that surely came into the 'virtues' category, but which she never mentioned, presumably because it was a boy's.

Whenever Aunt Hope said something derogatory about her own name in Jocelyn's presence, Jocelyn leaped to defend it. 'Hope is a beautiful name,' she'd say, 'beautiful. I won't hear a word against it.' Aunt Hope would laugh at that, her light, dismissive laugh, and busy herself with something, or leave the room.

Even so, Jocelyn wasn't above exploring the punning possibilities of Hope – 'We'd be Hopeless without you', that kind of thing. Once, when my aunt began a sentence, 'I hope you will – ' Jocelyn cut in, 'I Hope, you Will – that's Tarzan-speak.'

'No, it isn't,' I said. 'Tarzan never said "I", he said "me", so it doesn't work.'

'Hannah's a literalist,' Aunt Hope said to Jocelyn.

I remember one night at supper (this must have been after the move), another conversation about names. It had begun with dogs, and whether it was better – less patronising – to give them human names such as Jemma, or descriptive ones such as Patch or Trouble. Jocelyn said it was a pity in her view there'd never been a fashion for depressing names for humans because she fancied having boy and girl twins called Gloom and Despondency. Or a boy called Grief, which would allow one to exclaim, 'Good Grief!' Or even, 'Don't give me Grief!' And Aunt Hope pointing out that when Patience was on the monument she was smiling at Grief. 'Though she was a bit doolally, I suspect.'

Aunt Hope and words – her business, being an English teacher. They were the aspect of her I feared and, when I hated her, often hated the most. Where words were concerned, there was no pleasing her, in my experience.

For example, on my thirteenth birthday, I think it was, she gave me a thesaurus, a last-ditch attempt 'to improve your word power – as the *Reader's Digest* has it'. I tried hard with that thesaurus, which in fact I was pleased to have, and for a while I consulted it to pep up my essays, or compositions, as my school called them. One of my first word-power-improved compositions was about a girl in a garden, weeding a flowerbed while spied on by a peeping Tom in a high tree.

Aunt Hope glanced over my shoulder. ' "Pulchritude"? No, I don't think so. Never a good idea to reject a beautiful word like "beauty" for a word that's ugly in itself. "Deracinated"? If you mean "rooted up", you should say so. You get a picture of the action with "root up". "Lingulated"? "Contumacious"? *"Concupiscence"?* Fancy!'

Uncle Ber was twenty-one years older than his wife. Most of his adult life had been spent in the Royal Navy, but he'd had to retire early when it was discovered that there was something wrong with his heart, or rather with his two coronary arteries. These arteries began to be unreliable in the way they pumped oxygen-rich blood from the aorta to the heart muscle, and when this happened Uncle Ber had a really bad pain in his chest, and sometimes a pain in his shoulders, and occasionally a fizzy feeling in his arms. He had bouts of breathlessness so overwhelming he felt he was drowning, or that there was someone inside his chest squeezing his lungs together. Aunt Hope told me this when I was seven. I was on the young side to know such things, she said; on the other hand, knowledge was power, as someone wiser than herself had once said, and the more I understood about it, the less frightened, and the more helpful to my uncle, I was likely to be.

Coronary heart disease and angina pectoris were the full names for Uncle Ber's troubles. Angina was the short name for the acute chest pains he had. It was a strange name for a pain, I thought. The way Aunt Hope pronounced it, with a little upward lilt, it sounded like a girl's name – a pretty, fair-haired girl – and I used to imagine Aunt Hope calling for this girl (who was sometimes my little sister and sometimes

34

my best friend) in the garden or from the bottom of the stairs: 'Angina! Angina! Tea's ready!'

By the time Uncle Ber was sixty he'd been living with angina and the other symptoms for twelve years. Aunt Hope, then thirty-nine, had been living with them too, of course, and she also had the worry of my mother and she also, in termtime, had her teaching and all the marking of homework and the staff-room melodramas that went with it; and she also, I make myself remember, had the responsibility of bringing up me, her younger sister's child.

When he wasn't ill, Uncle Ber's face was a rosy pink, which on some days and in some lights contained a hint of blue, making it the colour of underdone roast beef; but when he had angina his face became greeny pale and damp-looking. If I was with him in his workroom, the first warning I'd have would be the sudden silence – he'd stopped whistling. Next, tiny bubbles of sweat would appear on his forehead, and these would soon break into thin rivers that ran down his nose or lodged themselves in his thick caterpillar eyebrows. He carried a round leather pillbox in the breast pocket of his jacket, and when the pain came on he'd shake a pill out of the box and pop it under his tongue in a casual way as though he were helping himself to a private store of peppermints. Then he'd carry on with whatever he was doing. If the pains were severe he'd stop work and make his way haltingly to the living room, where he'd lower himself into one of the two identical brown-flowered armchairs either side of the fireplace, and remain there, legs outstretched and eyes closed, for half an hour or more. If, instead, he made for the stairs and gripped the banister rail and began to haul himself up, stopping on every stair to fight for breath, I'd run in search of my aunt. She'd instructed me to do this.

'Uncle Ber's got a pain! He's gone upstairs to lie down!'

'Thank you for letting me know.' But Aunt Hope never went rushing after him. My instructions were to find her 'pdq'; or, if she could not be found or was out shopping, to run to Mrs Taylor at number 38 (she had once been a nurse and was nearly always in); or, if Mrs Taylor could not be raised, to ring Dr Havelock's surgery; or, should the surgery number be permanently engaged, to dial 999 and say 'ambulance' and then our address. So I could never understand why, when she'd digested my news, and while I hopped from one leg to the other and swung my arms round and round like a windmill, Aunt Hope went on calmly chopping carrots or firewood. She always let at least five minutes go by before climbing the stairs. 'Ber hates being fussed over, you know,' she'd say in a confiding tone as though to an adult or a friend, 'he can't abide fuss.'

Usually, when Aunt Hope came downstairs again, she'd go straight back to her task. Occasionally, she'd go to the telephone in the hall. Twice, in my memory, after Dr Havelock had been to visit, an ambulance arrived and took my uncle away to the new white-brick hospital in Shields Road, where he stayed for a week for 'observation' or 'tests'.

Uncle Ber's illness seemed intermittent to me because when not in pain he gave the appearance of ordinary, or better than ordinary, health. He was seldom still. I think of him in his workroom planing a length of wood, leaning his weight into every rhythmical push, and the impression I have is of confident energy and strength and great reserves of these. I see him sand the wood, pause to blow the fine dust off (his method the huff-puff, side-to-side one small children use to extinguish birthday candles on a cake), run his hand back and forth over the surface, sand again. There was a sort of weathered, all-weather fitness about him I've noticed some retirement-age cyclists and swimmers have. There's a seventy-five-year-old in our flats, Mr Holcraft, who reminds me of Uncle Ber. Mr Holcraft bicycles everywhere; to his sister in Walthamstow, to his married nephew in Peckham, to our nearest shops two blocks away. He wears shorts for these adventures, even in winter. Even in winter, his hands, forearms and neck are a ruddy brown, like Uncle Ber's. His movements are positive, his reactions sharp (the way he swings his leg over the saddle and glides away with a quick look over his shoulder impresses me), and in these too he reminds me of Uncle Ber, although my uncle didn't live to be seventy and never wore shorts.

I admire Mr Holcraft's courage in taking on city traffic, and I admire his refusal to be bound by the usual, and accepted, limitations of his age; at the same time there's something bothering – creepy, is it, or pathetic? – about his fake youthfulness. There's something creepy about his deft manner of fitting on his cycling helmet (symbol of daring, you think, more than of safety); the way he, holding the helmet with the flat of both hands, lowers his bald head into it, straightens up smartly, then snaps the buckles shut, one, two, three. And there's something pathetic about his unobtrusive buttocks in the little grey shorts; about his hairless thighs and calves, his outsize trainers and twinkling ankle socks. Mr Holcraft's leg muscles are being exercised daily, they're being pumped – yet they look wasted. Old.

Uncle Ber's workroom was at the back of the house. It was a large lean-to, made of wood and supported by four courses of bright orange brick (whereas the brick of the house itself was a dark maroon). Its outside walls were weatherboarded for extra warmth, and every April my uncle and I slapped on a reviving coat of stinking creosote, he from a stepladder, I from the ground, where I covered the small area of cladding within my reach.

I spent all the time I was allowed to in that workroom, which in the school holidays meant most of the day. To keep me occupied and from being a hindrance, Uncle Ber devised a series of tasks. Learning knots was one of them – that is, learning the name of all the knots sailors use, and how to tie them. To make it easier, he made me a knot board, on which he glued twenty-six varieties of knot (which he'd previously spent hours splicing and tying, in different thicknesses and colours of cord) with their names printed beside them. Then from time to time, without warning, he'd test me. Two sorts of test – name tests and practical tests.

'Tie me a thumb knot, Han; tie me a blood knot. Make me a sheet bend. Show me a bowline; show me a bowline on a bight; show me a rolling hitch; show me two round turns and two half hitches.'

Another task was cleaning the garden tools. Cleaning didn't just mean washing the mud off; it entailed rubbing boiled linseed oil into the shafts to prevent them from splitting; it meant burnishing the blades or prongs with glass paper and wire wool. The handles I only needed to wipe because the handles of all my uncle's tools, whether garden or house (hammers, screwdrivers, drills and saws), were canary yellow. He'd painted them himself with a tough enamel paint, the idea being that if a neighbour asked to borrow a fork, say, there could be no problem about identification, and no unpleasantness, when it came to getting the fork back. Even the buckets and watering cans in the potting shed had yellow rings, like the stripes of naval insignia on a sleeve, round their battered, galvanised outsides.

But Uncle Ber would have preferred me to be a carpenter rather than a cleaner. 'Your turn now, Han,' he'd say, after I'd watched him at work with chisel or rasp. I wanted to succeed, for his sake and mine. I wanted to be able to make a table or stool or, at the very least, a tray. More to the point, I wanted to make my own, unaided, seaworthy contribution to 'that collection of quinquiremes and Spanish galleons and dirty British coasters', as Aunt Hope called it, which filled the shelves above my head; but each attempt left me with sliced thumbs or glued fingers. It wasn't just that I was cack-handed. Having a picture of the finished article so clear in my mind made it difficult to concentrate on the fussy, frustrating processes that had to be gone through before I could get there. So much of the wood craftsman's time seemed to be spent in waiting – waiting for some vital and tricky section to be released from the vice; waiting for glue or varnish or paint to dry.

'You like Robbie Coltrane, though,' Finch said. Finch and I were watching television. (This was recently, a matter of weeks ago.) I was in the armchair and Finch was on the sofa, jiggling that wide, fleshy part of him that in other boys his age would be narrow and bony and called a knee. After the programme we'd been watching came to an end, there was a commercial break, and during the break I started laughing.

'You like Robbie Coltrane, though,' Finch repeated.

What? 'What?' Stop jiggling, Finch!

'You like Robbie Coltrane, though.'

'I heard you. Yes, I do. What does "though" mean? Though what?'

'You do like him.'

'I've said I do. I think he's very funny. Why?'

'D'you think he's sexy?'

'Sexy? Why? What is all this?'

'What is all this?' Finch mimicked. 'What is all this?' He heaved himself out of the sofa and padded to the door in his socks. When he returned he had a can of Coke in his hand, ice cold and sweating, as in the commercials.

'Thanks very much for the cup of tea,' I said. 'I really appreciated that.'

'What cup of tea?' He shrugged and sat down again, and the sofa ground its teeth.

I got up and left the room.

In winter, Uncle Ber wore green cord trousers and a jacket of smooth green tweed; in summer, lightweight trousers with a sheen to them, in green or brown, and clinging, almost see-through shirts which I suppose were nylon or a nylon-and-something mix. Aunt Hope hated ironing. Those were the days when clothing manufacturers and marketing men were beginning to cotton on to the truth that not every housewife was happy to spend her days pressing hubby's shirts. (When she was not in the kitchen, baking batches of fairy cakes, wearing high heels and a cocktail dress, and a miniature apron with a deep-frilled edge.) The easy-care revolution produced some nasty and smelly clothes for men, as I recall, and for women and children also: skirts that clung to your thighs when you didn't want them to, shirts that crackled and flashed when you pulled them over your head – and which, if they did get into the ironing pile, melted to burnt toffee at one touch of the iron.

I remember my own clothes at this time; a shapeless tabard-cum-tunic, usually, that went with a blouse and bobbly white nylon knee socks in warm weather. When it was cold, the blouse and socks were exchanged for a machine-washable jumper and ribbed nylon tights. The white knee socks would be grey after two goes in the washing machine; the tights and the non-wool, non-shrink, machine-washable jumper would grow and grow and stretch and stretch, and my body, legs and arms could never keep up with them. Not only did these garments expand; after one wash they became powerful magnets, able to attract and retain a whole carpet's worth of fluff, a whole dog's worth of dog hairs.

With his easy-care shirts and trousers, Uncle Ber wore two lanyards – one round his neck of thin white cord that carried a whistle and a key to the workroom, and one, of heavier rope, round his waist. On the end of the rope lanyard hung a jackknife and a fat Swiss Army knife with fifteen attachments. Aunt Hope made scornful fun of the lanyards and their trappings. Just a glimpse of the whistle, in particular, was enough to provoke remarks about Scout masters and football referees.

More than the lanyards and the tangible whistle (which swung below his shirt collar and banged against his chest), Aunt Hope deplored the intangible, breathy whistling noise my uncle made. He whistled while he worked, of course, but he also did it while he was reading the paper and when he was massaging dubbin into the leather of his heavy outdoor boots. The noise he made was just under the breath. It had a hiss in it and was achieved, as far as I could tell, by blowing air out and then immediately sucking it in, and by pressing the tip of the tongue to the roof of the mouth just behind the teeth. While tuneless, the rhythms of this whistling could at times suggest a tune – the opening bars of a dirge, perhaps. Surprisingly, Uncle Ber's habit didn't bother me (although if Finch were a whistler, I'd kill him, I'm sure).

But it did bother Aunt Hope. Uncle Ber was not a hero to her, and she could not cope with his whistling. After a few moments' suffering she'd get up without a word and leave the room. Or, suddenly beside herself, she'd scream, 'For God's sake, Ber, stop that filthy, filthy noise! Do you want to drive me *mad*?' When she exploded, he stopped at once. But within minutes he'd be whistling again.

The lanyards and the whistling aside, it seemed to me then that it was my uncle's desire to please my aunt; that he was continually trying to please her and usually failing. If, on one of his rare trips into the town, he returned with a bunch of florist's flowers, they would be the wrong flowers. She did not say so, but you could tell. There was something about the fold of her mouth as she stuck her nose into the paper cone and smelled the contents with such short, quick, peremptory sniffs; about her long sighs as she snicked the stems and stripped the leaves and then allowed the blooms (the colours of fire, always: Uncle Ber liked strong reds, oranges and yellows) to fall and arrange themselves any old how in any old vase she took from the scullery shelf, that had more to do with disappointment and resignation than with pleasure.

But the most spectacular failure of my uncle to please my aunt concerned the record cabinet he made for her forty-second birthday. Uncle Ber designed this cabinet himself. It was a long oblong box of coffee-table height, set on tapering splay legs that descended into black, laminated caps like the painted hooves of a rocking horse. The legs were not flush with the corners as I'd imagined they would be. Uncle Ber positioned them several inches in from the corners (and, underneath, several inches back from the sides towards the middle); and the effect, I see now, was typically 1950s of the Ercol style. Instead of knobs or handles, the cabinet had sliding doors with recessed finger panels; inside there were compartments for LPs, EPs and 78s.

Aunt Hope's birthday present was a secret, 'hush-hush' as Uncle Ber put it, and during its gestation she was not allowed in the workroom. If she wanted my uncle or me for any reason, she had to bang on the door and wait for one of us to emerge. When Uncle Ber was out of the workroom, it was kept locked. I enjoyed the feeling of importance I got from all this. I relished the undercover atmosphere in the work-room, and the conspiratorial signs and whispers Uncle Ber and I exchanged at mealtimes or whenever my aunt was near. Most of all, I relished our exclusiveness, the sharing of something Aunt Hope was forbidden to share. I think I forgot she was the cause of the long hours Uncle Ber and I spent holed up together, while he sawed and planed and chiselled, and I redistributed the sawdust with a broom.

Then, when our birthday gift – I thought of it as ours – was finished and the birthday was only a week away, I began to be anxious. To have doubts and fears. The wood Uncle Ber used for the cabinet was oak and ply: ply with oak veneer for the sliding doors, ply for the interior partitions, oak for the rest. At the carpentry stage, all the wood had seemed a more or less uniform whitish grey. When, at the end, varnish was applied, the oak parts – that is to say, everything that was visible without opening the doors – turned a greenish yellow-brown. Or perhaps a yellowish green-brown. A colour I was certain Aunt Hope, who on our shopping trips was in the habit of staring in the windows of antique shops and pointing at plum-coloured furniture and deciding, 'I'll have that, and that and that,' would not appreciate.

Even more worrying, the pattern of the grain, unremarkable before polishing, now leaped off the surface to dazzle and disturb. Straight, dark, broken, needle-thin lines, striping the length of the cabinet's tabletop, were crossed randomly by smooth, broad, unbroken waves, pale and shiny as scars. As scars? No, they were scars! Aunt Hope's birthday present was horribly wounded! I wanted to ask Uncle Ber, 'Is it meant to look like that?' and also 'What happens if it isn't what she wants?' I wanted to warn him (and therefore, if need be, to protect him), but my uncle's confidence prevented such questions. Recently his whistling in the workroom had had an exuberance, a tunefulness, even, I'd never detected before. If he had no doubts about the success of our present, how could I? And at least, I comforted myself, the cabinet was needed. How often had we heard Aunt Hope complain that the record collection had no proper home? (Its improper home was a shelf in the living room, on which the records were stacked flat, in piles according to size, the biggest ones overlapping the edge because the shelf wasn't wide enough. In order to reach the records, you had to push an armchair and a dicey standard lamp and a small table out of the way. When you'd done that there was still the problem of finding the record you wanted, which, in the way of these things, was usually at the bottom of a pile.)

'Open it,' Uncle Ber said after breakfast on the birthday morning, 'go on, open it.' For Aunt Hope seemed to be in no hurry to open her present. It stood on the stringy rug in the middle of the living-room floor, disguised by several sheets of wrapping paper. Several different designs and colours of wrapping paper. I had chosen the papers myself, and camouflaged the difficult parcel, and plastered it and my clothes with sticky tape, on my own, at Uncle Ber's insistence. Perhaps he felt it would be good for my morale to take some sort of creative hand in the enterprise.

'How many rolls of Sellotape did this take? Was it my Sellotape?' Aunt Hope asked in that dry way of hers that might be a joke, and again might not be. And still she did not open our present. Instead, she opened cards that the postman had brought, and took her time, reading out the messages and the rhymes when there were rhymes, holding the cards out for us to see. She sat on the arm of a chair to do this, and after each card had had its due, she got up and balanced it on the mantelpiece, rearranging the ornaments to make room. There were a great many cards, sent by staff and pupils at her school. There was a huge one with an embossed satin rose on the front that they'd all signed, and smaller individual ones; there were home-made cards from her favourites that had cryptic messages inside.

"Open our present now. *Now*.' My impatience was largely on Uncle Ber's account. It was wrong that he should be kept waiting. But I dreaded the moment of unveiling, even so.

'Just a minute.' Aunt Hope was going through the envelopes in her lap, turning them over, looking for something, not finding it. Finally she got up. Finally she walked round our present, slowly, with her head on one side and a finger pressed to her bottom lip, and examined it from every angle.

'Well. What elegant wrapping paper! Did you choose it, Hannah? Now, what can this be? It's very big. It's long. It's box-shaped. It's a coffin. Is it a coffin?' She looked first at my uncle, then at me. I wanted to kill her.

Aunt Hope got down on her hands and knees and started to tug at my elegant wrapping paper.

'I don't think I'm going to be able to undo this without tearing it – such a shame because it's so pretty.' She tugged at a double band of Sellotape. 'In fact, I don't think I'm going to be able to get at my coffin, I mean my present, at all without a pair of scissors.'

In a fury I ran to the kitchen to fetch the kitchen scissors, and ran back and handed them over; and then I stood beside my uncle and held his hand and my breath as Aunt Hope began to snip and tear.

There, at last, was our cabinet. Greeny-yellow in the morning sunlight, darkly grooved and brilliantly scarred. Aunt Hope stared at it. Then she clapped her hands.

'I was right, it is a coffin! I've always wanted one of those.

But where's the brass plate with my name on? And where are the handles?'

It took me days to forgive Aunt Hope. It was not just her cheerful cruelty that was unpardonable (the memory of those hours in the workroom spent on her behalf haunted me; I could not bear to think of my uncle's misplaced purpose and optimism). No, it was that, through the use of one word, she contrived to change the character of our gift for ever. In the same way that a lavatory bowl is art if the artist says so, so our record cabinet became a coffin the moment Aunt Hope decided that a coffin was what it was. That it was a record container too – later that day Uncle Ber demonstrated its usefulness in this – was secondary. What we had in our living room was a coffin on legs that for the time being housed thirty or so discs made from a shellac-based compound, plus twenty or so discs made from a vinyl plastic.

A few weeks after her birthday Aunt Hope came back from school with an embroidered linen throw which she threw over the coffin. 'To protect it,' she explained. Hadn't we noticed how scratched and stained the beautiful polished surface was getting?

After that, except when it was in the wash, the throw stayed where it was. It changed nothing, for we all knew what it concealed, and it was a nuisance. Its folds made a curtain over the sliding doors and got in the way of anyone who felt like putting 'Deep River' or 'Tiger Rag' or 'Don't You Rock Me, Daddy-O' on the turntable.

I had a father once. Everyone has had a father at some time. My father married my mother before I was born, which makes me the legitimate offspring of a legitimate union, a fact which at certain periods of my life has seemed important. My son Finch isn't legitimate, but I don't think it bothers him. Lots of his friends are love children, as bastards are now called.

For years I thought of myself as fatherless, as not having a father; and I also thought of myself as being an only child. But I had a brother once. My brother was my parents' first-born. He was three and a half years older than me and his name was Ivo. One summer's day when my brother and I were being driven to the sea, our car, bowling along the main road, was hit by a car that came out of a side road. (That is the picture I had: hot sunshine; blue sky; a car bowling merrily along; grown-ups in the front chatting and laughing; children in the back shouting and pointing. And then, out of a side road, out of nowhere, out of the blue . . .).

I was unhurt in the accident. I was strapped in a child's seat fixed to the back seat of the car; but Ivo, on the back seat beside me, unstrapped, was killed. He was four and three-quarters years old. I don't remember Ivo, I was too young when he died to remember him; and I don't remember the accident, although I feel I do because of the recurring dream I still have. This dream, the most recent versions, must be influenced by the anti-drink-driving 'commercials' the government puts out on television. I'm always a spectator, for one thing, never the infant in the kiddy seat. I'm outside the car. Another reason for suspecting the TV influence is the speed of the action in my dream and the behaviour of its soundtrack. Immediately after the car in the side road shoots out and hits our car, my dream goes into silence and slow motion. In slow silence our car doors cave in and the windows explode. In slow silence my rag-doll brother bursts from our car and sails into the sky before free-falling through a firework display of spears and splinters and stars.

That's the usual sequence, and usually my dream ends there, or else with the blue, jumpy lights of ambulances and police cars. But not long ago I had a different dream, or perhaps the same dream with additions and variations. I'm a journalist this time, at the wheel of a car that's following the car that has Ivo and me inside. I know from the start what to expect, and I'm afraid and keep my distance. (Not too much distance, however, because I have to be on the spot; I'm a reporter, commissioned to write a piece about this accident that has not yet taken place.) Next thing I know I'm at a table writing my report, trying to find the words. Aunt Hope is there, all of a sudden, leaning over my shoulder. 'Why do you keep using the word "accident"?' Aunt Hope asks. ' "Accident" is too long, too drawn out, too weak. There's no impact in "accident", it's not sufficiently onomatopoeic. What you want is "crash" and "smash", you should be using "shatter" or "crush".' Aunt Hope takes my pencil out of my hand and writes a word in my reporter's notebook. The word is 'smithereens'. She reads it out to me. 'Smithereens,' she says, 'an Irish word that Diarmid would use. No word has yet been invented that better describes the sound and sight of shattered glass. You need "smithereens" in there somewhere.' And that's when I lose my temper with Aunt Hope and start shouting. 'Fuck off!' I shout. 'Fuck off, fuck off, fuck off!'

I was still shouting 'Fuck off' when I woke up. (It was

most likely the shouting that woke me.) I made myself put the light on then, and write the dream down before it evaporated. There was a stub of a pencil by my bed, and beside it my Trip to Arizona notebook, and I wrote my dream in that. I wanted a record because I couldn't get over how real Aunt Hope was, how typically herself she was. She said exactly the sort of things, in exactly the same way, she would have said in life in those circumstances. That's what I thought when I woke in the night.

In the morning, I picked up the notebook and read what I'd written and was disappointed. The dream, as I'd recorded it, was nonsense. Aunt Hope was not real. For example, it was very doubtful that she would try to sell me 'smithereens', a word she would probably have considered so well-worn as to be a cliché. In my head I could hear her saying it. I could hear her saying, 'Smashed to smithereens. Well. Fancy.'

These dreams, these nightmares, about the accident or car smash are the inventions of my own subconscious. Of course I realise that. The bald facts of it were told me by Aunt Hope when I was five or six, when she considered I was old enough to take them in.

I blamed my brother when Aunt Hope told me. Not for the accident itself, I could see that it was not his fault, but for everything that happened afterwards. What happened afterwards was that my mother went off her head, and very soon into hospital. What happened when she went into hospital – and showed no signs of coming out or of wanting to – was that my father abandoned my mother and me and the animal-foodstuffs company he worked for. He bought himself a one-way ticket to Perth, Western Australia, and left his big and little troubles behind him.

' "The Dysfunctional Family" – that's you and me.' Finch was reading the paper, that section of it that deals with social issues and is called 'Family' or 'Health' or 'Life' or 'Living'.

(And in my experience is very often about break-up and deprivation and sickness and death and dying.) There was a bag of nuts and raisins on the table and he was helping himself from it as he read, putting a hand out from time to time and feeling his way into the bag with his fingers. I was ironing, and at the same time trying to watch the television over his head, but I kept being distracted by his hand as it stole from bag to mouth and back again, and by his baseball cap.

This cap is midnight blue with yellow detail. It has a yellow button top centre and a pattern of yellow spots, or suns, as I think of them, widely spaced, over the crown. The peak, too, is yellow. Immediately above the peak is a large letter M, and across the M a label (it looks like a label, but it's part of the cap itself and not stuck on) which says 'Michigan'. On either side of the cap is written, in smaller, sloping script, 'Wolverines'. Finch was wearing his cap back to front as a lot of boys do. Perhaps he imagined the back-to-front fashion made him look butch and streetwise. But Finch can't look butch whatever he wears. In his back-to-front cap and white T-shirt he reminded me of an eider duck preening its neck feathers.

Finch can't look butch whatever he wears. That's the key sentence, the root of the problem. (My problem with Finch; his problem, I suspect, with me; our problem together.) In the corners of Finch's tiny mouth, on his upper lip, black hairs are growing. I first noticed the dark smudges on his top lip about a year ago, and put it down to his nonstop eating and drinking habits. Coke, I thought, or hot chocolate. Ice cream. Soy sauce, maybe. I told Finch to go and wash it off. Over the following weeks I kept telling him to go and wash whatever it was off. Soon afterwards his voice started to crack. It kept slipping out of its usually smooth-running top gear. I discerned this gradually, while occupied with other thoughts and tasks and with private sadnesses I would have died rather than discuss with him. 'When's supper?' he would ask, lifting his head from his homework, or 'What is supper?'

or 'Is there supper?' – and in the course of these brief questions his voice would slip out of gear. It would stumble into third, plunge into second. I would hear him revving his voice, up or down, it was hard to tell which. At last I twigged – his voice sounded sore. A throat infection! And in termtime too!

'If it's not gone by tomorrow we'd better get you to the doctor,' I told him, 'throat infections can be nasty; you probably need an antibiotic. Let's have a look. Open wide. Say "Ah".'

Unusually for him, Finch seemed embarrassed. He twisted his head away. 'My voice is breaking,' he squeak-croaked. 'It's called puberty, I believe.'

Puberty! My son was fourteen, on the late side these days for the sex glands to 'become functional' and for the 'secondary sexual characteristics to emerge'. (After he went to bed I looked up 'puberty' in his dictionary, to see what it had to say.) Yet the idea that he might be 'pubescent' had never crossed my mind. The truth is, even though he'd grown recently, as much as two or three inches, so that he was taller than I was; even though I thought of him as a teenager, and at some level knew him to be an adolescent, I had not made the connection between Finch's bodily changes, his unreliable vocal chords and vestigial moustache, and sex.

Finch's femaleness is to blame. He has breasts, important ones, easily visible under shirts and sweaters. His breasts tremble when he walks. The distribution of his adipose tissue – on the chest, as I said, and also on the upper arms, the stomach, the hips, the buttocks, the thighs – is what you'd expect on a well-developed adult human female. (I hope 'femaleness' is the right word. 'Femininity' is not the right word, it's too strong, or maybe too weak. 'Effeminacy' isn't right. If it's 'semantically exact', as Diarmid would say, it isn't the word I want. I equate 'effeminate' with 'homosexual', and there are no indications, I've had no reason to suspect, that Finch is gay.) Sometimes, when I'm ironing or cooking and see, out of the corner of my eye, that white,

puffy hand stealing over the table towards a bag of nuts –
or crisps, or poppadums or Scrumptious Cheesey Chews – I
think, *There's another female in this room.*

Oh, if only Finch were female! If only he were a girl, we
would love each other then. I tell myself this and I believe
it. This girl-Finch and I would link arms on walks, like the
mother and daughter I followed in the High Street once.
Identically dressed in jeans and anoraks, this mother and
daughter skipped along the pavement. Heads together, gig-
gling, hooting – they might both have been schoolgirls – they
fairly danced along. At a tactful distance, I followed them. I
stopped when they stopped. I stopped outside the plate glass
of an electricity showroom, the steel mesh of a jeweller's.
While they chose microwaves and emeralds, and fell about
and hugged each other, I thought: this is what I want from
motherhood. What I wanted from daughterhood. This is
what I'm owed. This is what I deserve.

Finch, if you were a girl, we would be like those two, I
swear. You could forget the monstrous word 'dysfunctional'.
You and I would share confidences. We'd share clothes and
jokes and impossible desires if you were a girl. And your
fatness wouldn't matter. You could be as fat as you wanted.
Fat girls can be adorable. Believe me, I could love, I could
adore, a fat girl.

History and art and the history of art corroborate me on
this. Go into the National Gallery (as Diarmid and Finch
and I used to on wet Saturdays); wander through its halls,
and you'll discover a universal, centuries-old celebration of
fat female flesh, naked and clothed. Rubens and the Exal-
tation of Cellulite! Finch is a clever boy; he could write a
thesis on that.

'Words, words, words,' says Aunt Hope.

We've just finished lunch. It's a boiling afternoon and Uncle Ber has gone upstairs for what he refers to as a 'Harry Kipington', an expression he pinched from a young army officer he once shared a compartment with on a train. 'I'm Harry Flakers,' this young officer had said, seemingly by way of introduction, 'mind if I put my feet up on the seat? I'm desperate for a Harry Kipington.' Uncle Ber laughs whenever he retells this story, and since I got the point of it I laugh too, but it makes Aunt Hope sigh. I stand over her where she lies, stretched out on her back on a rug with a cushion under her head and with her dog prostrate across her feet. She's holding her book in front of her face, and is having to lower it and the balance it on her stomach each time she needs to turn a page. The council has just resurfaced our road and the air in the garden smells overpoweringly of tar. It's a smell that usually makes me happy, I suppose because, like the smells of hot grass and suntan oil, it's connected in my mind with day trips to the sea; but today nothing has been said about going anywhere and I'm annoyed with my aunt.

'That's not an answer,' I say, 'it's not a proper answer.'

'It's truthful, however.' Aunt Hope keeps her eyes on her book. Jemma keeps her wary eyes on me.

'It's not the answer I wanted. You know what I meant.'

'It probably wasn't the answer Polonius wanted – or was expecting. But it was the answer he got.'

So I'm right – 'words, words, words' are not Aunt Hope's words, she's borrowed them. I can tell when she's 'borrowing' because her voice changes; not dramatically but enough for me to know. Suddenly, for the first time, I see that Aunt Hope plays games with me. This particular game consists of saying something borrowed and mysterious and then, if I show any curiosity, if I so much as raise an eyebrow, keeping the mystery – and the solution to the mystery – to herself. She won't refuse to answer questions, she avoids the possibility of them by closing her eyes or by bringing in an extra something – Polonius – to confuse me further. Or she changes the subject entirely. It's an odd game for an aunt to play, I think; it's a very odd game for a teacher of English to play.

(But I see now that I played my own games with Aunt Hope. For example, I wasn't interested in her book, the title or the contents. I wasn't a reader, although I enjoyed being read to. She knew this; it was she who called me 'fozy', after all. She knew quite well that when I came and breathed over her and sweetly enquired, 'What are you reading, Auntie?' I was merely looking for an opening for my real question: Can we go swimming soon?)

'Can we go swimming soon?'

'No. We're having a lie-down.'

'Can we go later?'

'I don't expect so. Not today.'

Why not today? I sit down on the rug beside my aunt and begin to pull up tufts of grass. The ripping noise this makes is the noise horses and cattle make when they graze. We had a picnic recently in a field that contained one brown horse and several black-and-white cows. They moved in a line in front of us, grandly and slowly, ripping and crunching. One cow lifted its tail and messed itself, but kept on walking and eating (and flicking its tail, and twitching); and all the time it kept up that rhythmical rip rip rip.

'Could you stop pulling up the lawn, please?'

'I'm a horse.' (I feel like a horse because there's a fly that keeps landing on me. It's a horrible, silent fly; it swings to and fro silently, it lands silently on my bare leg and then, when I twitch, it takes off again without any sound at all.) I carry on with my grazing and ripping.

'Hannah. I said stop.'

Rip rip rip . . .

Aunt Hope lies tense and rigid on the rug. Her eyes are on her book still, but she's not reading it. I can tell she isn't, in the same way you can always tell when someone's awake, even when they're quite still and pretending to be asleep. I know she's longing to slap me, she won't be able to control herself much longer.

I go on with my task, but more quietly, less urgently. My grazing now has a melancholy air. After each slow sad rip I sweep the grass croppings into my lap. They're all colours – green or yellow at the tips, brown or whitish at the roots – and they're soft as feathers because it's not just grass, there's a lot of moss and clover in here. I shall make a nest with this stuff, I decide.

Bang! The sound of Aunt Hope's book shutting in a hurry and with force. The sound of Aunt Hope's temper getting lost.

I stop. I open my mouth to explain that I'm bored and lonely without a friend my age to play with – and close it again. Complaints (which is how my explanations will be perceived) will never work; they'll never achieve what I desire. For, as is always being pointed out, I have the whole garden to play in. I have a climbable apple tree. I have a pond, with a variety of oceans, to sail a variety of ships on. I have a hose with a sprinkler attached that two twists of the tap by the garage wall turns into a spinning, icy rainbow I'm allowed to jump in and out of. I cannot, not, not, not, be bored.

But (I suddenly see) I can be sad. I'm sad anyway. So I hang my head. I say, in an almost whisper, 'I miss my mummy.'

No sooner are the words out than they're true, I do miss my mother. Not the mother I have – and once killed by mistake – who spends her slumped days dropping ash on the day-room carpet, but the mother I do not have and have never known. The mother I've strenuously invented, whom I love and who loves me. That mother. The pretty, energetic, ready-for-anything one who, on a hot summer's day, will not just want us to go swimming; she will insist on taking me. ('Hurry up now, sweetheart, get your towel!') The loss of this mother, for ever, is terrible. Terrible and dreadful, quite dreadfully sad. In no time I'm awash with grief, crying my eyes out.

Aunt Hope sits up and puts down her book, moves Jemma off her feet and pulls me into her arms; she crushes me against her so hard I can scarcely breathe. The grass croppings in my lap fly everywhere, all over us. 'Poor baby,' she says, over and over, 'poor Hannah, poor baby.'

Aunt Hope isn't a natural hugger and endearments aren't her style. At bedtimes, a peck on the cheek or a quick ruffle of my hair are what I'm used to from her. (Sometimes, just before switching off the light and leaving the room with Jemma at her heels, she'll press the end of my nose, firmly, with a forefinger.) Our new, breathless intimacy is painful; the smell, musky sweet, of my aunt's body, embarrassing. Perhaps Aunt Hope's embarrassed too, for very soon – as soon as she decently can, it seems – she lets go of me.

'You must always tell me if you're missing your mummy – here, that won't do.' (With the back of my hand I'm wiping tears and grass and slimy snot stuff from my mouth and chin, at the same time sniffing everything within range back up my nose.) Aunt Hope conjures a handkerchief from the waistband of her cotton skirt and shakes it out. Then she folds it into a pad and begins to blot my face all over, blot blot blot. She stands up, pulls me to my feet and brushes the grass and moss from our clothes. 'We don't have to wait till Thursdays to visit your mummy, you know,' she says reassuringly. 'It's the holidays, so we can go and see her any time. Any time, any day you want. Of course we can! We'll go this evening, soon as you've had your tea.'

What? Oh, no! No, no, no, Aunt Hope!

Today is Saturday. We spent a hideous hour with my mother only the day before yesterday. If only Aunt Hope knew, if only I could tell her, how guilty my mother makes me feel. How guilty I am. It's my fault she's in that awful place, it's my fault she doesn't love me, it's my fault my brother is dead and my father went away. It's all, all, my fault!

'Did you say something, darling?' asks my aunt who never calls me darling.

I don't answer at once – I've got to get this right. If I get it wrong, within a few hours we'll be at the bus stop, climbing the stairs of the wrong bus. The right bus, a number 8, is the one that lets us off a few yards from the Pool Hall. Inside the Pool Hall are three pools, children's, Olympic and diving.

'Aunt Ho-ope, I would like to see Mummy.' This lie is risky, but probably necessary. 'I would like to. But, but shouldn't we go to the pool instead so Uncle Ber can have his swimming exercise? I mean, he didn't go yesterday, or Thursday, and you said the doctor said he has to swim three times a week at least. Three times at least, you said.'

Aunt Hope doesn't answer at once. She presses her hands heavily on my shoulders and stares down at me. I try to twist my head away, but she's not having it, no, she frees a hand from my shoulders and with it grasps my chin, forcing it upwards so she can have a good look at my face. At my eyes.

'Look at me. No, look.' She waits till I am, till I'm looking straight at the lie-detector eyes boring into mine. 'Are you false?' she asks. And then, 'Are you as crafty as I think you are?'

I don't remember how I answered her. I do remember that we did go to the pool, and my uncle did get his swimming exercise – as I did too, of course. I imagine that Aunt Hope had a tussle with herself about giving in to me, but she must have been relieved not to have to make that extra journey to the Rose Vale. For reasons I knew nothing of, she dreaded those visits at least as much as I did.

In Finch's opinion I'm a control freak. I have a neurotic need, he says, shared by most murderers and all serial killers, to control and be in control. This mania of mine was pointless, he told me recently, 'when you consider that, ultimately, human beings have no control'. Death was the first example he gave of human powerlessness, weather the second – typhoons, hurricanes and so on. As with death, we might know more or less when to expect them, but we couldn't prevent them. Earthquakes were another example. (All this because I'd asked him, please, to get his books off the table so I could get supper, his supper, on the table.)

We live in a dangerous age, he reminded me, dipping his little finger in the ketchup and then sucking it, far more dangerous than astrophysicists cared to reveal or governments dared to contemplate. Forget the Bomb, he said. (I wasn't thinking about the Bomb.) Did I realise the Bomb was only ever a metaphor for a different kind of megaton explosion? For a different quality of fear? A fear so terrible it has to be suppressed? If Jupiter could be hit by a fireball, well, watch this cislunar space! After supper, he polished the window with his sleeve and scanned the sky above the houses opposite for the coming, inevitable apocalypse. Out there were meteors and asteroids, comets and bolides, all heading our way. Booom! Like most people, I associate apocalyptic belief with weirdos and weirdo religious cults – the White Brotherhood, the Temple Cult, that sort of thing. Is Finch heading their way?

I'm not a control freak. No. Not to the degree my Aunt Hope was one when I was a child. For instance, she hated swimming (the sea was cold and an open sewer; public pools were public lavatories, afloat with fingerstalls and

Elastoplast); water was not her element. 'I can't abide it going over my head,' she'd say when I begged her to come in with me. 'I can't stand the feel of it up my nose and the sound of it in my ears, I can't bear that awful rushing deafness.' Yet despite these feelings she insisted on escorting Uncle Ber and me to the baths, as she called them, for our swim.

While my uncle was still in the process of sorting out his change, shuffling coins round the palm of one hand with the forefinger of the other, she'd be at the ticket booth paying for 'One adult swimmer, one child, one spectator'. That done, she'd supervise my safe passage through the wounding, cranking turnstile, propel me to the female changing cubicles, wait while I changed, check nothing had got left behind on the ledge or under the ledge, fold my clothes into my numbered locker, turn the key and then pocket it. I was capable of doing these things for myself, girls younger than I managed them. I wanted to swim with my locker key fastened to my wrist or ankle, as they did and as my uncle did, but she wouldn't have it. My wrists were too small, she said, the key would fall off. It would fall off and go straight to the bottom of the pool – and then where would we be? She couldn't follow me into the pre-swim showers that adjoined the Pool Hall; it was a Swimmers Only area, and a woman in a tracksuit with her arms folded across her chest enforced this rule, but she stood at the entrance, peering and waving like someone on a quayside, calling out instructions until I vanished from view.

Next sighting of my aunt, she'd be leaning over the guard wall of the viewing terrace, scanning the three pools for my, and Uncle Ber's whereabouts. The viewing terrace was reached via stairs and the cafeteria; it was a narrow passage that ran the length of the Pool Hall, high up, and jutted out from the interior wall. No chairs were provided for the viewers. If you wanted to sit you had to pinch a chair from the cafeteria, which Aunt Hope usually managed to do. Except when she was actively looking for us – leaning out and swinging her red neck scarf like a pendulum to attract our attention – Aunt Hope, on her chair, reading her book, was invisible from the water below.

I loved the Pool Hall. It was immense and grand as a cathedral. The sting-blinding chlorine apart, everything about the place pleased me: the pools themselves and their separate geometries (one square, one rectangle, one semicircle); the shifting, shrugging water with its fractured loops and plaits of light (this when we were early and the pools empty); and in peak, holiday hours, the echoing shouts and tremendous, plunging splashes, the sudden whistle blasts of the life guards who paced alongside with a head-down, sideways swing, like brown bears in the zoo. In the years before I could swim – that is, before I could do a full length of the Olympic pool unaided and without water wings – I stayed in the children's pool until Uncle Ber had completed his obligatory ten lengths. He'd come to fetch me after, and give me a lesson in breaststroke up the shallow end. Then, with one hand supporting my chin or stomach, he would glide me to the deep end and back again. Look at me, Aunt Hope, look, look, look, I'm swimming! But Aunt Hope had a talent for not looking when she should have been.

Uncle Ber turned into a different person in the Pool Hall. The transformation had to do with his eyes, chlorine-crimson instead of blue, and with his hair, normally white fluff, now dark and sleeked so closely to his head he might as well have been bald. This made his ears stand out and his nose bigger. It made him appear younger and resemble, more than he usually did, the portrait of himself in naval uniform a sailor friend of his had painted that hung in our hall. Another thing that made him different was his near-nakedness. I never saw him without clothes at home. Not once did I surprise him in the bath, or stripped to the waist for shaving, and I was never quite prepared for his body, for the shocking intimacy of it. The contrast between his ruddy face, neck and forearms and the dazzling whiteness of the rest of him was startling and fascinating. The exception to this whiteness was his feet, which were long, narrow and wax-coloured; his toes, yellow, his toenails, purple-green. When he stood on the wet tiled rim of the pool and flexed and curled his yellow toes, his tendons stood out in long fanning spikes. I know now that they were tendons, but at the time I believed them to be bones.

But my uncle's body was not the only body in the Pool Hall that interested me. Under cover of my dripping hair, between swims, hunched on the edge of the pool with my legs in the water, I watched all shapes and sizes and ages of bodies, swimming and diving, springing and arching and somersaulting. The ones I liked to look at best, that I found held my attention longest, belonged to boys. Any age of boy, it didn't matter. Eight-year-olds, twelve-year-olds, youths, young men. If asked, I could have listed the details I admired: powerful shoulders, slim waists, sharp knees, narrow wrists and ankles, high calves, flatly muscled chests and stomachs and upper arms.

Then there were the fat boys, or Fat Boys, as I thought of them, in capitals, as though they were a pop group or a comic strip. They always seemed to be there when we were there. They always seemed to be in the cafeteria afterwards, where I was allowed a Coke and a biscuit before going home. No grown-up accompanied them. Their tracksuit pockets bulged and jingled. From what appeared to be an unending supply of pocket money, they took turns to feed the Coke machine, the chocolate-bar machine, the fruit machine and the jukebox. They would slap and shake and kick the machines to hurry them along. I can't hear 'Ob-La-Di Ob-La-Da' or 'Honky Tonk Women' without a picture in my head of the Fat Boys. At the counter, they'd load their trays with crisps, bags and bags, all varieties, and Hula Hoops and pork scratchings, stack them on their chosen table and then sit and crunch their way through. 'Don't stare, Hannah,' Aunt Hope had to say often. They caught me staring once. One of them caught me, and he held his crisp bag out and shook it in a pretence of offering. Then he nudged his neighbour, and they all put their hands behind their ears and wiggled their fingers, yoo-hoo-hoo, and they shook their heads from side to side and stuck their tongues out. Yah-boo.

In the pool, the Fat Boys were noticeable because they stuck together; I never saw one of them strike out on his own. At first I assumed they were brothers. A family of fat boys, I thought. But then I wasn't so sure, because although they had features in common – secret eyes, button-snub noses, tucked mouths, puffball cheeks – there were five of them and they were all, near enough, the same height. As I understood it, they were all, at any one time, ten, or twelve, or thirteen years old. Another noticeable thing about them was that they didn't swim. They stayed close to the side of the big pool, where they floundered in rubber rings and water wings. Often they'd keep one hand on the ledge or rail. (They were cowards, I thought.) The only exercise I saw them take, if you could call it exercise, consisted of ducking and kick-splashing each other and innocent swimmers-by, and of driving water with their hands in a frenzied, backward arm-swinging way into each other's faces. The life guard's whistle blew a lot at their end of the pool. Sometimes the Fat Boys were ordered out of the water, and I'd watch them, one by one, trying to heave themselves up onto the side. I can see a Fat Boy now, his freckled shoulders and wide, slippery back, struggling to lever himself and getting stuck half in, half out, like a beached whale in a TV documentary. A life guard would have to pull them out in the end. As he despatched them to the changing rooms, he'd slap them, playfully but hard, on the bottom or thigh. I recall red finger marks on white, trembling flesh. There were other troublemakers in the pools – boys always; teenage usually; skinny, foul-mouthed, insolent – who were ordered out of the water, but the life guards never slapped them. Only the Fat Boys were slapped.

This is the painful part, remembering how I felt about the Fat Boys when I first began to notice them. Because, irony of ironies, I do remember. I felt sorry for them, one. It wasn't just the rough handling they received from the life guards, it was that their otherness, their unsightliness, demanded it. They were a group, yes, and cocky, but even so they were outsiders, anyone could see. I know I pitied them. Two, I felt shame on their behalf. (With bosoms like theirs, why did their mothers allow them to wear trunks? Why weren't they made to wear T-shirts or a one-piece cover-up bathing suit like mine?) Three, I despised them as cowards. Four – but this came later – I feared them.

The way I've told it, going on about the Fat Boys, Uncle Ber and I spent hours at a time in the pool, but we didn't. We were on an invisible leash – radio-controlled, it some-times felt, like model yachts on a lake. Forty minutes maximum in the water was what Aunt Hope allowed us. On the wall directly opposite the viewing terrace, under the words 'Swimming for All', there was an electric clock, and the first thing my uncle and I had to do on arrival in the Pool Hall was signal to Aunt Hope that we'd understood what the clock had to say. Ten minutes before we were due to come out, Aunt Hope and her red scarf would take up their positions on the viewing terrace. Ten minutes after that, she'd lean dangerously low over the wall and, like a policeman on traffic duty, start up a slow, rhythmical, beck-oning, backward wave.

When did Jocelyn first come to stay with us? Or, how old was I when I first became aware of Jocelyn's presence in our house? Or, what were my feelings about Jocelyn the first time we met? I've asked myself these questions and others like them many times, and I don't know. The answers, which I feel would be enlightening, elude me. If someone had said, at the moment of that first encounter, 'Look, this is Jocelyn, take her in, she's going to play a significant role in your life' – 'role' is the right word, Jocelyn was an actress – I'm sure I would remember. Memory is aided, fixed even, by such triggers.

I do remember, early on, noticing her luggage, unsurprising since the appearance of it, closed and stacked neatly in the hall, or open and overflowing interestingly on her bed, marked her comings and goings, her packings and unpackings. In the cupboard under the stairs my uncle and aunt's luggage stood on end: two dusty leather cases, sharp-cornered, stiff, cracked, scratched, with rusted locks and fasteners, which weighed a ton even when empty; a cardboard overnight case; a brown canvas holdall. Whereas Jocelyn's three pieces, big, medium and small, were all in the same lightweight, light-tan leather, squashy to the touch. The small one, a vanity case, attracted me. It contained colognes and lotions in screwtop bottles held in place by elasticated satin straps.

It was out of the middle-sized suitcase that on one visit she produced two books for me: *Fairy Tales and Legends* by Hans Andersen, and *The Great Panjandrum Himself*. They were her books, she told me, the only books she'd owned as a child. 'There were virtually no books in our house.'

The *Fairy Tales* was cloth-bound in red with a pattern of yellow scrolls on it, the terrifying stories inside exactly matched by the terrifying black-and-white illustrations. Jocelyn would read me one story a night, in bed, so that I fell asleep into dreams of skulls and urns and scythes and cloaked shadows.

The Great Panjandrum Himself was a thin, flat picture book. It was a very short story, and there were very few words on each page:

So she went into the garden to cut a/ cabbage-leaf/ to make/ an apple pie;/ and at the same time a great she-bear,/ coming down the street, pops its head/ into the shop./ What! no soap?/ So he died,/ and she very imprudently married the/ Barber:/ and there were present/ the Picninnies,/ and the Joblillies,/ and the Garyulies,/ and the Great Panjandrum himself,/ with the little round button on top;/ and they all fell to playing the/ game of catch-as-catch-can,/ till the gunpowder ran out at the/ heels of their boots.

'It doesn't make sense,' I said. 'None of it does. Who died?'

'No, well, that's the point, I think. That it shouldn't make sense.'

I was annoyed by the story and took it to Aunt Hope. 'Do you know this book?'

'Of course I do. It's a famous eighteenth-century nonsense – a playwright called Samuel Foote wrote it.' She frowned. 'His name isn't on the cover. Disgraceful!' She peered again. 'What? Great Panjandrum? It's the Grand Panjandrum! Grand Panjandrum's what it ought to be!'

At the beginning, whenever that was, I was required to call Jocelyn, who wasn't one, 'aunt'. This was not her idea, she thought the style ridiculous; although it seemed out of character, the idea was Uncle Ber's. 'Aunt' was a courtesy title, he explained, and courteous was what I should be. My courtesy aunt was a big woman, tall, big-boned, broad-shouldered, deep-breasted. She strode rather than walked, with her head high, loose-limbed and confident. I should have been a man, she sometimes said, take a look at these hands and feet, just have a feel of that muscle! She would roll her sleeve up and clench her fist and make me pinch the muscle in her upper arms and forearms. I was impressed by this evidence of strength, but the idea of her being masculine in any real sense was absurd. 'Womanly' is the word that comes to me now, when I think of the Jocelyn I first knew. Tender, warm. A mother figure. An earth mother.

Jocelyn had tiny teeth, perfect like first teeth, I thought. I couldn't get over this, having a mouthful of gaps and new tombstones myself. Had she never grown a second set? But yes, these were her second teeth, she assured me, opening her mouth wide.

Jocelyn wept easily. Her tears were sudden and brief and, unlike my tears, not prompted by self-pity. She was moved to tears by sad, true things she witnessed, or heard, or read about. ' "Moved to tears"? A bit too well-worn, perhaps?' I can hear Aunt Hope say, a hundred years ago, going through a school essay of mine. But I don't mind if it is a cliché. Jocelyn was moved; she did weep.

The eyes that produced Jocelyn's tears were blue – a fact, but what does it signify? 'Blue' covers such a multitude of colours. It includes a spectrum of tones and moods and personalities. Arctic, stony, steely, aloof, passionless, pitiless. Melancholic, lugubrious, disconsolate. Vague. Trustful. True. Sunny. All these will stand for blue.

The blue of Jocelyn's eyes was lapis lazuli, I think, or ultramarine. When she turned her gaze on you – that is how it felt, a gaze, a light almost, was being turned on you – you drowned in that intense and at the same time translucent sea. (Or if you couldn't face it, didn't feel strong enough, as I often couldn't and didn't, you turned your own head away.) This is hardly an exaggeration. And there was another quality her eyes had that by rights should have disproved the whole idea of sea and water: fieriness. In some moods, in some lights, her eyes were fiery in some way; they could burn you as well as drown you. Firewater then! Which is a paradox, an oxymoron – as Aunt Hope, refilling her whisky glass, once pointed out to me. Blue firewater is the nearest I can get to explaining Jocelyn's eyes.

One day, when the four of us – Uncle Ber, Aunt Hope, Jocelyn and I – were eating lunch in the alcove off the kitchen, a place where nothing matched, where the curtains were yellow with a pattern of red and black chianti bottles, the walls cream, the seersucker tablecloth checked orange with turquoise, the leatherette banquettes a sombre maroon, I laid down my knife and fork and announced, 'Aunt Jocelyn is beautiful.'

'Well, of course she is,' Aunt Hope said, but after a pause because her mouth was full.

'Only the prettiest girls dine at the captain's table,' Uncle Ber said – mystifyingly, for, as I'd heard Aunt Hope mention, his naval career had stopped short of that rank.

'My ears aren't beautiful, Hannah, look.' Jocelyn's heavy gold hair was worn up, in a French pleat, but there were unpinned curls either side of her face covering her ears as far as the lobes, and she now lifted these out of the way to reveal two huge, pointed things. Pixie's ears. Giant pixie's ears.

'You can't get much uglier lugs than these. I always keep 'em covered.' She covered them quickly. 'It's a bit of a bind in my profession. I'm so limited as to what I can do with my hair. Your Aunt Hope has very pretty ears, have you noticed? Perfect, hers are, like a black man's. Why do black men, black people, have such tiny, perfect ears, can anyone tell me?'

No one could. Instead, Aunt Hope pushed her hair back and turned her head this way and that so we could all admire her tiny, perfect, black man's ears.

'Bette Davis has ugly lugs, much to the fore in *Now Voyager*,' Aunt Hope said, 'so you're in good, or maybe bad, company. D'you remember her hairdo in that film? Dear me. Ugly ears don't seem to have affected her career at all; perhaps you should try putting yours on display.'

'Aunt Jocelyn's on the radio, you can't see ears on the radio, so what does it matter what they look like?'

'Not just radio,' Aunt Hope corrected me.

'I can't imagine why no one has yet mentioned my organs of hearing. Of, increasingly, non-hearing,' Uncle Ber said sadly. 'They've been much admired in their time, I can tell you.'

'Ber, your ears are wonderful!' Jocelyn cried, and she flung an arm round his shoulder and kissed him on the cheek. Great, smacking kisses. 'I'm completely crazy about those bat wings, I mean ears!'

Aunt Hope was sitting close beside me on the banquette seat, so close our thighs touched. When Jocelyn said those silly things to my uncle, and kissed him (making his red face and ears redder than ever), I felt my aunt's thigh tense, and I had the sense of her whole body tightening and tensing. I could not see her profile, her hair hid it from me, but I saw, under the table, the knuckles of her left hand whiten as she clenched and unclenched it on her knee.

Badinage. That's the word that comes to me now, thinking of those mealtime conversations when Jocelyn was staying. Silly, I thought then. Even Uncle Ber, normally a sane man, seemed to be infected. Of course the silliness, the laughter, was intriguing in a way, it was bound to be, it was so different from our usual mealtimes at home. Before Jocelyn came, and when she wasn't there, eating was a formal business, silent or punctuated by silence:

'Isn't it time the mower was serviced?' (Aunt Hope.)

'Possibly.' (Uncle Ber.)

Silence.

'Gayles give a discount for mowers brought in before February.' (Aunt Hope.)

'So I understand.' (Uncle Ber.)

'It's the 29th of January today.' (Aunt Hope.)

'It's the the 28th of January, according to today's paper.' (Uncle Ber.) 'Give the Adam's ale a fair wind, would you, Han.'

Silence.

'Can I leave this cabbage? I'm full up; I can't eat any more.' (Me.)

'You mean "may". May I leave this cabbage. Eat one more mouthful, then you may.' (Aunt Hope.)

'If she's had enough, she's had enough.' (Uncle Ber.)

Silence. (Which Uncle Ber might break with his whistling noise.)

'What a pity there's mandarin oranges and sponge for pudding.' (Aunt Hope.)

Silence.

I see now that these dull exchanges were almost invariably spiced with little cruelties and barbs – even the silences contained threats. At the time I don't think I worried, perhaps because, where I was concerned, Aunt Hope's brand of sadism – as over the mandarin oranges, my favourite – never amounted to much. I would always be given my pudding, when there was pudding, in the end. As to the dullness, dull equalled safe, and in those days safety was the condition that despite my complaints about boredom probably suited me best. ('On a becalmed ship there's always the risk of starvation, but at least you're unlikely to drown' – Uncle Ber.) And there was something else about those tripartite mealtimes: I was at the centre of them, whether pig in the middle or apex of the triangle. My aunt and uncle might play games

– 'fight' is too strong for the subtle, point-scoring tactics they employed – but without me, how would they have managed?

How different when Jocelyn joined us, when there were four at the table. I could be centre of nothing then. We had been foursomes before, on the rare occasions a friend came to tea, and when my mother came home from the Rose Vale, but for these I had a clearly defined role of host or body-guard. When Jocelyn was present I had no role. I was reduced to little more than silent spectator of a new triad, an unfamiliar game (rash and dangerous, it often seemed to me), with rules I did not understand.

Whose friend was Jocelyn, exactly? It was hard to know. She seemed to be Aunt Hope's. It was to Aunt Hope, not my uncle, that she addressed her frequent letters – almost the only personal letters, I think, my aunt received. The letters were several sheets long and written on both sides of the large, dark-blue paper. 'Expensive,' Aunt Hope would say, contriving to sound both disdainful and impressed. 'Classy. Just look at that watermark. I dread to think how much this paper sets her back,' she'd say. Aunt Hope did not offer to read her letters aloud, but from the quick-change expressions on her face as she first read, then reread, certain passages or a whole letter, you could guess her feelings. Elation, bafflement, amusement, mock outrage, disbelief, anxiety, disappoint-ment, all these and other emotions less easy to deduce went flickering by. From the way she folded her letter and slid it back into its blue envelope and then into her pocket, you could tell whether its contents had, all in all, pleased or failed to please.

Jocelyn seemed to be Aunt Hope's friend. And yet I some-times felt she was closer to my uncle. For example, she was far more demonstrative towards him than to my aunt. On Sunday afternoon walks, which I hated, she'd slip her arm through his; on the sofa after tea, watching *Thunderbirds*, she'd steal an arm round his shoulder and keep it there. She teased him, she made him laugh; something my aunt was incapable of doing. She was practical, a maker and a mender (she mended my pencil box and the strap of my sandals) who'd breeze into the workroom and pick up a carpentry tool. ('Excellent pupil,' I can hear Uncle Ber mutter to himself. 'Quick learner, damn quick.') She was a strong swimmer and a graceful, precise diver. (When Jocelyn came with us to the Pool Hall, Aunt Hope abandoned her book. Her dark glasses were trained on the diving pool, on Jocelyn climbing hand over hand to the high board, where she sprang, and dived, and entered the water like a bullet, and surfaced, and struck out for the ladder, and repeated this mesmerising sequence – up and down and round – again and again and again.)

Jocelyn was not driven insane by my uncle's whistling; she even thought the coffin-cabinet a splendid object. It was a crime, she said, to keep it covered. When Uncle Ber had angina, her show of unconcerned concern, of unflustered sympathy, was, I could see, exactly what he needed. 'I'll give you a hand up the stairs, Ber,' she'd say, casual and firm. 'I was going up anyway.' And, astonishingly, he'd let her.

Jocelyn had a car, and when she was staying, Aunt Hope and I seldom had to go anywhere by bus. She enjoyed chauffeuring us, Jocelyn said, she had to keep busy when she was 'resting', she needed to do something useful, otherwise she might wonder what she was for. Otherwise she might go mad. The car was a Volkswagen Beetle. An unpatriotic choice, according to Aunt Hope. Why didn't Jocelyn drive a Morris or an Austin? Or a Rolls-Royce? A French car would be crime enough – but a German car? A car designed during the Nazi regime? *Gott im himmel!* That aspect aside, the engine was noisy, the front seats agony, the back seat right on top of the wheels, and the daft beetle shape meant no room for your head or legs. No room to breathe. Nowadays, when I hear the expression 'Hell on wheels' I see Jocelyn's midnight-blue Volkswagen and I hear Aunt Hope's complaints. But her complaints about the back seat were nonsense, because my aunt didn't sit in the back. I did. Only when Uncle Ber came with us did she have to sit in the back. (My uncle's seniority, his masculinity, his dodgy heart, his long legs, all these determined his right to sit in the front passenger seat.)

The journeys to the Rose Vale were less awful when Jocelyn drove us there. No hanging around in the dark or rain; no fear of meeting a school enemy on the bus. And Jocelyn had the gift of making even dull food-shopping trips feel like an excursion. As soon as she switched on the engine you felt it, a prickle of excitement, a sense of the opening-up of pleasurable possibilities. She liked to sing at the wheel, an aid to concentration, she said. Her singing voice was sweet and somehow airy. It was not a powerful voice; a light soprano, I suppose.

Jocelyn's favourite driving songs were hits from ancient musical shows I'd never heard of, but on the Rose Vale trips she'd start on something endless and repetitive, and make Aunt Hope and me sing along with her. 'One Man Went to Mow', we'd sing, and 'Green Grow the Rushes-O' and 'Ten Green Bottles'. In the back seat I belted these out, shutting my mind to the purpose of our journey, ignoring the aspects, melancholy or sinister, of the words that at other times would trouble me. The lily-white boys, for instance, were tragic figures, so ill and pale and green; one was one and all alone and evermore would be so, the worst fate imaginable; and as for those hanging bottles, why should all ten of them accidentally fall off that – as I envisaged it – grey prison wall? There was a long-drawn-out emphasis on 'accidentally' that made you wonder if they hadn't been pushed.

When we arrived at the Rose Vale I always hoped Jocelyn would come in with us. I wanted her to meet my mother. That's what I told myself then. Jocelyn was the one person, I believed, who possessed the power to cheer my mother up. To cure her. She had only to step into my mother's room, to smile, to hold out her strong, workmanlike hand, and a miracle would happen. Within seconds, my mother would take up her bed and walk. But she had no need of it – there was a bed, a less hideous, more comfortable bed, made up and waiting for her at home. She would leave her bed, and her bedside locker, and her tobacco-stained chair, and her beetroot curtains and, on the windowsill, the melting freesias we'd brought the week before – and run. Towards me, with her arms outstretched. 'Hannah!' she'd exclaim. 'Hannah, my own, my only, my darling child!' And she'd rest her hands on my shoulders and examine my face with rapture. 'Why, you're beautiful!' (A delighted laugh.) 'And I never knew.' She'd enfold me then, and kiss me. And without a word to each other, without stopping for goodbyes to Matron or the nurses (kind Nurse Fitzgerald; sadistic Nurse Reeves), or the kitchen staff (batty Linda in her grease-floured overall), we'd run out of the Rose Vale, my mother, my aunt Hope, Jocelyn and I. We'd run out of the front door, down the steps and away. Never, never, never, *never* to return.

A night-time fantasy, a celluloid cliché, embarrassing and painful to think about now. What I really wanted from Jocelyn's presence in my mother's prison was protection. From my mother, from Aunt Hope, from myself, from the uneasy threesome we made. From the fake heartiness, the sealed, institutional warmth and the interminable silences that filled our visiting hour. (And also, though less urgently, from the rotten-sweet smell in the corridors and the 'Twelve Sunflowers in a Vase' on the wall.) Those were the reasons I begged Jocelyn so hard, every time, to come in with us. 'Please, Jocelyn,' I'd beg, 'please, please, please.' But she wouldn't. She wouldn't even get out of the car. 'I can't bear those places.' Once she'd dropped us at the steps, she'd drive to the furthest end of the car park, as far from the pebble-dashed façade as possible, and park there, facing the fence, under the dismal awning of laurels and macrocarpa I will for ever associate with the Rose Vale. When, after an hour, Aunt Hope and I emerged, we'd find our chauffeur asleep with the radio on, her head thrown back, her mouth wide open, all her tiny teeth on display, like a child in the dentist's chair.

'How did you and Aunt Hope meet? Where? How long have you known each other?'

I was eleven when I asked these questions, when I remember asking these questions, though it's inconceivable I hadn't asked them, or others like them, many times before. It was Easter Monday, I think, a bank holiday at any rate, and the women of the house were in the kitchen. My task was mashing the potatoes – the one job, Aunt Hope said, I could make a hash of with impunity – and Jocelyn and Aunt Hope were skirmishing round me, pushing each other out of the way of the chopping board which they both needed to use. At the same time they were arguing about a play they'd once been to together. The sets had been awful, Aunt Hope said, they had nothing to do with the play, they were entirely out of keeping with the spirit of the piece, the whole production had been a disaster. How could Jocelyn now stand there and smile and pretend otherwise? When she'd damned it as rubbish at the time?

While this was going on it suddenly struck me that my aunt and Jocelyn shared a history I did not share; that there was a whole world of plays and people, jokes and secrets, good faith and bad temper between them that I knew nothing of. They had each other and I had no one. So I asked my questions, more out of pique than true curiosity, and I asked them of Jocelyn because of the two she was the one, I thought, more likely to break off the argument and turn her blue eyes and attention on me.

Jocelyn put down her chopping knife. 'Haven't I ever told you that?' She sounded amazed. 'D'you mean to say Hope hasn't told you? Well. Well, it was a shipboard romance. We took one look at each other and whoof! wham! that was it.' She'd been on the promenade deck, she explained, leaning over the rail, smoking a Passing Cloud, gazing at the moon in the sky and the moon on the water; the orchestra was playing 'Blue Moon' – 'as ships' orchestras are wont to' – and all of a sudden Aunt Hope had appeared in a long satin evening dress. 'You're the person I've been looking for all my life,' Aunt Hope had announced. 'May I pinch one of your cigarettes?'

'Not surprisingly,' Jocelyn said, 'I fell overboard with a capital O.'

Aunt Hope had never been a smoker to my knowledge. I could not see her in a satin evening dress. I said, 'Where did you meet really?'

Jocelyn looked at Aunt Hope. 'Can't remember, Hope, can you?'

'The Kardomah café in Brighton rings a bell with me,' Aunt Hope suggested, 'or it might have been the ABC.'

'Don't think so,' Jocelyn said, 'they never played "Blue Moon" in the Kardomah.'

This version of their first meeting had to be the right one, though. I could see the two of them in the crowded café, peering over their trays, searching for a place to sit. Eventually being forced to share a table. ('Mind if I join you?') Strangely, although I know now that Jocelyn and my aunt didn't meet that way, I still have a picture of this scene exactly as I imagined it when I was eleven; it still has reality for me. In my picture it's raining, the café windows steamed up, the place smelling of wet mackintosh. Umbrellas by the entrance weep into little puddles on the woodblock floor. Aunt Hope's wool headscarf is coated with a luminous mist; she takes it off and hangs it on the back of her chair, then shakes her curly head like a terrier. I watch her eat damp chocolate cake with a fork while Jocelyn smokes, tapping her cigarette on a gold cigarette case before lighting up. Jocelyn wears hard lipstick and soft black gloves to the elbow. She wears a tiny red hat with red and green feathers swept round the front and a wisp of spotted veil. I can't hear what they're saying to each other, if they are saying anything to each other.

Eleven. I was eleven that time in the kitchen, a black age for me. Or perhaps it was the year itself, 1971, that was black. If I look back over the years I've lived through, thirty-four in all, a lot of them seem to me grey, but a few leap out as black – 1979 is another one, a black bitch of a year – and fewer still I recognise as red, as being red-letter years. Something similar, to do with recognition, not colours, happens when I look at photographs of myself. Sometimes I know myself in photographs and sometimes I don't. Age has nothing to do with it. Likeness has nothing to with it. For example, I can recognise this child in the sandpit, with her bright, tight smile and pigtail-tortured hair; I know what she thinks and how she feels. I accept that she is me. But that moody girl, young woman, mother, of nineteen, head and shoulders in close up (so that I can see, too clearly, the three moles, evenly spaced, like Orion's Belt, on her cheek that I have on mine) – who is she?

If 1971 was a black year, 10 August was the blackest of days. But it doesn't start off black. It starts early with a shimmering haze that by ten in the morning has evaporated, leaving behind a sky of steady, unclouded blue. Jocelyn, whom we haven't had sight of since Whitsun, is with us. She arrived yesterday, and we've all cheered up. Until she came, the long, shapeless summer holidays had been getting us down – though 'holidays' is inaccurate, Aunt Hope says, what's holy about them? 'Vacation', the American word and the university word, is nearer the mark she says. But 'vacation' can't be right either, not in my opinion. How can it be when we never go anywhere? When we never vacate this house, this garden, this cul-de-sac, for more than half a day? It's a running sore with me now, that we never go away. I used not to mind, or even think about it, but last year, when I was ten, I realised I did. Last year, at the start of the autumn term, when the other kids in my class were recounting their adventures in Benidorm and Tenerife and Weston-super-Mare, I told them I'd spent my holidays, five weeks of them, in Africa. With my godfather. In the bush. (Africa's a big place, whereabouts in Africa? – You wouldn't know if I told you. – What was it like there then? – Hot. – What animals did you see? – Oh, you know, giraffes, elephants, hippos, tigers – Tigers? Tigers in Africa? Sir, sir, Hannah saw tigers in Africa!) Why don't we ever go away? Why can't we? Because it's impossible, Aunt Hope says. There's no money for holidays, as I'm old enough to realise; and, I'm old enough to realise, Uncle Ber must be within reach of the hospital. In any case, we live on the coast, we go on day trips to the beach, what more could anyone want?

A lot more, Aunt Hope. A lot, lot more. So many things, places, people, you have no idea.

As I say, this day, 10 August, starts off well. Jocelyn is with us and we're going to the seaside. We're going to the cove we think of as our cove. It's small, stony, difficult for the ordinary tourist or holiday-maker with a road map to find. Access is difficult. It's not a place for the old, the unfit, the very young or the carless (the bus stop's two miles away). Even with a car, you still have to trek the best part of a mile along the cliff path, single file between a corn field and the sky. After that you've got to get down to the cove, which you do by way of a near-vertical, chalk-crumbly and slippery, zigzagging track, no wider than a sheep run. It means having to turn your back on the sea, and after that it's like descending a ladder – a ladder that has several rungs missing. Too perilous and exhausting a journey for Uncle Ber, you'd think, and Aunt Hope certainly thinks so. She says so every time; but Uncle Ber says thank you, he can manage; he was a sailor once, remember, he's used to ladders and companionways. If she thinks this descent tricky she should try getting down from the crow's nest of a destroyer in a heavy sea. He says that, provided he's allowed to take his time, he can manage. The climb back up at the end of the day, with picnic bags weighted with shells and pebbles, is good, he says, because it exercises his heart. It's good for him provided he takes his time. So he starts back before we do, a half-hour earlier at least. There are two ledges on the way just about wide enough to sit on, and he stops and rests on these and shades his eyes and looks out to sea.

(Twenty years from now our near-deserted cove will be peopled throughout the summer and also on fine days at other times of the year. Easier access will be the cause. It will take the form of a new motorway, a coach park with amenities, concrete steps cut into the cliff side. The semisecret places under cover of overhanging rocks where we picnic, the caves and hidey-holes Aunt Hope runs for when the wind gets up, will be littered with Coke cans and condoms and syringes. Just like the rest of the world. There will be seaweed still, but few shells to hunt for. Almost no shells. I know this because I took Finch to our cove last year.)

There's another seaside place we go to occasionally, where we always used to go when I was very small: the Big Beach, all sand and no pebbles, a twenty-minute bus ride from Hilldown Parade. (That's the trouble with it, Aunt Hope says, it's an urban beach, it's easy to get to so everybody goes.) Above the Big Beach is an esplanade we stagger along in winter, and behind it a row of shabby ice-cream hotels, vanilla, strawberry, pistachio. I like this seafront and the Big Beach. The sea may be a sewer, as Aunt Hope says, but in summer it's shallow and, I consider, warm, rising slowly as you wade out until, lapping your waist, it lifts you off your feet and sets you down. There are dinghies and pedal boats here that you can hire. There's a whelk 'n' cockle 'n' mussel stall, a hot-dog stall, a Mr Whippy caravan.

But today we're going to our cove, and we're all ready. The yellow plastic beach bag with our swimming things is stationed by the front door, and alongside it the two carrier bags that contain our two picnics; one is lunch, the other tea. We're in the hall, Jemma's whining and panting and making rushes for the door, we're all ready to leave, when Uncle Ber says he doesn't feel too grand. Wiser, he thinks, for him to stay behind, especially given the heat. It'll be even hotter later.

'What does "not too grand" mean?' my aunt asks, icy

sharp. 'Have you got angina, Ber? Have you got a pain? Do you need the doctor?'

No, he hasn't got a pain. No, he doesn't need the doctor.

'What, then? What do you feel, exactly?'

'Queasy,' my uncle says, 'seasick.'

'I wish you'd told me before. Before I made all those sandwiches.'

'I felt all right before.'

'Let's have a look at you in the light.' My aunt squints up at my uncle. 'You do look sallow, Ber. You'd better go and lie down. You'd better go and have a Harry Kipington. As you would call it.'

My uncle shrugs. The shrug could mean anything. It could mean yes or no or Go to hell and stay there.

'Right,' my aunt says, tapping her foot, addressing the ceiling, her tone so brisk the word 'right' sounds like 'wrong', 'I'm staying behind with Ber. Jocelyn and Hannah can go.'

'That's ridiculous,' my uncle says calmly, 'I don't need you to stay. I haven't asked you to stay. I'm fine.'

'Fine? I thought you said you were ill.'

'Hope,' Jocelyn says in a warning voice, the first time she's spoken. 'Hope.'

'It's impossible to make a plan in this house.' My aunt frowns and sighs.

'Listen,' my uncle says, 'there is no need for anyone to stay with me. I have not got a pain. I am not ill. I feel a bit queasy. I feel – not quite myself. It's a hot day, it's a long walk and a long climb, and I wish to stay here. That's all. There's no need for anyone else to change their plans.'

'Her plans,' my aunt snaps, 'not *their* plans; "anyone" takes the singular. And who do you mean by "anyone"? Me? Or Jocelyn perhaps? Perhaps you'd like Jocelyn to stay. Is that it?'

'Hell's bells,' my uncle murmurs, shaking his head.

'Shut up,' my aunt says to Jemma, whining at the front door. 'Shut up and sit. Lie.'

'I have an idea – ' Jocelyn begins.

'I've decided. I'm staying. And there's an end to it. I'm not that keen on the seaside anyway.'

Not keen on the seaside? It's true my aunt hates swimming and bathing, but she loves the sea. The sea fascinates her; horizons, especially. She and Jemma are always the first down into the cove – 'so I can catch you if you fall' – and the last back. As soon as their feet touch the beach, Jemma runs off to explore and Aunt Hope stands face to the sea and sniffs or deep-breathes. Aaaaah. She may fling her arms wide at this point and cry, 'Break, break, break, On thy cold grey stones, O Sea!' or, less understandably, for there is no sand in our cove, 'Come unto these yellow sands!' Only when the tide's a long, long way out do you get a glimpse of sand. High up the beach, under the rock ledges where we eat our picnic, there's a coarse grey grit with glittery black specks in it like coal dust – quite comfortable to lie in, but you couldn't call it sand. It's useless for building anything. No, what we have in our cove is stones. Big, flat stones, too heavy to lift and useful as seats or pillows, eggshaped stones that fit your fist, pebbles, fine shingle. All shapes, grooved and smooth. All colours, not just grey by any means. In among the greys and opaque creams and blue-veined whites are black pebbles and red ones, brown, purple and slate. There are plain stones and marbled stones, stones with white rings and markings, striped ones like humbugs, peppermint and aniseed.

While Uncle Ber investigates the sharp and slimy rocks; while I hunt for shells or lie on my stomach in the boiling foam and wait for the waves to roll me in to shore (and snatch me back and roll me out to sea) over and over and over; while Jocelyn strikes out for the Broad Stone (and swings her arms in signal before swimming home); while the three of us play a version of deck tennis with a smelly quoit – a spiteful version that involves forfeits and punishments, foot-stamping and hysteria – Aunt Hope watches the sea. She sits on her coat on the stones with her knees drawn up, her elbows on her knees, her head on her hands, and watches the waves, pushing and shoving. She'll do this all day. If you see her head nodding and her lips moving (so she looks crazy as any inmate of the Rose Vale), she's reciting poetry again. Odd lines of it, whole verses. Running up for a towel – scrambling, I should say, you can't run on this deep-piled shingle, it trips you up and pulls you down – you'll catch her at it. 'I love all waste and solitary places,' you'll catch, or 'Listen! you hear the grating roar Of pebbles which the waves draw back.'

'You are keen on the seaside,' I tell my aunt. 'You like the sea. You love watching "the water massing for action on the cold horizon". You do want to go.' I hope, by flattering her, by quoting a line I've often heard her quote, I'll persuade her to come with us. I'm afraid, if she stays behind, that Jocelyn will decide to stay too. That none of us will go.

'Shut up, Hannah,' Aunt Hope says, and, 'Ber, for the last time, will you go and lie down. What's the point of hanging round here if you're not well?'

Without a word, my uncle turns and starts to climb the stairs.

The sun beats down on the carpet. It slants in through the little round window, the porthole, it's known as, on the left of the front door, high up in the alcove where the sticks and umbrellas are kept – Uncle Ber's rolled black one he never uses, Aunt Hope's unfastened brown one with the two cream stripes round the edge – and strikes the lustres on the table, throwing rainbow diamonds round the walls. All the time we've been standing here, all the time the grown-ups have been arguing and Jemma alternately whining and panting (and getting up and wagging her tail and lying down again with her head on her paws and her eyes on Aunt Hope), the sun has been beating down on the carpet. And on me, on my ankles and feet in their red, new on today, open sandals.

'I want to go,' I say, 'I want to go swimming.'

'Off you go, then.' My aunt moves to unlatch the front door, but Jocelyn stops her. We don't want to go without her, she insists, how could we enjoy ourselves without her? Jocelyn's suggestion is this: she'll take me off to the Pool

Hall for a swim before lunch. Then we'll come back and eat the picnic – in the garden, maybe. Then, if Ber's feeling up to it, we can all to go the sea. Around five, when it'll be cooler. We could go to the Big Beach, couldn't we, which after all is no distance and unlikely to be crowded in the evening and doesn't entail a climb.

My aunt says she supposes so. If that's what Jocelyn wants. But does she realise what the baths will be like on a day like this? At this time of day? She whispers something in Jocelyn's ear. Then she catches sight of me. 'Don't pick your arm, Hannah. And don't you dare scowl; you're eleven years old, don't you dare.'

Aunt Hope's right about the pools: you can't see the water for heads; you can't hear yourself speak for the screams and rifle-crack splashes. The only pool that's not crowded is the diving pool, but I'm not allowed in there. On her last-but-one visit Jocelyn said it was high time I learned to dive. She would arrange lessons for me with the diving instructor, and pay for them, she said. I've wanted to remind Jocelyn of this promise. I keep thinking I'll remind her, I gear myself up to mention the subject, the insides of my hands get sticky, I dig a new hole in my arm – and then I don't. Somehow I can't ask her.

Jocelyn and I stand side by side on the edge of the big pool. Round our right ankles, on an elasticated bracelet, anklet rather, are our locker keys. It's the first time I've swum with a locker key. I'm eleven years old, and it's almost the first occasion I've set foot in the Pool Hall without Uncle Ber. It's strange. The knowledge that Aunt Hope and her red scarf and her book aren't somewhere up there on the viewing terrace is strange.

Jocelyn bends down and lifts my hair. 'This place's a nightmare,' she bellows into my ear. 'A quick dip only, don't you think? Just to cool off. Then home.' And I agree. It is a nightmare. I've always imagined I could swim in anything,

81

milk, soup, champagne, but this morning I don't like the look and the sound of the big pool at all.

'Mind if I have a dive first?' Jocelyn bellows. 'Just a couple of dives. Then I'll join you. Come and watch if you want to. Then we'll do a length together. If there's room to.'

I do mind, Jocelyn. I don't want to watch you dive when I can't dive. But I don't say so. I follow her to the diving pool and watch her do a couple of dives. Then a third. This isn't fair. Then a fourth. She waves to me from the diving board this time, but I look away. When, for the fifth time, she swims round to the ladder and starts pulling herself up, smiling to herself, shaking the water from her hair, I walk away. She'll notice I'm missing soon, I reason, then she'll get out of the diving pool pdq and come looking for me.

I wander back to the big pool and prowl the sides searching for a gap in the heads. For a gap in the screams. I lower myself onto the edge and sit for a while, head down, fingers in my ears, staring at my feet in the water. In the water my feet are larger than they normally are, and give the effect of being broken in several places. I flex my feet and toes, up and down, side to side, and they break up into new patterns, re-form and break up again. I prop myself on my arms and lower myself so my bottom's balanced right on the rim of the pool, and my legs in water as far as the knees. I examine my thighs. They're brown and mottled. I hate these mottle-blotches on my thighs. In winter the blotches are pink and purple; in summer suntan turns them a sallow green, the colour of an old bruise. That's how my thighs look – as though they're covered in old bruises. They have ugly hairs on them, too, tiny glinting hairs I've more than once tried to remove. I'm examining these hairs in disgust, tweaking them, when something, somebody, grabs my ankles. A quick grab, a forceful tug. It's so sudden, it happens so fast, there's no time to protect myself. At the first tug I slip into the water and under. I slide in like a ship or a submarine – in, under and down. Down. No time to take a breath, and I kick and kick to get free, I've got to get up to the air, and I beat the solid water away with my hands, and kick and thrash. When at last the ankle clamper lets go, I shoot to the surface and fill my lungs. But immediately there's a weight on my head, a flat weight, pressing hard, forcing me under again, crushing me down. Each time I surface (Uncle Ber! Save me, Uncle Ber!) and snatch a breath, the flat weight descends and pushes me down.

I never saw the Fat Boys in the pool. I never noticed them before they tried to drown me. (They wasn't trying to drown me, the oldest Fat Boy, Billy Cooper, explained to the supervisor afterwards, they was trying to save me. They was trying to get me out of the pool, wasn't they? They wouldn't of touched me otherwise, would they?) I didn't see the Fat Boys before I entered the pool, but at some point during my journeys to the bottom and back, I became aware of white shapes closing in, of white bodies and legs and arms, of stifling pillows of flesh, and I knew it was them.

'Do you want to press charges?' The supervisor has sent the Fat Boys out of his office, ordering them to wait in the passage outside. 'Do you want the police involved in this? Or are you happy, would you be prepared, to let me handle the incident?'

Jocelyn doesn't answer at once; she's upset and angry and doesn't know what she wants. She's flustered. Finally she says no, she doesn't think the police need to be involved.

'I think they should. It's not the first time. These lads need to be taught a proper lesson.' It's the life guard, the one who pulled me out of the pool, who's speaking. He's standing in the doorway of the supervisor's office, sideways on so he can keep one eye on the Fat Boys. He's had his fill of the Coopers and the Batleys, the life guard says, they're nothing but trouble, he's had it up to here (he biffs his chin) with their lies. 'Have you seen the kid's face? We're talking about assault,' the life guard says, 'that's the least of what we're talking about.'

'Horseplay. Rough-housing. High spirits that went a bit

far – that's how it could be seen in court,' the supervisor says, 'that's how it would be seen by some I could mention. Juveniles can get away with murder these days. And then again the magistrate might blame you. They might decide – '

'We need more pool staff peak times in the school holidays, as I say, as I keep saying,' the life guard says. 'Me and Alison can't be everywhere at once.'

'Then again, the court might decide it was unfortunate the child had no adult with her at the time, that her auntie – is that right? – was in the diving pool when the incident occurred.'

'I'm going to take Hannah home now,' Jocelyn says. 'She's had a horrible experience, I'm going to take her home.'

The supervisor says of course, of course. He says that what he intends to do is impose a six-month ban on the Coopers and the Batleys. He has the power to do this and he will. He's going to ban them from all the new sports facilities, not just the Pool Hall. He's going to ban them from the building. Will that be acceptable? We have his assurance the Coopers and the Batleys will not be here next time we come to swim – which he hopes will be soon. Then he writes something on his desk pad, tears the sheet off and hands it to Jocelyn. 'This is a free swim pass, valid for two sessions. It will admit one child and one adult. Choose your time of day and stay for as long as you like. Just hand it to the receptionist on entry.' This morning's incident is very regrettable, he adds.

'You watch out, grasser,' Billy Cooper says behind his hand in the passage. 'You – watch – out.'

On the way home Jocelyn drives with one hand. She keeps her right hand on the wheel and her left hand on my right hand, holding it. Every two seconds she takes her hand away to change gear, but afterwards she returns it to mine. 'You all right, darling?' she keeps asking. 'You feeling OK?'

I say 'Yes', because that's what she wants to hear. She's in a stew and that's all she wants to hear. But I'm not all right. How could I be? I swallowed a gallon of chlorine in the pool. When they got me out I was sick, and I was sick again in the changing room. This happened in front of the supervisor. (He'd had to open my clothes locker with his master key because my own key was somewhere at the bottom of the pool.) I was nearly sick when the medical attendant was checking me over – listening to my chest, stinging iodine onto my nose – and I feel sick now. There's no air in the car. If we could only get some speed up there would be, but our journey's traffic lights and roundabouts, jams and hold-ups. Everyone in this town's making for the sea, it's stop go, stop go, all the way.

When we get there, Jocelyn doesn't turn left off the main road into our road; she pulls the Volkswagen right, up into the parking bay outside Hilldown Parade.

'I thought we'd better clean you up a bit. Have you seen your poor nose? Have a look.' She twists the driving mirror so I can see.

My nose is a mess. Swollen and bright orange-yellow with a scratch running through. On the tip there's a raw dent, and round my nostrils are rusty smears of dried blood. There's more of this on one side, under my nose. I have half a moustache, half a bloody moustache.

'Spit into this tissue,' Jocelyn says, 'and I'll clean you up.' She does it gently, dabbing and patting, 'just to get the worst off'. She can't imagine why those thugs did this to me, she says, how they did it, what sort of monsters they must be. She'd like to kill them, she says, she really feels murderous about them.

It wasn't the Fat Boys who scratched my nose. It was the cement bottom of the pool that did it. I remember this now. I remember going down, somersaulting down, the bottom of the pool floating up, my nose landing. I remember a dragging, gritty scrape, and pushing off with my fingers – and then, suddenly, the water lifting me. From under my stomach, like a hoist, it lifted me up and sideways, up up up.

'How about an ice cream?' Jocelyn says, turning her blue eyes on me, but I feel sick, I've got a headache, my nose

85

throbs, I don't want an ice cream. I'm dying of heat in this car. Let's go home now, Jocelyn, please.

'A lolly-ice, then. Drink-on-a-stick, as they say. That'd be refreshing, that won't hurt you.' She doesn't wait for an answer, she's out of the car and into Pearson's the newsagents in a flash.

'Who's been in the wars then?' It's Mrs Taylor, who lives in our road and used to be a nurse. She wags a finger in my open window, laughs delightedly and wheels her bike away.

'I've been thinking,' Jocelyn's back, peeling off the wrapper, handing me my drink-on-a-stick which is melting already, dripping onto our knees. 'I've been thinking, and I've decided it's best, it's probably best if we don't tell your aunt what happened in the pool. Not all of it. You know what she's like, you know what a flap, what a worrier she is – '

What's this you're saying, Jocelyn?

' – we don't want to upset her, do we? She wasn't in the best of moods when we left. Of course we'll have to tell her something because of your nose. She'll want to know how you hurt your nose. But we could say the pool was crowded and someone barged into you by mistake. We could say that when you were barged into, you banged your nose against the side of the pool. Couldn't we? Something along those lines.'

And she pauses, anxious, waiting for me to agree. I don't agree but I don't say so. I'm shocked by Jocelyn and by her plan. Its sweeping omissions and mean lies are shocking. Its naivety is shocking – Aunt Hope is bound to discover the truth in the end. You're a coward, Jocelyn. But I don't say anything. My tongue's trying to catch the drink which is running away from its stick, escaping into my hand, over my thumb, my wrist, my forearm. My tongue has to be everywhere at once, I'm licking so hard I can't answer; I don't have to agree with Jocelyn's lies or disagree.

Aunt Hope's in the garden, in a wicker chair in the shade,

reading a book. In front of her is the garden table, laid for lunch. The table, surprisingly, has a cloth on it; we don't normally bother with a cloth when we eat outside. Also surprising is the jug of flowers, white daisies and pink roses, at the centre of the blue cloth.

Aunt Hope must have heard us arrive. It's inconceivable she didn't hear the noisy Volkswagen in our quiet road, or the car doors slam, or Jocelyn fighting with the front gate (it sticks and you have to kick and kick the base until it opens with a rush, tipping you forwards); she must surely be aware of us walking towards her over the grass, but she doesn't look up. Even if, lost in her book, she did not hear any of these noises, Jemma heard them. Jemma was barking as we got out of the car. Aunt Hope must have heard Jemma because the dog's here now, panting, huhuhuhuh, huhuhuhuh, at her feet.

Without looking up, Aunt Hope turns a page. By now Jocelyn and I are only feet away – and I think, How tedious, what a tedious game this is, all because we're a few seconds late for lunch. For a sandwich lunch! Hell's bells, I think. Hell's bells.

'I'm afraid we're a bit late,' Jocelyn says when we're standing, side by side, in front of the table. 'A bit later than we said we'd be.'

Aunt Hope puts her book down and takes her specs off and folds them and places them on the book. She leans back in her chair and the wicker creaks and groans. She slots her fingers together and rests them on the stomach of her denim skirt. Her eyes are closed. On her top half she's wearing a short-sleeved shirt I dislike – maroon and spinach stripes with a V neck and wide lapels. It makes her look businesslike always, even now when her eyes are closed. It makes her look middle-aged. A teacher preparing to conduct an unpleasant interview, I think, and of course that's what she is. A teacher about to punish two naughty eleven-year-olds, Jocelyn and Hannah, Form 3.

'Twenty past two a bit late? For lunch at twelve forty-five? I suppose that's one way of putting it.'

How cold and sarcastic the teacher sounds!

'I hadn't any idea it was after two. Hope, I am sorry. I expect you were worrying –'

'Worrying? Why ever should I be worrying?'

And Aunt Hope opens her eyes and sees my face.

Until this minute I haven't been sure whether I'll play along with Jocelyn's version of how I hurt my nose. I can see that if I do I won't get the reaction – horror, concern, sympathy, admiration, a mix of these – I need and have a right to expect. It's when Aunt Hope says 'worrying' in that bored and crushing voice, and repeats it, I make up my mind.

'Someone bumped into me in the pool,' I tell her before she can ask. 'They did it by mistake. And I hit my nose on the side.'

'I can see you did.' She stares hard, first at me, then at Jocelyn, then at me. Then she gets up out of her chair. 'What bad luck,' she says, her voice gentle, so gentle and sympathetic you wouldn't believe. 'You poor old thing, that does look sore. I think we ought to let the doctor have a look at it,' she says, touching my nose lightly with the tip of her finger. 'I hope it isn't broken.'

My aunt does this: she changes mood fast. You never know where you are or what to expect.

'How's Ber?' Jocelyn asks on our way into the house to bring the picnic out, and Aunt Hope says he was snoring last time she looked in. He's had a good rest, she says, maybe he'll feel like having a little something to eat now.

'Not a lot you can do with chickweed.' We've stopped outside the back door while Jocelyn inspects the herb bed. She wants something to chop into the salad dressing – her responsibility when she's here. (When she's not with us, salad consists of lettuce, tomatoes cut in quarters, hard-boiled eggs, sliced, and cucumber, ditto. Plus spring onions, whole. The dressing we have is Crosse & Blackwell Salad Cream from the bottle. This is the salad, and the dressing, I like and Uncle Ber likes. But Jocelyn says how can we? Salad cream? Disgusting! Hard-boiled eggs in with the lettuce? Disgusting! Quartered tomatoes? Unspeakable. Tomatoes should be left as they are, if decent; if they're not, if they're less than wonderful, well then, sliced and served in a separate bowl. Sliced tomatoes should be eaten with basil; failing basil, parsley. When Jocelyn comes to stay she brings garlic and wine vinegar, and olive oil in a tin. She puts our salad cream at the back of the cupboard and turns our salad – our lettuce and our separate, sliced tomatoes – upside down.)

It's when we're in the kitchen and Aunt Hope's uncovering the sandwiches, cheese and pickle, ham and mustard, made at breakfast, that I know for certain I won't be able to manage.

'I can't eat any lunch, Aunt Hope. I've got a headache and I feel sick. Can I go and lie down?'

'D'you think Hannah and Ber can have caught a bug? Gastric flu or some such?' Aunt Hope asks Jocelyn as I make for the door, and she calls out to me, 'Hannah, as you're going up, would you put your head round your uncle's door and see if he's awake and ready for some lunch?'

I walk through the dark and cool hall, deliciously cool now that the sun has moved up and over the house, and the lustres on the table tinkle on their stand. As I climb the stairs I think, I'll tell Uncle Ber what happened in the pool; if he asks me, I'll tell him. Why not?

If I hadn't insisted on going for a swim, if the Fat Boys hadn't tried to drown me, I shouldn't have been the one to find Uncle Ber sprawled and awkward on the floor, his top half face down in the bathroom, his legs on the landing, his right leg bent under his left leg, no shoes on. A little hot breeze was blowing the bathroom curtain in and out of the case-ment, furling and unfurling it like an ensign, but Uncle Ber was still. He didn't move at all.

He was buried at sea, according to the instructions in his will. Not a popular choice, the undertakers Aunt Hope first contacted said. They had to refer her to a firm that specialised in alternative burials.

It was not popular with my aunt, either. It meant she had to get a licence from the Ministry of Ag and Fish, and an Out-of-England form from the coroner. There were all sorts of regulations for burial at sea, apparently. The coffin had to be lead-lined and made of solid but soft wood (with a specific number of holes, of a specific diameter, to ensure it sank). The body, not embalmed, had to be naked, and certified free of fever and infection. Identity discs had to be strapped, with metal strapping, to all the limbs. If, after that, the coffin was not of the prescribed weight, a concrete mix or iron bars had to be added.

Uncle Ber was dropped overboard from a launch somewhere off the Needles (another regulation: burials must take place at least four miles out to sea). Aunt Hope did the voyage alone; she refused to let me or Jocelyn go.

But really, it made no difference because I have a picture of the scene clear as a memory – the clergyman's robes billowing like sails as he raises a hand in blessing (while trying to stay upright in the rocking, oily boat), and then the coffin sliding and splashing into the sea, and drowning.

I went back to the house in Green Copse Road four years ago, and I made Diarmid go with me, and it was a mistake. I chose a weekday so Finch would be at school (I couldn't bear the idea of his trampling on my childhood), though it meant Diarmid having to take a day off work. To begin with, he said he didn't mind taking time off. It was OK, other people's roots were always interesting at some level. But then suddenly, on the drive down, he did mind. It wasn't OK. There was a clock in front of him on the dashboard, but he started looking at his watch in a mean, meaningful way. He started tapping the steering wheel with one finger. At the same time his jaw tightened, untightened, and tightened again. I knew these signs and was wary of them. Things hadn't been right between us for weeks.

We stood on the opposite pavement, as far from the house as possible, in order to get some sort of perspective on my roots, but it wasn't far because the road was only a narrow suburban road.

I saw at once that my roots had shrunk, as Diarmid had warned me they would. Number 5 and its Sandtexed Siamese twin were shorter than when we left, the windows smaller, the front doors meaner; the privet hedge, fat and impenetrable under Uncle Ber's punishing shears, scrannel now with holes showing the daylight through. Some of it must have died, there was a chunk missing, and in its place was an anaemic brick wall with a castellated top.

'That's my bedroom.' I pointed at a window where flowered curtains bloomed.

'Was.' Diarmid had his hands cupped, lighting a fag.

I remembered the bedroom curtains I'd had, the pattern of Chinamen on them. I suddenly saw the Chinamen – their pigtails and tunics and shoes with turned-up toes.

We crossed the road.

The house was much nearer to the front gate than it should have been – so astonishingly near that for a moment I was convinced it had been shunted forwards several yards. The gate was new: cream-painted iron, the top bar a heart shape of intertwining scrolls. There were absences, too, distorting gaps it took a few minutes to work out. No laburnum trees! No leggy rose! No lilac by the steps. Another disconcerting thing: Green Copse Road itself was half the length of the road I used to bike or skip or drag my feet along.

'That was lawn in my day.' We were peering into the side garden, purple-paved and pebbled now. 'There was an apple tree on the left where that whatsit is.' I was not sure if I could bear all this.

We walked along the hedge. Diarmid knew about Uncle Ber's pond and the oceans it had been; he wanted to see it, he once said; but the pond, if there still was a pond, was round the back at the far end of the garden, not visible from the road. The words 'leeward' and 'windward' came into my head, I could hear them in my uncle's voice. I could see the two of us, Uncle Ber in the yachting cap Aunt Hope despised, kneeling in the sopping grass to launch a tall ship; and I could see him hoisting his old White Ensign to test the wind. When the wind blew from the south, I suddenly remembered, it brought with it a whiff of yeast from the brewery in Horsefell Lane.

'If we stand over there,' I said, 'we should be able to see a corner of Uncle Ber's workroom.'

But when we stood over there, all we could see was sheet

glass and tan polished wood, the curved outcrop of a conservatory.

While we were leaning and peering, while I was grieving, a woman came out of our front door and marched up to us.

'I've been watching you,' this woman said. 'May I enquire what you're doing? This is private property.'

The road wasn't private property, though, was it? Diarmid asked; the pavement wasn't. And we were on the pavement. As she could see.

I'd imagined, before we made this excursion, that at some point I'd walk up the path and ring the bell and tell whoever answered that I used to live here and could we please look round the garden. I'd decided to disarm this person (whom I'd envisaged as male, a house husband or pensioner) with a frank expression and shy smile; but when I tried these, and explained my interest in the place, the woman frowned. How was she expected to know that? She angrily pushed the straggle of hair off her face that the wind kept blowing across it. Why should she believe it? People shouldn't be allowed to go peering into other people's property. We'd been acting suspiciously – how was she to know we weren't casing the joint? Did we have any idea how many break-ins they'd had in the area in the past twelve-month?

And she vanished in a puff of fag smoke.

'Neighbourhood witch!' Diarmid shouted after her.

We walked past the row of 'home improved' semis to the cul-de-sac end of the road. No replacement doors or windows here, no jazzy roofs and hacienda plasterwork, no sun lounges. The detached houses were just as I remembered them. They weren't uniform, but they had features in common: hung tiles and lead casements; curved brick steps or brick-arched porches; discreet, weather-boarded garages. Their gardens hadn't changed. As in my day, they revealed a shared nursery catalogue of cotoneaster and berberis, pyracantha and prunus. As in my day, the oak gateposts had brass plates fixed to them. Despite the recent break-ins, the detached end of Green Copse Road was still a place where dentists and chiropodists and veterinary surgeons wanted to live.

'Aunt Hope used to say there was no danger of being struck by lightning in this road.' I thought Diarmid would be amused by this. I imagined he'd have something insulting to say about the smug houses and their insulating greenery, but he hadn't. He needed a pee and a beer, in that order, he said.

So we walked back to the main road, faster, keeping our heads down, because a squally, horizontal rain had started to blow. As we did so, I began to feel uneasy. The squashed berries and chalky dog pellets nestling under the privet were too familiar. The smell of evergreen was too familiar. I could see my eight-year-old self setting out for school along this pavement. Autumn term, new shoes like conkers, dithering leaves. Leaves that on wet days stuck to the asphalt like cornflakes to the bottom of a bowl. I spent the psychedelic years here, I thought. All the time I lived here, Eng-a-land was swinging like a pendulum do – but not here, not in Green Copse Road.

At the junction of our road and the main road, we stood in the rain, waiting for the lights. The pillar box was still there on the corner. I touched it from old superstition, and at once saw Aunt Hope posting a letter. She'd had a strange way of seeming to hurry past the box, while at the same time contriving to pull a letter from her bag and slip it in. She never lingered over her postings, didn't bother to check her letters were stamped and the envelopes stuck down; they disappeared into the fixed black grin so fast I never had a chance to see who they were addressed to.

We drank our beer in the Cross Keys. Like the rest of Hilldown Parade, the pub was fake half-timbered, the roughcast plaster of its upper storey crisscrossed with tacky, tacked-on beams. In the days when I knew the pub – saw it, rather, every morning on my way to school – there'd been an enormous gold cock in bas relief on the outside wall above the entrance; and for years I believed the pub was called the Cock. Or the Cockerel. Or the Gold Cock, or the Golden Cockerel.

'Ham?' Diarmid called from the bar. 'Or you could have cheese. Cheese and pickle, cheese and onion, cheese and tomato, cheese?'

'Whatever.' I didn't care what I ate; I wished we hadn't come.

'White or brown?' Diarmid called again. 'Toasted or untoasted? Fested or infested?'

We sat at a round black table near the fire – not a real fire, a gas one, with regulated flames and simulated coals. 'Weasel piss,' Diarmid said when he'd tasted his beer; and after that we were silent, he twisting round in his chair to take in the people and jokes and conversations at the tables behind, I watching the dog that lay, stretched out on its side, in front of the fake fire. I don't like dogs as a rule, and I knew this one would be smelly if you got too close, but I felt sympathy for it. It was old and had a white-whiskered face; there was something pathetic about its narrow, bony chest and hairless stomach. I watched its ribcage rise and fall. This pathetic old dog was talking in its sleep, making little grunts and snorts. Now and then its open mouth emitted a shuddering sigh. Its back legs twitched and trembled, and now and then one of them would kick out, a jerky, involuntary kick. When this happened its balls – his balls – came into view, black and shiny and heavy-looking. Weighty as iron, it came to me, as iron doorknobs. I imagined the old fellow struggling to his feet, the spider legs collapsing, pulled down within seconds by the weight of those extraordinary iron balls.

Diarmid stretched a hand to the sandwich on my plate. 'You going to eat that?'

I shook my head.

'I'll tell you something sad,' I said eventually. 'I think it's sad. Uncle Ber used to paint yellow stripes on his tools, his house tools and his garden tools. He did it to mark them so that if anyone borrowed and forgot to return them, he could prove they were his. But no one did borrow them, I've just realised, not to my knowledge. Not so much as a spade.'

A man at the far end of the bar suddenly leaned right back on his stool and guffawed. Diarmid swung round, then turned back to me.

'I don't see that as sad. Not necessarily. It's more likely he marked his tools in case they were stolen. Or to prevent them being stolen. A lot of people, careful people, do that.'

So I explained to him, tried to explain, how lonely my uncle must have been. (A new thought, new to me.) He'd spent all those years in the navy, where he must have had friends, and then there was nothing. No one. Only Aunt Hope and me. I couldn't recall anyone coming to the house, I told Diarmid. Imagine it, I said, no one coming for a drink even, let alone a meal. Just imagine.

'Jocelyn did.' Diarmid examined his beer glass. 'D'you want the other half? Thought I'd give the Boys' bitter a go this time. Can't be filthier than the Best.' As he got up, he said; 'Don't know what makes you think a sailor has to be gregarious, Evie. Sailors go to sea to get away from the world. That's why they go, why a lot of them go – to get away. I expect your uncle Ber was one of those.'

Fuck you, Diarmid.

I watched him at the bar, pulling his wallet from the back pocket of his jeans, slapping it on the counter. Not wallet, I remembered, billfold. For some reason best known to him, only known to him, he called it a billfold. Not all Englishmen, sorry, Irishmen, call a wallet a billfold, Diarmid, so fuck you.

But I didn't really mean it. Part of me meant it, part of me thought, You cocky bastard, screw you, fuck you, while another part, equally strong, meant and thought and felt something else, equally strongly: I love you, Diarmid. You are the only man I've loved. I don't care what you call your wallet, you can call it a purse if you want to, you can call it a sow's ear.

'What sort of watch would that be you're wearing? Is it a watch?' Diarmid was still at the bar, leaning forward on his elbows, chatting up the barman's assistant, a pretty boy of eighteen. 'Don't you dare give it me in a glass this time,' I heard him say, 'I'll have my beer in a mug. If it's all the same to you.' When the beer came he drank it where he was, straight off, in one long swallow, while the potboy looked on. Pink-faced, smiling. Impressed.

You're a show-off, Diarmid. A show-off and a flirt.

I remembered another time in a pub with Diarmid. It was soon after we'd decided we were in love, and we kept touching each other, we couldn't leave each other alone. We didn't kiss, snogging in public was not for us. What we were doing was semiprivate, semicovert, conspiratorial. Little palpations and strokings under the table, little knee and leg and ankle rubbings, tiny pressures that turned the quiet blood in our veins into urgent rivers. Not embracing, we held each other with our eyes, unable to let go. Meanwhile, the egg and chips we'd ordered hardened into novelty keyrings on the plate. We were hungry, of course, but not for food; we were thirsty, but it wasn't a thirst that a pint of real ale was going to satisfy.

The waitress hadn't liked our behaviour. All the world loves a lover, but this waitress hadn't. Perhaps it was our exclusive, excluding absorption that annoyed her; perhaps envy was her problem. Or perhaps she had PMT. Whatever the reason, she slammed the plates down in front of us, later returning to remove them, along with our knives and forks (still wound in their paper shrouds), the salt and pepper shakers and tomato-shaped tomato-sauce dispenser, with contemptuous sniffs and sighs.

'Something wrong with your meal, was there, sir?' she challenged Diarmid finally; and when he shook his head, happily, not taking his eyes from mine, she stumped muttering away.

And we smiled at each other, wide, delighted smiles. It was

the old cliché about love, about being in love: no one existed but us.

'Right. Let's go.' Diarmid, back from the bar, brisk and decisive, unhooking his jacket from the back of his chair.

On the way to the door, he paused for a moment by the fireplace. 'There's a fockin' oggly dog fer yew,' he said without malice, 'there's a dog that's had its day.'

Would we be near the sea still? was the first question I asked Aunt Hope when she told me we were leaving Green Copse Road. (Not just the road but the town, the whole area.) And she said no. She was sorry about it; she knew I'd miss the sea.

No sea! This was too terrible to think about, so I asked another question: Where would I go to school? Would she be a teacher at my new school?

A comprehensive school, not unlike the one I was already at. She'd been to see it, she thought it would do. She thought I might even tolerate it – 'as much as you'd tolerate any school'. It was strong on woodwork and metalwork, she added. And no, she wouldn't be teaching there. She wouldn't be teaching anywhere.

I must have looked surprised at this, because Aunt Hope, who never went in for long explanations, or certainly not to me, sat me down and explained that she was giving up teaching because she wasn't allowed to teach the way she wanted to any more. The things she minded about, spelling, grammar and learning by heart, were no longer considered relevant. Uninhibited self-expression was what she was expected to encourage, 'and as you know, I don't believe in self-expression. Not in the classroom.' So she was giving up. She didn't intend to teach again, ever.

I think she was hoping for some reaction to this speech,

but I didn't say anything. The more she went on about traditional teaching methods and values, the less I believed her when she said she was giving them up. Anyway, what else was she fit for?

'It's all right for you, Hannah, you should be pleased. Education's going your way, your own fozy way. It's going out of the window – which I seem to recall is where you go during lessons.' And she laughed an unkind, unamused laugh.

Aunt Hope was referring to my last school report; in particular, my form teacher's summing-up remarks:

Hannah's disappointing exam results reflect the amount of time spent 'out of the window' this term. This is a pity as she's a pleasant girl and not without ability. Come on, Hannah, stay with us in the classroom and show us what you can do!

My form teacher's 'chummy rallying call' had made Aunt Hope very angry. And 'disappointing' was not the word for my exam results. As a teacher herself, as my aunt, she felt humiliated by them. Again, if I spent all my time 'out of the window', why hadn't they moved me to a desk away from the window? As for my being a 'pleasant girl' – what had that to do with it?

I hated Aunt Hope's sarcasm and her bitter laugh, but what she said was true – I did spend lessons out of the window, though I never planned to. I'd start off in the classroom, concentrating on the teacher and the blackboard and the open textbook on my desk, but within minutes my eye would be drawn to the enormous rectangle of plate glass on my right. There was a cherry tree out there. There were clouds – cirrus, nimbus, cumulus and what was the other one? – which on windy days bowled, or raced, across the sky. There was the sky itself, as interesting, in my opinion, as any landscape. (I was getting to be an expert on skies.) There was the semicircle of kerbed grass, to the left of the school gates, where clockwork sparrows hopped and pecked. In the far right of my picture, if I craned my neck, was the black brick back of the Science Block with its fascinating downpipes. Bang in the middle lay the car park and the teachers' cars, maroon, navy, navy, cream, salmon, powder blue and rust, lined up on the tarmac like fishes on a slab. When the sun hit them, the windscreens turned into sheets of blinding tinfoil; in a cloudburst or downpour, the rain trampolined tirelessly on their roofs, down and up, up and down. I was never bored watching the rain, heavy rain, bouncing and spinning on those car roofs. I was happy to spend whole mornings and afternoons watching the rain.

'Is Jocelyn coming with us when we move?'

I asked this to change the conversation, but I was also keen to know. I could see no reason why Jocelyn should want to be with us, but I prayed that she would. Aunt Hope was less awful when Jocelyn was around. Less disturbed and disturbing. Since Uncle Ber's death, my aunt had been behaving in disturbing ways a lot of the time. For example, she'd always detested clumsiness of any kind – my kind, Uncle Ber's kind – but now, extraordinarily, she'd become a dropper and a loser herself. Pie dishes full of pie slipped from her hands and exploded on the floor. Plates and glasses made suicide leaps from the shelf as she reached for them. Her specs, her royal-blue and gold fountain pen, her favourite peeling knife, repeatedly vanished. (Stolen, she insisted. And she knew who the thief was.) She'd become a collider, colliding with Jocelyn and Jemma and me and strangers in the street, also with tables and chairs and doors and chests of drawers. But most disconcerting, I found, was her new habit of pacing. She paced obsessively, indoors and out. Watching from behind the sofa or the crab-apple tree, I'd see her stop and clap a hand to her mouth, as people do when they've forgotten something. Or remembered something. I'd see her sway, side to side, forwards and back, dangerously, as though she were about to fall. I'd hear her mutter, 'Oh no, Oh no', or 'Oh, Christ, oh, God, oh, my God!'

Once she caught me watching her. She swung round then, in mid-pace, and pointed, her outstretched arm levelled threateningly at my head. 'Don't stare, Hannah! Leave your face alone!'

I was picking again, not just my face and arms, but my hands and legs as well. As soon as a scab formed, or looked like forming, I ripped it off. I bled into school shirts and home sheets. One morning after breakfast, after a particularly bloody night, I found Aunt Hope in my room, stripping my bed. 'Why didn't you tell me, dear?' My mouth was open, I was ready to argue or at least explain, but a mournfulness in her tone prevented me. I took the paperbagged parcel, squashy as a new loaf, she handed me and put it in my underclothes drawer. I was nearly thirteen; there were bumps the size of marshmallows on my chest; there was a twist of hair 'down there' I could curl with a finger; I'd be needing the parcel soon anyway.

It was grief, Jocelyn explained when I asked her. It was grief that made my aunt behave so weirdly. Grief took people different ways.

Well, all right, I could accept that. Jocelyn had wept for Uncle Ber; I'd seen and heard her. My own grief had been dumb and tearless. I was getting over the worst of it now. But Aunt Hope's craziness and clumsiness, her pacing and muttering, her vile temper?

'Anger comes into grief, you know,' Jocelyn said. 'Anger's often what people feel. Guilt and remorse are often a part of it. It's not unusual, when someone dies, for those closest to them to feel guilty. Even when they have no reason, no real reason, to feel it.'

I remembered all the times Aunt Hope had refused to make Uncle Ber figgy duff and custard, his favourite, and I thought, She has every reason to feel guilty.

Rather late in the day, several days after she'd broken the news that we were leaving, I remembered to ask my aunt something else.

'What's going to happen to my mother?' (I'd by this time given up referring to her as 'Mummy'; I couldn't get my tongue round the word.) 'What's going to happen to her?'

'Your mother?' From the way Aunt Hope said it, you'd think she'd never heard of this person. She shook her head vigorously, perhaps to clear her brain. When she did answer it was fast and jerkily, the words tripping over themselves. My mother would stay where she was. For the time being. We would visit her as usual – no, Aunt Hope would visit her. She wouldn't force me to go. She was aware that recently I'd found the visits, well, shall we say, difficult. Which they were. Yes. We, she, would go on the train. Oh, and when she found a suitable hospital, nursing home, nearer, we'd move my mother there.

I thought, but did not say, My mother hates change. We both know she can't cope with change. What if she doesn't want to leave the Rose Vale? What is she refuses to move?

But I still hadn't understood where Aunt Hope and Jocelyn and I were moving to, because Aunt Hope had been so vague. I thought it unwise to press her for details: she might see my interest as an excuse for a geography lesson, for poring over Ordnance Survey maps or testing me on the counties and county towns of England. In the end, I consulted Jocelyn.

'Jocelyn, where are we going to when we move?'

Jocelyn was standing at the kitchen table, spread with a double sheet of newspaper, cleaning shoes: her red slip-ons, Aunt Hope's tan courts, the old black lace-ups I wore for school. Lately she'd taken on the jobs Uncle Ber had always done, jobs like hedge-cutting and brass-polishing and button-sewing. Shoe-cleaning.

'This has had it,' Jocelyn said, shoving the black polish tin in my direction. 'We must get some more.'

I picked up the tin and fingered the hard, whitish lumps that were left. I held the tin to my nose. I was addicted to the smell of cleaning stuffs – Brasso and Silvo, turps and Windolene, furniture polish and shoe polish – and to most sorts of glue. It surprises me now that I never took up sniffing in any serious way.

'Jocelyn, where are we going to exactly?'

Jocelyn had her hand inside one of my smelly old lace-ups. She spat on the toe and breathed on it so it went cloudy; she rubbed it furiously with a duster, and it shone.

'Don't you know? We'ze a-goin' to Arizona, child. We'ze a-goin' to the Wild West countree.'

Arizona. Ariz. Or (with zip code) AZ. The Grand Canyon state. The Grand Canyon is a mile-deep gash, or gorge, of the Colorado River. Formed by vertical river erosion cutting though the multicoloured strata of a high plateau, the canyon extends from its junction with the Little Colorado River to Lake Mead, some two hundred and seventeen miles away. It has three parts: the popular South Rim, the North Rim and the Inner Canyon. By mid-April the temperature in these parts is in the seventies, the sky *National Geographic* blue . . .

The Arizona we moved to wasn't this one. It was a house, a series of ugly outbuildings and a tussocky field called Arizona. It was a place in the West Country, in the sticks, at the back of beyond, in the middle of nowhere, called Arizona.

Of course Aunt Hope didn't give it that name. The old man who'd owned the place before she did had done that. He was ninety-three when he died in the house, and he hadn't done anything to it in the way of repairs or decoration for fifty years at least. Local people had a lot of stories and theories about Jack Bowdell. Some said he was penniless, lived on bread and dripping, couldn't pay his bills or taxes, the bailiffs were always on his back. Others swore he was filthy rich, a miser. He might have appeared poor, but that was because he didn't want anyone to know about the money – in stocks and shares, in diamonds, in race horses, in oil: opinions varied – he'd stashed away for years. One story doing the rounds was that he'd been a gold-washer in his youth, and that he'd buried his haul somewhere on his land. It was still there, that story went, under a tree, at the bottom of the well in Big Meadow, waiting to be discovered. A farmer neighbour told Aunt Hope soon after we got there that he'd called in on Bowdell without warning once and caught him on his knees in the parlour, sorting out contract notes. The house was squalid, the farmer said, no woman had ever been allowed to clean it, there were hens and pigs running in and out – and yet here was old Bowdell, on the floor, counting his paper millions! Even those who weren't convinced Bowdell had money agreed about his being a woman-hater. Never had a female in the house, to his knowledge, the postman told my aunt when we were moving in. If the old boy knew it was a lady had bought his place, and that there was going to be three females living in it . . . well! He just hoped for our sakes there wasn't such things as ghosts.

From time to time during our life at Arizona, I went looking for Jack Bowdell's treasure, but all I found was a black button that, when polished, turned out to be brass, hundreds of cartridge cases, green and red, a musket ball (Aunt Hope said it was), three Victorian pennies and a dozen or so sexagonal bottles that had 'Poison' or 'Not to be taken' in raised letters on their blue glass sides. The well in the Big Meadow I kept away from. It was protected by a stone slab I'd never have been able to budge on my own, but in any case I discovered soon after our arrival that I was terrified of wells. There was a well much nearer to the house than the Big Meadow one; it was just outside the courtyard, and in dry summers and wet winters Aunt Hope would check up on its level. This well had an iron trap over it, and always after Aunt Hope had shifted the trap her hands and the knees of her corduroys were orange with flaky rust. Standing behind her as she knelt and peered, I'd be repelled by the vertical stone tunnel that apparently had no bottom – but mesmerised also by the glittery disc, the distorting water mirror, I glimpsed over my aunt's shoulder, miles down, it seemed to me. How cold water must be that never felt the sun! How easy it would be to fall! In nightmares I did fall, and Jocelyn (who never went near the well if she could help it) fell, and Aunt Hope's horrid terrier, Jemma, fell; and I struggled, or they struggled, in the stone-icy water – and no one ever heard our cries, and none of us was ever rescued before I woke up with a backbone aching with fear. Aunt Hope seldom featured in these nightmares. But it was her name I, or Jocelyn, called from the bottom of the bottomless well.

Nothing is so beautiful as spring . . . Spring is massing forces, birds wink in air . . . Spring, the sweet spring, is the year's pleasant king . . . This is the weather the cuckoo likes . . .

The daffodils on the hump of grass at the back of the flats are over, melted into toffee or dried to crepe paper. *Fair daffodils, we weep to see You haste away so soon*, and now it's the tulips' turn – not on our patch because there aren't any, but in the circular beds of the public parks and gardens I peer down on from the bus. *The city financier walks in the gardens, Stiffly because of his pride and his burdens*. Tulips and blossoms, prunus, malus, magnolia, *cherry* – pink and double, single and *hung with snow. The glassy pear-tree leaves and blooms. Hark, where my blossom'd pear-tree in the hedge/leans to the field and scatters on the clover/Blossoms and pear drops* – no, *dew drops, to* (or is it at?) *the bent spray's edge . . . The battlemented chestnuts*, in these parks and gardens, *volley green fire*. But not for long; what you notice, when they're new, is how limp they are, how they hang down, thin and limp. Having shot their bolt, they appear exhausted, before summer has even got off the ground.

This is Aunt Hope's legacy, this is what she's left me, and left me to deal with: bits and pieces of poems, snatches of them, misremembered lines, gaps – that's to say, words I'm not sure of, phrases that have gone missing altogether. These bits and pieces come into my head unasked for, and interfere with my life. I hear them in my aunt's voice, exactly the way she declaimed or murmured them. I can't see a thrush singing its head off on some TV wildlife programme without Aunt Hope's insistent commentary in my ear: *That's the wise thrush; he sings each song twice over.* I'm sure if I were to discover a thrush's nest – unlikely round here – it couldn't be without the reminder: *Thrushes' eggs look like little low heavens.*

Aunt Hope knew who wrote all this stuff, of course. The stuff that interferes with my life was the fabric of hers, or perhaps its underpinnings. I used to think all that quoting and reciting was showing off, but it can't have been just that because so often when she did it she was alone – or believed herself to be alone. You'd hear her murmuring in the bathroom, at the sink and the washing line. And she did not always do it aloud. You'd ask her a question, an ordinary question such as 'Have you seen my tracksuit bottoms anywhere?' And she'd stare at you, her brown eyes unnaturally large behind their specs. She wouldn't answer at once. There was something going on behind that creased forehead that had to be resolved before she could reply matter-of-factly and, it would turn out, accurately, 'In the airing cupboard, under the yellow towel.' She couldn't help herself, I think now. She had her reasons, I know now, for keeping all that stuff going. I don't blame her for that.

What I do blame her for is for not sharing. She didn't share, and she didn't explain. One evening when she and I were together in the kitchen at Arizona I charged her with this. It was after supper, quite late. Finch was in bed, Jocelyn away, working on a radio programme. My aunt had a book in her lap (open, but she wasn't reading it, she'd had too much to drink), *The Poetry of the Thirties* it was called, something like that, and I took it from under her hands and held it up. 'This book is to blame,' I said. I'd had a lot to drink too that evening, I'd been matching my aunt glass for glass. 'It's to blame for all our problems! For everything!'

'How can it be?' Aunt Hope said, startled. 'I've hardly begun that book, I'm only on page 3.'

'I don't mean *this* book,' I said, 'I mean poetry, poems,

books of poems. The thing that matters to you, the thing that rules your life!'

'Rubbish!' Aunt Hope said. 'It doesn't rule my life. What an amazing amount of tosh you talk. Especially when you're drunk.'

'Drunk! Just listen to who's talking!'

And we went on like that, ding-dong, until I accused her of shutting me out always. Of sharing everything with Jocelyn and Finch and nothing, nothing, nothing with me. Of keeping me at a distance. Of using silence as a weapon. Her silences had always been very threatening to me, I said, I'd never known what was going on in them.

Then she got serious. Sober, suddenly. She hadn't meant to shut me out, she truly hadn't. But the truth was, I and she were very different sorts of people, weren't we? For example, I'd never shown the slightest interest in reading novels, let alone poetry. I'd never, to her knowledge, of my own volition taken a book, any book, down from the shelf and read it through. She'd felt she couldn't force me to read – why should she? Some people weren't natural readers. There were people – interesting people, some of them, intelligent, no doubt – who managed to get through the whole of their lives without ever reading a book. Nothing wrong with that. Ber hadn't been a great reader. If she'd been my mother she might have done more to encourage the habit, but she wasn't my mother. She'd felt she hadn't the right to push me in ways I so obviously didn't want to go. 'Anyway, Hannah, I've shared messy quotidian life with you – what else can human beings be said, really, to share?'

You're lying, Aunt Hope (I thought but did not say); you're deceiving me and yourself. Your contempt for nonreaders has always been boundless.

These leftovers of Aunt Hope's are unfinished business. They're like unsatisfactory sex, when the man you're in bed with has got his rocks off and fallen asleep and left you to kick the sheets and thrash the pillow. They're like that last piece of chocolate you've got your eye on which, just as you're about to eat it, someone else pops into their mouth, leaving your tongue, your saliva glands, your stomach, all of which were expecting chocolate, cheated and dissatisfied. If I knew who wrote these bits of poems and where they came from, they might go away, but with one or two exceptions, I've no idea.

I see at last that all the knowledge I wrung from the darkness – that the darkness flung me – is worthless as ignorance: nothing comes from nothing . . . I got into a stew about this snippet once. What came into my head first was 'nothing comes from nothing', and then I worked backwards from there, as far as I could. Which was not far. It took a while because I had problems with 'flung'. To begin with I was saying 'threw', but it didn't sound right, and eventually, after half an hour or so of repeating it out loud, I came up with 'flung'. Aha! But I still didn't know who'd written it, or where it came from.

'Look it up, Evie. Go to the public library and look it up. They'll have anthologies there and dictionaries of quotes.' Diarmid's suggestion. He was exasperated and bored. He'd already been up and down his own shelves on my account.

I did what Diarmid suggested: I went to the library. It was a hot afternoon, and I had on a T-shirt and an old cotton skirt I was fond of, faded blue. Clean on but, after the bus ride, after being squashed up against the window for half an hour, damp at the back and crumpled. My legs and feet were bare and I was wearing sandals, black with crossover straps and a little heel. Pretty shoes, but painful – the buckles cut into my ankles. (It hadn't happened when I'd tried them on in the shop.) Before putting on the sandals I'd run a hand up and down my legs to check they were smooth, and I'd painted my toenails with the plum nail polish Diarmid insisted on. He was adamant about such details. There was no more disgusting sight in summer, according to him, than hairy female legs, unless it was yellow female toenails in sandals. I took exception to these remarks. I believed, and still believe, that women should not be dictated to about their appearance, certainly not by men. Women should be free to grow underarm hair if they want, if that's where their body hair naturally grows. I feel this even though I don't like these hairy sights myself and – I would never have admitted this to Diarmid – find them offensive. But toenails? What harm, what possible offence can an unpainted toenail cause? I painted mine, in the end, for my own reasons. That's what I told myself and how I got round it. But the need to please, to please men, the fear of disappointing them and having to witness their disappointment, has always got in the way of other, possibly nobler, instincts.

After the bus ride and the baking pavements, it was deliciously cool in the library. The reference section was down the stairs. There were three dictionaries of quotations on the shelf and I pulled them all out. Important-looking tomes, handsome, heavy to carry.

Most of the tables were occupied, but I found a seat at a table where there was just one other person, an old man reading a newspaper, across the table from me. In my pocket was a piece of paper, and I unfolded it and placed it beside the stacked dictionaries. It had occurred to me that the seriousness of the surroundings might cause my bit of poem to evaporate, so I'd scribbled it down before I left home. Another thing I'd done was underline the key words – what I hoped were the key words – to look up in the indexes. Then I got to work. The words I looked up in those three dictionaries were 'knowledge', 'darkness', 'ignorance' and 'nothing', and there were a lot of entries for each, and it took time.

While I was doing it, checking and rechecking and not finding what I was after, I felt a sudden pressure on my right foot. The old guy opposite had inadvertently trodden on my foot. Sorry, I murmured, the automatic reflex when some part of your anatomy collides with some part of a stranger's, but he didn't say anything. He was busy with his newspaper, spread out on the table. Plump, hairless hands. A pale face and colourless lips. Spectacles – but then most old people have those. Thick, very white hair on his head and a pointed beard, the sort you don't see very often. Goatee? Was the beard tufty enough to be described as a goatee? Was it too trim and dapper to be goatee? He was dapper. There was nothing about him of the grubby sheen, the stale and stained, neglected look some old folk have – the look, and the smell, it can be, of chronic loneliness. The look that speaks of incontinent stumblings and fumblings in unsafe kitchens, dire plumbing arrangements.

I took in the spruce jacket and dazzling shirt cuffs and thought: he has a woman at home. A wife or a daughter, or perhaps both. He was turning the pages slowly – licking his thumb beforehand – right to left, right to left, and then turning them back, left to right. Right to left, left to right, slow and careful, scanning each page. Concentrating. Searching for something. As I was. If he catches my eye now, I thought, I'll smile. I'll smile and I'll mouth 'Any luck?', and when he shakes his head I'll shake mine: 'Me neither!'. By this time I'd discarded dictionaries one and two; and I was running my finger down the 'knowledge' entries in the index of dictionary three when it happened again: a pressure, unmistakable and determined, on my right shoe.

What? Oh, give me a break. Do me a favour, *please*.

An ankle rub came next, side to side, and after it a calf rub, up and down, slow and rhythmical. Then a leg lock. A travesty of what lovers do. And I couldn't say anything. Stop, for instance. Fuck off. I couldn't make myself break into the silence of that place, which had a notice saying 'Silence' in large black letters on the white wall; and I couldn't move my legs – to kick him, or tuck them out of his reach – or any particle of my body except my eyes. These saw that he was absorbed in his paper still. What he was doing under the table hadn't affected his expression, his pallor, his breathing even, one jot.

"'Scuse me, is that yesterday's *Chronicle* you got there?

There isn't one in the rack and there's somethin' I need to find. Could I have it after you? No hurry.'

It was a man who rescued me. Young – a student, possibly, his face hidden, bent over my abuser's shoulder.

'I have finished with it. And with my chair. You can have both.' And without a glance in my direction, the old man got up and unhooked a walking stick from the back of his chair and, leaning heavily on the stick, walked away.

On the bus journey home I decided to make a joke of this incident to Diarmid. A jokey anecdote. Here was I, I'd tell him, trying to get to grips with English literature for once, and here was life, in the shape of that old guy, geezer, bloke, fellow, goat, determined to prevent me. Ironic, if you like! Another irony I could make something of: the freshly laundered, pristine appearance of someone who turned out to be a dirty old man. I decided to make my dirty old man older than I'd guessed him to be in the library, which was seventy-something. For Diarmid's benefit, to make the episode more disgusting and preposterous, I would describe a ninety-year-old. (Both feet in the grave, with one foot over to play footy-footy with me.) Then there was my ninety-year-old's walking stick. There had to be mileage – lewd or pathetic – to be made out of that stick.

But hobbling home from the bus – my sandals were agony by now, the buckles had rubbed the skin off both ankles – I decided it wouldn't be wise to tell this story to Diarmid, or not with the embellishments I'd planned. The story could backfire. Early on in our relationship I'd confided to him a lot about my sexual history – the variety of it, the numbers involved, the three-in-a-bed experiments I'd gone in for at one stage. I'd also told him about the troubling or hilarious attentions most girls and young women have to endure from faceless strangers in cinemas and stand-up comedians on tube trains. The greedy fingers , the rubbings and thrustings of invisible parts, the bad breath and body odours. I'd told him about these, confessed them, partly because I believed he had a right to know, partly because I wanted his sympathy, but also because I felt safe. For the first time since Uncle Ber died I felt safe, really safe, with another human being. Here was a man I could trust myself and my secrets to, and with no fear of betrayal or punishment. But I was wrong, of course. Not to begin with, but eventually. As soon as the arguments that crept into our life together developed into fights, the detailed evidence I'd volunteered was used against me. In our fights it came out that I was, and always had been, a whore.

And Diarmid was clever. From the start he'd been guarded about the specifics of his own sexual past, sketching the scenes with only the broadest and vaguest of brush strokes, so now I had nothing concrete to accuse him of in return.

I never found the quotation I was looking for that day in the library. On subsequent visits it became clear that most of the bits of poems that plague me aren't in those dictionaries. I gave the anthologies in the poetry section a miss. If you don't know the name of the poet and you don't know the title of the poem, if the lines you're haunted by aren't the first lines – what use is an anthology?

'Ask Finch,' Diarmid suggested. 'He reads poetry. He'll probably know.'

It was spring when we arrived at Arizona. The end of March, but you'd never have guessed. We'd left behind blossom trees in Green Copse Road and forsythia out in our own garden, but there was nothing out here, and I learned something then: spring in the country is a late business, a largely green and yellow business. What happens, almost imperceptibly, is that the grass starts to get a bit longer, a bit greener. The buds in the thorn hedges turn whitish and break, patchily, over weeks, into a different, sharper green. The ditches and roadside puddles begin to reflect this green. Tiny prickles of nettle, tiny feathers of cow parsley, tiny spears of lords-and-ladies push up on banks and verges. That accounts for the green. The yellow expresses itself in, first, celandines; second (where these will grow), primroses and cowslips; third, dandelions. Other signs that winter is over include an expectant quality in the light just before dusk, just before the light goes altogether; and noticeably noisy jackdaws, crows and rooks.

'We are not going to be hippies,' Aunt Hope said. We'd been in the house for perhaps a fortnight and were camping still. There were unopened tea chests and packing cases in the living room; there were no carpets down and no curtains up; our beds had blankets but were so far without sheets (somewhere around but no one knew exactly where), and she was frightened, I suppose, that we might be getting used to this unsettled, picnicky way of living. That we might be enjoying it and might want to carry on with it. Jocelyn had a bohemian streak Aunt Hope was wary of.

All I thought, all I remember thinking, was: What a weird place, what a lonely place, why have we come here? I was disappointed by our new house. It was long and narrow and low, and the windows were small, which meant dark rooms. From a distance you'd think it was a bungalow, but in fact there were two storeys. The front was cemented and at some time had been whitewashed, but the whitewash was more green than white and whole areas of it had flaked off. Bright-green stains, like bath stains, ran down from every junction and joint of the guttering. The top window frames were painted black, but here again much of the paint was blistered or had flaked off, leaving bare, grey wood. The ground-floor windows you could hardly see, they were hidden by a porch – or was it a veranda? – and this, I decided, was the most interesting thing about the house. It consisted of a corrugated iron roof, very rusty, supported by four rustic pillars, and was enclosed at both ends by rough wood panelling. It had a floor composed of narrow planks, a lot of them rotten. To get at the front door you had to climb four rickety wooden steps and then pick your way across this chancy boardwalk – like the boardwalk in the waterlogged fairground Jocelyn took me to once. In the corners against the house wall were heaps of curled dry leaves, little sleeping creatures they looked like, and when the wind blew, which it did every day that first week, some of these would detach themselves and scuttle for cover on the other side.

'Don't worry,' Aunt Hope said when she caught me eyeing the veranda, 'it's coming off; it's only tacked on, it shouldn't be there. It's rotten, and it's coming off.' And she showed me a gap in the boards where, if you squinted down, you could see the original front doorsteps – stone and slimy, a home for snails.

But Jocelyn said the porch had to stay. It might be Hammer House of Horror at the moment, but we couldn't get rid of it. What we had to do was restore it and paint it. It was part of old Bowdell's cowboy dream, his idea of Arizona. How could she consider getting rid of it?

'Bowdell doesn't live here any more,' Aunt Hope said. 'He's dead. It's our house now. I cannot live in a house called Arizona. On the estate agents' particulars it said "formerly known as Goosewell Farm". We should revert to that.'

'It isn't a farm now,' Jocelyn pointed out. 'It hasn't been for a long time. It'd be pretentious to call it anything farm. Unless Cold Comfort,' she added. 'Or Funny.'

It looked like a farm, though. It had outbuildings like a farm, breezeblock pigsties, a dungeonlike milking parlour with hooks and rusty chains. It was surrounded by farmland. It was separated from the road by a runway – Aunt Hope said it was – of ribbed concrete half a mile long. The concrete was in six-foot slabs, badly joined, so that grass and weeds, docks mostly, grew in the joins. It was isolated like a farm. Lonely as one.

The person who sold Arizona to Aunt Hope was Bowdell's heir, a nephew. He'd flown over from Halifax, Nova Scotia, for the funeral – and also, of course, for the reading of the will. 'Nephew' always sounds young, you think of toddlers or schoolboys when you hear the word 'nephew', and I remember being surprised when Aunt Hope, who met him during the sale negotiations, told Jocelyn in my hearing that Bowdell's nephew was a man in his sixties, red-faced and heavily built. Not a personable man, she said. Charmless and extremely brusque. She put his brusqueness down to having to do business with a woman – though he wasn't really doing that: there was an estate agent present and two solicitors, all of them male – and to disappointment at discovering the house he'd inherited wasn't a mansion. Far from a mansion; a small, down-at-heel farmhouse, barely habitable. She gathered that quite a few people had made enquiries about the place but that most of them, when they saw it, had driven away without bothering to get out of their cars. The ones who did step inside had stepped out in a hurry, with angry or relieved looks. Aunt Hope's offer, well below the asking price, well below the property's real value (it was the estate agents who said this), was the only one submitted in the whole six months it was on the market. After contracts had been exchanged, one of the many young men in the estate agents' offices, a trainee, confided to Aunt Hope that they'd found the vendor a tricky customer. He'd accused the agency of mishandling the sale; he'd accused his own solicitor of malpractice. The truth was, the trainee said, he'd ignored their advice. If he'd only emptied the place and cleaned it up, if he'd only been prepared to pay out for minor repairs and necessary paintwork, if he'd only waited until the magic month of May before putting it on the market – who knows what price they'd have been able to get for him? 'Anyway, his loss – and ours – is your gain,' the trainee agent told Aunt Hope. 'And I have to say you've got a bargain. Once those few structural problems we both know about are taken care of, and the place renovated, there's a tidy profit could be made. So if, in a couple of years' time, you feel like selling the property on, I hope you'll remember us.'

'He had a nerve,' Aunt Hope said to Jocelyn.

Bowdell's nephew took his revenge, in a petty way, for his disappointing inheritance. I didn't know this at the time, such details would not have interested me, but it had been agreed between the vendor's and purchaser's solicitors that Arizona should be empty of furniture, and clean, by the time we moved in. He carried off the best pieces, pieces he knew he could sell – Bowdell had owned a few surprisingly nice things, Aunt Hope said – and then flew back to Halifax, leaving the junk, and the filth, behind for us. A fiendish gift from the other side of the Atlantic.

Aunt Hope had to pay the removal men extra for taking the junk out before they could carry our furniture in. They hadn't wanted to do it. Cheerful and efficient when loading our furniture in Green Copse Road, crackers of jokes, sharers, with Jemma and me, of tea-break snacks, tuneful singers and fancy whistlers, Jeff, Bri and Mick had turned surly and unsmiling when we got to Arizona.

I had chosen to ride with them in the removal van, in convoy behind Jocelyn's Volkswagen, and they were my mates by this time, wide-eyed listeners to the tragedy of my parents' death. In a plane crash. Aunt Hope, no relation, well-meaning but mad, had rescued me from the orphanage. The dramatic change in their behaviour, the scowls and muttered curses, upset me greatly. But it was their disappointment more than anything else – more than their rudeness to Aunt Hope and Jocelyn, more than their coldness to me, more than the sight of Jeff, a George Best lookalike, landing a kick on Jemma's backside when he believed no one could see – that was so painful. Three hours' journey in the van had made me stiff-legged and sleepy, but the removal men appeared fresh as a sea-breeze. They'd jumped down from the cab rubbing their hands, eager to get started – and finished, it occurred to me later. They'd trotted round to the back of the van, slid back the bolts, swung open the doors, lowered the ramp. They'd taken the rickety steps of the porch in one leap, danced over the dodgy boardwalk on tiptoe, with behind-the-hand asides, and jogged on the spot outside the front door, impatient for Aunt Hope to produce the key. And then . . . when she had produced the key and turned it in the lock and pushed the door first with her hands and then, when that didn't work, with her knee and, finally and successfully, with her backside . . . what happened? The smiles froze on their faces. Or, it may be more accurate, the smiles were wiped off their faces.

I knew about the freezing and wiping of smiles. I'd witnessed it on the occasions my uncle had given flowers to my aunt and she hadn't liked them. More recently, I'd encountered the phenomenon the time Jocelyn took me to the fair.

The evening of the fair, a Friday, we have someone else with us, a girl the same height as me but a year and a half younger – a bad combination. Not a girl from my school or anyone

I know, the daughter of a teacher colleague of Aunt Hope's. A member of their family's ill – the grandmother? – and it's the job of this girl's mother, a maths teacher at the high school, to go to the ill person's house and look after her. Can my aunt have Toni for the night? Possibly two nights?

Aunt Hope says she can. 'How could I refuse?' she asked Jocelyn.

The funfair's in our town this week, and although it's been raining all day and is drizzling still, Jocelyn says she'll take us. (We've been begging since tea.) Aunt Hope says Jocelyn's out of her mind. The fairground will be a lake. Nothing would induce her to go, even if she had no marking to do. Strangely, she makes no mention of the homework Toni and I have, but she's loopy at the moment; it's only two months since Uncle Ber died.

Jocelyn spoils Toni and me at the fair, as she tends to spoil me when Aunt Hope isn't around. She buys us hot dogs and candyfloss and white soft ice cream in cornets with sticks of chocolate Flake stuck in the sides. The sweet-sweat smell of hot dogs and onions follows us from booth to booth, there's no escape; the smell's trapped in the stifling, deafening air that weighs down the fairground. We have fifty pence each to spend the way we want, and we lose it at games of chance in these little booths, which are lit by flashing bulbs, red, yellow and blue. There are more bulbs above our heads, strung on wires, so you can see your way along the slippery duckboard passageways. The rain's held off but Aunt Hope was right, the fairground is a lake. When we've spent our money and won nothing, Jocelyn digs into her purse again. All three of us ride the motorbikes on the merry-go-round, the switchback and the waltzers; and after that we drive the dodgems, which Jocelyn calls bumper cars.

'Can we go on the Red Devils next?' It's Toni bleating. She has a round face with freckled cheeks, a turned-up nose, also freckled, round blue eyes, pale, almost white hair and eyebrows. American kiddy-movie-star looks, disgusting to my mind. Disgusting behaviour too, considering all the treats – two goes on the dodgems – she's already had.

'No. That's it.' Jocelyn's had enough. To my relief, for the Red Devils are terrifying. Just to see them in action is enough to scare me to death. I've never flown in them or wanted to. The Red Devils are a boys' ride. The people who climb into those planes are mostly teenage boys and young men, singly or in pairs. The only girls you see embark are accompanied by boys – the sort of show-off boys who get a kick out of scaring girls; who, when the girls are thoroughly scared, get a kick out of comforting them. 'Enough's enough,' Jocelyn says. 'It's late. We're going home now.'

'Please. Pleeeese. Just one more. The Red Devils are my favourite.'

Toni jumps up and down while she pleads with Jocelyn, and I think, What a waste of time! What makes you imagine Jocelyn will give in, you pathetic person?

But after five minutes more of this performance, Jocelyn does give in. She sighs and opens her purse. 'This is the very last,' she says, 'the very, very last. I've only money enough for two, so I'll stay and watch. Off you go.' And she gives me a little push. She hasn't asked if I want to go on this ride. She must know from my face, from my expression of horror and astonishment, that I'm less than keen.

I despise you, Jocelyn, I thought. I'll never forgive you for this betrayal.

The Red Devils are two-seater aeroplanes, red, naturally, with a mock jet engine in the front, attached by steel rods to a central column. You notice a lot of complicated-looking cables and oily mechanisms, greased pistons and ball bearings. The planes fly in a diagonal arc, soaring into the sky one minute, plunging towards the earth the next, while at the same time the individual aircraft rotate. It's like the waltzers, this dual, neck-breaking movement, except up in the air. Like the waltzers, like all rides, this ride starts off misleadingly slowly, with music to match, and works up to sickening speed before winding down. During its fastest circuits the music can't keep pace and cuts out, and at that point a scream, the type military jets make, cuts in. Cuts in and drowns the screams of the terror-struck passengers in these spinning, plunging, pilotless planes. No child under ten – but how can they prove this? – not even accompanied by an adult, is allowed on the Red Devils. There's a notice, in wonky hand-printed letters, to say so.

If only I were under ten! If only Toni were, but she's already informed Jocelyn, twice, that she's eleven and one month. I wish I'd refused to go on the Red Devils – it's not too late to say no now, as Toni and I stand in the mud beside our chosen aircraft – but I didn't, and I can't.

There are three people, two men and a boy, working this ride, and one of them helps us into our plane and straps us in. (Seat straps and crossover shoulder straps, both necessary because for some of the ride we'll be flying upside down.) He chats us up as he sorts out the buckles. All the men and boys in charge of the rides chat you up if you're female. It could be offensive but isn't because without exception these men and boys are attractive. This one's in his twenties, I imagine. He has a thin face and a wide smile, black hair, greased and quiffed, black eyebrows, sideburns. He's wearing a T-shirt and over it a cracked leather jacket, open, with a busted zip. It's hard to know what colour his jeans are because they're stained, saturated, with oil. Most of the people who work the rides, I've noticed, even the young ones, have long sideburns, and most of them look like this – like Elvis with oil stains, like rockers and bikers from way back before I was born. It must be fairground style to look and dress the way they do.

'So who's the pilot and who's the navigator?' the Red Devils man asks, and I say 'pilot' quickly, before Toni has a chance. Not that it makes any difference. Toni and I are passengers. There are no controls in this cockpit, not even fake ones, jut a curved guard rail in front of us at chest level.

'Remember to keep both 'ands on the joystick, all the

time,' the man says, and he taps the guard rail. 'No messin', me loves – keep 'em on and don' let go, OK?' Then he says, 'What you two gorgeous girls called then? Let me guess – Marilyn Monroe' (he points at Toni) 'and, and Elizabef Taylor.' (He points at me.) 'Am I right?'

We both giggle, as we're meant to. We shake our heads and giggle again. We tell him what our names really are.

'Tony!' He feigns falling over backwards in surprise. 'Well, wo' a coincidence! Tony's my nime! It's a fella's nime – but you're never a fella wiv tha' beau'iful 'air. Tell you wo', Tony, seein' as you an' me's go' the sime nime, seein' as gen'lemen prefer blondes, you can ride 'alf fare. Jus' this once. Which reminds me – 'aven't taken any money off you two lovely ladies yet, 'ave I?'

After he's pocketed our money, Tony gives the plane a spin, a last-minute, casual flick with a black-oiled hand. ''Old on to yer 'ats, darlin's,' he calls, blowing a kiss as he swings away, though neither of us is wearing a hat.

> 'I'm leaving on a jet plane
> Don't know when I'll be back again,'

sing Peter, Paul and Mary – but mostly Mary – as we sit in our Red Devil, waiting for takeoff. We have to wait what feels like a long time. Maybe it's the weather that has put people off this ride, or maybe it's the cost – the Red Devils is the most expensive ride of the fair. Each time the three planes nearest the ground take on passengers, our own plane jerks up a notch, and eventually we're high up, five to twelve if this were a clock, motionless, suspended above the fairground. Side by side in the stuffy cockpit. Toni and I sit tight and don't speak; she's gone silent for once and I've got nothing to say. I grip the bar and concentrate on the next-to-near future. I tell myself that before I know it this ride will be over. As soon as we get going it'll be as good as over. I have to repeat this, chant it, to shut out another voice in my head that keeps butting in to ask questions. How well

are these planes fixed to their rods? the voice asks. How
well are the rods fixed to the central machinery? Is all the
machinery, are all those cables, in good working order? Do
they get checked over from time to time? What would happen
if, when the ride's at its fastest, split-arse, Uncle Ber would
have said, one of the bolts on one of the planes, on this
plane, worked loose . . .? I look up at the sky, dark and heavy
with rain clouds. Thunder clouds, could they be? Thunder
and lightning clouds? I look down. A little crowd has gathered to watch the aerobatics the Red Devils are famous for,
and I can make out Jocelyn's scarlet mac. I look straight
ahead, and there's the Ferris wheel, stationary a moment
ago, now on the move. Ferris wheel? Catherine wheel, it will
be, any minute now.

Over soon. Over soon. *Already I'm so lonesome I could
cry* . . .

'Hannah, Hannah!' Toni wailing.

'What?'

'Don't wanna go on this ride. Don't like it, frightened,
wanna get off.'

What?

'You can't get off now. Don't be stupid. You can't get out
up here.'

'Feel sick.'

She does look green, but that may have something to do
with the lights, green and yellow, strobes and flashers, that
make everyone look queasy. I tell her to think about something else, and I wave my arms about, trying to get Jocelyn's
attention. The red mac's vanished. You cow, Jocelyn. You
coward. Where are you? How could you stick me up here
with Toni, who, it's quite obvious, has never been on the
Red Devils in her life?

> 'Those magnificent men in their flying machines
> They go up diddlyum up, they go
> Down diddlyum down . . .'

And we're off. The moment Pinky and Perky take over, we're away. Up diddlyum up for a second or two, and then – it's like being on a swing – down diddlyum down. As we near the ground on the first circuit, I spot the Fat Boys, three of them, shoving their way to the front of the crowd, and my heart stops. (I haven't seen them since the day they tried to drown me, the day Uncle Ber died. Since that terrible day I haven't been near that Pool Hall once.) The presence of the Fat Boys confirms it: our flying machine is doomed.

But it isn't doomed. Not in the disaster-movie manner I've imagined – plane breaking free, zooming into sky, stalling, nose-diving into crowd, killing Toni and me and Jocelyn and the Fat Boys, maiming innocent bystanders for bad measure. No, all that happens, early on in the trip, is that the navigator throws up. Undigested hot dog and ketchup and candyfloss and Coke and ice cream land first in her lap, then in mine. On subsequent circuits she rids her stomach of better digested, looser, smellier stuff: the scrambled egg and baked beans we had for tea, plus whatever was on her school dinner menu this morning. When the music cuts out and the jet scream cuts in, when the Red Devils break through the sound barrier while at the same time they execute their dizzy rolls and spins, looping the loop and defying the ground, when the G force weights our legs and arms with lead and does its worst to snap our heads off – guess what happens to the stinking heaps in our laps?

All at once, it's over. Screaming jets and passengers give way to Pinky and Perky for the final, half-hearted laps. Slow, slower, slowest. Stop. Toni and I sit in our puke-sprayed hellhole and wait to be released. The stink is appalling. There isn't a surface or crevice of the cockpit Toni's puke didn't reach. And it's in our hair, it's down our necks. It's inside our socks, it's inside our shoes. We want to get out, we're desperate to get away before this infamy can be discovered, but the bile-soaked harness has defeated both of us.

And now – and for ever, probably, for whatever else goes, I'm unlikely to lose this image – over the muddy grass towards us lopes Tony. Grinning, arms flung wide in a gesture of embrace. He calls out, 'All right, darlin's? Good flight? and 'Ow was it for you, Toni gal?'

He must be stopped, someone must stop him. Stay where you are, Tony! Don't come any nearer! Stay there, please! Stop!

He takes no notice. Of course not. It's his job to get us out of the plane and to get new fares aboard; so he keeps on coming and he keeps on grinning until. Until the grin freezes on his face.

What wiped the smiles off the removal men's faces that first day at Arizona was not the junk Bowdell's nephew had left behind – the clapped-out chairs and settees and pipe-smoked curtains and sodden carpets – much of which had to be brought out of the house before our furniture could be moved in. It was the rubbish they tripped over and the dog shit they skidded in. No, it would have been the smell in that sealed house that struck first. Aunt Hope worked out that Bowdell's nephew – for who else could it have been? – must have lugged the four bursting dustbins she'd seen on earlier visits across the porch, and up-ended them just inside the front door. (This explained the trouble she'd had trying to get the door open.) And he must have got hold of a dog, a dog with a serious bowel incontinence problem, and let it loose upstairs and downstairs and in my aunt's chamber.

'We're not contracted to work in these conditions,' Mike, the senior removal man, said for the umpteenth time when the three of them had sullenly done the minimum they were prepared to do.

'I believe you,' Aunt Hope said.

'Diabolical's the only word for what we've found 'ere.'

'I wouldn't argue with that,' Aunt Hope said sweetly.

'Hardly a fit place to bring a young girl, to bring your adopted daughter, is it?' He paused. 'I wonder what the authorities would have to say?'

'I wonder.'

'We'll be off then.' He stood his ground and held out his hand, palm upwards. Aunt Hope fetched her bag and crossed the palm with several pound notes and a fiver, which he squinted at and fingered suspiciously before folding into his back trouser pocket. Then he and Bri and Jeff left. Not a smile, not a word, not a wink or a glance at me.

I stood on the porch and watched their grim and disappointed faces as they closed the van and swung themselves into the cab. I knew they knew I was watching them. They'll wave now, I thought. Now that Aunt Hope's out of sight, they'll have to call goodbye. But they didn't. I remembered our journey to this place, the stories and the jokes. I remembered how, when the van was scarcely out of Green Copse Road, they'd done their best to sell me the countryside and the country way of life:

'Lookin' forward to life in the sticks, eh, Hannah?'

'No.'

'Aw, come on now, that's not the right attitude. The country's the best place to live. We'd like to live there, all things being equal, jobs 'n' that. Wouldn't we, lads?'

'You bet.'

'Cer'ainly would.'

'Roses round the door, fresh air, village pub, pond with little ducklin's swimmin' around, trees to climb – '

'I've got a pond, and a tree to climb, at home.'

'Well, there'll be more trees where you'se goin', loads more, whole woods full of trees. An' birds.'

'There's no sea where we're going. I'm used to living near the sea.'

'Rivers, though. You got rivers in the country. Bet yer anything yer like there's a river nearabouts. You'll be fishin', and swimmin' . . .'

I said nothing.

'New-laid eggs, milk straight from the cow, cream – you're not goin' to tell us yer don't like cream?'

I was going to, I was just about to, when it suddenly struck me that a positive answer was required. So I said I did like cream. 'Sort of.'

'There y'are, then.'

Disappointment. It was disappointment that turned my mates Mike and Bri and Jeff into stony strangers. To cheer me along, these three town dwellers had listed the virtues of a way of life they probably despised or, if not despised, would assuredly not have wanted for themselves. But something happened on that journey, I think. The more they enthused about the pleasures of rural living – their picture-book, pre-war, pre-first-war version, that is – the more they began to believe in its reality. That's how I understand it now. They'd painted a picture, they'd created expectations, as much for themselves as for me, and Arizona let them down. A lot of men aren't good at dealing with disappointment. Disappointment makes them feel foolish, and feeling foolish makes them cold. Or aggressive. Murderous, even. Perhaps men start off with more expectations, and bigger ones, than women. Perhaps they want more. They want more, they expect more and when life disappoints, they are unforgiving. Bowdell's nephew was such a man. Tony, the Red Devils hand at the fair, was. 'You fuckin', fuckin' little bitches! You dirty, disgustin' little cunts,' he'd hissed at Marilyn Monroe and Elizabeth Taylor when he got near enough to see and smell them. It wasn't what Toni's puke had done to his plane that so enraged him – people must often throw up on those rides, beer drinkers surely are candidates, he must have been used to that, they probably have hoses and disinfectant on standby for the puke merchants. It was disappointment. In us, his darlings, and especially in his namesake Toni, whom he'd let ride half fare. In himself, for lack of judgement. He'd believed us to be innocents abroad and allowed himself to get involved, and we'd proved ourselves corrupt.

I remember, one evening, Diarmid looking forward to the fish pie he'd asked for, and then after a couple of forkfuls pushing the plate away. 'I'm sorry,' I said. I'd spent hours making this pie; haddock aside, it contained leeks and carrots and prawns and hard-boiled egg and white sauce and mashed potato, and there was nothing wrong with it that I could taste. 'Let me make you something else.' But the man who minutes earlier had been pacing the kitchen, suddenly wasn't hungry. There was nothing I was able to offer him that he wanted to eat; and I thought, It's not just the pie, it's more than that. It's life, it's life with me that hasn't lived up.

Aunt Hope and Jocelyn came out on the porch in time to see the removal van roar out of the courtyard. Dumped any old where on the boards was our garden furniture, deck chairs and wicker chairs, the wooden bench Uncle Ber made that had spent my lifetime under the crab-apple tree, the iron table with the bobbly glass top. Jocelyn freed one of the wicker chairs, the rocker, and sat down on it. In an attempt to keep the dust and muck out, she and Aunt Hope had tied tea towels over their hair, and Jocelyn undid hers and arranged it round her shoulders like a shawl. She set the chair at a steady rock, folded and tucked her top lip in a way that made it seem she hadn't a tooth in her head, rolled her eyes around like a lunatic.

'Well, I declare, I'se plumb tuckered out.'

This performance made Aunt Hope smile, the first wide, sane, genuine smile I'd seen her smile in months.

'I sure hope that dawg shit ain't a bad omen,' the toothless old woman in the rocking chair went on. (Jocelyn, I'd noticed, appreciated an appreciative audience.) 'How'se us folks ever gonna manage t'sleep with that thar smell?'

It was cold on the porch, and getting dark. We went inside and brewed up, and ate the sandwiches left over from lunch. Then we cleaned the kitchen. It took hours. There was a lot of mould on the walls. When we tried to brush it off, flaky paint and plaster flew from our brushes and settled like dandruff on surfaces we'd already cleaned.

'That'll have to do for today,' Aunt Hope tipped a bucket of black oily water down the sink. She'd just finished the floor, swept it and scrubbed it on her knees, though really when it dried you couldn't tell the difference.

'A girl could die of thirst around here.' Jocelyn went out to the car, and came back with a whisky bottle and two picnic beakers and set them on the table. I looked on critically as she poured.

'How can you drink that stuff?' I'd tried whisky, naturally, at the first opportunity. I'd tried it several times since, to check if it was as nasty as I'd remembered, and it always was, it always tasted like a punishment.

'Very easily – my answer every time you ask that irritating question.'

Drink, spirits rather, was new in our lives. It had first entered the house the day the Fat Boys tried to drown me and Uncle Ber died. The doctor had been and gone ('What have you done to your nose? Dear me, that does look sore,' he'd said, vague and hearty, catching sight of me in the hall), the undertakers had creaked up the stairs – and, after an interminable time behind a shut bedroom door, creaked painstakingly down. Saying, 'Stay with your aunt a minute,' Jocelyn had nipped out to the off-licence in Hilldown Parade. She came back with Napoleon brandy. 'Doctor's orders – best thing for shock,' she'd explained. (I was in shock on two counts, my teeth wouldn't hold still and my legs kept twitching, but she did not pour brandy for me.) That night my nightmares had been interrupted by weeping and laughter, in bursts, from the kitchen. By teatime the following day a new, full bottle had replaced the empty one on the sideboard. Whisky this time. Whisky thereafter. One bottle a week to start with, soon two. Before long two and a half. My aunt and her friend were turning into drunks.

Wide-open windows and Jeyes fluid got rid of the dog-shit smell eventually, but not that first night. Aunt Hope, Jocelyn, Jemma and I slept on mattresses on the floor of the one upstairs room the dog hadn't visited, but the smell crept up through the floorboards, sweet and terrible, and invaded my dreams.

It took months to get Arizona halfway habitable. The roof leaked, and as soon as the weather improved scaffolding went up and, after it, two roofers, who felted, rebattened and retiled the weakest areas. Fuses blew regularly; we ate cold suppers in candle-dark. The electrician who came discovered that some of the wiring, ancient in any case, had been eaten by rats: the whole house had to be rewired. In the course of rewiring, traces of saprophytic *Basidiomycetes*, the fungus that causes dry rot, not mentioned by the surveyor in his pre-contract survey, was found in the skirting of the little room off the scullery Bowdell had used as his office, which my aunt planned to use as a workroom. When the fumigators moved in, we moved out, to a bed-and-breakfast place on the main road.

Aunt Hope hadn't reckoned on these extra expenses, and you'd catch her, in spare moments, making hurried calculations on the backs of envelopes; but strangely she didn't seem really fussed by the problems, uncovered almost daily, that caused the workmen to shake, or scratch, their heads. We were without a telephone for weeks (it had been promised for moving day), a lack which annoyed the workmen – who needed to be in contact with their bosses, or whose bosses needed to be in contact with them – and infuriated Jocelyn. Every time she wanted to ring her agent she had to get the car out and bump down the runway, and then drive a mile to the crossroads, to what she called 'that broken-down sedan box in the stinging nettles', usually out of order. Aunt Hope refused to get het up about the telephone. Rather, she seemed amused. 'A relief to be without that damned machine,' I heard her say, and 'Do we really need a telephone? I've half a mind to cancel it.'

We were not going to be hippies. We were not going to be flower people. It was she who'd said it, and I found her relaxed attitude mystifying. It was as if, in changing house, she'd changed into another person. Gone were the rages, the clumsiness, the demented pacing and muttering. It wasn't that she returned to the exacting and tight-lipped aunt I'd known before my uncle died. This person who looked like my aunt and continued to wear her grey cardigan and neat wool skirts was tolerant of mistakes, even mine. She hummed about that dismal house. She ran lightly from room to room – like a girl, I was about to say, but girls don't run lightly; they mooch or sleepwalk, as I did. Her smiles blazed like log fires. (Like some log fires; the windfall branches we collected from the lane sizzled and smoked but would not burn.) In the evenings when she and Jocelyn sat late over their firewater, planning and playing cards, the only shrieks that reached me in the room above were of laughter.

Was my aunt's nonchalance – short-lived, as it turned out – real? Or did she fake it out of need to keep Jocelyn at home? Would she have been capable of such conscious fakery? She certainly convinced me; on the other hand, it is possible to act happy and carefree when you're not. Some people can. Clowns bend over backwards to that end although, as everyone knows, there is no such thing as a happy clown. I've wondered about this because throughout that period when my aunt reinvented herself as someone light-hearted and benign, her troubles were still there. Out of sight, maybe (my mother), submerged (in more senses than one, my darling Uncle Ber), but not gone away. Perhaps she was able, in those first weeks, to deceive herself that a new life meant just that. A shedding of old ways, old ties, old fears, old responsibilities. A ridding of old, terrible guilts I at the time knew nothing of.

All the interior walls of Arizona – yellow originally? it was hard to be sure – were the greenish brown of dark stone, while the doors, skirtings and even the windowsills had been stained an ugly brown that in evening light appeared black. Against this background Jack Bowdell had hung – that is, pinned or stuck – his exhibition of the Old West. Posters, maps, diagrams, photographs, articles cut from magazines: his obsession collared us in every downstairs room. Gunmen and lawmen, bandits and bounty hunters, bootleggers and cardsharpers. Boom towns and ghost towns. Canyons and creeks.

You had to stand close up to those washed-out sepias and black-and-whites to see the details and to tell the difference between Wyatt Earp, say, and Doc Holliday. All the white men wore down-in-the-mouth moustaches. You had to peer and peer at Bowdell's minute, hand-printed captions to learn that what you'd understood to be a massive stove (that tubelike object reaching to the ceiling was a stovepipe, surely?) a few feet from the bar of the 'Oriental Saloon, Tombstone', was in fact a safe. I did peer and peer those first days after the move. I found Bowdell's fixation comforting and distressing by turn. His careful drawings of 'Rawhide Reatas' and 'Manila Lariats' reminded me of Uncle Ber's knot board. His photographs and diagrams headed 'Guns used in the West' took me straight back to my uncle's work-room. I saw our model ships on the shelves, and the prints and diagrams on the spare spaces of the walls and on the back of the door. There had been two diagrams on the door, 'The Sails of a Ship' and 'The Yards and Running Rigging of a Ship', and I remembered how for years my uncle had tried to teach me these. 'Show me the lower mizen topsail,' he'd say after one such lesson, or 'Put your finger on the main topgallant staysail.' Or on the crojik – 'spelt "crossjack", remember' – or the spanker.

> A charming young girl called Bianca
> Fell asleep while the ship was at anchor
> She awoke in dismay
> When she heard the mate say,
> 'Pull off the top sheet and spanker!'

Spanker boom, spanker boom topping lift; spanker sheet; spanker gaff; spanker vangs – Uncle Ber's limerick was no help when it came to locating them on the diagram; I got nothing right in his tests, except by accident. The rectangles and triangles and arcs and parallel lines of rigging resembled nothing so much as the theorems in my geometry textbook and were just as unfathomable. All you could be certain of was that, goosenecks and whiskers and boom and bumpkin apart, a line that wasn't a brace – or a lift or a yard or a guy – had to be a halliard.

Walking round Bowdell's exhibition, staring at a coloured illustration of 'Chaparejos or "Chaps" ' (shot-gun chaps, bat-wing chaps, angora chaps, rear and side views), I remembered the day, some weeks before, when Aunt Hope had cleared out my uncle's workshop.

She did it one afternoon when Jocelyn had taken me to the skating rink. (Now that I refused to go to the Pool Hall, the rink had taken over as the place to go for exercise.) She set aside the house tools and garden tools and a few things she thought I might like to keep – my uncle's White Ensign, half a dozen of the best (as she thought) of the model craft he'd slaved over – and made a bonfire of the rest. Unused balsa and chippings, old glues and paints helped fuel the flames. The diagrams of sails and rigging I've mentioned went onto this pyre, as did the *Kon-Tiki*, Uncle Ber's yachting cap and the sea pictures he'd loved: the Montagu Dawson reproductions that had been his favourites and the set of four Hely Augustus Morton Smiths, the size of extra-large postcards, that were mine. Never again would I be able to lose myself in 'Roll On, Thou Deep and Dark Blue Ocean, Roll', 'The Fog Horn', 'The Blue, the Fresh, the Ever Free' and the one I liked best, 'Westering Home': a white three-master, square-rigged on the fore and main masts – the mizen's obscured – sails full, listing slightly to starboard, heads to the bottom left-hand corner of the painting. Heads into the sunlight, heads for home. The sky is enormous, cloudy, a mauvish white; the sea, or ocean maybe, choppy and a dark, deep blue.

A few years ago, hunting in a stationer's for a birthday card for Diarmid, I found a greetings card of 'Westering Home', and my heart keeled over. It wasn't a birthday card, the message inside read 'Bon Voyage!', but what did that matter?

I watched him as he took the card out of its envelope. He said nothing, just stared. 'Is it a joke?' he asked eventually. We usually chose jokey cards to give each other, crude ones to do with sex or unkind ones to do with age, though occasionally he went for old masters.

'No,' I said, 'it isn't a joke, why should it be? It's one of my favourite paintings.'

'You're having me on,' Diarmid said.

'No, no, I'm not,' I said, 'I mean it.'

Diarmid shook his head and started to smile in a disbelieving way.

'Look at it again,' I said, 'no, look at it properly. You can smell that sea, can't you? You can tell it's deep. It's heavy and solid, like Turkish delight or uncooked jelly – the way really deep sea always looks. You could cut a piece out if you wanted. Also, the ship's going at a tremendous lick, isn't it? You can hear the noise it makes, the creak and flap. You can hear those heavy waves, slap-slap-slapping against the bows.'

Diarmid scratched his head. 'Well, I dunno,' he said, 'we seem to be looking at different pictures. What I'm looking at – and no, I can't hear anything at all – is a really naff, really kitsch example of nautical so-called art. Let's see what Finchy makes of it.'

The know-all was in his bedroom, but when Diarmid called him he waddled in.

'Whaddya make of this, Finchy?'

Finch was nine years old then, nine or ten. He frowned and pursed his little mouth as he examined the card. 'Could be a ship,' he said. 'Strictly speaking, a ship's a vessel with three masts, all square-rigged, but there's only two sets of sails here that you can actually see. The mizen may well be fore-and-aft rigged. Probably is. In which case it's not a ship but a barque. But of course we have no rigorous proof, let alone complete proof on that. Is that what you wanted to know?'

When Finch, nothing more to add, had gone back to his room, Diarmid opened the card. I'd crossed out 'Bon Voyage!' and substituted 'Happy Birthday', but he chose to ignore the amended message. 'Oh, I get it,' he said, 'you're trying to get rid of me. That's what this card is all about.'

I won't let them be burned, I told myself after I'd examined every item in Bowdell's Arizona collection; these things must stay where they are. But they couldn't stay. Before the electricians and plumbers could get to work, everything had to come down. That wasn't all. When the workmen finished – if they ever did finish – there'd be the decorating to do. Jocelyn pointed this out to me. We could hardly paint walls that had bits of paper stuck all over them, now could we, Hannah dear?

I followed her from room to room as she went round the walls pulling out nails with the prong end of a hammer and prising the glued pieces off with a knife. It seemed to me that as one exhibition came down, another went up, a phantom exhibition of blank geometric shapes that proved the walls had once, a long time ago, been painted cream. The posters were easiest to remove; the heaviness of their paper ensured that, having pulled out a strategic tack or two, all Jocelyn had to do was give one tug with finger and thumb at the bottom edge, and they slid to the floor. Where I retrieved them.

'Hey, Hope!' Jocelyn called, peering at something on the wall. 'Hey, Hopey, come here.'

My aunt came running from the kitchen.

'There's a piece here about the Hopi tribe. I'm learning all about you. You live in northeast Arizona – well, that's true. You have a peaceful philosophy, it says here. You're a very private people. Your clan system keeps you together. The Rattlesnake clan – are you a member of that? That doesn't sound too peaceful to me.'

'You're very silly,' Aunt Hope said.

'I'm relieved to learn you keep to your traditional ceremonies. That Snake Dance you always do in August – we shall expect that, come the bank holiday. But why haven't we been treated to the sunflower-seed bread the Hopis are so famous for?'

'You shouldn't make fun of them,' I said. 'You shouldn't make fun of Indians.'

'Oh, my gawd,' Jocelyn said. 'I wasn't. I was making fun of your aunt. OK?'

'Don't tell me you intend keeping all that stuff?' Aunt Hope said to me.

'Yes.'

But I had no idea how or where. My bedroom was minute. There was just room enough for a bed, a chest of drawers, a chair. No room for a table, no room for a clothes cupboard. No room to swing Jemma, not much bigger – though a lot heavier – than a cat. The few dresses I owned would have to hang in Aunt Hope's cupboard in her bedroom. Either there or on hangers on the back of my door. The cramped feeling upstairs was due to the back roof which, in contrast to the shallow front roof, was absurdly deep, sloping to within a foot of the lintels of the back door and ground-floor windows. Viewing the house from the side, you had the impression of a square of greenish cheese from which a substantial wedge had been sliced away.

There were two decent bedrooms, however, at either end of the house. They were identical, or perhaps I mean mirror, twins, each possessing a fireplace with a rusted iron fire basket on its far, outside wall. Both had two windows. Aunt Hope's windows faced east and north, Jocelyn's east and south. A narrow, low-ceilinged passage, running along the back of the house, connected the two, and in between, opening off it, was the bathroom, or what passed for a bathroom (next to Aunt Hope's room), a lavatory and finally my own cubbyhole (next to Jocelyn's room), with one small window, facing east. At first, my aunt and Jocelyn seemed pleased with these sleeping arrangements, but as time went on they began to argue about the merits and disadvantages of their rooms in a childish way.

'It faces south,' Aunt Hope would murmur ruminatively, as though to herself, 'it gets all the sun. It's the master bedroom, of course.'

'What's that?' But Jocelyn would have heard her perfectly well.

'The master bedroom – yours, my dear, yours.'

'Mine? You had first choice, as I recall. As I recall, I wasn't even consulted.'

'Generosity on my part,' Aunt Hope would sigh. 'Self-sacrifice.'

At this, as at all similarly outrageous remarks made by my aunt, Jocelyn would open her extraordinary blue eyes extraordinarily wide.

'I suppose it was generosity on your part made certain your bedroom was next to the bathroom? Which is where master bedrooms tend to be. There isn't a basin within spitting distance of my room. I have to walk a mile every time I want to clean my teeth. Let alone have a bath. But if you'd like to swap, it's fine by me.'

Aunt Hope would stare into the distance then, as though she hadn't heard.

I Blu-Tacked the best – the most arresting, the least damaged

– items from Bowdell's exhibition onto my own bedroom walls and door, and the rest I shoved under the bed. Jocelyn, who fancied herself as a handyman, put up a high shelf on three of my walls, and on its rough and jumpy surface I placed my treasures: shells and stones collected from the Little Beach, what remained of Uncle Ber's model craft, my mother's assortment of china bears. My bed, almost the length of the wall it pressed against, faced the door of this snug museum, so that when I woke in the mornings light from the little window above my head illuminated the collaged heads and moustaches and stick-up collars and broadcloth shoulders of the Earp brothers: Wyatt, James, Virgil, Morgan and Warren. Turning my head a little, I would find myself in Red Rock Country, surveying from the top of the world 'the crimsons and blood reds and ochres of Sedona's sandstone spires'. 'Not bad alliteration, not bad at all,' my aunt said, reading Bowdell's caption when she came to say goodnight.

Eggshell Arch, Chino Valley, Copper Creek, Haunted Wilderness – these names would mean nothing to me if it weren't for Jack Bowdell. The Painted Desert and the Petrified Forest are world-famous, Finch says, but if it hadn't been for the old man's obsession, I doubt I'd have known where to open the atlas to look for them.

In the block of flats where Finch and I . . . live, I was going to say, but my son says he doesn't live with me, we occupy the same cage, that's all.

Of course the line isn't original; Tennessee Williams wrote it and it comes from *Cat on a Hot Tin Roof* – from the movie, at any rate, I haven't seen a stage production. Watching movies on TV, old black-and-white melodramas, films noirs, thrillers, Westerns, is the only interest my son and I share, although 'share' is not quite the right word for the way we view, silent – save for the cracking-open of Coke cans and the rustling of crisp bags – and separate, he in his small corner, me in mine. Nevertheless, after a fashion, we watched *Cat on a Hot Tin Roof* together. I'd seen the film on television once before, but it was a long time ago and I'd forgotten a lot of it. I'd forgotten, or perhaps hadn't realised, how good it was. I do think it's good. Despite the fudging of the real reason for Brick's drinking and Maggie's sarcasm and frustration, the film struck me, second time around, as excellent. Witty, harrowing, moving, awful; all of these. Terrific performances, also. Liz Taylor was terrific. The child actors, those appalling No-neck Monsters – who reminded me of Finch at that age, so much that I flushed with embarrassment each time they hit the screen, wondering if he recognised himself – were terrific. And Paul Newman, in those pyjamas, refilling that whisky glass, hopping painfully round the room on that crutch . . .

It struck me too how modern the film still is in some ways, in some visual ways, how up to date the appearance of the male characters, in particular, seems. The short-back-and-sides or crew-cut hair, the straight-legged trousers – they aren't all that different from the look you see in the street now. I remarked on this to Finch during a break for commercials. Odd, wasn't it, I said, that a movie made in 1958, before I was even born, should be more accessible, more easily recognisable than a movie made in the mid-seventies, say. Nothing now seemed more foreign and ridiculous than those Robin Hood haircuts and suede jackets. Whereas, conversely, I could remember, as a child, in the seventies, watching a fifties film and thinking –

'How many drinks have you had?' Finch asked. 'Three? Four? I ask because you make that observation every time. Every time we watch a seventies movie – or a fifties movie, or a sixties movie even – I have to listen to that. Tee-di-us.'

Later, during another break, digging deep into a crisp bag, one eye on a sun-struck saloon powering over a mountain range, he asked me if I fancied Burl Ives at all.

What a question! Why would I, why would any woman, even consider Burl Ives when Paul Newman was on offer? There had to be more to it than met the ear.

'He's a bit old for me,' I said cautiously, 'more like a father or a grandfather. And anyway, I'm not that keen on beards.'

'My father was big, I imagine? A Big Daddy? I must have inherited my size from him?'

'Well, I'm . . .' Not sure, was the truthful answer, but I didn't want to say that. Over the years, in response to my son's infrequent but, when he sprang them, anxiety-inducing interrogations, I'd built up a picture of his father, a hazy picture, not too specific, just enough substance, I hoped, to make the figure believable. I'd been fearful of inventing too many details in case I later forgot them or got them wrong – Finch is a quick spotter of discrepancies. I realise now that what I should have done, very early on, before Finch was of an age to ask anything, was invent a character and a context, write it all down, learn it off by heart and stick to it. As it was, the few facts about his father that we could both be sure of were as follows: His name was Michael Jones (millions of M. Joneses in the phone book, was my thinking, should Finch ever feel an urge to try and trace his father). He had blue-grey eyes and crinkly hair. He had webbed toes (I'd read an article in a mag about people who had webbed toes). He was neither especially tall nor especially short. He was left-handed (this had been an easy decision: Finch was himself left-handed). He was bright, of course. But fat? Or thin? Finch had never asked, and I had no idea.

'I see him as big,' Finch said, 'like me. I imagine him to look like me, though you've never said so.'

'He did look a lot like you. A lot.' It wasn't a lie; Finch's father might well have looked like Finch. If I'd known who Finch's father was. If I could work it out.

'What I find weird,' Finch said, 'is that I'm almost the age he was when he fathered me. The fathers of the guys I know, the ones who've got fathers, are all old men, really old, some of them.'

When Finch was nine or thereabouts, he'd suddenly shot at me, 'Why didn't you and Dad get married? What made him go off before I was even born?'

It wasn't the first time he'd asked, but up till then I'd fobbed him off with who-can-say gestures or vague remarks about the relationship just not working out. This time he meant business, I could see. My answer, unrehearsed, had seemed sent from heaven, it was so inspired: 'Because he was still at school at the time. Because he was only sixteen. I couldn't ruin his life, could I? Anyway, his parents would never have allowed it. They were professional people. I was waitressing then, as I'm sure I've told you. I had no qualifications, no prospects. So when I knew for sure I was pregnant I left the area. Without saying anything.' At one stroke I'd conjured for us both an image of innocent young love destroyed by cruel adult rules, and at the same time given Finch an incontrovertible and, on my part, selfless excuse for his father's abandonment.

That's what I'd thought I'd done, if only because Finch had accepted the story. More than accepted it, he'd seemed relieved. Recently, though, I'd had the uneasy feeling, from various things he'd said, sly, disingenuous things, that my son had begun to impose some revisionist thinking, as Diarmid would put it, on his youthful interpretation.

'Your dad would be an old man man now, anyway,' I said. 'A very old man.' (I was trying to make a joke of it.) 'Almost as old as me. He must be thirty by now, the poor old fellow.'

I waited. He jiggled his leg and said nothing. Don't jiggle, Finch. I'll kill you if you don't stop jiggling.

In the block of flats where Finch and I inhabit our cage, there's a married couple in their early forties who have two adopted children. The couple's names are Sandy and Paula, their surname's Peterson, and their adopted children, aged nine and six, are Matthew and Julie-Ann. Matthew and Julie-Ann aren't a real brother and sister, they're not related in any way. Sandy and Paula adopted them separately, Matthew first, when he was four, and then, after a two-year gap, Julie-Ann. Paula now feels it might have been better if they'd adopted children of the same sex, two boys or two girls, and she suspects girls are easier to handle in the long run. Children of the same sex are more likely to have shared interests and to want to play together, Paula now thinks. Another advantage is that they can sleep in the same room right through puberty, until they leave home if need be.

Matthew is a beautiful child by any standards. He's tall for nine, narrow-bodied, with long, thin legs and arms. He has wide-set, immense green eyes with lashes so long and thick you'd think them false if a woman had them. He has loosely curly hair the colour of ripe barley, a straight, delicate nose, a curvy mouth, an amused smile. In summer his ivory skin turns an even Marie-biscuit brown. Film-star looks. You'd never guess, from looking at him – I never guessed, and I looked at him, stared, at the beginning, whenever he came into view – that this boy has problems of any kind, but he does. Poor bladder control, severe behavioural problems and learning difficulties. Early on in his life he was diagnosed autistic, though subsequent tests by a different set of medics revised that diagnosis.

Julie-Ann is not beautiful, her features are unremarkable. What you do notice is that her head seems too big and heavy for her puny body, and that her hair is wispy and thin, the amount and texture of hair you'd expect a toddler, an eighteen-month-old, to have. Julie-Ann has problems also. Epilepsy is one. Extreme short-sightedness and astigmatism another (she wears spectacles, I forgot to mention). And she's partially deaf, which means that, like Matthew, she has socialising and learning difficulties.

Paula told me these facts about her children – the hidden medical facts, not the aesthetic ones I was able to observe for myself. She and I live on the same floor, her flat is just across the landing from mine. The flat had been empty for ages when the Petersons took it. (Our block was originally a council block, but after that right-to-buy business came in, a lot of people bought their flats and now can't sell them, can hardly give them away, except to the desperate.) When the Petersons moved in, I thought, Oh, perhaps we'll be friends. For I'm short of friends here; the people in these flats are chary of intimacy, I find, there's no one I could really call a friend. The nuclear family, I thought when I first saw the Petersons; Mum, Dad and two kiddies, just like in the commercials. And I felt cheered and envious, both.

I rang their bell that first evening with the idea of making neighbourly noises. Were they all right? I was going to ask. Did they need anything? Was there anything I could do? Was there anything they needed to know? (About the building, I meant, and the lift that's always breaking down; about the caretaker who takes no care unless you make it seriously worth his while. About Mr Dowsett, the schizophrenic from 55a who, when not ill enough to be sectioned, patrols the corridors all day shouting obscenities while at the same time he wraps – or is it unwraps – brown paper parcels. I wanted them to know that he was harmless. Or had been so far. And it had occurred to me there might be other sorts of information they'd be grateful for: where to go for milk and papers; the times of buses when there are buses; the short cut, via Muggers' Alley, to the tube.)

Sandy opened the door. He had a hammer in his hand. Of course I didn't know his name was Sandy, or anything about him. 'Yes? Yes? What can I do for you?' His tone was so aggressive, so off-putting, I forgot what it was I'd planned to say.

'Look, we've only just moved in. Unless it's important, this is not the moment. We're too busy beating up our kids just now. As you can hear.' He cupped his free hand behind his ear in a theatrical, and rude, fashion. I could hear screaming in the background, a high-pitched child's scream, and a sound like the drumming of heels on a hard floor.

'It's not important. I just – ' But he'd shut the door already.

Paula excused Sandy's rudeness later. He'd feared I might be a social worker or child-welfare officer, come to check up, she explained. He'd had it up to here with them. The truth was, they were frightened they might lose their children, that Matthew and Julie-Ann might be taken into care. At the time of the adoptions, Sandy had been a senior manager in a plastics company, and until Matthew arrived she'd been a paediatric nurse in a general hospital. Another thing that had weighed with the adoption authorities was their home, a four-bedroomed semi with a garden in a leafy road. The ideal place to bring up children! The ideal couple to bring up children with special needs!

Then, last year, the plastics company had made a loss and Sandy been made redundant. I could guess what happened next, couldn't I? I could imagine the whole train of events from that point?

The first time I spoke to Paula was about three weeks after they moved in. I was on holiday from work and had been out grocery shopping, got home to find the lift out of order. I was shouting, 'Bugger, bugger, bugger!' and kicking the lift door with rage, when Paula turned up, weighed down with carrier bags.

'The lift's fucked,' I said. 'Fuck it.'

'Oh.' Her eyebrows shot up into her very yellow hair, and I sensed it was my language, more than the lift's not working, that had sent them there.

We started to climb the stairs. Very slowly, side by side. Floor six was our target. It was a hot, humid morning and by the time we'd reached the second floor we were puffing and gasping. We kept having to stop and put our bags down. Between floors four and five Paula stopped again.

'I'm going to have to sit down for a minute. Take no notice.'

'Me too.' And I sat down beside her on the filthy concrete step. A clanging, banging noise far below echoed up and round the ribbed concrete walls.

'See my fingers?' and she showed me. They were claws. They had red, deep grooves in their undersides where the fingerholds of her plastic carrier bags had cut in.

'Look at mine.' I uncurled them slowly.

We sat there for a while, straightening and flexing our sore fingers, getting our breath back. Eventually Paula got to her feet. 'Come and have a coffee,' she said, 'if you've the time, if you don't mind the mess.'

There was no mess. When you considered that they'd hardly had time to unpack and that there were two adults and two children living in that small space, the flat was tidy and organised. Toys in the living room were stacked in a painted box. There was a large, healthy-looking busy Lizzie on the window ledge and another in the kitchen. There were curtains in the windows. Obviously new shelves had ornaments on them, precisely arranged.

The flat was empty of people save for Paula and me. Sandy was at work. I learned later that work meant standing around with one other sober-suit in an electrics showroom, waiting for a customer to fill in a form for a buy-now pay-later fridge or nought-per-cent-finance dishwasher – one of a number of vacuous, ill-paid jobs he'd had since his redundancy. But a job at least, as Paula laughingly said. Matthew and Julie-Ann were at school. That's to say at their respective special schools, miles away since the move and in different directions. As far as I could see, Paula spent most of the morning taking her children, via a series of buses, to their schools, and most of the afternoons bringing them back again.

'Have you got a job, Hannah, may I enquire?' The minute I'd told Paula my name she used it repeatedly, and soon I found myself listening out for it – in the same way that I waited for the laughter that punctuated most of her remarks, even sad remarks.

I wanted to answer 'I'm in retail', as I'd heard a woman on a radio phone-in programme do (it transpired eventually that this woman was a shop assistant in a chain-store chemist's), but the words wouldn't come.

'I work in a hardware shop.'

'Well, that's an unusual job for a woman. Still, it's a job, Hannah, isn't it? It's better than nothing!'

'I like my job.' I felt defensive. 'I like hardware. We've got a big DIY section too.'

'Do you take milk, Hannah?' The milk, in a jug, was hovering over my cup.

'Not as a rule,' I said, 'it's stealing.'

Paula laughed, but after a pause. 'You're a sharp one, Hannah. I see I shall have to watch my step with you.'

Next time Paula and I had coffee together it was in my flat, cleaned and tidied for the occasion, and it was then she told me the details about her children, their adoption, the problems each had. The worst thing about losing their house, I learned, had been losing the garden: there was nowhere safe now for her children to play. She couldn't let them out by themselves on account of the stranger danger. Before we got on to that, however, we talked about nothing much because Finch was in the flat; his school had broken up the day before and he kept shuffling in like an actor with a sinister walk-on part, looking for something, and shuffling off again. Eventually he exited for good, in his back-to-front baseball cap, in a bosom-enhancing T-shirt.

'Home for lunch?' I called.

With his back to me he lifted a hand and kept it there, an ambiguous gesture intended to annoy.

'Kids, Hannah – who'd have 'em?' Paula said. And laughed. Then she told me about her own. Or rather about how she couldn't have her own, and the decision she and Sandy had made first to foster, then to adopt. It was tragic, wasn't it, she said, how many unwanted children there were in this world. How many mothers there were who did not love their own babies. Imagine it. When at the same time there were all those women who longed to be mothers but who for one reason or another couldn't be. None of it made sense. That was one of the reasons they'd decided to adopt – to make some sense out of a senseless world.

I asked her what had made them want to take on children with handicaps. It was a brave thing to do, I said.

'Matthew and Julie-Ann aren't handicapped, Hannah! They have difficulties, but yes, I see what you mean.' And she explained to me at length what a long and difficult process adoption was, what hoops you had to go through, how many hurdles you had to face – unless, that is, you were prepared to take on a child, or children, with special needs. Most couples wanted to adopt babies. Not too many couples were prepared to adopt children, disruptive ones, ones with disabilities. There was never a queue for those.

Unless they were pretty, I thought. Like Matthew. There must surely have been a queue to adopt him.

I left the room to make more coffee. When I came back, Paula was standing in front of the window. She said, 'Your view's really quite pleasant, isn't it? Compared to ours. Look, Hannah – ' when she'd returned to her chair – 'I love Matthew and Julie-Ann. Don't misunderstand me, I really do. But it's no use pretending it's the same as having your own flesh and blood. It can't be. I don't mind admitting I get envious sometimes. Pregnant women upset me even now. And I can't bear to see a mother breast-feeding her baby. You breast-fed yours, I'm sure. I wish I'd had that bonding experience. It must be wonderful.'

She had her eyes on me, intently, so I nodded – what else could I do?

'Your Finch – is that a nickname, Hannah? A pet name? It's very unusual! He looks a lot like you. It's the eyes, I think, or the mouth. Family likenesses are fascinating, aren't they?'

'Have some coffee,' I said.

I offered to baby-sit for the Petersons. Guilt was the spur, probably. (I did feel guilty, and sad, after listening to Paula. Guilty about Finch, sad about Matthew and Julie-Ann.) It was something I could do, give them a chance to go out for the odd evening, alone. At first Paula declined the offer; she was worried that Matthew might have a tantrum, or Julie-Ann a fit, and that I wouldn't be able to cope. But after a lot of humming and ha-ing it was agreed that provided both children were in bed and asleep, it would probably be safe for her and Sandy to go for a walk or to the pizza parlour for an hour or two. If anything went wrong, if either child woke, if there were problems of any kind I couldn't handle, I was to phone Finch (he had to be at home, that was part of the arrangement), who would go at once and bring Paula and Sandy home.

'What d'you want to baby-sit for?' Finch asked. 'Baby-shit, I expect it will be. You don't like babies.'

'They aren't babies,' I said, 'you've seen them. They're quite big children.'

'Oh, one thing,' Paula said when I arrived, eight forty-five on the dot as requested, 'we'd rather you didn't smoke in the flat. If you don't mind. Apart from the fire hazard, there's Matthew's asthma to consider.'

The plan worked. I thought it did. The children slept through. And I was able to watch TV on a better set and a bigger screen than we had at home. But after the second session, as I was leaving, Paula said, 'Look, Hannah, this is embarrassing, but have you been drinking, may I ask?'

Of course I said no. (But what harm could a little drink do? Most adults have a drink or two in the evening, and why not?) The next time I baby-sat I didn't slip a drink into my bag – vodka and tonic, ready mixed in a couple of tonic bottles – I drank Paula's decaffeinated coffee instead. But the time after that I thought, This is ridiculous, and before crossing the landing I made up the mixture as before, adding a squeeze of lemon juice to each bottle.

'Sorry, Hannah, game's up. We know you've been drinking. We can smell it.' Sandy speaking.

But vodka doesn't smell! That's the whole point – everybody knows vodka has no smell!

'It was kind of you to offer to baby-sit, Hannah, and we're grateful, but we can't do this again. We daren't take the risk, you see. I'm sure you understand. We daren't take that sort of risk with Matthew and Julie-Ann.' Paula's turn.

I picked up my bag with the dead men inside and walked to the door. There was no clinking because I'd wrapped the bottles separately in a T-shirt. On top of them was a book of Finch's I'd taken from his shelf for the purpose. I didn't say a word to either of them.

Paula laid a hand on my arm. 'Hannah, you can't even walk straight. You're in denial, dear, d'you realise that? That means it's serious. That means you've got a real problem. Isn't it time you sought professional help? For Finch's sake, if not your own?'

That was the last time I went to the Petersons' flat. When Paula and I bumped into each other the following day, she said, 'Hello, Hannah, how are you? How's Finch?' in a bright, busy way, without waiting for an answer, and she still does. The most I ever say is 'Hi'.

Sandy I avoid. If he gets into the lift when I'm in it, I get out.

Paula doesn't know this, but not long after the baby-sitting fiasco, I did find myself in the lift with Sandy. I'd just got in from work and was tired and had my eyes shut, and when I opened them, there he was. Grinning faintly, so that I noticed, in the seconds before I shut my eyes again, how ugly and stained his teeth were. 'No hard feelings, eh, Hannah?' I heard him say, but my feelings were hard and resentful, and I didn't reply.

When the lift stopped he flung out his arm in an after-you gesture; but as soon as we were in the corridor he grabbed me and swung me round. He pushed me up against the wall. 'I've seen the way you look at me,' he whispered, with breath to match his teeth. 'You randy little bitch! You're dying for it, aren't you? Aren't you?' He snatched my hand and pressed it on his fly. 'Hard feelings,' he said, 'these are the kind a bitch like you appreciates.' He grabbed my other wrist and held it down. With his whole weight he crushed me into the wall. He plunged his tongue into my astonished mouth.

A door banged, sudden laughter gusted from the landing. It was these sounds, not anything I did, that made him drop off me. (Like a bloated leech, I afterwards decided.) I'll report him to the police, I promised myself, I'll do it tomorrow first thing. But the next day I knew I wouldn't. What would the police care? In any case he'd say my accusation was all lies, my motive revenge. He'd say I was drunk and had accosted him. I had to fight her off, he'd say. It's pathetic, really. My wife and I did our best to help her, and this is how we're repaid. But I'm not one to bear a grudge. Don't be too hard on her, officer.

I did not tell Paula. And Sandy must have known I never would.

Paula did something useful for me. She showed me a truth that until that moment had been hidden. It happened that time she came for coffee and talked about adoption. She was talking and I was listening and suddenly a voice in my head said, 'Adoption', remember that word, ring it round, pull it out later, there's something in it for you.

I did pull it out later and what I learned was this: if Finch were not my own flesh and blood I'd love him. If he were an adopted son I'd be able to love him.

A revelation. Or, a word Diarmid was fond of using, an epiphany. The familial bonds of blood and flesh and genetic history Paula minded not sharing with her children were the very bonds that kept Finch out of my heart. (For I do have a heart. Most mornings when I wake, I say, Please God, let me love Finch. Please. I uncurl myself and lie on my back, arms by my side. I breathe deeply, slowly. I breathe in hope for Finch and me, one two three four. I breathe out despair, one two three four. Let it happen today. Let the miracle, let the thaumaturgy – another of Diarmid's words – happen today.

Then I get up and go to the bathroom. On the way, or on the way back, I meet Finch. And at once it's gone. The sweet calm, the cleansing oxygen, the good and peaceable intent – vanished. Within seconds of seeing my son – he doesn't have to say one irritable or irritating word – I want to murder him.)

If I'd adopted a child it wouldn't have mattered what sort of child, my revelation revealed. Personality and physical appearance would have counted for nothing. This orphan needs you, I'd have realised. So what if he's a no-neck monster? So what if he spits in your face? His problems and defects are no fault of yours. You can love this child and will do. Relentlessly. No matter what.

I saw that I had proof to back my revelation – the stray cat I'd rescued once. This cat hung around the dustbins for days before I managed to lure it, a starving, matted glove that cowered when you approached. Not an affectionate cat; it didn't go in for purring or leg rubbing; if you tried to pick it up it spread its claws. It stayed under the sofa and slunk from its hiding place only for food and to misfire on the cat tray. Not a pretty cat. Apart from a split ear and a stumpy tail, its short back ensured that its fore and hind legs were awkwardly bunched. But as the days went by it grew sleek, and after a week or two it grew bold, and came out to wash itself on the windowsill. And each time I saw it there, absorbed, fastidious, indifferent, getting on with its life, my heart swelled. I did that, I said to myself. I am responsible for that small *thaumaturgy*.

Visitors came those first weeks at Arizona, not invited ones but strangers whose motive seemed more nosy than neighbourly. These visitors didn't knock on the door – there was no bell. They walked straight in and called coo-eee.

'Coo-eee!' having entered via the front door, or occasionally the back. 'Coo-ee! Anyone at home?'

Such liberty-taking was unheard of in Green Copse Road.

'Coo-ee!' walking from downstairs room to downstairs room.

In Green Copse Road the front door had a bell, in working order, and if a visitor rang the bell and got no answer, he or she, unless a burglar, went away again. A printed card or written message might be pushed through the letter box if the caller's business was urgent.

'Coo-ee! Anyone there?' In the country, total strangers seemed to think it admissible, when there was no sign of life on the ground floor, to continue their search up the stairs.

I remember a husband and wife in their forties. The wife's green, woollen, patterned tights (it was May), the husband's checked tweed cap (which in the kitchen he pulled off and stuffed into his pocket). Both so tall they had to duck their heads under our doorways.

'Coo-ee! Mind if we come in?' (But they're already in.) 'We're dying to see what you've done with old Jack's place! He was the most extraordinary chap! A real character!

Larger than life, you might say! I only came here once, collecting for Dr Barnado's – the old boy refused to play, wouldn't cough up so much as sixpence – and I couldn't get over all that black paint in the hall. As for the smell! Gosh, what an improvement!'

It was a Saturday lunchtime, and we had our mouths full when they arrived. Otherwise our jaws would have dropped, Aunt Hope said. Speechless, we troop behind them as they peer out of windows and throw open doors.

'Which of you sleeps in this room? Goodness, someone's a reader!' The husband flips a hand to his eyebrows and scans Jocelyn's bed. 'What've you done with the man of the house?' (He opens a cupboard.) 'Is he in hiding?'

Jocelyn finds her voice then. 'No,' she says, stepping forward into the room, 'you're looking at him. I'm the man of the house.' She bends her right knee and her right elbow and clenches her right fish. 'Feel that muscle,' she invites him. 'Go on, have a feel of that iron.'

I escort the intruders to the front door. (They've suddenly remembered an important engagement.) 'How old did you say you were?' the wife asks, vague, in the doorway.

'Fourteen,' I answer, adding a year as usual.

'Oh, Tessa's fourteen – we must try and get you together some time . . . By the way, did you know this place used to be called Goosewell Farm? I'm sure you're going to revert to that.' And then, to her husband, as though I were deaf, 'Hideously poky upstairs, Johnnie, but I dare say if you got rid of the veranda the place wouldn't be quite so dire. It's pure Charles Addams as it is.'

I reported these remarks to Aunt Hope and Jocelyn. My aunt said, 'That's it then, the porch stays, *and* the name – Arizona it shall be.' Jocelyn said she was concerned about the hall and the lack of black paint. Would we remind her to get some, Monday morning first thing?

And I remember a girl on a horse.

It's a scorching afternoon when she rides up – bareback,

at a drowsy walk, her head nodding in time with the horse's nod, one hand on the reins, the other resting on the horse's shiny rump.

I've been asleep; I woke up confused, and am now in the bathroom splashing water on my face.

From the open window I watch, as in a dream, the horse and rider's dreamlike, rhythmical advance. I see the girl pull up, slide to the ground, then loop the reins over the courtyard gatepost – the action, careless and efficient, of a cowboy in a film. But she's not wearing jeans or riding clothes. She has on a sleeveless cheesecloth shirt, tied in a knot above her waist (a fashion that summer; Jocelyn ties her shirts that way), and a wide, ankle-length cotton skirt, plain brown except at the bottom where there's a frieze of lozenge shapes in black and cream. She has nothing on her feet.

The horse throws its head up and down and paws the dust, as tied-up horses do in Westerns.

The girl is beautiful and has waist-length hair, like a princess in a fairy tale.

'Teatime!' My aunt's voice, calling from somewhere. From some other world.

Downstairs I say nothing about the girl. She was a ghost; or else I dreamed them, her and her horse.

She comes in as Aunt Hope's pouring out, through the back door, straight into the kitchen. Not a girl, not beautiful, not even young; a woman in her thirties. Slim, and her thin arms are youthful, but the skin of her face isn't young. Her brown eyes are huge and somehow weird, they're too far apart, right at the edge of her face.

'I'm a back-door person,' she says by way of explanation, head on one side, smiling a sad half-smile. Her peculiar eyes rest on us in turn. (How can you focus properly with such wide-apart eyes? I think. How can you get them together enough to focus?)

'I've come for some water for my mare.' She takes her time to tell us this.

At once Jocelyn finds a bucket, fills it and carries it out to the yard. We follow and stand round watching the level in the bucket go down as the mare draws the water into her mouth – a silent, submerged process, more like snuffling than drinking. On her wet-suede muzzle are spiky hairs like pins, which when she lifts her head have tiny pearls attached to them.

'We're having a cup of tea,' Jocelyn says. 'Would you like one?'

'I'm a coffee person, not a tea person.' The same sorrowful and sweet half-smile. 'Unless you have jasmine?'

'I dare say we can find some coffee,' says Aunt Hope, very dry.

I press my face against the mare's sunshined neck (hard underneath, wrinkled silk on the surface), and breathe and breathe. I can't get enough of the smell. It's intoxicating. The smell of horses may be the best thing about them.

> 'For sideways would she lean, and sing
> A faery's song.'

Mary, or Mouse 'as some people prefer to call me', had just ridden away – in the same half-sideways manner as she'd arrived, one hand on the reins, one hand on the horse – when Aunt Hope started quoting. It was the first poetry we'd heard from her in months, and I thought, Oh, God!

'She was fey,' said my aunt. 'Fey equals dangerous. I cannot stand fey people. I'll bet she leads that husband of hers a dance.'

We'd learned a lot about the visitor over tea. That she was a bread-and-butter person, not a cake person. That Jack Bowdell had been a friend of hers and supplied her with eggs, regularly, for free. That she had a husband called Tim and a baby called Jake. They owned a smallholding five miles south of us, where Tim bred rare breeds of sheep for their wool, and kept goats for their milk (which they made into cheese); and she grew wild flowers and dried them and sold them to smart department stores for the Christmas trade. All this in answer to Jocelyn's interested 'Have you ridden far?'

'She was a liar,' said Aunt Hope. 'Jack Bowdell never had a woman in the house. Everyone's agreed about that.'

'She was pretty.' Jocelyn always liked to say something kind when there was anything kind.

Aunt Hope snorted. 'If you like that sort of thing.'

'I'm not saying I like it, I'm not saying I personally found her attractive, just making a statement of fact.'

'Perhaps you think she's pretty because she said you were. All that guff about your eyes.'

'I didn't hear her.' (She must have, though. Mouse had gone on and on about Jocelyn's eyes, the colour of them. They were like tourmalines, according to Mouse, and round-headed rampion and several other things I hadn't heard of.)

'What did you think, Hannah?'

'I'm a watching person, not a thinking person.'

I'd had no time to plan my answer. The words just came out, in Mouse's voice. Afterwards I put my head on one side and smiled in a daffy way. 'Is there room for my little bottom?' I enquired. Mouse had asked this question of the kitchen bench, before sitting on it at the table.

Aunt Hope and Jocelyn laughed and laughed. Jocelyn almost fell over. For the first time in my life I knew what success was and how it felt to be one; and it felt wonderful, just as sweet as they say.

At one time, Jemma would have barked at the approach of visitors and, at the slightest encouragement from Aunt Hope, seen them off with a curled-lip display of her nasty little teeth. But by then she was old, older than I was in human years, ninety-eight in dog terms, and in the year since Uncle Ber died had lost her hearing, her sight, her voice and most of her teeth. I preferred this new, old, silent Jemma to the old, young, garrulous one, and was no longer jealous. All she did now was lie in a basket in whichever room my aunt happened to be, and doze and snore her life away. If Aunt

Hope looked like leaving the room, she sensed it and lifted her head; to other people's comings and goings she turned a deaf ear and a blind eye. Her old adversaries, flies, could taunt and dance and settle on her nose as they pleased, and she would not snap.

The loss of our guard dog and alarm system was a disadvantage, though. It was the day Aunt Hope and Jocelyn and I were stripping wallpaper in the Long Room, as we'd started to call the living room, simply because it was so long.

The paper on the Long Room walls was several layers thick, and underneath it was crumbly plaster, so we were having to soak the walls first, then scrape off a layer, then wet the walls again before trying to remove the next. Tedious and laborious but, whenever my spatula found its way under all the layers at once and a huge strip came wetly and cleanly away, satisfying, I found.

Aunt Hope and Jocelyn have their faces to the wall when the stranger appears, Jemma's snoring in a corner and I, dipping my brush in the water bucket, am the only one to spot him, standing motionless on the bare boards between the door and the window. A ghost, I think he must be, the ghost of Jack Bowdell. Beside him on the windowsill is the radio, and as I watch the ghost reaches a white hand to it. Mozart – the concerto for flute and harp Jocelyn loves and has been looking forward to since breakfast – dies a sudden death.

Jocelyn shouts at me to turn the radio back on. What do I think I'm up to? 'At once, you imbecile!'

'I'm afraid it's me who's the imbecile.' But the stranger, not a ghost after all, does not look afraid. 'Could I have a word? Peter Huntley, father of the local flock.'

'Now which farm would that be?' Aunt Hope asks. 'Nearly everyone we've met seems to be a sheep farmer of sorts.'

The stranger laughs. He says she's misunderstood him. (She hasn't.) He's not a farmer, he explains, he's a father. 'Of the Christian flock.'

Aunt Hope looks him up and down. 'You're not wearing a dog collar.'

'Always wear mufti when I'm not on duty. It's an ice-breaker, I find.'

'It's misleading, however.' The schoolteacher voice, cold as unbreakable ice.

At this point Jocelyn puts down her brush and leaves the room, taking the radio with her. '*Excusez-moi,*' she says, stepping round Mr Huntley to get at the windowsill. '*S'il vous plaît.*'

If Jocelyn can go, I can go. I don't want to listen to my aunt announcing we're not churchgoers, which is what she's about to do. (I know exactly how she'll put it. 'We're not churchgoers, we're cathedralgoers. So unless you've got a cathedral up your sleeve –') I don't want to see the vicar's disappointed face.

'Can I get you a cup of coffee?' I ask at the door. Someone has to have some manners.

'Well, that would be –'

'Or a glass of sherry?' Aunt Hope and Jocelyn aren't great sherry drinkers, but there's a bottle in the kitchen they use for cheering up unsatisfactory soup. Prune juice is Jocelyn's name for it.

' – very acceptable. Sherry, perhaps.'

I felt sorry for Mr Huntley. He'd seemed harmless to me. And he was a man. I was missing Uncle Ber.

For a long time now, ever since he'd died, I'd shut my uncle out or, perhaps more accurately, put him off. Later, I'd tell myself, when an image or memory arrived unbidden; I can't deal with you yet, later. (A part of me, I suspect, fearful of pain, was hoping that 'later' would never have to come.) But recently I'd begun to dream about him, distressing dreams in which he gave every sign and appearance of being alive while I knew for certain he was not. 'You're dead,' the dream me would inform him silently. 'You don't know it but you're dead. You're at the bottom of the sea.' I was sad in these dreams, but I also felt superior, knowing what my uncle clearly did not know, and because I myself was alive. Waking, I would feel more shame than sorrow. But there was another kind of dream I had that was far more distressing to wake from. In this kind, I had no superior knowledge to protect me. My uncle, indubitably alive, whistling under his breath, sleeves rolled for action, would lean into his plane while I, leaning on my broom, watched the blond curls collect on the workbench and spiral to the floor. Everything would be in order – the sea pictures, the tools, the knot board, the glues and paints, his paperback collection of C. S. Forresters and Alexander Kents (the only fiction he'd told me he enjoyed), our model fleet sailing along the shelves . . .

I missed Uncle Ber, and in a wider sense I missed men. The builders – cowboys, according to Aunt Hope – had left by this time, and we were on our own; the house was quiet and empty-seeming; our voices, whenever we opened our mouths, shrill and ugly to my ears. It was a man's voice I felt the lack of most; but there were other aspects of masculinity I missed – unfaltering hands, significant shoes, a firm tread on the stairs, that aura men had (that Uncle Ber had had) of purposefulness and solidity.

I felt sorry for Mr Huntley because, when he'd gone, Aunt Hope tore him to bits. He was a secular priest, she insisted, there was nothing whatever of the spiritual about him. He'd stayed for the best part of an hour and in all that time there'd been no mention of God or Jesus or faith. He was a coward. He hadn't even asked if we were C of E. 'In the end I said, "It's not clear what you believe in, vicar, so I shall tell you what I believe in – the holiness of the heart's affections!" '

'He said "Christian",' I defended, 'he used the words "Christian flock". I heard him.'

'And he was a snob, Hannah. Only one subject was he prepared to talk about – the Senior Service and your uncle Ber's part in it. As soon as he discovered, via a series of impertinent questions, I was the widow of a sailor, he quizzed me about the ships your uncle served in, and where, and when. When I mentioned the River Plate and the *Ajax*, he got very excited. "Then your husband must have known my old friend Bill Tiddlypush!" he said.'

'So I told him it was unlikely. Very unlikely, unless his old friend Tiddlypush had served on the lower deck. And that, as I knew it would be, was the end of the conversation.'

(So triumphant, she might have been slapping the ace of spades under Jocelyn's nose.)

I stared at my aunt, a snob in so many ways herself. I knew, as my uncle had known, she despised the years Uncle Ber had spent on the mess decks. The fact that he'd made it to the wardroom in the end seemed not to count with her. At home, that is, with him. In other places, in other company, she played it differently. 'My husband was a naval officer,' she'd confide, in a voice I did not recognise, whenever a question made the answer possible. '*Royal* Navy.'

'A gentleman would have finished it,' she said now. By 'it' she meant Mr Huntley's glass of sherry, abandoned on the window ledge. Three-quarters full, the colour of pond water. 'If he'd been a gentleman he'd have drained it to the last drop.'

Mr Huntley didn't call again. But then, very few of the people who came to see us – spy on us, Aunt Hope said – repeated the experience. None of them invited us to visit them. The telephone, finally connected, remained silent save for outgoing calls or when it rang for Jocelyn. She took her calls in private, on the red extension phone next to her bed.

It was our manlessness that kept people away and invitations from arriving. That must have had a lot to do with it. What could be done with us, really? What sort of occasion could it have been that would comfortably have accommodated two women in their forties, one of them an actress, the other a retired schoolteacher, one very attractive (so that women were wary of her), the other sharp-tongued and peculiar (so that men were frightened of her), and a girl of thirteen?

Besides, Aunt Hope did not want a social life; she had no gift for friendship, that was obvious.

Jocelyn had, I believed. She was outgoing; in shops and public places, she slipped into conversation with old men and toddlers as easily as she slipped into her old canvas garden shoes. She was a flirt, and could strike sparks off the most unlikely material. One remark from her, one dark-blue look, one smile, and the frozen unfroze, the closed opened out like daisies in the sun. (And then, having performed her flirtatious, incendiary miracle, she'd walk away.)

A person like Jocelyn would need some sort of social life, you'd think.

On the other hand, as was soon evident, the reason they'd moved to Arizona, the whole point of going there, was to escape.

Aunt Hope and Jocelyn weren't unusual in wanting to escape. Getting away from the rat race and, by the same token, back to nature, growing your own and being self-sufficient were phrases you often heard in the early seventies. And they weren't unusual in attempting to make the fantasy a reality. From cities and suburbs throughout the land, hard-nosed materialists, couples mostly, were selling up and moving out. They left their offices and boardrooms – not factories, not building sites; it was a middle-class exodus – took their children out of school, threw away their TV sets and became goat-breeders on Welsh hillsides or crofters in the Scottish Highlands. Getaway people, or breakaway people, they were known as.

According to Finch, at any rate. He did a project on 'The Seventies, a sociological and demographic study of a decade', and my information, including the phrases that were apparently on everybody's lips – though not on Aunt Hope's, nor on Jocelyn's – came from him. According to Finch's study, nature got the better of these new ruralists. By the end of the decade 90 per cent of them had returned to their original habitats and employment. In the meantime they'd given birth to a generation of incurable country-phobes who, as soon as they got back to civilisation, became TV junkies. Junkies whose philosophy could be summed up as *Video, ergo sum.*

Finch got A- for his project. Groovy, man. But I didn't recognise his 'getaway people'. The expression was familiar but not the context. As far as I'm concerned, *Getaway People* is the title of a musical Jocelyn had a part in in 1970. She played a barmaid – the biggest female part in the show, I gathered. I never saw the show, which closed after three performances, and neither, I think, did Aunt Hope, but I remember one of the numbers:

> Oh, I was a Getaway Person,
> My girl was a Breakaway Girl,
> And we were both switched-on people
> To the nineteen-seventies whirl.

> We broke us away from Dullsville
> To the swinging London scene
> For we were both turned-on people
> And we knew what might have been.

> Goodbye to the semi in Salford
> Goodbye to yer dad and yer ma,
> It's blacker than 'ell in Salford,
> We've gone where the bright lights are . . .

There was a lot more to that song, which had no tune to speak of and which Jocelyn chanted in an exaggerated Lancashire accent, verses and verses of it, which I've forgotten, though I remember the story line. These getaway-breakaway people meet a man in a café who gives them a funny glance, who says, 'Excuse me and begging your pardon, Can you sing by any chance? My name is Jeremy Jackson, I manage the Boys in Blue, I'm looking for new material, and I like what I see of you.' They become pop stars; they get into drugs and booze and gurus. One of them, the girl, ends up dead; the other, our hero, flips out and winds up in the bin.

'But the good news is, neither of them had to go back to Salford,' said Jocelyn, who'd been born and brought up in that town.

In some ways, Aunt Hope and Jocelyn were the getaway people of Finch's study. They did grow their own at Arizona. They did keep goats, or rather a goat, though not for long because the goat, Angel, was a jumper and jumped daily out of her home ground into the vegetable patch, where she ate every green thing growing. They did keep hens always – and ducks and geese until the fox got them. But they did not keep a cow, and therefore were never, in the terms of Finch's project, self-sufficient.

The weather was hot and humid that first summer, and my bedroom, with its oppressive ceiling and one small window, unbearably airless. I moved out as soon as I could to an outbuilding in the garden. I say garden, but it was a hayfield, riddled with anthills and impossible to mow with our small mower; Jocelyn gave it two cuts with a hired motor scythe, but it was months before the humps and tussocks (and docks and thistles) began to resemble lawn.

My new sleeping place, an outbuilding in the sense that it was not joined to the house, was a railway carriage. Half a railway carriage. There were a lot of freight trucks and bits of carriages in the neighbourhood then. They were leftovers from the branch line that, until the sixties, ended up in Long Clovell, our nearest town. I imagine there must have been a sale, after the line and the station were closed, of mail barrows and platform seats and unrailworthy rolling stock, because these relics turned up all over the place. And Old Bowdell must have been at the sale, bidding with the rest: apart from the carriage, his garden boasted a seat, in wood and iron, that had a wire litter basket attached to one end.

In farmyards, the trucks and carriages were usually wheelless, and shored up off the ground by means of bricks or sleepers. They stood in for poultry houses or were used as storage sheds. Two I used to see, which had retained their wheels, had been turned into wayside shops, one selling farm produce, the other, whose outside the owners had decorated in Gypsy caravan style, house plants and ice cream and garden ornaments. Wheels gave the shops an air of impermanence, and sure enough, the shop that sold garden ornaments, a landmark on my bus journey to school, was one morning simply not there, vanished in the night, like a Gypsy caravan or funfair trailer. The only evidence of its tenancy was a sickly rectangle in the fertilised dark green.

From the house, you couldn't see Bowdell's Pullman half-carriage because three big ash trees grew in the way. To reach it you had to cross the courtyard, turn left out of the gate, then walk a few yards along a rough concrete path between a thorn hedge and the vegetable patch. The path ended abruptly in a tangle of weeds, grass, elder and nut bushes. The washing line was here, and the compost heaps and, beyond them, half hidden by elder, the railway carriage. It had its wheels and bearings still, but they had sunk into the ground, and at first sight you had the impression of something secret and abandoned, and at the same time rooted and domestic. Unusually for a railway carriage, there was guttering running under the roof, and at one end a downpipe descending into a rain barrel. Only half its former self, it had been halved again inside by a partition, and consisted of henhouse at one end and henfood store the other. In the henhouse half, its floor a litter of hen feathers and hen shit and black, musty straw, all the seats had been ripped out to make room for perches and nesting boxes. A door on the end had a ramp up to it so the hens could walk in and out. The roof had an air vent, like a small metal chimney, necessary, I could see, because all the windows in the henhouse half were boarded on the outside.

The other half, the half I made my room, had, in addition to glass windows, all intact, a large Perspex skylight shaped to the curve of the roof. Inside, at the partition end,

I discovered seats – eight of them, four on each side, the two pairs facing each other with a table in between. Otherwise, there was nothing – just a few old sacks the rats had got at, and rat droppings and leaves and caked grey mud with boot prints in, and dust.

I slept in that carriage – train, as I thought of it – May till September every year. Why was I so determined, so quickly, to sleep there? Wouldn't I be lonely? Wouldn't I be terrified? Of the dark? Of noises? Of ghosts? I was always seeing ghosts. Aunt Hope asked these questions, though she didn't try to prevent me. Moving room was a palaver. All my possessions, including Bowdell's cowboy exhibition, had to move out with me and, because there was no heating and the place, in winter, freezing and damp, all had to move back again the moment I did.

Sometimes I think myself back into that train. Sometimes I'm despatched there by a smell – uncut moquette with the sun on it has the power; old cigarettes and old ash in metal ashtrays can do it. Either way, I'm lying on my back in Uncle Ber's camp bed, positioned under the open skylight, half asleep, watching the clouds puffing by. Or the dot-to-dot planetarium stars. Or the moon – in the course of a month, a cut fingernail, a slice of honeydew, a misshapen, then gradually restored, tinfoil ball. Or, wide awake, I'm waiting for the first, intermittent, staccato pings of rain on the closed skylight. I wait in what feels like a huge silence, the tense hush that, we're told, precedes a battle, and have a sense of things, powerful things – arms and forces, elements – gathering and massing.

And of course when the barrage gets going it is like warfare. (Which would explain why, conversely, arrows always rain, while gunmen die in a hail of bullets.) But as soon as the initial rattling and clattering settles to a steady drumming and thrumming and hammering, as soon as the rain in the gutters begins to gush and gurgle and burble and tinkle, the martial imagery fades. It's music I'm listening to now, a junior-school percussion band, it sounds to me, of drums and triangles and xylophones and tubular bells. 'Fancy,' Aunt Hope said, when I offered her this simile. 'Tubular bells. Fancy.'

The downpour nights are the ones I like best. They make me shiver, not with fear, as Aunt Hope suggested, but with pleasure – the pleasure of being safe and dry and warm in bed, in the knowledge that everything outside, trees and bushes, leaves and grass, the train itself, is caught in it, being inescapably rinsed and soaked and drenched and polished.

And wind, accompanied by rain or on its own, doesn't bother me. When it blows strongly, the train sways and rocks, and we are travelling at great speed on a long journey. Across America, from the east coast to the west – to Phoenix, Arizona, the place Glen Campbell repeatedly heads for (en route to Oklahoma, and in order to get away from an obviously faithful, perfectly OK-sounding wife) on Jocelyn's record player.

It's only thunder I can't handle. One distant rumble, and I'm sprinting to the house, up the stairs to Jocelyn's room. She fears thunder and lightning quite as much as I do.

The first time a thunderstorm sent me to Jocelyn's room, it was empty. I groped my way down the passage to Aunt Hope's. Two heads lifted themselves from the pillows of my aunt's double bed. 'Guessed you'd be along,' Jocelyn's voice, American version, said. 'We're all in here, babe. Come 'n' join us.' She patted the eiderdown. I crept under it at the foot of the bed and curled myself out of the way of Jemma, her bloater-paste breath and her snores.

It surprises me now that Aunt Hope allowed me to sleep outside, so far from the house. Perhaps she was relieved to be rid of me, and my stare, those long, light evenings. Without me, she and Jocelyn were free to talk about whatever they wanted to talk about, and to do whatever they wanted to do: read; play cards; tell dirty jokes; drink whisky. Whatever they wanted.

Finch still sees Diarmid; I don't.

A bald, unbearable fact I have to bear.

He doesn't talk about Diarmid, neither of us does – as neither of us talks about Aunt Hope and Jocelyn, it's too difficult – but he sees him. The meetings are regular, but without a discernible pattern: he goes to Diarmid's place once every ten days or so. I never know when it will be. I cannot tell myself: Finch is seeing Diarmid this Tuesday, say, or next Friday week. The arrangements are made, I imagine, like this: at the end of a visit Finch says, 'When can I come here again?' or Diarmid says, 'How are you fixed in the next fortnight?' and then they get out their diaries. Diarmid, an organised man, prepares his ballpoint for action. Finch, an organised boy with an efficient memory, having got out his diary to check it, will memorise the date they agree on. He won't write anything on paper for fear of his mother's prying, spying eye.

It's true I would pry and spy. I have done. I do. And there is never anything in Finch's diary, nor on the backs of envelopes, nor on the screws and balls of snack wrappers in his pockets, to give me a clue.

The first clue I have that Finch is off to see Diarmid is the sound of taps running, the smell of hot water. A bath or wash is under way, and not at bedtime. Next, he appears before me in a clean shirt, with slicked hair and pink-and-white cheeks.

'Going out,' he says. And he lifts his anorak off the hook.

I have choices at this point. A *whole range of options*, as politicians put it, unwilling to specify. I can say something like, 'OK, what sort of time should I expect you back?'

I can say, 'Who's the lucky girl, then?' Knowing there isn't one, there couldn't be.

Or I can come straight out with it. 'Are you going to see Diarmid?'

If, unable to help myself, I choose the last, Finch answers, 'Yes.' Or 'Yep.' Unemphatic, matter-of-fact. Final. He zips up his anorak, adjusts the starred baseball cap just so, and is out of the door.

'Yes.' (Or 'Yep.') What sort of answer is that?

Fuck you, Finch. Fuck you, Diarmid. I hope you both rot in hell.

But it may be my fault Finch and Diarmid continue to see each other. In one of the last fights we had before we split up, when he was wanting us to split and I wasn't, I accused Diarmid of being a traitor. It was Finch, not me, he'd betrayed, I told him. For nearly six years he'd played father to my fatherless son. For nearly six years he'd convinced Finch he loved him like a son. And now he was preparing to abandon this son he loved so much. Just like that. Great! Marvellous! Wonderful! Terrific!

Diarmid said, sarcasm was demeaning, it never got anyone anywhere.

He sat me down then, and spoke kindly and slowly, as though I were ill or retarded. He said he did indeed love Finch, as I very well knew, and nothing would change that. He said love was an emotion I didn't know too much about, but that was not my fault, probably. He said that after a while, when he and I had had time to cool down, he hoped I'd allow him to see Finch. On a regular basis, if that was what Finch wanted.

I said, 'Oh, so you fancy him, do you? Is that it?'

He hit me then. A ringing, stinging slap across the face.

When Finch leaves the flat for these rendezvous, I don't know what to do with myself. I pace up and down, I turn on the TV, I turn it off, I lie on my bed, I get off my bed, I take a book off Finch's shelf, I put it back, I pick up the phone, I ram it back, I kick the fucking phone.

When kicked, the phone laughs a brief, bell-like laugh. Sometimes it shrieks, like someone in pain.

How do you stop your imagination working?

I imagine, I see, Finch arriving at Diarmid's place. 'Hello, hello, great to see you, Finchy! Come on in.' I see Diarmid, courtierlike, helping Finch off with his anorak, leading him to the kitchen or the living room. A room I know. A room I know so well I could make an inventory of its contents here and now. I could take a test on the exact whereabouts of every chair, table, picture, rug, photograph, stack of paperbacks, and score 100 per cent.

But then I stop. For Diarmid's flat cannot look the way I remember it. My own stuff, the only passable stuff in the flat, I always thought, is no longer there. Moreover, there's someone new in Diarmid's life, and for all I know this person may have strong views about how a living room should look. Views very different from mine. Not from Diarmid's. He has no views about rooms. Strangely, for someone in his line of work, he doesn't seem to notice his surroundings at all. 'You go ahead,' he said when I asked if I could have a go at injecting a bit of style and comfort into his hard-rock hotel living space and try and make it into a room he and I might want to spend time in. 'You go ahead, Evie. Feel free. Do whatever you want to do.'

What I did was move some of the real junk out to a charity shop, and move the best of my stuff in. Then I went shopping, to a place in his road that sells ethnic cushions and Kelims and tablecloths. (And beaten silver earrings, leather necklaces, wooden giraffes, plaited *kikapus* and environmentally friendly greetings cards.) There was a sale on in this shop, which is called Libra, or maybe Gemini, and I bought several bright, smelly cushions (the musty, spicy Indian smell – of the dyes, is it? – that's still there after ten washes), a small Kelim in orange and brown, and four tiny-patterned table-cloths. I draped the tablecloths over one ugly sofa and two ugly armchairs and one hideous table – yellow oak with barley-sugar legs. Then I painted the room, ceiling included, Indian red. It was avocado before, with white trim.

When Diarmid and I split up, I took my own stuff back, but I refused to take back the things I'd bought. He asked me to, he thought it was right I should keep the things I'd paid for, although he couldn't remember exactly what they were. I thought, How humiliating, why should I? They were presents to us. Somewhere in my mind was the hope that the vibrancy and warmth I'd left behind would act as a reminder, a symbol even, of my own colourfulness and warmth; that Diarmid would come to miss these qualities and want them back.

Pigs might fly.

Much more likely: the things I bought are in the charity shop already, bundled there by Diarmid's new person to make room for her's – or his? For I knew nothing about his friend – reproduction Empire sofa or genuine Lloyd Loom chairs.

I drink when Finch is with Diarmid. Often, as a result of the drink, I weep. Sometimes I start laughing in a mad way, like Bette Davis or my mother, and can't stop, and frighten myself.

But, in fact, the present tense is misleading: I don't behave in any of the ways I've described. I used to, but I don't any more. That sort of demented behaviour is demeaning, and it's exhausting. You can't keep it up for ever. Unless you're a masochist, there's a limit to how long you can go on loving and wanting and thinking about someone who's stopped loving and wanting and thinking about you.

Anyway, I'm not certain I did love Diarmid. I think a lot of me hated him and resented him, a lot of the time.

One evening when Finch had left on his semisecret mission, and I was about to clamber aboard the familiar switchback ride of wrath and anguish, jealousy and self-pity, it suddenly came to me: Really, how absurd!

Really, how absurd. The realisation left me weak and grateful, like a convalescent. I made myself some pusser's kye, the stuff Uncle Ber used to drink at sea after a watch-on, watch-off night, and which he and I used to brew up, to Aunt Hope's disgust, on cold days sometimes. (Slice slab cocoa – or dark chocolate if you don't have that – into a mug; add two big spoons condensed milk; pour on boiling water.) Then I took trouble preparing an interesting sand-wich. Then I got out my atlas and guide books and the copies of *Arizona Highways* magazine I stole from the Health Centre waiting room; and between bites and sips I began to plan my trip to Arizona.

Because my uncle and aunt did not own a car during the Green Copse Road years, and because I never saw Aunt Hope take the wheel of any vehicle, I'd assumed she couldn't drive. I was wrong: my aunt could drive, and had a licence; so it had to be a case of wouldn't rather than couldn't. Or didn't enjoy it, or didn't see a need. But of course nondrivers are at a disadvantage in the country. Even in those days there were only two buses a day into our nearest town, their times variable, their performance unreliable, and I wonder how she ever imagined she'd manage without a car, whether she'd really thought it through. She and I had our bikes, and rode them in the lanes for blackberrying and sloe-picking and nut-gathering purposes, but not for shopping. Long Clovell was seven miles away, and you can't carry much shopping on a bike. Besides, the main road – not really main, a B road – was dangerous in the way only so-called quiet country roads are (as roads in Ireland are, according to Diarmid): drivers, believing they had the road to themselves, would drive breakneck in the middle of it, careless of bends and crossroads and farm entrances and cattle crossings. Minor accidents were routine, and showed themselves in the number of injured cars and vans and pick-ups you saw parked in Long Clovell; but once every two months or so a more calamitous collision would occur. I got used to the screams of ambulances and police cars. You could hear them, on a still day, from our porch.

I suppose my aunt was relying on Jocelyn to chauffeur us, but not long after we arrived, Jocelyn, who for years had played bit parts and character roles in radio and TV plays, accepted the offer of a regular job as one of three readers in a weekly poetry programme. This meant her spending one night a week in London. Sometimes two nights.

No, Aunt Hope said, when the question of her taking to the steering wheel again first came up. No. Never. She shook her head so violently I thought she'd do herself damage.

'I don't have to,' my aunt said, 'you cannot make me.'

But Jocelyn could make her. She talked of responsibility and emergencies. Say, when she was away in London, Jemma was sick and needed to get to the vet in a hurry. Say there was a crisis at the Rose Vale. Say little Hannah here had an accident, fell out of a tree or into one of those horrible wells – what then?

In the end she won. She made my aunt drive her up and down the runway, and practise reversing and three-point turns. Then she made her drive on the road and in the lanes, in daylight and in the dark. Finally she made her drive us all into Long Clovell. This car wasn't the old blue Volkswagen; Jocelyn had sold it by then. It was a third-hand Morris Traveller, cream-painted and half-timbered, with van doors and a lot of room behind the back seats for the bags of poultry corn and spades and boots and the mud from boots, that go with country living.

We celebrated our safe arrival in Long Clovell with lunch – roast meat, three vegetables and two sorts of potatoes, roast and creamed – in the empty dining room of the Dragon. There were brown velvet curtains at the dusty windows, and on the wall behind our table a group of brown photographs showing how the town looked 'before the Great War 1914–1918'. I left my chair to get a closer look at Market Street on market day, at horse-drawn floats outside the Town Hall at Carnival, at the cattle market packed with cattle. There were also solo portrait photographs: tradesmen wearing the fancy dress, as it seemed to me, of their trades; town characters posed beside a lamppost. Women in long aprons, small boys in boots, girls in pinafores, babies in bonnets. A fat dog lying flat out outside a butcher's. All ghosts, I told them, you're all ghosts. You were alive then, at that moment, and now you're dead. (A pessimistic judgement, I think now. Some of the people in those photographs, the boys and girls and babies, would have been in their sixties or seventies the day I made them into ghosts. A few of them were still living in the town, probably, not all retired by any means; living active, committee-driven lives.)

Above the fireplace there was a large stuffed – or plaster? – fish in a glass case. The smell in the dining room was warm and unpleasant.

'A deafening silence,' Jocelyn whispered, plucking her napkin from her glass. 'Wouldn't you say?' She filled her glass with water from a jug, and raised it. 'Here's to our driver. An excellent performance, I thought – didn't you, Hannah? I wasn't frightened at all.'

'What's a deafening silence?' Aunt Hope turned to me.

It was a trick question, it had to be. I thought hard. Does silence really deafen you? No. Was it an exaggeration then? A, whatsit, hyperbole? Not exactly. A nonsense? Yes. And the word for that? It began with p. Paradox. No, wait, hang on, don't tell me, oxymoron. But I wasn't sure if this was the answer she wanted. It might be too obvious. A deafening silence. A deafening silence. It sounded familiar. Too familiar? Was it a cliché perhaps? Was that what she meant?

In the end I came out with oxymoron, and a shrug.

'Well, well. Wonders will never cease.'

Jocelyn leaned across the table. 'What d'you make of wonders will never cease, Han?'

'Cliché.' No difficulty with that one.

'Irony,' Aunt Hope muttered. She hated being teased, as she hated any sign of conspiracy between Jocelyn and me. 'Don't you recognise irony when you hear it?'

Our food arrived, meat and gravy already on the plates, vegetables and potatoes fussily apportioned with an ice-cream scoop from silvery partitioned dishes.

The emptiness of the room, the deafening silence, made it impossible to talk in our natural voices. We felt compelled to whisper. We whispered even when the waitress had gone back to the kitchen and there was no one to hear what we said.

Incredible, wasn't it, Jocelyn whispered, that people could still do that to roast beef? And to cabbage. And to carrots! And had we taken in the cauliflower, my dears? It was pink mush. It was pink purée.

Aunt Hope whispered back that she was enjoying hers. This had to be politeness, I imagined, because Jocelyn was paying for our treat. Then, in her ordinary voice, cancelling out her manners and professed enjoyment, 'Anyway, what else can you expect from a one-horse town?'

Long Clovell was a one-horse town. A hick town. It consisted of not much more than a single street of sad-looking shops. Probably not many people chose to shop in Long Clovell. They went there for the same reason Aunt Hope and Jocelyn did: because there was nowhere more exciting for twenty miles, and also because parking wasn't a problem – on either side of the street lay a sandy parking strip which was seldom full even on Saturdays. The town, which from our direction you came across without warning, after a bend, at the bottom of a slowly descending hill, was a wind tunnel (wind geat, Aunt Hope called it) between hills: a stiff, maddening wind blew through it all year round. Despite the wind and the down-at-heel atmosphere, or it might have been because of these things, I felt there was something romantic about Long Clovell. In August especially, and in late-afternoon sun, it seemed as though a sandy wash had been painted over the town. And the wide main street, the disproportionately tall and leaning telegraph poles, the flaky shop fronts, even the beached cars and their dazzling windscreens, made me think of the cow towns and mining towns and ghost towns in Bowdell's exhibition. Tombstone, I thought.

In those days, the early seventies, Long Clovell's only garage was a weather-boarded shack; it didn't take much imagination to see it as the saloon. Then there were the sawdusty French fancies in the window of Barstow's bakery; the haberdashery counter of Eileen's, the draper's (where Aunt Hope bought my Terylene skirts for school), with its cards of fancy buttons and bolts of flowered satin no one, surely, would ever buy; the pitchforks and spades and brooms and wicker baskets stacked on the pavement outside A. W. Swale & Sons, hardware. All these fitted the Wild West picture I had. Trailing after Aunt Hope with a shopping bag, I'd convince myself that into this windy one-horse town not one horse but horses, a tight bunch of them, would at any moment come galloping in, the cowboy riders firing into the air before reining their mounts to a snorting, rearing stop outside the saloon.

My new school was in Long Clovell, on the outskirts of the town. To get to it you turned off the main street, Market Street, into a narrow side street. This was Cheap Street, one of three streets on that side (the right side, for anyone coming into town from our direction). There were shops at the Market Street end; a small, dark greengrocer's that we supplied with eggs and vegetables, a tobacconist's, a betting shop with naively painted, anatomically impossible greyhounds racing across its blanked-out window.

After the shops the street widened into something that seemed to me more like a road, though it continued to call itself Cheap Street. On the right, the recreation ground; on the left, a breezeblock council estate; straight ahead, and end of the line, Cheap Street Comprehensive (until the late sixties Cheap Street Secondary Modern). A long, black-and-white and plate-glass building set in a rough green sea. The school resembled a ship in some ways – a low in the water, possibly sinking ship. It had a funnel at one end, to do with the heating or ventilating system; and it had decks, two boarded, covered walkways that ran all the way round it at ground and first-floor levels, where on wet afternoons we were encouraged to go for runs. Not forced, however; forcing was no part of the 'do your own thing, go at your own pace, discover your own strengths' liberal principles of the head teacher, Mr Downley.

I was not happy, nor truly unhappy at that school, a comprehensive only in name, whose curriculum, as Aunt Hope had diagnosed, was geared to the practical. No professional people, apart from the teachers who taught us, sent their sons and daughters there. Few business people did. The doctors and dentists and solicitors of the town, the librarian and the manager of one of the two branch banks, preferred to send their children on a fifteen-mile bus journey to the one comprehensive in the area that had academic ambitions – a former grammar school. Not just academic ones; their netball, football and hockey teams regularly smashed (and verbally abused) our chaotic and cheerful volunteers. The fathers of the boys and girls in my year were farmers or farm workers, postmen and post-office clerks, small shopkeepers or people who worked in those shops. Most of the mothers had part-time jobs – hairdressing, office cleaning.

I'd come from a school whose intake was urban and sub-urban, varied and transitory, which had included black children and Asian children, Scottish, Irish and Welsh and combinations of these, and to begin with I was confused by the indigenous, complex network of ties and blood links that existed in Cheap Street Comp. Links which, like veins and arteries, ran up and down and sideways through the school, invisibly connecting pupil to pupil, pupil to teaching staff, pupil to kitchen staff and maintenance staff. Take Helen Butterwick, the girl I sat next to. Her father, Dan, worked at Home Electrical and Repairs where he mended, or failed to mend, the TV sets, radios and toasters of the entire community. He was also a star swimmer and coached the school swimming teams on Wednesday evenings. Her mother, Margaret, manageress of Stay-prest dry-cleaner's, took time away from her wire coat hangers to give weekly housecraft lessons to the third and fourth years. Her uncle Ray, Dan's brother and head cowman on the Sheepwood estate, whose wife caused an earthquake in my second term when she ran off with the school janitor, a married man of sixty-three, had a son called Scott who, although older than Helen and I, was two forms below. It was said that Scott wanked incessantly in class; also that he would not, or could not, learn to read.

There were links you were permitted to know about, that were spoken of out loud in public places, that you could see or work out for yourself. Some you could not avoid knowing, because of headlines in the local newspaper. (The janitor made the front page twice in six months; not long after the elopement he killed himself.) And there were other links an outsider could only sense or guess at, that only an insider would truly know. Bad links, you sensed, to do with bad divorces, perhaps, or bad debts. Or with bad feeling between neighbours on bad estates. Old, terrible bitternesses and disappointments. Inconsolable griefs. Feuds whose origins went so far back no one alive could remember what had started them.

In that liberal, easy-going, friendly-on-the-whole school, there were people who never spoke to each other, and not for reasons of shyness or indifference; not because of natural hierarchies of age or seniority, nor because the parties concerned had nothing in common. These people, pupils or staff, or a combination of both, deliberately avoided one another. I witnessed it. In corridors, in classrooms, in the light, bleak dining hall, on the covered decks, in the playground at break, you could see this cold recognition, followed by a just-perceptible pause – before one or other passed by on the other side.

October

The dews are heavy and cold. The runner beans left on
the poles are like curled black tongues. Spiders webs make
giant fingerprints against the window pane. The Red
Admirals have flown from the buddlia's rusty spikes. In
the early morning the yew outside our kitchen is swagged
with glitter like a Christmas tree . . .

and so on and so on. One of the first essays I wrote at
Cheap Street Comprehensive. I found some of my old exercise books among Aunt Hope's things, and this essay
('composition' was the word we used, or 'story') was in one
of them.

'Very nice, Hannah,' Mr Swinnerton, English and history,
has written underneath in red. There's a huge red tick in the
margin, but no mark. Except when it came to exams, there
was no marking system in that school. If there had been,
some people would have been awarded Bs while others in
the same class, perhaps older, would have had to get by with
Ds or even Es. Which would have been wrong. Education
was not a competition. The only person you should be com-
peting against was yourself. A big red tick – the bigger and
more flamboyant, the better – was the most you could hope
for.

There were no ticks, and no crosses either, for what was

considered substandard work. The standard in question being your own imaginative best. ('Disgraceful!' – Aunt Hope's comment when I tried to explain this policy to her.)

Under Mr Swinnerton's red-letter praise of my composition is one blue-ink word: 'Yes!' Aunt Hope wrote that. She also underlined, in blue, the words 'buddlia' and 'spiders', and put in the margin alongside them a big blue S for spelling mistake.

Mr Swinnerton did not consider it helpful to correct minor spelling mistakes. Punctuation, also, was an individual thing. He was following the school's stratagem in that. A child's imagination could be killed stone dead by too much nit-picking criticism. This explains the pages of misspelled, unpunctuated, uninformed, misinformed ramblings in the English exercise books I found; it accounts for the enormous number of ticks, the minimal amount of corrections and suggestions.

When I opened that first exercise book and discovered that first essay, and read my aunt's exclamatory comment, I sat down and held the book against my heart.

I sat – no, knelt – on the floor, and rocked backwards and forwards, embracing my book. I swayed from side to side, holding it. She loved me, I thought. She really cared, all along. I have the proof here, in my arms.

For I understood that 'Yes!' wasn't just an objective verdict on a piece of work; it was her verdict on me, an affirmation of everything that was Hannah Eve Wickham. It was a blessing from my aunt to me, one she knew I would eventually find. It was benediction. It was absolution. It was a sign.

'Yes!'

I went through the exercise book slowly, page by page, searching for more of my aunt's handwriting, more blue-ink corrections, more signs of her love.

Nothing.

I found poems in the exercise book. Although we were not taught poetry as such, and seldom read poems in class – poems in books by famous and dead poets – we wrote a lot of poems ourselves. Even I did. We'd spend the first half of the lesson writing, the second half reading out loud what we'd written. In turn we had to walk up to the blackboard, face our classmates and read out our poem. 'Throw your voice to the back of the classroom,' Mr Swinnerton would instruct us, 'pretend you're on stage!' We were all poets, he said, and should feel confident. Every single one of us in that room was a poet.

I found a poem called 'The School Bus':

> The school bus is
> a grumpy old woman
> overweight and out of breath
> staggering weezing complaining
> stumbling and grumbling and
> groaning
> moaning
> she stops on the hill
> to get her breath back
> then at the top
> wheeeeeeeeee
> downhill she comes
> down down down
> fast faster faster
> wheeeeeeeeee
> like a boy on a toboggan.

How touching and true, I thought when I read it; and I believe I wept. A big red tick in the margin from Mr Swinnerton for this touching and true poem. Nothing from Aunt Hope.

But I was drunk that day I found the exercise books. Not incoherently drunk, but drunk enough to rock and sway and feel emotions I wouldn't ordinarily feel; and to have convincing, untrustworthy convictions. I'd had to have a drink in order to drum up the courage to go through my aunt's desk. Before she died she'd burned her personal stuff, letters and so on, but there were papers here pertaining to Arizona: the deeds, records of the sale and the building work that was done. I was going to have to lift the piles out of the drawers, go through the piles, and then decide what to keep and what to throw away. You need a drink or two for that sort of work.

Bollocks. That's what I thought when I was sober, about my aunt's 'sign'. The poem, also, was bollocks. When I read it again, I remembered that I was thirteen at the time. Thirteen! What I had in my hands was the effort of an average eight or nine-year-old. Finch was writing better, more effectively and accurately, at six.

Finch's cleverness. I thought about it, and a picture came into my head of the kitchen at Arizona as it was in the mid-eighties. That kitchen went through various metamorphoses during the twenty-odd years Aunt Hope lived there. The cold, impractical white we first slapped on the walls gave way first to fierce blue, then a flower-pot red. The floor changed from pebble-patterned vinyl laid over concrete to steel-blue farmhouse tiles, paid for by Jocelyn with earnings from her part in a radio soap they scrapped after twenty episodes. Furniture moved about. Rugs came and went. The rickety, square table we'd brought with us from Green Copse Road buckled at the knees and was replaced by a trestle that got in the way of stove at one end and sink at the other. A room that my aunt and Jocelyn had made functional and clean, but could be cosy too when the curtains were drawn, that smelled appetising and felt warm, transmogrified, with the advent of hens and ducks, into a draughty outhouse-cum-scullery, a place of buckets and bins and swill and slop; of eggs in egg boxes awaiting transport into town, of eggs in baskets awaiting a scrub. A bad cabbage-stalk smell hung around in it. And it began to accumulate a litter that had little to do with cooking or poultry-keeping: bills and letters, old newspapers, buttons, corks and bottletops, spectacles, special-offer tokens that were never taken up, empty cigarette packets that had served as ashtrays, exhausted felt-tips. These things were washed into the kitchen on a daily invisible tide which, receding, left them high and dry on every surface, even the top of the fridge. No tide ever swept them away again. Meals, which I had once looked forward to, which Aunt Hope had once taken pride in and time over, became increasingly perfunctory. Before sitting down to eat we'd have to shift all the debris off the table. We'd pile it up on spare chairs or on the floor.

It was this scuzzy, shambolic kitchen that came into my head. And here we were, Aunt Hope, Jocelyn, Finch and I, eating our early supper – it had to be early because of Finch – at the cleared-of-shambles table.

At this time Aunt Hope must have been nearly sixty and looked it; Jocelyn, a few years younger, looked mid-forties at the most and was beautiful still; I was twenty-six or so; Finch was – what? – seven. Diarmid had yet to walk into my life, though he was just about to.

'I'm thinking of selling the cheval glass.' Aunt Hope had just returned from a trek to the 'you-know-what', and was settling herself back into her chair when she made her announcement. 'It's in good condition apart from the missing finial. Should fetch a bob or two.'

The cheval glass had belonged to my suicide-grandfather. It was handsome, the only decent piece of furniture my aunt owned. She'd pointed this out many times. The cheval glass lived in her bedroom and always had done. Its reflection was kind.

'Don't sell the cheval glass. It's the only mirror in the house that doesn't make me look hideous.'

'Me, me, me. What about us? What about Jocelyn? What about your poor old aunt? Doesn't it matter what we look like?'

'Mirror, mirror on the wall, who's the ugliest of all?' Finch enquired smugly of his distorted image in the biscuit-tin lid.

'Poor old aunt,' Jocelyn murmured. 'But there aren't any

aunts any more, are there? Haven't you noticed? Aunts are a thing of the past.'

'What's this nonsense? Of course there are aunts. I'm an aunt.' Aunt Hope turned to Finch. 'Have some more ice cream, darling. Go on, do.'

'Aren't any aunts,' Finch repeated, puzzling over it, thinking about it. 'Arrren't any aunts.' He handed his pudding bowl to Aunt Hope, his tiny, intent eyes following the scoop as she piled his bowl for the second, or it might have been the third, time.

And I looked away. Because such beady-eyed, lip-smacking, quivering greed is a nauseating sight. And it was nauseating the way my aunt and Jocelyn fed this greedy child as though he'd never been fed; and fussed over him, and vied with each other at every meal to keep him supplied with ketchup and mayonnaise and orange squash and 'anything else you fancy, Finchy darling?' No one asked my opinion or permission. It was as though I didn't exist. And why did they do it? Why did these two late-middle-aged women indulge Finch in this loverlike way? I thought I knew the answer. Because he was male. Because he was clever. And also, it occurred to me, because they were guilty.

'I meant aunt aunts, if you get me,' Jocelyn said. 'Maiden aunts, great-aunts. They had status once. "Aunt" was a serious title when I was young. And there were courtesy aunts. Every woman in our street was auntie to me. There was Auntie Joan and Auntie Beryl and – '

'Coffee?' Aunt Hope directed the question at me. Jocelyn never drank coffee in the evening; she couldn't sleep if she did. When my aunt said 'coffee' with a question mark, it wasn't an offer. She meant, would I get up and make it?

I got up and made the coffee. Ordinary instant for me; decaffeinated for her. Real coffee kept her awake too, but she liked the taste and, I thought, needed the illusion.

'Hannah calls me aunt, don't you, Hannah? Even now, when she's grown-up.'

'Finch doesn't, though.' It was a sore point with me. Finch

had called Aunt Hope and Jocelyn by their Christian names from the word go. Neither of them had questioned it. Neither of them had ever talked to me about it.

'Perhaps that's what I meant. Perhaps I didn't mean anything very much . . . Will you excuse me a moment?' Jocelyn stubbed out her cigarette and made for the door.

I felt a pang watching her go. It was two years since Jocelyn had had her hair cut off, and I still hadn't got used to her back view. I didn't like it. You couldn't really tell from the front, and sometimes I convinced myself that that heavy gold stuff was still there, massed behind her ears (which, because they were ugly, she kept covered by little curly side pieces). I remembered the way she used to pin her hair into its pleat – by feel, without looking in the glass – so deftly and quickly. So casually. Duchess and barmaid and tart, no, courtesan, that old-fashioned hairstyle had made her seem. But I'd been frightened of her, or by her, when her hair was down. She'd looked witchy then. I'd go into her room before breakfast and find her drinking her early-morning tea, and see all that hair spread over the pillows, and it was frightening. Her face was too narrow, not young enough, her features were too strong for that long, thick, heavy hair.

'I've been trying to think of words that sound like aunt and are spelled like aunt, and I can't think of any,' Finch said. 'All the words that've got "aunt" in are pronounced "orn't".'

'Is that so? How interesting,' said Aunt Hope, smiling, clearing the plates.

'If you put a consonant in front of "aunt", you get things like "taunt" and "gaunt",' Finch explained.

'Fancy!' said my aunt (but in an admiring way, not in a squashing or satirical way). 'You know I don't believe I've ever noticed that.'

'What haven't you noticed? What have I missed?' Jocelyn was back. From the lavatory, she wanted us to believe; she'd left the bathroom door open so we'd hear the flush. But I wasn't fooled. Jocelyn had left the kitchen to get herself a drink. Whenever I brought Finch to Arizona, there was this charade. No drinks before supper, no wine on the table at supper, all booze out of the way until after he'd gone to bed. It was daft. It meant I never got offered even one glass of anything stronger than tonic water. It meant that these two old soaks, who were incapable of surviving for more than half an hour without their fix, bobbed up and down from the table like corks. Did they want us to think they were incontinent?

Later, after the washing-up, after a glass or two, I put my head round Finch's door to see if he was asleep. ('Have you been to see Finchy yet?' Aunt Hope had asked me. 'Have you said goodnight to your little boy?')

He was lying on his stomach, writing in a notebook.

'You ought to have your light off. You're supposed to be asleep.'

'Want to see what I've written?'

Not much, no. 'OK. Quickly, though.'

He handed me the notebook. There were a lot of crossings-out, then a blank couple of lines, then underneath:

The Aunts, A Romaunt
Undaunted by taunts from vaults, the gaunt aunts saunter jauntily from their haunt. Avaunt!

'I wanted to make a story out of all the words that have "aunt" in,' Finch explained. 'But there are only ten. As no doubt you're aware.'

'It's very clever,' I said. 'Romaunt. Well. That is clever.'

'Of course my story – sentence, rather – isn't a romaunt, but I couldn't see another way of getting the word in.'

'No. Of course not.' Though I had no idea what a romaunt was. Eventually I said, 'How did you know there were only ten words? How did you know where to start looking for them? There could be hundreds in the dictionary, they could be anywhere.'

Finch sighed. 'I used a rhyming dictionary. I looked up "aunt", ending first, as you have to, and there they all were.'

'Even so, it's clever,' I said.

But I was relieved. It wasn't that clever. All it proved was that my seven-year-old son knew how to find his way round a rhyming dictionary. I could have done that myself if I'd thought of it. If I'd wanted to.

'A romaunt is a tale of chivalry, according to *Walker's*,' Finch went on, unrelenting. '*Chambers* gives "a romance". The *Shorter Oxford* says it can be a poem or a form of speech. The *OED*'s got all sorts of stuff, different spellings, examples, quotes. Chaucer, Byron, Scott – all sorts.'

It was then I saw the pile of books on the floor beside Finch's bed. He'd spent time on this aunt investigation, all the time, two hours or so, since supper. He'd really thought about it, the little bugger.

I said, 'You'd better put those books back where you found them. First thing tomorrow.' At the door, I said, 'Have you cleaned your teeth?'

'Yes.'

'Then what's that in your mouth?'

'A sweet.' He took it out to show me. 'Hope gave it to me. When she came to kiss me goodnight.'

On the face of it a straightforward, truthful answer. But it wasn't, believe me. What he was really telling me was that there were some people, my aunt, for example, who appreciated him far more than they appreciated me. Who were sufficiently fond of him to give him sweets and kiss him goodnight. So screw you, Mother dear.

And I have not mentioned his smile, which was enough to freeze the blood.

You're a liar, Finch. (But I didn't say it.) Aunt Hope would never have done that – give a child a boiled sweet at bedtime when he could fall asleep and choke on it. No. Jocelyn might, she was capable. Her desire to please and to be thought well

of was strong enough to overrule more important consider-
ations. Danger, for instance. But Aunt Hope? No.

I don't worry so much about Finch's cleverness now that he's
in his teens. It's less obvious now. It doesn't threaten me the
way it did when he was small. He does his own thing and I
do mine. He doesn't ask questions any more. It's not just that
he has no expectation that I'll know the answers. Somewhere
along the line he got bored with his subtle baiting game.
There isn't enough input from me to make it worth while.
There isn't enough reactive bad behaviour on my part. There
isn't enough feedback.

It was when he was between the ages of three and twelve
that I felt most threatened by Finch. A mother expects to
teach her young child, not the other way round. She expects
to be several jumps ahead of him or her in just about every
department. That's the normal order of things, the order
through, by or from which mutual respect and, who knows,
even love can grow. I imagine it can grow. As it was, as soon
as he could read, I lived in daily fear of being found out by
Finch, of having my ignorance exposed in all its depth and
variety in a million humiliating ways. He was a skilful and, I
believed, disingenuous inquisitor. A question at breakfast,
deriving from an article he'd read in the paper, say; innocent-
sounding and sufficiently general in shape to allow me to
bluff my way to some sort of answer, would be followed, at
later snack- and mealtimes (the times when we were
together), by more specific and deadlier questions, often concerning my original reply. Stripping a banana or a chicken
bone, he would take even greater pleasure in stripping skin
after skin off me. 'So it's your opinion, is it,' he would begin,
oh so innocently, between mouthfuls of flesh. Or 'If I've
understood you right . . .?'

*

A week or so after the aunt episode, Finch and I went back to London. Back to work, me, back to school, him. I was sleeping badly, as I tend to when there's no one to share my bed, and there was no one at that time. What I mean is, there was no one to fuck, and next to outdoor exercise, sex is the best insurer of a good night's rest I know of. I'd go to bed about eleven and turn off the light and listen to the radio. I'd listen to politics-talking heads and repeats of old unfunny comedy shows and the bedtime serial. All enough to send you to sleep. But however sleepy, I had to try to stay awake for *Sailing By* and the shipping forecast. A habit that I'd slipped into by chance had become a ritual, an act of remembrance, a prayer, it sometimes felt, for Uncle Ber. As soon as the music started, I could see my four-year-old self standing beside my uncle on a windy headland. The headland was somewhere off Plymouth, and we were watching the Tall Ships' Race. I was holding his hand and we were watching those tall, magnificent ships sailing by. What Uncle Ber had taken me to see, on a blustery morning so long ago, was the start of the race, but my sleepy imagination saw evening sunlight, like gold leaf, on everything; and the ships weren't setting off anywhere, they were westering home. Billowing sails, billowing clouds, sparkling billows, soft pillows, sweet dreams . . .

And then, two hours later, I'd be suddenly, fiercely awake. In those two hours I'd have dreamed dreams that were far from sweet. Nightmares. I'd have dreamed I was drowning in a well. That I was being drowned in a pool. Or that Uncle Ber was being drowned, held under the water by invisible suffocating softness, while I ran barefoot up and down the hard, wet concrete of the Pool Hall screaming my head off and waving (but, it being a dream, no one could see or hear me). I'd have dreamed that a fox was murdering hens and ducks – as in fact happened all too frequently at Arizona, and not only when I'd forgotten to shut them up; a bold daylight raider and serial killer, a dog fox or, more probably, a series of these, haunted our time there.

Waking from these dreams of violent death, from a panic

of blood and feathers or a stifling billow-pillow of water, I'd be convinced that I was about to die. My thunderously thumping heart was about to stop. It was only a pump, I'd realised; pumps could stop pumping; like car engines and outboard motors and faulty valves that no one knew were faulty, they could conk out without warning. I was going to die, we were all going to die! Any minute now (thump thump, bang bang, flutter flutter) I was going to be dead! I was going to experience – no, not experience, that was the terror of it – the blackness of eternity.

I would lie perfectly still then, frozen, deafened by the racket of my panicky, faulty heart.

One night, soon after we'd returned to London, I had woken from such a nightmare, turned the light on and looked at a magazine to try and make myself dozy; turned the light off and worried about how I was going to pay the electricity bill; given the pillows a hard time, wondered how Finch and I could go on living together, and thrown myself all over the bed, kicking my feet into corners, searching for a cool place.

And then suddenly my body had had enough. It began to go slack and feel heavy, and my mind began to drift about in weird, disconnected ways. Sleep, the brink of sleep. I was almost there, so nearly there, when the word 'chaunticleer' floated into my head. At once I was awake again. Chaunticleer. What did it mean? What did it signify? Should it be spelled 'cleer', as I first saw it, or 'clere', or even 'clear'? And then I understood. The ending was unimportant. It was the beginning that mattered. 'Chaunt' contained 'aunt'. And Finch hadn't used 'chaunt', or 'chaunticleer', in his romaunt. He hadn't discovered them in any of his bloody dictionaries.

After this victory I slept dreamlessly till morning.

But Finch and I had a problem that had nothing to do with his mental superiority, or his looks. My dislike of him, his dislike of me – for it was not a one-sided thing, you know; it never was – started long before he revealed himself as a clever suet pudding. It started the day he was born.

Aunt Hope didn't throw away our television (as the getaway people of Finch's survey threw away theirs); it wasn't a moral or lifestyle decision, the thing just fell apart. A black-and-white set, with a big wood surround and a very small screen, it was on its last legs when we left for Arizona, and never recovered from the journey. Dan Butterwick of Home Electrical and Repairs did his best, with new valves and implants and bypass surgery, to extend its life and to stop the continuous whining hum it made, but his cures, which often entailed lengthy home visits, seldom lasted more than a week.

'You'd do better paying out for a new colour TV,' Dan advised Aunt Hope. When he said 'new', he meant good-as-new. He kept a stock of renovated second-hand colour sets in his shop, and was always encouraging her to invest in one. It would be a saving in the long run, he insisted, since all his sets came with a six-month guarantee. Aunt Hope said she'd keep that in mind.

When our television died and could not be resuscitated, Jocelyn and I carried it out and buried it in the dustbin.

'We never watched it anyway,' Aunt Hope said. (But how could we when it didn't work?) 'What time have we got to watch television?'

It was the start of summer then, and it was true that in summer we had no time. We were grass-cutting and hedge-cutting and potting up and planting out and pricking out till late. We were weeding and watering till darkness fell. After all this effort we were too tired to watch television; and in termtime I had to get up at seven. So I'd leave them to their whisky bottle and go off to my wagon-lit.

But in winter tea and telly were what I expected when I got home from school. Everybody else had them. It was already dark by the time the bus let me off on the main road. In really bad weather – thick fog, heavy rain, gales, snow – Jocelyn would meet me in the Morris at the end of the runway. Otherwise I biked home. The bike was hidden in the hedge. I'd beam my torch along the hedge to find it, load my kit into the panniers, and race home under the creaking, dying elms. They'd started dying that first summer after the move. Dutch elm disease. Aunt Hope was distraught about our dying trees – about all the dying trees. She would never have moved to an elm landscape had she known, she told us. She would never have bought Arizona if it hadn't been for those 'beautiful, beautiful elms' on either side of the runway.

Sometimes I forgot to take my torch; and sometimes I'd hidden the bike too well. Often, disentangling the wheels from blackthorn and bramble, I'd discover a flat tyre.

When Jocelyn was at home, there was something to come home for. The courtyard light would be on; the downstairs windows, curtains drawn, were squares of muffled warmth. The back door might open on a smell of toast, on a conversational radio, on the record player singing its head off.

When Jocelyn was away, my headlamp wavered over a ghost house of blank, black, silent windows. One icy-white light in the kitchen was the only intimation that anyone, other than ghosts, inhabited the place.

No television meant games after supper when Jocelyn was around. There was no choice for Aunt Hope and me, except what game we were going to play. A card game? A board game? A pencil and paper game? An acting game? Come on, come on, make up your minds! The ringmaster would pluck the book my aunt was reading out of her hands and make room for it on some high surface, way out of reach. She would unsnap the card table and shunt our chairs into position. When she manoeuvred the chairs, with us inside, the rugs were dragged along behind, ruckling and bunching into ugly ridges. I would feel compelled to get up and straighten them.

The card table: moth-eaten baize, its green, except at the edges, bleached to a dirty grey. The moth holes were really sizeable, round and dark, like cigarette burns. I used to stand my pencil in the holes and swivel it between my finger and thumb, while keeping my eye on Jocelyn's huge hands, deftly and flamboyantly shuffling the cards. Or dealing the cards, with her head high and her eyes screwed up to avoid the smoke from her own cigarette. Slap, slap, slap. Confidence and nonchalance and expertise – would I ever acquire them?

'Your turn to deal, Hannah.'

'Must I? I'm no good at it.'

'You certainly won't be if you don't practise.'

But sure enough, as soon as the pack was in my hands the cards stuck together like glue. Like lovers. Lovers were much on my mind at this time. I longed for a lover, by which I meant someone to love and to love me, a relationship which might, or might not, include sex. When I was the dealer and we picked up our cards, there'd be discrepancies in the number each of us had. Big discrepancies that caused Aunt Hope's eyebrows to shoot into her hair. I'd be asked to deal again.

Aunt Hope would be peering at her hand, sorting it, frowning a deep frown (or smiling a little secret, worrying smile), sipping her whisky, tapping her fingers on the baize, sighing. Such deep frowns, such awful sighs, nothing about them of relief. Aaaaaaaah. When she sighed, her shoulders rose to great heights, then fell correspondingly low. Her chin dropped to her chest; her whole body slumped. The sighs were triggered by whisky, I thought. Periodically during our game, Jocelyn would get up, pick up her glass and Aunt Hope's and waltz out to the kitchen. 'Tra la la-la-la-la,' she'd trill, opera-style, up the scale. 'Tra la la-la-la' – down. I'd hear the tap gushing and the pipes cranking. Then she'd be back, on skates, seemingly, gliding into the room, holding the glasses high, at arm's length. Two full glasses, the colour of first-of-the-day pee. Chin-chin.

Towards the end of the game, and the evening, Jocelyn would not waltz or glide. Concentrating on one glass at a time, gripping it tight, she'd weave her way to the door, her free arm outstretched for balance or clutching the furniture for support – like a landlubber on a rolling deck. Whoops!

'Don't you dare spill my drink!' Aunt Hope would call after her.

Who were these dangerous old women? I was always staring at them, asking myself that. What had they got to do with me?

But there were times, just after supper, the wind roaring in the trees, the trees waving like wands, the fire roaring up the chimney, when a feeling of wellbeing would spread over me. A delicious, safe feeling, the nearest to bliss I could imagine. It never lasted long. There was nothing I could do to retain it. After it had gone, my imagination could never recapture it.

The games we played: I remember a betting card game, Oh Hell, for which we used matchsticks for chips. I remember whole evenings of Cluedo and Scrabble and Monopoly and Rhyming Consequences. I remember mime games – in turn we had to act words or combinations of words for the others to guess – and the embarrassment of these.

Aunt Hope never wanted to play anything as a threesome. She complained that most of the games that were possible for three to play worked better with four players or more. But it was clear to me that she enjoyed being bullied by Jocelyn. When Jocelyn took the book from her hands in that bossy way, or pushed the chair she was sitting in up to the table, my aunt, while covering her eyes or waving her arms in protest, would be secretly – not so secretly – pleased.

We were all cheats at these games, when we spotted an opportunity to cheat, if we thought we could get away with it. Cheating gave the games an edge, and kept us watchfully on the edge of our seats. We were all bad, bad-tempered losers.

'I'm bored with Monopoly,' Jocelyn announced one evening, having lost her shirt as well as all her hotels, pushing the board away. 'I'm going to invent a game of my own.'

'Tautology.' Aunt Hope pounced at once. 'If you're doing the inventing, who else's could it be?'

I said, 'Could it be about cowboys? A cowboy game. An Arizona game.'

'OK. If you like. If you help me.'

We called our game the Arizona Board Game. It was going to be about a cattle drive. Once upon a time, at Green Copse Road, I'd watched an old, exciting film about a cattle drive, on TV with Uncle Ber, and I had a picture in my head of treacherous rapids, whizzing arrows, stampeding herds and broken wagon wheels. As I saw it, our game would work something like this: each player would start off with a herd of cattle that had to be driven west. From Chicago, Illinois, say, to Tombstone, Arizona. (From what I'd gathered from Bowdell's notes on Wyatt Earp, Tombstone wasn't so much a cow town as a mining town, a silver boom town. But cattle must have been driven through it, if not to it.) The first person to drive his cattle into Tombstone would be the winner, and collect ten bags of gold or whatever.

Having agreed on the get-yourself-and-your-cattle-from A-to-Z aim of our board game, Jocelyn and I argued about the details.

I knew from the start that I wanted our game to be logical, and rooted in a believable world, in the same way that Monopoly was. I wanted the players to have to think about the moves they made, to have to make choices and decisions. Difficult choices that would have a bearing on the success or failure of the cattle drive. The kind of decision-making I envisaged had to do with practicalities, such as how much food and water to take and which route to go for. The short, dangerous cut through Navajo country, for example, or the longer, safer route which might lose you precious time and supplies. Money would be another choice: how much, out of an initial handout, to spend on what. And I wanted moral choices, the sort you always get in Westerns, concerning loyalty and betrayal, involving wounded comrades, marked cards or sick cattle. Bowdell's material would provide the details. Our cowboys would drive their cattle through a real landscape with real place names. Coffee Pot Rock, Iron Springs, the Dragoon Mountains – names such as these, though I hadn't done any homework on it yet.

Another idea, brainwave, I had was that the players could be Goodies or Baddies. Before starting, you'd pick a card from a pile of cards that had the single word Goody or Baddy on it, and have to act accordingly. No one would know what you'd picked. You might all pick a Goody card; you might all pick a Baddy card, but no one would know. Baddies could be as devious as they liked, disguising their intentions till well into the game. What did Jocelyn think of this brilliant idea?

Jocelyn said, 'Oh, my gawd.' She said my game sounded like *The Pilgrim's Progress*. It sounded like hard, serious work to make and to play. The rules would take years to work out. What she had in mind was something simple and amusing. A sort of Wild West version of Snakes and Ladders, with dice and tiddlywinks, but no game cards and no money.

Snakes and Ladders was a pathetic game. I told her I'd make the dollar bills we'd need, no problems there. I'd draw and paint them and cut them out. Or I'd get a printing set from the stationer's in Long Clovell and print them.

Aunt Hope glanced up from her book. She said, 'That I must see, Hannah. That I really look forward to seeing.'

It was Jocelyn's version of the Arizona Board Game we eventually made (out of double-thickness white cardboard, marked out and illustrated with felt pens. For lettering we used those peel-off, stick-on letters you can buy). There was no logic to her version. There was no skill required to play. And I saw that her game would be almost impossible to win because the 'snakes' outnumbered the 'ladders' to a farcical degree. Another thing: in order to escape jail – or a lynch mob or a scalping – players were going to be made to pay out the sort of sums they were unlikely to own. (We did play with money, it was Jocelyn's only concession to my original idea. We used the Monopoly notes. Pounds became dollars at Jocelyn's say-so.)

Jocelyn's game had its roots, if you could call them roots, in Westerns and cowboy songs. Nothing wrong with that, perhaps, if you'd seen all the films and knew all the songs. If you understood all the jokes. Long before the board was completed, I walked out and up the stairs to my room, slamming several doors along the way. Why should I help when it wasn't my game?

Aunt Hope would never play it, though, I comforted myself. She disliked silliness in all its forms. Her boredom threshold was low.

The evening arrives when Jocelyn's ready to unveil 'our' game. We're going to give it a trial run, she says over supper (beans and bacon, to 'get us in the mood'). If there are things that need changing, well, then we'll change them. We'll adapt or change anything that doesn't work. Won't we, buckeroo?

Buckeroo is me; but I don't answer. What I think is, Why ask me? It's your bloody game.

'Oh, it's beans and bacon most ev'ry day
I'd as soon be eatin' prairie hay –'

sings Jocelyn as she clears the plates.

Aunt Hope squares up her reading spectacles to examine the board, kept hidden from her until this moment. She's wearing a neckerchief and a 'cowboy' hat, as we all are. These hats aren't real stetsons or ten-gallons, they're not made of felt or leather or even straw. They're hard white plastic, out of a mould. Jocelyn bought them at the toy shop, in the Party Corner, where you find balloons and squeakers and paper serviettes and policemen's helmets made of cardboard. The hats, which have exaggeratedly curled brims and the names ROY ROGERS in red and TRIGGER in blue stamped round the base of the crown, were intended for five-year-olds. They perch on top of our heads, and would slip off if it weren't for the jolly red-and-white cord that goes under, and cuts into, our chins. (On a five-year-old, the cord would hang down at chest level, weighted by its central knot – 'the authentic cowboy knot', the toy-shop owner assured Jocelyn.)

When Aunt Hope tried on her hat – which until that moment I was certain she would never do – she said, 'How do I look?' and turned her head from side to side for us to admire. She said, 'The Milky Bars are on me, by the way.'

I watch her face as she examines the board. Her mouth begins to twitch. She's trying to keep a straight face. 'This game's all stop and no go by the looks of it.'

'It's a silly game,' I say, 'there's no point to it. It's got bugger all to do with Arizona.'

'Very silly indeed.' But she sounds delighted.

As in most board games you have to throw a six to start. When you've achieved that, you have another throw.

I'm the first to throw a six. A six followed by a four. I tap my green counter along four squares. (I always choose green in board games. For some reason I have to have green.) Tap, tap, tap, tap. 'Take time off to Paint Your Wagon,' I read. 'Go back six squares. Miss a turn.'

'But that's stupid! I've only just begun this drive. Why would I want to paint my wagon? If it needed painting, I'd have done it before I started. Wouldn't I?'

'Hannah's a literalist, remember.' Aunt Hope to Jocelyn.

'Anyway, how can I go back six squares when I've only gone forwards four?' (I've just noticed this.) 'There aren't six squares to go back on.'

'Don't worry about that, cowpuncher. It isn't important.

Just go back. Back to Chicago. Chicago, Chicago, my home town!'

'Do I have to throw another six before I can move?'

'Naturally.'

But I don't throw a six my next go, or the one after, or the one after that. I sit with folded arms while Jocelyn and my aunt, who have managed sixes, get nowhere in ridiculous ways.

' "Cactus hurts your toes – better get some rest. Lay up in Calamity Jane's cabin for a while",' Aunt Hope reads. 'How long is a while, can anyone tell me?'

'As long as you want. As long as your toes still hurt. As long as Calam's prepared to have you.'

'By Calamity, I hope you mean Doris Day?' Aunt Hope says. 'I loved *her* in buckskins, of course. I don't mind being shacked up with *her*. However, if you mean the original, good grief! I saw a photograph of her once.'

Jocelyn, meanwhile, is having a Bad Day at Black Rock. For no reason I can see she has to give two mules to Sister Sarah before she can get back on the Navajo Trail.

' "High Noon. Time for a siesta. Miss a turn." I'm always being made to lie down in this game,' Aunt Hope complains. 'I'm sure this isn't how the West was won. I don't feel tired at all.'

'There's nothing that says you have to lie down alone. The Magnificent Seven are in town – and the Wild Bunch. Those guys are game for anything. Your turn, Hannah. Ride, tenderfoot, ride.'

I take off my idiotic hat. I drop the dice into the shaker.

Jocelyn lifts her head and sniffs the air. 'It's quiet,' she says, 'have you noticed? Too quiet.'

Shake shake shake. The dice rolls out over the board, hovers on six, tips over. Four.

'Shall we let her off?' Jocelyn to Aunt Hope, in a stage whisper. 'Shall we allow that maverick to start with a four?'

But I've been there, remember. I know where a four lands you.

Aunt Hope throws a six. It sends her yellow counter into unknown terrain, further than any counter has been. ' "Annie got your gun. For a Fistful of Dollars you can get it back. For a Few Dollars More –" Dang me! I ain't got a fistful of dollars! I only started out with two bits and a quarter.'

Nobody won the Arizona Board Game that first playing; no herd made it to Tombstone. It wasn't long before the red and yellow counters were back in Chicago with the green. Sixes seemed impossible to come by. Not just for me; Aunt Hope and Jocelyn couldn't throw one either.

'That's it. I'm headed for the bar.' Jocelyn stubbed out her cigarette. She picked up her tumbler and Aunt Hope's.

'Well, I really enjoyed that game.' Aunt Hope smiled, stretched her arms above her head and leaned far back in her chair. 'It's so unlike life. In life everyone gets to Tombstone in the end.'

Jocelyn said that was the whole point. That was why she'd devised all those delaying tactics. 'It was Hannah who was set on Tombstone; she pooh-poohed all my alternative suggestions. So I thought, OK Corral, if you must; but I'm going to make damn sure we don't get there in a hurry.'

From time to time after that, Jocelyn's game was brought out, though I usually had something better to do with my time. (Daydreaming about boys; boning up on mascara and tank tops in the teen mags I was spending my pocket money on at that time.) When I refused to play, Jocelyn and Aunt Hope played by themselves. 'See if we care,' they'd say. 'Just see if we care.'

The game changed over the years. Some of the moves, and the movie and song references changed. Updated or downgraded. Lone Rangers and Midnight Cowboys came and went. Singing forfeits were introduced for players who couldn't pay their dues. A player who ran out of bucks might be made to sing 'Ghost Riders in the Sky' or 'I Was Born Under a Wanderin' Star' or 'Mule Train' or 'Empty Saddles on the Old Corral'. Or 'Ragtime Cowboy Joe':

'Out in Arizona where the bad men are,
Th'only thing to guide you is an evenin' star.
Roughest, toughest man by far
Is Ragtime Cowboy Joe . . .

'How they run
When they hear the feller's gun
Because the Western folks all know
He's a high-falutin', skootin', shootin'
Son of a gun from Arizona –
Ragtime Cowboy Joe!'

It helped if you were drunk, I decided, to sing those songs. You probably wouldn't have attempted them unless you were paralytic.

Over the years, the game got sillier, or so it sounded to me, tucked up with my mag in my armchair. It struck me that the jokes got more suggestive. Dirtier.

'Is that a Winchester rifle in your pocket? Or are you pleased to see me?' I heard Jocelyn ask Aunt Hope.

The magazines I was spending my pocket money on: their cosmetic content, I see now, was just that, a cover for the sex they were also peddling, which was the main reason I bought them. There were in-depth exclusives on film stars and pop stars and sports stars; there were hunky, chunky boys showing off knitwear and underwear – and biceps and pectorals – on every page.

'I really go for him.' Jocelyn leaned over my chair. 'Take a look at those shoulders!' Like me, she had a thing about shoulders. She snatched the mag out of my hands and carried it off. She spread it out on the table, under the lamp, to get a sharper view of all those high-voltage power packs. Wow!

'What's this?' Aunt Hope, passing through, pausing to look, rested a hand on Jocelyn's shoulder. 'Oh, that.' Speeding away.

A normal reaction, exactly what you'd expect from a middle-aged retired schoolteacher and widow. Quick exits or opt-out clauses, an easy and airy dismissiveness – these reactions of hers to anything remotely sexual were in keeping. I found them reassuring.

It was only when she was the worse for wear that she played along with Jocelyn.

One evening, late, when I'd been dozing in my chair and the fire had gone grey, and I was trying to make myself get up and climb the freezing stairs; and, at the table, Aunt Hope, specs folded on her abandoned book, eyelids at half-mast, was nursing her empty glass; and, at her feet, Jemma was twitching and shuddering; and, at the other end of the table, Jocelyn was humming and leafing through my current mag, I heard a soft exclamation. 'Cor!' it might have been. Or 'Coo-er!'

I knew at once what Jocelyn had discovered – four pages of photographs of swimmers and divers. 'Olympic hopefuls make a splash,' the headline read, and underneath, 'British boys go for gold'. According to the caption, two of them were only fifteen.

I can see those photos now – boys on the diving board, poised for takeoff; boys in mid-flight; boys, arms round each other's monumental shoulders, legs in the water, a row of white grins at the edge of a pool. Boys in profile, parading in military file. Massive necks and shoulders and chests; slim hips, tiny, disturbing, overloaded swimming briefs.

I'd spent an hour after tea on my bed with these boys, admiring and comparing. No detail of their individual anatomies, no pearly, decorative, drop of water, had escaped my examiner's eye.

'Choose one.' Jocelyn, walking round, slid the spread pages under my aunt's nose.

'What d'you mean?'

'Pick one to take home.'

'What for? Do I want one?'

'Yes, of course you do. But you can't have that one, he's mine.'

Aunt Hope sighed and unfolded her specs.

'Hurry up, you can't take all night. You're only allowed one.'

Aunt Hope hummed and ha-ed. She said, 'Well, they're all big, handsome boys, aren't they? They're all – '

'Get on with it!'

' – well-endowed . . .'

'Choose!'

'That one, then. I'm having that one. Now there's a young man who by the looks of it would be excused shorts in the navy. Ber was, you know. They told him to drop his trousers, they took one look, they got our their tape measures to check . . . "Excused shorts!" They wrote it down in some kind of log. "Ordinary Seaman B. W. J. Eastman – Excused shorts." '

'Boasting,' Jocelyn said. 'Wishful thinking.'

'Ber told me that story when we were engaged. D'you know, I didn't know what he meant. I hadn't any idea what he was talking about. Isn't that a joke?'

But she sounded bitter rather than amused, and she pushed herself up from the table and started to pace about the room, stagger about in the way I feared.

'Hope,' Jocelyn began.

'You know what?' My aunt stopped pacing and thumped the table so that the glasses trembled. 'You know what?' She thumped it again. 'That husband of mine was sick. I'm not talking about heart disease. Oh no, no, no. I'm talking about penile dementia.'

At this point I got up from my chair and made straight for the door.

'Leaving us so soon?' Her mouth looked wrong; it was the wrong shape, dragged down at one corner, twisted in the movie-villain way it always was when she'd had too much to drink.

'It's nearly midnight.' I brushed her hand off my arm.

'You're the one who's sick. And don't you dare talk like that about Uncle Ber. You hated him anyway. You think I don't know. Well, I may be a moron, but at least I know that. I couldn't fail to know that.'

It was the first time I'd done such a thing, spoken out to my aunt, and I lay in bed and shivered. Excitement, fear, exhilaration, the icy sheets, all these contributed to my shakes.

Knock, knock. Who's there? Jocelyn.

She came into my room and sat on the end of the bed. She was quite sober, suddenly. 'I'm sorry about that, Hannah. I thought you'd gone to bed. I had no idea you were there. I thought you'd gone to bed hours ago.'

I said nothing. I'd already decided they were going to get nothing more out of me, certainly not apologies. It was Aunt Hope's job to apologise.

'Mind if I switch that light off?'

I turned my face away from her, to the wall. She switched off my bedside light.

'Extraordinary strong smell of soot in here. Does your room always smell of soot? We must do something about it.'

You can't win me over that way, I thought.

'Look, Hannah, I know you loved your uncle Ber. And I know he was a good father to you, and I'm very glad about that, of course. But. But marriages can be more complex than they seem, you know. Than they seem to an observer. To a child – as you then were.'

Silence.

'Look, I think you're old enough to be told a few things. I mean facts. I think that if you knew them, you might understand your aunt better, be more sympathetic. You're not very nice to her, are you?'

Silence.

'I need a cigarette for this. D'you mind if I smoke in your room? I won't if you object.'

Silence.

'OK then, I'll just go and get myself an ashtray.'

When she returned, she said, 'What I'm going to tell is between you and me. You're never to mention it to your aunt. She mustn't know I've told you. You're going to have to promise this before I leave your room.'

I didn't reply to this threat, and she told me anyway.

My Uncle Ber was a philanderer. A womaniser. A stud, if I preferred that word. He was never faithful to my Aunt Hope, not even at the beginning. It wasn't just a question of a girl in every port. No, there were girls, women, at home. On his own doorstep. In Green Copse Road. Until he got ill, there were –

(In Green Copse Road? No, that couldn't be true. What attractive women had I ever seen in Green Copse Road?)

Of course some husbands were chronically unfaithful, as were some wives. But faithless, promiscuous, however you liked to describe it, didn't necessarily equal cruel. Uncle Ber had been cruel.

While Jocelyn told me these facts and truths, I concentrated on the red light of her cigarette, flaring and fading, breathing, it seemed to me, in the dark. I will not listen, I told myself, I will shut my ears and concentrate on that breathing red light.

There was something else I should know, Jocelyn said. Had I ever wondered why my aunt had never had children? Well, she had wanted a child. She could have had a child, she was perfectly healthy, there was no reason at all why not, but my uncle Ber wouldn't let her. He didn't want children.

Of course people could always get out of bad marriages; it was probably the best thing to do in those circumstances – split up, get the hell out of it.

But Aunt Hope hadn't been able to do that. First there was the accident, when my brother was killed, and then there was my mother . . . and then – but it might have been before the accident, she couldn't remember the exact order of events, it was all so long ago – my uncle developed heart disease. So then there was no choice. My aunt had to stay.

She had to make a home for me, for one thing.

'There's one good part in this bad story, Hannah. Your Uncle Ber loved you. Against all the odds he did. I think you changed his mind about children. You brought out the best in him, I noticed that. So that's good. That's something good and positive you can think about.'

That expression of Aunt Hope's, 'penile dementia'. When I ran away from Arizona and went to live and work in London, it was my party piece for a while. I used to bring it out at parties and pretend it was an original bon mot, something I'd just thought up. 'See that guy over there? That tall dark guy?' (Or that short fair one.) 'You want to watch out – he's got penile dementia!' Shortening it to PD, as I sometimes did, the 'P' often misheard, in a crowded room, as a 'V', caused tight lips and consternation in some company.

But in the crackpot company I was keeping then, laughter was the reward I mostly got, from those who weren't too out of it, on crack and pot and speed and coke and bombers, to laugh.

Later, PD was connected in my mind with bad sex, my own experiences of it. By bad, I mean injurious or humiliating, the posturing bang-marathon some men go in for and believe women enjoy; the perfunctory, unfriendly lust I associate with middle-aged, married types.

I never saw it as having anything to do with Uncle Ber.

'Excused shorts', on the other hand, that other phrase of Aunt Hope's, can make me laugh out loud. And I do connect it with my uncle. I think of it when I look at his portrait on my bedroom wall. (This is the portrait a friend of his painted, which hung in the hall in Green Copse Road, and, at Arizona, in the kitchen passageway.)

In this portrait, he's wearing the uniform of a lieutenant commander, Finch says it is, and sits half sideways, gazing into the distance, scanning the horizon probably. At his right elbow, on a table, are the instruments you associate with the Senior Service, a compass and a sextant and a telescope; and his left knee is partly obscured by a globe on a mahogany stand. I look at my dignified Uncle Ber and his serious instruments of navigation, and I think of his other instrument, not on display here. Was it as impressive as Aunt Hope believed?

'Why Arizona? Why would you want to go there?'

Finch had found the maps and plans for my trip open on the table. I'd meant to put them away.

'I should have thought it was obvious why I might want to. Could you get out of my light, please?'

His bulk gets in the way of everything, light included. Lamplight, windowlight, starlight, moonlight, the light at the end of the tunnel. It comes between me and any hope of freedom.

'Arizona's hot. Too hot for a paleskin. For your pale skin. I should've thought.' He picked up a leaflet. ' "The Haunted Wilderness," ' he read. ' "Extending from Oak Creek Canyon in the west to Sycamore Canyon in the east, taking in the Coconino National Forest on its way south to the Verde Valley, the rugged wastes of the Haunted Wilderness exert their paranormal power even today. This is the land of murders and mysteries, of lost legends and . . ." Ooooooh aaaaah.' He flapped his arms. 'I'm exerting my paranormal power over you. Oooooooh.'

'Fuck off, Finch.'

'You know what Arizona is, don't you? A giant theme park. Dust park. Trailer park. Outsize picnic area. Just like those other tourist paradises – New Mexico, Colorado, Texas . . .'

'Leave.'

'They're all hard-line right-wingers, you realise, those middle-aged new frontiersmen in ten-gallons and belt buckles who drive their Ford Bronco pick-ups to the out-of-town superstore. If that's what you –'

'I said leave.'

'Washington State might be a better bet for you, it's more New-Agey. Or Montana. The Glacier National Park really is wild, there really is a chance of being eaten by grizzlies in the Gla–'

'Get out of this room.'

'Don't shoot. For Gawd's sakes, don't shoot.' He raised his hands above his head and backed to the door. At the door, he said, 'Why not Idaho? What's wrong with Idaho?'

Finch has never been to Arizona or any of the American states he mentioned. Apart from a school coach trip to Normandy, he has never left this island.

He went to Wales once; Diarmid rented a cottage in the hills outside Llandovery, Dyfed, one wet summer, and we all went. For a fortnight in the rain. Like me, he has not been to Scotland. Like me, he has not been to Ireland, although Diarmid was always promising we'd go – to Donegal, where he was born and brought up.

I know more about Arizona than Finch does. I'm interested, Arizona goes back more than twenty years in my life, I know more.

I have to tell myself I do because Finch has the ability to pick up information as a Hoover picks up fluff. He picks it up – or sucks it in – holds it in his headbag, and then, when the time is ripe, in optimum conditions, he spits it out. He doesn't have to be interested in whatever it is. It's wise to keep any passions you may have to yourself. I remember when he was at the primary school, he brought a boy home for tea once. This boy, an endearing little chap with knobby knees and a wholehearted smile, had a thing about vintage motorbikes. At tea he told me about the motorbike rallies his dad had taken him to, and the models, Airfix kits and so on, he'd made. Finch bided his time, clearing the plates of sandwiches, before wading in. Before quizzing this child and disconcerting him. Humiliating him. There was apparently nothing my son did not know about vintage motorbikes. He had the whole history, the engineering facts and figures, the successes and disasters, at his podgy fingertips.

It's the destructive use he puts his catch-all, remember-all mind to that gets me down: the negative take he has on everything. Nobody wants to be reminded, as they're setting off into rush-hour traffic, that the world is fundamentally unstable and unpredictable, that harmony is a myth. You don't need to be told, when you're checking the locks at bedtime, that there are all these viruses and diseases working overtime to get you. (Anthrax, malaria, TB, the Ebola virus, which liquefies human tissue and causes you to haemorrhage – from the arms? I'm sure he mentioned arms.) I had a sore throat not long ago. Finch filled the bathroom doorway, watching me gargle. (Go away, Finch, go away.) He waited while I spat out the gargle, rinsed the basin and turned off the taps. He drummed his fingers on the wall to get my attention. Was I aware, he finally asked, there was a new, virulent strain of antibiotic-resistant streptococcus going the rounds?

After that ding-dong Finch and I had about my trip to Arizona, he unhooked his anorak and went out. When he came back he said, 'By the way, I'm thinking of moving in with Diarmid and his friend for a while. The atmosphere there is more conducive to revision.'

'That's fine by me,' I said. 'And you won't have to divorce me either, seeing as you're nearly sixteen. You can live any-where you like at sixteen. Some people get married at sixteen.'

Finch stared at me. I think he was surprised by my response. I think he'd been expecting a drama of some sort.

'No, really, Finch, it's fine. It makes sense. Diarmid'll be able to give you all the support you need for your exams. So it's fine. And you don't have to worry about him being out of pocket because you can pay him. You've got money of your own, remember, so you can pay him rent. That would be the right and proper thing to do.'

'You never wanted me anyway,' Finch said.

Finch has got the money to pay Diarmid because Aunt Hope left Arizona to both of us – him and me, half and half. Mischievous, I considered her decision at the time.

Arizona took a long time to sell, and sold badly, on two counts. It was in very bad nick, the agents said; and the house market had collapsed by then.

Finch's half is deposited in a high-interest building-society account. 'High' is a relative term, the interest rate being low at present; nevertheless, Finch has money he could spend if he chose. Unlike most boys his age.

My half is bespoke. A monthly standing order spirits it away to the Grange (private psychiatric) Nursing Home, where my mother now is.

When I picture my mother, and when I dream about her, she's always at the Rose Vale, although the Rose Vale Psychiatric Hospital doesn't exist any more. Not long after Aunt Hope died, they closed it down. Not long after that, they razed it to the ground and sold it off. Not long after that, twenty-four holiday-home, chalet-style bungalows sprang up in its place. 'Five minutes' walk to the sea', the advert said. No mention of the seven-league boots you'd have to buy. In dreams I still walk along its corridors or sit on a hard orange chair, trying to count twelve sunflowers in a vase.

Now that Aunt Hope can't go, I go to see my mother sometimes at 'The Grange' – in inverted commas on the noticeboard. She sits in a chair by a window, her head canted over to one side, half hidden in a cushion. She shows no recognition when I enter, nor at any time during my visit. Her left hand rests by her side; her right hand plucks at the cellular wool blanket tucked loosely round her – or pushes fiercely down at something inside the blanket, push, push,

push. 'Don't, darling,' I tell her, 'you'll make yourself sore,' but she takes no notice. (Perhaps she can't hear me; I have considered that.) I get down on my knees beside her and try to stop that punishing hand, but there's surprising strength and determination in its frail bones. It has a mission and won't be stopped. In an effort to distract her, I take her other hand and hold it, and stroke its swollen joints. She may submit to this – or she may withdraw her hand at once. It depends. Some days she has a lost, unfocused look. Other days she stares into my face for minutes at a time with a dismaying intensity. 'That's a very smart cardy,' I'll say, hearty and terrified, 'that yellow really suits you – is it new?'

Finch says I never wanted him, but that's not true. I did want him before he was born. I wanted him badly, and I wanted him to be a boy.

At the time I discovered I was pregnant I hadn't been near Arizona for almost three years, and was under pressure from Jocelyn to go. 'Make it SOON,' she wrote, caps underlined, 'Hope's desperate to see you – but she won't tell you that. She only wants you to come if you want to come. Well I say bugger to that! You get your butt on that train whether you want to or not!!' (Subtle pleas had given way to head-on jokey directives, expressed in a language that was not Jocelyn's own. It was my language she was striving for, I imagine.)

I didn't answer that letter, nor the one that followed, which told me that the last of the elms had been felled. 'Hope's sad about that, but they had to go. And don't tell her I said so, but it's a lot less depressing without them. Anything's better than having to look at a row of skeletons. Anyway, we've got wood for a hundred years now!!'

Reading Jocelyn's letters, I got a picture of their lives together that was cosier and more companionable than the one I remembered. They sounded like a retired married couple, and I saw them walking arm in arm, like the muffled-up old folks we used to see on the seafront, leaning into the steady onshore wind. 'We've planted a cedar of Lebanon –

don't laugh!' 'We're both on the wagon at the moment, have been for a fortnight. Hope says she feels better – fitter and more energetic. I, on the other hand, feel worse.' 'Went to the flea-pit on Saturday and saw *Kramer vs Kramer* – I know you'll have seen it. What did you think? Are you still enamoured of D.H.?!'

Inspecting those dark-blue envelopes addressed in Jocelyn's extravagant hand, examining the postmark as though it might contain a coded message, I felt disappointed. I thought, Why doesn't Aunt Hope write? It ought to be her writing. If she really wants to make up. If she really wants to see me.

But in the end, after more letters and phone calls from Jocelyn, I did agree to go. For the Whitsun weekend, which meant three whole days, Saturday, Sunday and the bank holiday Monday.

I was nearly three months pregnant when I made that visit. I'd given up dope and even straight cigarettes because just the smell of them made me sick. I'd had to move the waist buttons of the two skirts I owned, and recently I'd decided I'd be more comfortable wearing a size up in jeans; but my condition didn't show, I thought. In those days my career in retail ironmongery and hardware hadn't yet begun. I was working for a wholesale stationer's, filing and invoicing, packing and unpacking boxes of school exercise books and files and file paper. There were two others of my age in that warehouse, a girl called Mary and a boy, Russell, who drove the forklift.

Between trips up and down the aisles, when he was unloading stuff onto the packing bench, Russell plagued Mary and me with jokes, the question-and-answer variety that have to do with lightbulbs or custard or how many elephants can fit in a Mini. It was he who laughed at the answers (which we allowed him to supply), even though he had nothing to laugh about, you'd think – he had painful and disfiguring boils on his face. When Russell first joined Mary and me in that cold yet stuffy warehouse, I was so embarrassed by the boils that I avoided looking at him. After a while I thought this policy might be a mistake, that he might consider it unkind, and so from time to time I made a point of staring at him straight in the face. There was invariably one of these awful volcanoes erupting or about to erupt on his nose – on a nostril, the most painful place to have any kind of spot – and within seconds I'd find my eyes watering and have to look away.

Mary and Russell appeared not to notice any change in my appearance. I was having to bolt up the stairs to the staff toilets on the first floor (it was the smell of the glue we used that made me throw up, that and the sea-grass matting that covered the concrete floor of the office area), but no questions were asked about my abrupt exits. No jokes were made about them by Russell, not in my hearing.

It was May when I went down to Arizona, and the apple blossom was out. Under the apple trees the cow parsley was frothy as waves, and just visible among it were bluebells (not all blue, there were white ones and some pink) and late, wild tulips, yellow and purple, and a few hybrid aquilegias, mauve and yellow, pink and white. I remembered Aunt Hope plant-ing the aquilegias, which I think are also called columbine. I had a picture in my head of her pricking out the seed trays in the greenhouse while I hovered beside her with a watering can.

Jemma was buried there somewhere; Jocelyn had written to tell me. Beneath the cow parsley and bluebells, three feet deep in the black earth and mouldering leaves lay what was left of Jemma, wrapped in her smelly plaid blanket.

I was led round the garden by my aunt and her friend.

In the vegetable patch thin red stalks were pushing out of chimneypots and dustbins; curled green fists were opening into limp, poisonous umbrellas.

'Can you take some back to London with you? We've got far more than we can eat. Or sell. You get practically nothing for rhubarb these days. No one can be bothered to cook it.'

'We didn't do too well with the globe artichokes last year, I don't think we fed them enough. I didn't dare use offsets from those woody plants. We've had to start again from scratch.'

'We've put in some Dura onions here. The blood reds are nicer, of course, Jocelyn will tell you the Dura are inedible, but too bad – they're better keepers by far. As you'd expect.'

They took it in turns to tell me these things. Like polite, formal children wanting approval, they waited their turn to tell me their achievements.

'As you see, I've earthed up the potatoes. Not such a good job as you used to make of it.'

It had been my job to earth up the potatoes. Making sure that the ridges were even, patting the sides smooth with my spade, was a task I'd enjoyed. I'd liked the ridges to look just so.

We continued our slow perambulation. A new hen run, twice the size of the old one, had to be inspected, and new hens. In among the familiar Leghorns were Black Orpingtons and Rhode Island Reds, and some speckled hens – Sussex, I think they were – which Aunt Hope said were disappointing layers. I looked for the three Marsh Daisies, Daisy One, Daisy Two, Daisy Three, which had been my favourites, but the fox had had all three. 'We daren't let them out of the run now. The bugger lies in wait. On one raid he killed two pullets inside the courtyard. In front of my nose.'

'He's very beautiful.' I meant the Rhode Island Red cockerel, picking and pecking fastidiously over the grass, his jerky movements those of a wooden Russian toy. But Jocelyn said he was a bastard, a little martinet, he gave the hens hell, he was almost as much of a menace as the fox. She said *coq au vin* would be on the menu if he didn't mend his ways. I knew she meant it. We didn't eat the chickens, which all had names, as a rule, it was the eggs we kept them for, but from time to time there had to be a mercy killing. Sick hens, injured hens, geriatric hens and vicious cockerels were candidates. Killing them was Jocelyn's job; Aunt Hope was incapable. When the Angel of Death pulled on her boots and rubber gloves and strode out to the hen run with no-nonsense, purposeful strides, Aunt Hope ran up to her room and shut the door.

'I hope you weren't planning to sleep in your carriage tonight, Hannah? As you see, the hens have rather taken it over.'

I had seen, and I was relieved. In the train coming down I'd thought, I'll be sleeping in my train tonight. Then I'd remembered the darkness of Arizona nights, and the owls. The total silence when there were no owls. I was used to streetlight nights by now, the orange glow no curtain can ever entirely stifle; I'd become accustomed to shouts and sudden laughter at all hours and door-slamming; and furious car engines revving and roaring.

We went on with our tour in the spring sunshine, and as we did I began to feel uneasy about the secret I was carrying. For I saw that this garden walk, organised to take place at once, before I'd even set foot indoors, was their way of forgiving me and welcoming me back into my old life, and back into their lives. Walking round a garden under a blue sky, with birds singing and buds breaking, what more healing way back, they must have thought, could there be?

Lunch was prodigal, and fit for a prodigal: nettle soup made by Jocelyn; Aunt Hope's famous fish cakes with roast parsnips and purple sprouting; apple snow. A bottle of wine was produced. They were on the wagon at the moment, Aunt Hope explained, but they thought they'd break out today. Just for today.

The kitchen was as I'd last seen it, except cleaner and tidier. That was the effect being on the wagon had always had with them: a sudden elbow-grease of spring cleaning, whatever the season; rugs on the line thumped by a besom; the air in every room smelling of self-righteousness and spray-on lavender.

Also unchanged in that kitchen: the slow, slow-ticking schoolroom clock and a preserving pan of hen food, simmering and steaming, the windows steamed over as a result, running with condensation.

'We thought we might go to the traction-engine fair at Burdon End tomorrow, if that would amuse you,' Jocelyn said, ladling a second helping of sieved nettles into my bowl.

'Read any good books lately?' Aunt Hope asked me sweetly, as I lifted my spoon.

That was the good part of my visit, painful to remember now, because after it things went bad and wrong.

Between Jocelyn's soup and Aunt Hope's fish cakes, while Jocelyn was stacking the bowls and my aunt was dishing out the purple sprouting, fussily ensuring we had three prongs each, the stink of that hen food hit my hormonally affected gut.

'Is there anything you'd like to talk to me about, Hannah?'

It was after lunch, the lunch I'd been unable to eat – except for the soup, which had stayed down for five minutes. Jocelyn, at a signal from Aunt Hope, had left the kitchen.

I said no. No, there was nothing. Why?

'You've put on a bit of weight, you know. You've got a bit of a tummy on you. And then you were sick, without – '

I opened my mouth to lie. Not lie, exactly; I was going to tell her I'd put on weight because of all the doughnuts I was eating. There was a bakery across the road from the warehouse, and Russell would dash out in our coffee breaks and come back with a hot paper bag containing four dough-nuts oozing with jam or cream – one each for Mary and me, two for him. But suddenly I thought, No, she's on my side, they both are, I'll tell her the truth. She's guessed it anyway. So I told her I was expecting a baby. ('I'm expecting a baby,' I said, not 'I'm pregnant'; I thought she'd be more likely to respond sympathetically to the humanity of that, to the sense of responsibility those words implied.)

Aunt Hope asked two questions: Who was the father, and how far gone was I?

I couldn't satisfy her on either count. Presumably, if I'd known the answer to the first, I'd have had a good idea about the second.

Well then, if it wasn't already too late, I'd have to get rid of it, my aunt said. She'd pay for the abortion, of course. If I could find the name of a good private clinic, she'd pay for everything. While anti-abortion as a general principle, she was for it in specific circumstances. Young, single women with no qualifications and no earning power, no prospect of support – those circumstances.

Financial support, emotional support, she meant both. Ideally you needed both of those to bring a baby into the world.

Having a child without that support would ruin my life, Aunt Hope said. What chance would I have of finding a husband with a baby in tow? How could I earn money to live if I was tied to a baby?

Had I thought about this at all?

Had I any idea what real poverty was like?

Had I considered how it might be for the baby?

'I want someone of my own to love,' I said. 'I want a baby of my own to love.'

'Give me strength,' Aunt Hope said, and she shook her head. 'Give – me – strength.'

Jocelyn drove me to the station. I'd demanded to leave now, at once. And no one had to take me to the train, I'd walk. But it was twenty-two miles, and when Jocelyn got the car out I didn't argue.

'Hope was thinking of you, Hannah. You must understand that. It's your future, your happiness she's concerned about, Truly.'

I didn't answer. Neither of us spoke for the rest of the journey.

There was no train in the station, no London train for an hour, and when one did come it was a stopping train.

The midwife who helped me unpack said, 'Did you remember to bring a ring with you, dear? If so, I suggest you wear it. The older mothers can be a bit, well, sharp sometimes with the unmarrieds.'

(We were in the labour ward then. I'd be moved to the delivery room for the birth, it was explained, then to the maternity ward. After my baby was born. With my baby.)

I shook my head. The contractions were by now so strong and regular, the pain each time so extraordinary, I feared the baby was about to come out while I was standing up, in my clothes.

The midwife was in no hurry. She sat me on a chair and asked me questions, writing the answers down on a green form. She used to top of the locker to lean on.

Not knowing who else to say, I gave Aunt Hope as next of kin.

Each time a contraction started, I gripped the chair with both hands and pushed myself up off the seat. There was a flimsy door between my legs and the baby was hammering on it. Kicking it down.

'Right, that's fine. Now we'll have a little listen to baby. We'll have a look-see what that baby of yours is up to.'

The metal rim of the listening instrument was icy and pleasurable on my burning skin. 'Good strong heartbeat. Excellent.' She laid her head against my stomach and listened again. 'Hey, you in there – are you Joe or Josephine? Well, we won't have to wait too long for the answer!'

I told her it was Finch. It was Finch in there.

'Finch! You're not serious!' She put her head out of the curtains. 'Nurse!'

A nurse pushed in through the curtains.

'This baby's a Finch. A goldfinch, maybe. That's what they're going to call him. Have you ever heard the like of that?'

They laughed together for a while. 'Do you remember when we were on G Ward, there was a baby they called, what was it, Pericles? "How would you be spelling it?" I said. The mother wrote it down for me, and I thought, you might as well call the poor wee chap Testicles. It's a shame, really, when you think of it, what some parents will do to their children.'

'But wait a mo – who's so certain he is a boy? She hasn't had an ultra sound has she, Sister?' The nurse wore a green uniform, the midwife's was blue. She stood with her arms folded, looking down at me. 'I'll bet you anything you like you've got a dear little girl in there. And what'll you call her if it is?'

'It's a boy.' (But I was beginning to feel unsure and unreal. I, the pink curtains, the nurses, the baby – everything except the pain was unreal. The nurses' faces were too big and too close, their teeth were too big. Their voices were too loud, or too soft, I couldn't tell which.)

'It's a big baby, whatever,' the midwife, who was also a sister, said. 'Nurse here will make you comfortable. Later on we'll give you something to help with the pain. You'll be fine. You're a healthy young girl. You've nothing to worry about. It's all going to be fine.'

Nurse making me comfortable. This involved a razor and a bowl of soapy water, it included an enema and an enema dish. When she left me, the nurse said, 'Baby's head's engaged, it's well down there. Chances are your waters'll break soon. Things'll speed up when they do.'

Break, break, break. On thy cold grey stones, O Sea! I saw Aunt Hope sitting on the stones on the Little Beach, hugging her knees, her woolly hair blowing all round her head. *And I would that my tongue could utter The thoughts that arise in me.*

I concentrated on that poem for a while. I repeated the first line over and over. I thought if I said it often enough, and if I could really think my way back onto that beach, so that I could see the waves rushing in and breaking, my waters would have to break. They would have to.

But when they did it was fifteen hours later, and I was in the delivery room, and the baby about to be born.

They laid him on my chest before the cord was cut. I did not recognise him. He was not my baby. It was not just the colour that was wrong. I only needed one look to know he wasn't mine.

I remember, hours or minutes later, a woozy certainty imprinting itself: they'll bring me the right baby soon. They'll bring me my beautiful black Finch.

'You've got to keep persevering, dear,' the nurse said, pushing my nipple into the foreign baby's mouth. 'He'll get the hang of it soon. Cuddle him close.'

The foreigner turned his face away. He filled his lungs and emptied them repeatedly in convulsive rage. This was the third time he and I had been forced into this intimacy, and with the same result.

'I don't want to breast-feed,' I said, after fiasco number four.

'What's all this nonsense? You'll feel a lot more comfortable when baby's taken some milk off you. Your boobies are like rocks, dear.'

When I said no, Sister was summoned.

'Breast milk's best for baby. It's the natural thing. It's easy to digest. It contains antibodies that help protect baby. You want the best for him, don't you?'

Changeling – the word that came to me while Sister was reciting her spiel. I shut my eyes and pulled the sheet over my head.

'She's gone, doctor.' I'm sure she said it.

Of course they couldn't let baby starve. They made up a bottle of cow's milk and boiling water, and cooled it to blood temperature. A nurse sat beside me with the changeling in the crook of her arm and showed me how bottle-feeding was done.

At the first pressure, the weeny mouth opened, then fastened, on the teat. All two and a half ounces vanished, hardly a pause for breath or wind. 'Who's a clever boy then?' Nurse was over the moon.

They gave me pills to stop my own, rejected milk.

The night nurse who brought them was tight-lipped as she handed me the cup and watched me swallow.

From a long way away I watched the maternity-ward movie unroll. The mothers in this movie were a lot older than I – in their thirties, I thought; one at least had to be over forty. The babies asleep in the cots beside their beds were their second, or third or fourth efforts.

These mothers wore pink, hand-knitted bedjackets. They had husbands and mortgages and school-age children, and a lot to say to each other.

The conversations they had, side to side or diagonally across the ward, which missed me out entirely (unsurprisingly, for I was outside, and invisible to them), were carried on from their beds, where they sat, propped against the pillows, knitting, or feeding their babies. They wandered the ward on their way back from the bathroom, stopping to perch on the ends of each other's beds, or to peer into each other's cots or at each other's greetings cards. They wore quilted or candlewick dressing gowns; on their feet, fluffy slippers without backs, which I later decided were mules.

What did they talk about? Their husbands' eating habits, or their children's, was one topic.

'Malcolm won't touch fish,' one of them said.

'Have you tried disguising it with mayonnaise and ketchup and curry powder?' another suggested. 'Here's what you do – as Jimmy Young says on his prog. First, you chop two onions . . .'

The mother in her forties said she remembered the days when Jimmy Young had been a singer, and sung a hit song called 'The Man from Laramie'.

The nurses addressed me as Hannah, but the other mothers were addressed by their married names – Mrs Jones, Mrs Johnson, Mrs Barford, Mrs Webbly. The nurses couldn't teach them anything – how to bring up baby's wind, how to bath or change baby – because they knew it all already. They were old hands, as they were fond of saying. 'Don't worry, nurse, I'm an old hand at nappies!' 'I've seen worse sights than this, nurse, believe you me!' When her baby cried, Mrs Johnson, in the bed opposite, would put down her knitting (or slip it into a knitting bag), lift the baby from the cot, tuck in it beside her and unbutton her nightdress – all in one casual and practised movement. While the baby was feeding, she'd flip through a magazine, or check out her knitting pattern, and continue her conversation: 'But as I say, you have to shop around. For my money, Keymarkets' tasty cheddar is tastier and better value than Tesco's.'

One of the mothers, Shona, Mrs Barford, I think, who had very fair hair, kinked up at the ends in a fashion you didn't see too often but familiar to me from Green Copse Road days, always drew her curtains round when she fed her baby. She said it was important to have peace and quiet at this very special time.

My feelings of unreality grew by the hour. The smug milky aura surrounding the mothers, that normally would have disgusted me; remarks they made that my real self would have despised – which at the very least would have triggered a superior if secret smile – I witnessed with this same indifference. When the nurses brought me the baby to feed they insisted was mine, I held him out from my body, balancing him on the very edge of my knees. Then, as soon as the teat had found its target, I looked away, straight ahead, anywhere, to avoid sight of that urgent mouth, those grotesque dilating nostrils.

Aunt Hope and Jocelyn came to fetch me from the hospital. I wasn't expecting them. Visiting was fathers only, I'd said. This was true, except in the cases where there was no father. In those cases, a mother or a sister – or an aunt – was permitted to visit; but I had not relayed this information to Aunt Hope.

Jocelyn and Aunt Hope and Sister and I stood in the corridor outside Sister's office. The carrycot, with the changeling inside, rested on two chairs.

'She's still in shock,' Sister said to Aunt Hope. 'Her body hasn't come to terms yet with such an upheaval. She's an immature girl, isn't she, emotionally? She's going to need a lot of encouragement in the caring for that baby. She had a rough time, mind you – nine and half pounds is very big, not the ideal size for a first one, as I mentioned on the phone. She'll be needing a saline bath daily on account of those stitches – but your district nurse'll see to that. In the meantime, she's to take two of these tablets three times a day. Oh, and the blue ones – one a day of those.'

'Goodbye and good luck to you, Hannah,' she said to me. 'Next time you have to come into hospital for any reason, get yourself a dressing gown, will you? I don't like to see my mothers slopping through the ward in their outdoor coats.'

'Goodbye, Finch,' she said to the carrycot. 'He's bonny, isn't he?' she said to Jocelyn.

I agreed to spend a month at Arizona, but the month turned

into two months, then three. Aunt Hope always found some good reason, each time I planned to leave, for my not leaving. When I eventually returned to London, Finch was two and half years old.

There were no drugs to speak of in Cheap Street Comprehensive during the time I spent in the place. No one offered me a purple heart or a more than usually interesting cigarette. In those days drugs in schools were seldom found outside the big cities, or boys' public schools. You saw headlines from time to time: 'Peer's son sacked. "I will not tolerate drugs in my school," headmaster says.' That sort of thing. (We smoked, of course, and we drank whatever we could get hold of: canned beer, bottled beer, rough cider, home-made brews of dandelion and chickweed.)

No drugs; but sex? That was different, that started early and was everywhere. This has always been so in country areas, I imagine. What else is there to do? In our school, thirteen or fourteen was the age most girls started out on their sexual careers, though at any one time there were usually a couple of precocious twelve-year-olds with big breasts and ditto reputations.

The boys were later starting, fifteen on average, as they were late in most things. Even so, there were exceptions. Darren Hickey, whose voice had broken while he was still at the primary school, was the Cheap Street Lothario well before his fourteenth birthday. He was not especially tall or good-looking, and he was slow in class, but what did that matter? He was a wag and a mimic; people laughed out loud at the one-liners he came out with. More critical were the green eyes with heavy, sexy lids (like Robert Mitchum's, I realise), a beard that had to be shaved every day, luxuriant leg hair and forearm hair – attributes visible to all. Other virtues only the privileged could vouch for: twin curls of chest hair, apparently, one on each nipple; a furry trail that ran down the middle of his flat, muscled stomach as far as, and disappearing into, his pubic hair; a truly monstrous dick.

Darren's sex appeal was beyond question, he was a 'star stud' as the expression went in our school, though I told myself, and let it be known, he was not my type. (It was something we did when the star studs failed to pick us out for their attentions. 'I can see he's attractive, yeah,' we'd say, 'but I don't fancy him. 'S nothing personal.')

Darren was rank as a fox, and not through misfortune or carelessness. According to him, deodorants were for perverts; what really turned females on was the raw smell of the male animal. His success seemed to confirm the truth of this; however, the hot stink of wool sweat that clouded the air each time he flourished his comb was too much for some.

I was fifteen when I first went with a boy; up till then I was the oldest virgin in my class by a mile. Lack of opportunity was the excuse I gave. There was no bus back to Arizona after the ten-past-four school bus. I couldn't very well ask my aunt to drive out and fetch me, could I?

It was Pat who changed my fortunes (and who would supply excuses and, indirectly, alibis and transport). She arrived at the school, in my class, halfway through the summer term.

Pat sought me out, not the other way round. At the time I was flattered; but I see now, she didn't have a lot of choice. By our age most girls could boast, if not a best friend, two or three allies, or maybe a gang, whereas I hovered on the edge of various groups and couplings, sometimes included, more often not. She spotted possibilities in me, I think. She saw I was ready and ripe for significant change. Given sufficient doses of flattery, I could be led.

Pat's appearance was exotic, and when she arrived she caused a stir. She was tall, the tallest in our class, and had black hair – truly black, not the very dark brown the unobservant call black – cut in a sharp fringe on her forehead, hanging straight and smooth at the sides to shoulder level. Her hair never had ragged ends; that was because her mother had been a hairdresser, and trimmed it once a week with hairdresser's scissors. I read or heard somewhere recently the phrase 'smooth as a blackbird's wing' – it may have been a raven's – as a description of hair, and immediately saw Pat.

Her face was broad and flat and oriental-looking, and her eyes were oriental too: wide-set almonds, slanting upwards. Her face was very white, her lips very red, so red that she was frequently ordered to 'go and wipe that lipstick off before you come into my class' even when she wasn't wearing any. She did wear make-up out of school. She kept a vanity bag in her shiny PVC school bag, and after lessons would retire to the cloakroom and apply eye shadow and mascara and lipstick. Before long she was applying them to me, standing me against the wall to get proper purchase, working colour into my cheeks and eyelids with the tips of her fingers, her mouth open in concentration. I found her nearness disturbing, as I did her hand on my shoulder holding me still, and her breath, sweetly scented with violet cachous. She sucked these in lessons to 'keep boredom at bay'. 'Throat sweets, doctor's orders,' she'd reply with a false smile when challenged.

The teachers did challenge Pat; they were unanimous in their mistrust of her. Whenever money or possessions went missing, she was the first suspect. The male staff fancied her and that made them aggressive. The female staff accused her of insolence. 'Bad attitude' is the expression talking heads always come up with in any discussion of schools and disruptive pupils. Pat's attitude was bad, but I don't remember anyone putting it that way.

Before Pat had been in the school a week, I'd learned a lot about her and her family. She was an only child. She and her mother lived in a caravan in the back garden of her auntie's bungalow in Wilsom Road, Long Clovell. They'd moved there only recently from a rented flat in Braintree, Essex. Money, a lack of it, had been the reason for the move (bailiffs were mentioned). Her mother had lost her hairdressing job through illness. Cancer. Her mother had had cancer of the stomach, and operations, and had lost her job.

'What about your dad?' I asked her.

Her dad? Well, that was an extraordinary story, that was really unbelievable and weird. Two years ago, her dad, a businessman, had set off for work one morning as usual – and not come home again. His clothes were still in the cupboard, he'd left his pyjamas under his pillow and his razor on the basin. When her mother phoned his office, they said he hadn't been there. No one knew where he could have got to. Since the day he left home they'd heard nothing – not one phone call or letter, nothing.

They'd lived in a big house before her dad's disappearance, Pat said. They'd had posh furniture and holidays abroad. A heated swimming pool in their huge back garden.

I felt bonded with Pat when I heard that story, it was so close to my own experience of how fathers carried on. The difference was, I had no memory of my father, and we did at least know what continent he'd vanished to because for a time envelopes with a Perth postmark had arrived, containing a money order – not a cheque, for a cheque would have shown his bank-account number – made out to Aunt Hope 'as a contribution to the upkeep of Janey and the child'. Pat's confidences made me want to confide in her. When I started at Cheap Street Comp I'd decided it wise to simplify the circumstances of my life, and had told the curious that my parents were dead, and that I lived with two aunts. But now, with friendship in my sights, I felt a need to confess facts and details, and so I told Pat about my brother's death, my father's abandonment, my mother's resulting mental illness, Uncle Ber, everything. I remember I jazzed the story up in places. Jocelyn had lovers in London only I knew about, I said. Aunt Hope made me sleep in a railway carriage all the year round, even when there was snow lying. Someone who lived in a caravan and disliked it, as Pat said she did, would be sympathetic to that, I reckoned.

Pat asked me just one question: 'Do you visit your mummy often in the home?'

When I hear her words in my head now, I hear the deviousness in 'mummy' (why not 'mum' or 'mother'?) and the slight, nasty hesitation before 'home'. The entire question was disingenuous; but I didn't spot it then.

All I remember is wishing I hadn't told Pat the truth about my mother, and the realisation I'd made a mistake. Because I wanted Pat to like me, any answer I gave needed to show me in a caring light; but the truth was, I hadn't been near the Rose Vale for two years, even though Aunt Hope went once a month and would have appreciated my company. The journey she had to make was as follows: car drive to the station, which she dreaded; two hours on a train, change at Southampton; taxi to the Rose Vale. Then, after an hour of hell, the whole business reversed. Aunt Hope always gave me advance warning of her visits, letting the information drop without emphasis into mealtime conversations. But I shut my ears to any mention of my mother. I did not want to be made to think about that awful place, the wet-knicker loonies who wandered the corridors, the smell. So when Aunt Hope mentioned her visiting plans, hoping I'd pipe up with an offer, I concentrated on my plate, or asked Jocelyn to pass the biscuits please.

'I'm not encouraged to visit my mother,' I told Pat. And it was true, Aunt Hope never did encourage me.

The exaggerations and half-truths I fed Pat were nothing to the downright whoppers she fed me (and everyone else). She was someone who *did not know what the truth was*. She was someone of whom it might be said *the truth was not in her*. A person who was *unable to differentiate between truth and fiction*. Perhaps that last sums it up best, because with her truth and fiction were plaited together so neatly and indissolubly you couldn't unravel them.

Pat's mother didn't have cancer; she never had had it. She hadn't even been ill. I learned that the first time I climbed the steps into her caravan (that part of the story was true). Pat wasn't an only child; photographs of her two married brothers, and their wives and their children, were Sellotaped to a partition door.

Pat's father had been foreman in an engineering works, which I thought not the same as a 'businessman'. The family had not been rich.

But there were true things in Pat's story. The first time she took me to the caravan, her mother walked round me and then lifted my hair and pulled strands out and examined them. 'Woolly, isn't it?' she said. 'And so dry. Could do with a good cut and reshaping. I'll have a go at it if you like.'

And, extraordinarily, the 'unbelievable' tale about her dad's disappearance was true. Her mother showed me cuttings from an Essex newspaper.

Did Pat mind being caught out in her lies? Apparently not. If you said anything, she'd shrug and smile and change the conversation. The new conversation would contain new lies, bigger and better and more convincing ones.

Pat was bound to betray me in the end. Girls and women like her – when I say like, I don't just mean liars; I mean liars who use other people for what they think they can get; who slag their 'friends' off behind their backs; who set out to steal other women's boyfriends or husbands just to see if they can; who swap allegiances as easily as grandmothers swap anecdotes of their grandchildren; who are dyed-in-the-wool cheats and turncoats – always do betray you.

When eventually Pat turned coat on me, she did it in style. She put it round the school that my mother was alive and raving mad in a lunatic asylum. (In a straitjacket, in a padded cell.) My father meanwhile was doing time for gross indecency, I think it was – it might have been rape. As for the 'aunts' I lived with, they weren't even related. They were two old alcoholic lesbians who, when they weren't completely arseholed . . . (the next bit would be whispered, while she kept her sly eyes on me).

But her betrayal was still in the future. In the present we were sharing then, I thought Pat wonderful, glamorous, exciting, mysterious, dazzling. Her lies didn't bother me once I'd got the unpredictable hang of them; they were part of her fascination, like the heavy perfume she sprayed on her neck and wrists, which rocked the cloakroom.

Of course Pat was an old hand at sex. She'd been on the pill for more than a year now, she told me, and to prove it showed me the packet, with its tinfoil enclosures of tiny press-out discs. The guys she went with were men, she said, men knew what they were about. You wouldn't catch her messing with infants. The men she'd discovered so far in Long Clovell weren't up to much, but the air-force guys up at the camp – had I seen them? Had I taken in that talent?

I had seen them occasionally. You couldn't avoid noticing them and knowing what they were because of the haircuts. Only army boys, air-force boys or convicts had short back and sides in the seventies.

They had monthly socials at the camp, Pat said. She could wangle me an invite. A blind date with a gangbang – was I on for that?

I told Aunt Hope I was going to a party with my friend Pat. I didn't know how late I'd be but I'd be given a lift home. Aunt Hope said eleven thirty at the latest. Jocelyn said, 'Well, well,' and raised her eyebrows at me in a knowing way.

We drank Coke at the social, which took place in the mess hut; nothing alcoholic was on offer. This was because the camp was a junior training camp, and the 'men' Pat had spoken of were no older than seventeen. She and I had spent hours in the caravan perfecting our appearance – her mother, more or less my height, had squeezed me into a black satin miniskirt and a magenta top with sequins round the neck –

but when we got there we found the other girls were wearing jeans.

Our hosts were polite and awkward. They introduced themselves – 'I'm Joe'; 'I'm Mick, pleased to meet you' – before offering us 'refreshment'. You had the impression they'd been instructed to say these things.

A disco had been set up in a back room. There was a whole lot of shaking going on; the whole joint was jumping, even the floorboards in the bar. Long Clovell didn't have a disco at that time, there was only Old Tyme dancing for the old folk at the Carnival Hall, the place where blood donors gave blood when the mobile units came round, but, though curious, I couldn't bear the noise and shook my head when they asked if I'd care to dance.

The one called Mick didn't want to dance either. Not to that rubbish – fifties and sixties pop, out of the Ark. The commanding bloody officer's choice, all they ever got. He offered me a smoke and lit it, but wouldn't have one himself. 'We're in trainin',' he shouted in my ear, 'and Sarge is watchin'.' Later he told me he could have a smoke if we went outside. He had a bottle of something worth drinking outside. 'Just say the word when you wan' a breather.'

The something worth drinking was cooking brandy. We took turns from the bottle, sitting on the cold ground with our back to one of the huts, out of the way of lights and sentries, as far from the thumping music as we could manage.

In between swigs Mick told me he hated the life he'd got himself into. He'd joined up because he wanted to be a pilot, but so far they hadn't been allowed near an aircraft. What they got was drill and kit inspection and cross-country runs and nothing but, every effing day. He might as well have signed up for the army, there was no difference.

I was happy sitting on the wet grass with Mick, listening to his complaints, having a smoke and drinking. I had this idea in my head that we were taking part in some black-and-white Second World War drama. We were star-crossed lovers in this movie, making our last, forbidden goodbyes before Mick went back to the front to be killed.

'Did you take the Michael then?' Pat asked the following day. (Jocelyn had had to drag me out of bed to the phone. I was ill, and had stayed in bed all morning.)

I said, 'What?' My head was breaking; I was dying. 'What d'you mean?'

She meant sex. Had I taken the Michael meant had I taken Mick. It was, like, a pun. Anyway, forget it. What she wanted to know was, Had I had him? Had I had sex with him?

I said I was ill, I'd phone her back later. I forgot they weren't on the phone in that caravan. Pat must have been in a call box when she phoned me.

I didn't want Pat to know about my failure. Mick hadn't laid a finger on me, not even attempted to. We'd been sitting there, talking, when suddenly he'd said, 'Think you've had enough of that,' and screwed the cap back on the brandy bottle. He told me to wait there. He was going to see if a mate of his, who had a car, could drive me home.

Nobody spoke on the journey. I'd felt very sick, and I remembered wondering where Pat was and how she was getting home; and feeling sad, and thinking, That's it, I've blown it.

They dropped me off outside the courtyard. But as the car reversed, Mick leaned his bullet head out of the window and called, 'Fancy a walk some time, then?'

When ten or so years later Diarmid asked me, 'Who was the first person you went to bed with?' I said Mick. He was a young airman called Mick. I don't remember his other name.

But of course I didn't go to bed with Mick – there were no beds to go to. We did it on a walk, in a patch of brambly grass just inside a copse, just outside the chain-link perimeter fence of the airfield. In order to get into the copse, which Mick said was an OK place for a picnic, we had to walk for a mile along a pocky, dung-spattered path. Just thinking about that walk, I'm back there, trailing behind Mick, the carrier bag with our tea things knocking painfully against my leg. The path is narrow and we have to walk in single file. It's a hot September afternoon, the sunshine red gold, the sky dark blue and cloudless. I'm wearing a summer dress, red with tiny blue daisies all over, and pretty shoes with soles so thin that I can feel every stone and ridge and bump. Close against us on the left is the rusted chain-link fence with a view of grass and runway and, in the far distance, following us like the moon, a bobbing yellow windsock. On our right is a loose hedge, and through it I can glimpse jigsaw pieces of field and bullock. Mick has cut himself a stick, and he's using it to poke any cowpats – bullock pats, they must be – he comes across. There aren't too many solid pats among the green explosions, but whenever Mick meets one he stops and levers the crust off. We take turns to stir the spinach-coloured purée underneath. Then we walk on again, escorted by squadrons of dung flies, Mick in the lead always, cheerful and purposeful, swishing his stick at the flies, thrashing the nettles. He's taken his sweater off and tied it round his waist by the sleeves, so that it hangs down like a wool miniskirt over his jeans. I know what Mick's purposefulness is about, but I'm not worried by it. I'm outside myself, right outside, able to observe the crumbling orange rust on the fence, the sloes and elderberries, the fizzy, gone-to-seed nettles, Mick's little swinging skirt and my own progress along the path with curiosity and detachment.

'Did you enjoy it the first time? With that airman?' Diarmid asked me, all those years later. I hoped the question was prompted by jealousy, though it was more likely to be polite-ness or prurience, or even envy.

I said, 'No, not a lot, no.'

I'd been asked this question before; every man I'd had a relationship with had wanted to know about 'that first time'. It's astonishing, really. How could any female be expected to enjoy that painful and messy business?

Breaking and entering is what the first time is about. Breaking and entering and looting.

I understand why men like doing it with virgins, why some men only like doing it with virgins – which must be tough for them now, with virgins in such short supply. Breaking and entering sounds fun to me. I imagine I would enjoy it, if I were a man.

I told Diarmid that although I hadn't enjoyed the sex, as such, that first time with the airman, there were things I had appreciated. His strong arms round me beforehand, when we were lying in the clearing; his hard, impatient kisses; the sweet, fresh, masculine smell of his neck. The weight of him. I had felt lustful, I told Diarmid, before things got going and then out of hand.

The bird calls in that clearing were something I remembered, and told him: the silence in the wood after the noise we'd made, and then the sad late-afternoon bird calls starting up again; and looking up through the dark leaves; and seeing laser beams of sun striking down through the leaves.

Diarmid wanted to know if there'd been a repeat performance, if it had been anything more than a one-afternoon stand with that airman and his joystick; and I said only a couple of times because soon after we started going out, Mick went AWOL from the camp, and didn't warn me he was going to, and that was the last I heard of him. (I never did learn what happened to Mick; whether he was caught and clapped in irons, or escaped to a more rewarding life elsewhere. I like to imagine he became a civil airplane pilot and is flying jumbos on some exotic route. I picture him as a middle-aged man with a paunch and a string of bimbo stewardesses in tow; I think of him as coming up for retirement, when in fact he'd only be thirty-sevenish now. I keep forgetting he was only two or three years older than I was then.)

I told Diarmid about sexual partner number two, who lasted six weeks. He was the forecourt attendant at Long Clovell garage, that shack I used to pretend was the saloon in my Wild West version of the town. I got to know him because his mother was Pat's auntie, the one in whose garden the caravan was parked. I liked him because his Gypsy looks and style reminded me of the boys who work the fairground rides. Jimmy Denton was his name. He had a car, an old Austin Cambridge estate, a squeaker and bone-shaker, and a lot of the exercise we took was taken in the back of it.

Jimmy was an oily boy, I told Diarmid; he stank of motor oil and something called nipple grease ('for a grease nipple'); his hands and nails were black with oil. 'He looked like John Travolta, now I come to think of it.'

I told Diarmid how I used to get the giggles every time Jocelyn drove the Morris to the garage and asked Jimmy Denton to 'fill her right up, would you, Jim' – because those were the words Jimmy said to me when we were in the back of his estate (or in whatsit Woods, where we went in good weather). 'I'm going to fill you up,' he'd say, 'I'm going to fuck you into the ground.'

I described the underwear Jimmy had favoured when I knew him. I remembered it because it had been such a surprise. You'd expect a boy as oily as he was to wear oily old Y-fronts, but Jimmy had worn these weeny briefs like the ones you see illustrated in the small ads of Sunday newspapers. One pair had a seagull motif on a blue ground. He used to pile his equipment into its inadequate silky holder, and then arrange it, a bit here, a tweak there, as though he were arranging flowers.

'Why do you wear those?' I asked once. (They looked so uncomfortable; also, I'd read an article in a mag about the dangers of too tight underpants: how they can make a man sterile; how, if they're to do their job properly, the testes need to have cool air circulating them at all times.)

''Cos you love it,' he said, ''cos you girls love it, that's why.'

I told Diarmid how long it had been before I could truthfully say I enjoyed sex; that for years any satisfaction I derived from it had more to do with the feeling that I was being useful and providing a service than anything else. (Women aren't supposed to think the way I did then; it's subservient and demeaning to think like that. We're supposed to go for what we want, to demand it and not to put up with anything we don't. We're supposed to say no to sex if we don't want it, and not feel guilty about that decision. But I had it in my head from early on that it was wrong to disappoint men. That in most circumstances it was cruel and unjustifiable to turn a good man down.) I had had no desire to be one of those girls who lead a man on and don't deliver, I told Diarmid. I had had no wish to be one of those girls who accept presents from a man, who are happy to eat and drink their way through four-course lunches and dinners the man is paying for, and then, while his back's turned tipping the doorman, leap into a taxi: 'Home, James, and don't spare the horses.'

I knew my duty in such situations, I told him. I always understood what was expected of me and what my obligations were.

'When did anyone ever buy you a four-course lunch, Evie?' Diarmid said. 'You've got a very fertile imagination for a girl in ironmongery. You must have seen a lot of terrible movies in your time.'

'I was taught by masters, as Olivia De Havilland would say,' I replied.

'Or Henry James, even,' Diarmid said. 'Evie, you're a card – as my Uncle Sean would say.'

Evie, you notice, not Hannah. Diarmid always called me Evie, from the first day I met him. I remember being pleased because it made me special, and because it made him special, separating him from everyone I'd ever known in my life, for whom I was Hannah or Han.

Now when I think of the way he reinvented me, without asking permission, I feel angry at Diarmid and resentful. I now see that changing my name was an arrogant and patronising thing to do. Sometimes I wonder if he had a darker motive than the mere need to dominate; there are days when I believe that if he did not deliberately set out to rob me of my identity, he at least intended to confuse it.

That first meeting with Diarmid, when I was renamed, or restyled or reinvented by him, happened like this:

He came into G. L. Bardon & Sons, Ironmongers and Hardware, where I was by then senior sales assistant, and walked straight up to the counter. He wanted a whole lot of items, some of which I remember. Four- and five- and six-inch wire nails – he wanted quantities of those. Two corner braces and one large fluted angle bracket, though I don't recall the exact sizes. Half a dozen drills, assorted screws, Rawlplugs.

He had a Northern Irish accent, which I was used to and liked. Among our regular trade customers there were several with accents and pronunciations like this. I liked their habit, in particular, of turning 'u's into 'o's so that 'but' became 'bot'; 'rubbish', 'robbish', 'trust', 'trost'.

He was charming in the way the Irish, even Ulster Irish, can be charming.

Most of the items he listed were to be found in the ancient wooden drawers (with brass handles it was my job to polish) behind my head; but others were kept in a collection of old ammunition boxes on the shelves on my right.

He was fascinated by the ammunition boxes, and also by the beautiful drill box, with its sliding partitions and fitted brass measure that ran the length of the box's interior and allowed you to see at a glance the drill you wanted – all the sizes from one-sixteenth of an inch to a half-inch. He took the box out of my hands and examined it minutely.

'It looks torrn of the century, must be nineteen-twanties at the latest – will you look at that craftsmanship! If this goes missing, you'll know where to look for it.'

While he was examining and exclaiming, Mr Tweedie, the manager (old Mr Bardon, grandson of the original owner, was by now too old to run the shop himself, though he came in regularly to annoy us all) called to me from the gardening section, up three worn wooden steps to my left, 'Hannah! Have you finished that order for Maplethorpes? They're coming for it at twelve!'

'I've done it, Mr Tweedie, but we're six hook bolts short – I've put in an order, OK?' I called back.

The young man leaned his arms on the counter and peered up at me through his hair, which was white with plaster dust. 'Hannah – so that's you, is it? Don't like your name, sounds hard-hearted to me. Are you hard-hearted, Hannah?'

I shrugged and blushed; how was I to know?

'Do you have another name I could call you?'

'Eve.'

'Eve.' He repeated it, trying it out. 'Eve. Evie. That's better. Evie. That's a foxy name for a foxy girl.'

'My aunt thinks I'm a moron.' I'd assumed that by 'foxy' he meant clever or cunning.

'Well, you may be a moron, your aunt may well be right, but that doesn't stop you being foxy. You're a foxy moron, maybe.'

When I'd collected all the items he wanted on the counter, I did my sums, subtracting the usual trade discount. It never occurred to me he wasn't a builder, even though no builder I'd served in that place had ever shown an interest in the drill box, only in the drills. The drill box should have alerted me, and the fact that he wasn't wearing overalls but cord jeans and a holey grey jersey several sizes too small.

On the other hand, he was cheeky enough, and flirtatious enough, for a builder. I thought him very attractive – his grey eyes, his smile, his square small hands. He was not tall, five foot nine perhaps, but he had big shoulders, and the rest of him was slim and muscular.

'Well, I'll be seeing you then, Evie,' he said at the door. 'Do you know that Jimi Hendrix song, "Foxy Lady"? I'll play it to you if you don't.' The bell jangled cheerily as he went out.

The next time he came in, for masonry nails, he asked me if

I had a lunch hour I was allowed out in, and when I said yes, he asked if I'd have a jar and a sandwich with him.

In the Bricklayers' Arms three streets away I learned his name was Diarmid. He pronounced it Dermit.

'Dermit,' I said, weighing it. 'Dermie.' It sounded like a skin disease, I told him; hadn't he another name I could use?

But no, bad luck, he hadn't. Just – jost – the one.

Not long after, he asked me to supper to see his new flat.

The tiny hallway was made narrower by stacks of books and newspapers, floor to ceiling. In the living room, a whole wall had been bookshelved, and there were books on the floor too. Three separate piles of heavy ones stood in for seats. There were only two, uncomfortable, chairs in that room.

I had believed him to be a builder of sorts, and nothing he'd said in the Bricklayers' Arms had led me to suppose differently. His father was a builder. Two of his four brothers were in the trade. One of his sisters had married a plasterer. (This was in Killybegs, on the coast of Donegal, Republic of Ireland, where most of his family had remained – though one sister had gone to Australia and married an Australian, and lived in a posh suburb of Melbourne.) So I felt depressed and betrayed when I saw all those books. I like men who make things or – like electricians and plumbers – make things work. You know where you are with men who work with their hands.

I felt even more depressed when he told me he was the author of two books. The first, a novel, had been published two years ago; the second, a collection of stories – 'or fables, as I like to think of them' – he'd only recently delivered to his publishers.

DIY – that's what he'd wanted those nails and drills for. I'd given him a trade discount every time, I realised, just for DIY.

Someone who introduced himself as Brian put his bald head round the door and said supper was ready. Diarmid's flatmate. I'd not been warned about Brian.

We ate the supper in the kitchen-diner, where there were chairs to sit on. We had artichoke soup, which Brian called fartichoke, with croutons and cream; afterwards lamb chops with a shiny, sharp sauce, baked aubergines, and potatoes boiled in their skins; then Brian's home-made ice cream.

Over the soup, Brian told me he was a freelance cook, and he described the pricks he had to cook for and the dreary, pretentious menus he was always being asked to provide for boardroom lunches. 'Have you ever tried frozen melon balls with crème de menthe? Don't.'

I liked Brian, he amused, me, but I kept thinking, Why is he here? Why didn't Diarmid ask him to go out for the evening? Or for the night?

At some point it struck me that Brian was gay. His manner was not camp especially, it was nothing he said, just something indefinable about his mouth, and a feeling I had.

We got to the coffee and the third bottle of chianti. Then, as I'd feared it was bound to, the subject of Diarmid's new book came up.

'Has the title been sorted yet?' Brian asked him. To me he said, 'I hope you're not a bookish type, Hannah? The only way I survive in this place is by never, ever opening a book – except cookbooks, of course.'

Diarmid said no, it hadn't been sorted, he and his publishers were still at loggerheads over his chosen title. It wasn't his editor's fault, he explained to me – his editor liked the title, he thought *Faecal Smears* the right, right-on, attention-grabbing one. His editor had actually read the book and was smart enough to see that the title was accurate, embracing as it did the shits and shitty behaviour and smeared reputations his fables treated, as well as, and more obviously, the stained lavatory bowls and underwear that marked so many of the pages.

'But the publishing director thinks it's a crap title. She wants gravitas, darling. She thinks my book should be called *Visceral Concerns*. And she's not the only one I'm fighting. The chief executive says that females, "who buy more books than men, remember", might have a problem when it comes to asking for *Faecal Smears* in the bookshops. In a memo to my editor, he wrote, "The proposed title would scupper any hope of building on the mini-success we had with the author's novella *Conceit*." Mini-success, please note. Not even minor!'

'Drink up,' Brian said, refilling Diarmid's glass.

'Let's try it on Evie. She's a female, female equals book-buyer, let's see what she thinks. Would you buy a book called *Faecal Smears*, Evie? Because my publishers don't think you would.'

'Well,' I said, 'well.' I wasn't sure how to answer. It didn't seem the moment to confess that I steered clear of bookshops, crossing the street to avoid one if need be.

'It doesn't matter anyway, because the consensus now is it's going to be called *A Cruise Down the Alimentary Canal* – that's the title of one of the fables. And you know what that means? It'll be stocked under Leisure or Inland Water-ways.' He put his head in his hands – in despair, I thought.

Brian *was* gay; I learned that later. He and Diarmid had been lovers for a short while, but that was a long time ago. They were friends now.

Diarmid was bisexual. An unsatisfactory word, he said, for feelings that had as much to do with emotional needs as they had to do with lust. His sexuality usually went in cycles – a period of feeling and behaving hetero would be followed by a period when he had eyes only for men. Not just eyes, obviously; other parts of his anatomy were involved. But this pattern he'd discerned in himself wasn't infallible. There'd been times in his life when he'd had a woman and a man on the go simultaneously, and had not been able to work out where his real commitment lay, and had not been able to choose.

His inability to choose had led to a lot of messiness and pain all round, he said.

Brian was one example of a person who hadn't been able to handle the messiness.

There'd been periods when he'd been sexually promiscuous, but only with men.

He'd lived with the knowledge of his dual sexuality since he was fifteen, when he'd discovered there were two people at his school he fancied equally – a girl called Kathleen and a boy called Thomas.

He wanted me to know about his sex-stroke-emotional life because he thought he might be falling in love with me. He didn't want me to be hurt. He thought I should be given the opportunity to get out now if I wanted.

'I'd like to be a family man, a part of me would,' Diarmid said. 'I'd like to marry a nice, beautiful girl and raise kids. But as things are it's as likely to be a nice, beautiful boy on my arm when I walk down that aisle. A boy in a white lawn shirt and a bolero jacket.'

He liked kids a lot, Diarmid said.

I was not as worried as some would have been by these revelations and fantasies. I did not immediately think: I can't handle that kind of messiness. And HIV and AIDS weren't a worry because at that time the plague was only a dark rumour to most of us in this country; I'm not sure I'd even heard of it. I think Diarmid's confession was a relief in a way; it made me feel better about things in my personal history I hadn't told him yet – Finch, for example. Up to that moment I'd feared he'd do a runner if he knew there was a giant eight-year-old cuckoo in my nest.

I felt more threatened by Diarmid's literariness than by anything he had to say about his sex life. I'd felt a fool when, soon after that first supper in his flat, he told me that the saga about his book titles had been a fiction. All of it? Well, most of it. He had written two books, that was true, and the second was at his publishers, but it wasn't called *Faecal Smears* or *Skid Marks* or whatever he'd said. It was called *Paradigms and Epiphanies*, and there'd been no problem with the title at all.

'It was just a joke, Evie, a bit of fun. I was helping Brian peel those bloody artichokes, and I said, "Let's have a bit of fun with Evie. Let's see if we can shock her." It was just a joke.'

Epiphany. Was Diarmid's book a religious work? As I understood the word, it meant the arrival of the Three Kings at the stable in Bethlehem. I looked it up in Finch's dictionary to see what other meanings it might have. Then I looked up 'paradigm'. Those two words and their meanings, taken separately or together, offered no clue to what Diarmid's stories might be about.

But I needn't have bothered; it didn't matter. It made no odds to Diarmid that books were not an ingredient in the pease pottage of my life. His mother didn't read, except their local paper; nevertheless she was one of the most intelligent and perspicacious people he'd ever known. There was nothing wrong with my intelligence. It was hardly my fault if I had no education, when my aunt had elected to send me to such a piss-awful school.

'I love you. I adore you.' I said these things to Diarmid when finally we went to bed, and I meant them, but the words sounded shopworn to my ears. I'd said them too many times before, not meaning them, to other men. Now, when I really meant them, they'd lost their power. I wanted new words, and there weren't any. Kissing Diarmid's mouth, I'd be haunted by all those other mouths I'd kissed, aware, as I examined his face, and touched and stroked his eyelids and his nose, or pushed his hair back to see the way it grew – springily and coarsely – from his forehead, of other faces, other hair, I'd fingered and scrutinized in just this way. I'd feel cheated then, and cheating. Sick with myself and also, unfairly, with him.

Finch-and-Diarmid, Diarmid-and-Finch – a hyphenated duo I think of them as now. And really, it was so from the beginning, it was friendship at first sight. And I was torn –

on the one hand their compatibility made our life together possible, particularly when we moved into Diarmid's flat (and Brian moved out); on the other, I'd experienced three-somes before, good ones and bad ones, and was wary of them. There was always this feeling of betrayal each time I saw those two heads close together, bent over something, intent on something I was never invited to share.

I took Diarmid down to Arizona to meet Aunt Hope and Jocelyn. They both came to the station to meet us, Jocelyn, as usual, at the wheel. It was January and the countryside lay under snow, the heaviest fall I'd seen in that landscape. They'd been cut off for three days, Aunt Hope said, before the farm tractor came by and dug them out. She said the northeasterly that had followed the first fall had driven six-foot drifts across the runway and in several exposed places along the road.

'We've got a toboggan for you, darling,' she said, twisting round in the passenger seat to Finch, pig in a bobble hat between Diarmid and me.

I left Finch in the kitchen and led Diarmid out on the snow-banked porch – an exit, and entrance, we never used in winter. I was going to walk him round the garden and show him my railway-carriage bedroom (where the hens had been shut in, Aunt Hope said, on account of the snow). I thought that unless he was made to beat the bounds of the place, and to view Arizona from the outside as well as in, he would get no real idea of what life had been like there. I hoped he would see how cut off from the world we had always been – and not just by snow.

But I couldn't show him anything. Here, on the garden side of the house, where the snow plough hadn't ventured, all that was visible was a deep, levelling whiteness that gave no hint of where the paths ran, say, or where the banks climbed, or where those two terrible wells descended. And the walls and hedges, the bushes and shrubs and shrubby trees, that old station seat Bowdell had got hold of – things I knew must be there somewhere – had been transformed into a great white bedding sale of pillows and eiderdowns and enormous, suffocating duvets.

A picture of my mother's white bed at the Rose Vale flashed onto my screen. And I remembered her white toothbrush, which had always frightened me; and for a moment saw it in its clinical glass, fixed to the wall by a chrome bracket, above the cold, white basin.

Aunt Hope took to Diarmid within minutes of our arrival. He homed in on her bookshelves, exclaiming and admiring. He pulled volumes out and leafed through, searching for particular passages, which he then placed under her nose. Which they then discussed. After lunch, we went for a walk through the hard-packed, glittering tunnel the tractor plough had made of the runway, he and she walking together in front, Diarmid a horse, pulling Finch on the toboggan, from time to time neighing and snorting and stamping the ground.

Jocelyn, who had a headache, stayed at home, and I had no one to walk with. The tunnel was too narrow for three to walk comfortably abreast. So I trailed behind, deliberately keeping my distance from that mutually admiring threesome of my lover, my aunt and my son, going slower and slower, so that the gap between us grew wider and wider. Colder, too, it felt – though that was my intention; I wanted it to be cold.

'What's become of tail-end Charlie?' I heard Diarmid's mocking call.

When they reached the road, the convoy about-turned and stopped. They stood, banging their gloves and stamping, waiting for me to catch up. I wouldn't look at them; I kept my head down and shuffled forwards as slowly as I dared.

But of course I couldn't avoid it, I was bound to get there in the end.

'What kept you?' Aunt Hope was banging her gloves still. 'D'you want us to freeze to death?' As we moved off again, she turned to Diarmid. '*My little horse must think it queer To stop without a farmhouse near,*' she remarked conversationally.

'*Between the woods and frozen lake, The darkest evening of the year,*' Diarmid said. He said he was thinking of giving *his harness bells a shake to ask if there was some mistake.*

'There are no woods,' I said, furious, 'look around you. There are no big trees, now that the elms have gone.' I hoped, by mentioning the elms, to wound my aunt. 'There's no lake either. Not even a piddling little pond.'

But I couldn't touch her, let alone wound her. Aunt Hope was the Snow Queen, and she'd stolen away Diarmid who already, like Finch, had a splinter of ice in his heart. Their sleigh flew faster and faster through the white, frozen tunnel, and grew smaller and smaller, the toboggan, with Finch in his bobble hat, swinging wildly behind.

And little Evie was much frightened and began to cry, but no one besides the sparrows heard her.

'They're not at all as you painted them.' Aunt Hope and Jocelyn had gone out into the snow to feed the hens, and Diarmid and I were washing up. 'Your aunt Hope's great, Evie. I like her a lot. I like that air she has of jocund gloom. And Jocelyn – what a beautiful woman she is! Imagine how she must have looked at eighteen. You never told me. You never even mentioned those eyes.'

At supper, asking Jocelyn about her theatrical career, chatting her up with all sorts of nonsense, he asked her, 'I hope we're going to play the Arizona Board Game? Because I've devised a diabolical game plan. I'm going to get to Tombstone if it kills me. If I have to kill the lot of you to get there.'

'He's a charmer, isn't he,' Jocelyn whispered. The potboy was in the kitchen replenishing glasses. 'If anyone'd asked me to guess, I'd have said he was an actor. Tell me – it's just a feeling I have – does he, as they say, kick with both feet?'

'What?'

'AC/DC. Ambidextrous. You know, Hannah – bisexual. I wondered.'

That night we slept in Aunt Hope's bed. Extraordinarily, she'd given up her room to Diarmid and me. She'd put Finch in my old room as usual, insisting that she herself would be perfectly comfortable on the camp bed in Jocelyn's room. After we'd made love – so sweetly and energetically that the splinter in Diarmid's heart melted as though it had never been – I told him what Jocelyn had said. 'It was mischief, you realise. She's a great mischief-maker. You should have seen the way she carried on with Uncle Ber. But don't worry. She got nothing out of me.'

But Diarmid wasn't worried. He laughed out loud. 'Takes one to know one, ducky.' He pulled the pillow over his head and laughed some more.

I was upset. He was as bad as Pat, I thought, and I said so: 'You're as bad as Pat.' Naturally I'd told him about Pat and her lies and treachery.

'Oh, come on now, Evie – what d'you think their relationship's about? Really? Why d'you think they've spent all these years together, up this track. Use your wits. You only have to look at them when they're together.'

'You're quite wrong,' I said coldly. 'You've got it all wrong. It was nothing like that. I was there. They slept at opposite ends of the house, you know. They still do.'

'You were too young to see it, and too close. But just consider for a moment. Consider Jocelyn. She's an unusually good-looking woman even now. She could've had any man she wanted, always – if she'd wanted a man. Look, I feel like a ciggy. Is it all right to smoke in this room?'

I switched on Aunt Hope's bedside light and, naked, got

out of bed and found Diarmid's cigarettes and matches in the pocket of his coat, hung over my aunt's dressing-table chair. It was freezing out there, and I dashed back to bed, lickety-split. 'There's no ashtray. We'll have to use the packet.'

'I love your body,' Diarmid said.

We lay back against my aunt's pillows, her eiderdown tucked under our chins, and puffed in silence. At the foot of the bed stood grandfather's cheval glass, and within its oblique frame was Diarmid, the part of him I could see. I watched a reflected arm and hand, his right hand, with the cigarette. His right, miracle-working hand.

(If I want to hurt myself, I picture Diarmid's hands and I remember the power his fingers had. They weren't beautiful hands, the fingers, though slim, were on the short side, yet they had this power to electrify. Just one touch – but I can't bear to think about it. And I can't bear to remember his strong, almost elastic limbs. I've known men whose sensitive-looking fingers turned out, in bed, to be agents of paralysing boredom, or irritation, or torture; whose protective arms became iron bars designed to crush hips and ribs and breast-bones. Whose sexy torsos were dead and bruising weights. And I've known Diarmid.

If someone were to tell me there are no other hands and fingers in the whole wide world that can work the miracles Diarmid's did, I'd give up sex – the idea of sex, of ever having it again – tomorrow.)

Having stubbed out our cigs in the packet, my lover and I settled ourselves for sleep. I on my right side in the foetal position, Diarmid behind me echoing my curve, his knees under my knees, so snug you'd think they'd been custom-made to fit there. I could feel his prick, knocking on my back door. 'How'd you feel about buggery?' he'd whispered to me once, in this position.

'D'you know, Evie, your aunt Hope reminds me of you, and it's not just the funny hair. That's mostly why I took to her, of course: because she looks and moves and laughs like you.' He mumbled this into my shoulder, punctuating the words with little noisy kisses. 'I'd like to see a photo of her when she was your age. I'd like to see you with her specs on.'

'You're wrong about her and Jocelyn, by the way.' I manoeuvred myself to the edge of the mattress, out of reach of that persistent battering ram. 'It's not love that keeps them together, it's guilt. It's guilt and fear – the fear of being left alone with the guilt. I learned that when I was fifteen. I'll tell you about it.' And we slept.

Aunt Hope unhooked her car keys from the mug rack above the stove. She was dressed in her Rose Vale visiting clothes, summer version. They consisted of a floppy pale-green dress (button-through, elbow-length cuffed sleeves, belted with a self belt), a fawn cardigan, fawn tights, tan courts. She carried a lightweight mac over her arm, though the sky outside the kitchen window was unbroken blue.

The dress was made of some sort of cotton and man-made fabric mix that didn't crease, a good thing to wear on the train. It was a shock always to see my aunt in a dress because for over a year now she'd worn trousers every day – terrible sludge-coloured trousers that made you think 'slacks'. She bought them at the draper's in Long Clovell; they were wide-legged, which, although in fashion, looked old-fashioned on her; they had big turn-ups and a side zip. Jocelyn wore trousers too, they were the obvious choice for garden work, but hers were jeans, the kind I wore, fly-front Levis or Wranglers, flares naturally, a stone-washed blue.

'I suppose you wouldn't like to come with me?'

I was buttering a piece of toast for my breakfast. All I had on was the mid-thigh-length black T-shirt I'd recently decided was the only possible nightwear. I'd come as I was from my wagon-lit, barefoot through the sopping, glittering grass, and had yet to wash or untangle my hair. My aunt had long ago given up asking if I wanted to visit my mother, so on two counts I knew her question wasn't serious. It was the question she invariably asked Jocelyn at the very last minute – to which Jocelyn invariably replied, 'Thank you, no; I've got to hoe', or some similar refusal. But Jocelyn had been in London all week. (She was due back that day, to my relief; I'd heard Aunt Hope on the phone, planning their homeward journeys: they were going to meet at the station at eight and drive home together.) Aunt Hope's question was just a pointless habit she'd got into.

So I went on buttering. I don't think I even bothered to reply, though she was still standing there.

'You might quite enjoy the train journey, Hannah. You never go anywhere by train. It's really quite fun.' She looked at her watch. 'I've got ten minutes in hand. If you were very quick, if you nipped upstairs now and – '

'No!' It was almost a shout, firm and rude – but then she'd taken me by surprise. Suddenly my bare foot touched the dog basket under the table, and there she was, my entirely rational excuse. How could I go off for the day when there was no one at home to look after Jemma? I asked. Surely Jemma had to be let out every two minutes to pee? And we couldn't take an old, incontinent dog with us on the train, could we? We couldn't take her into the Rose Vale – dogs weren't allowed.

After the Morris had bucked and groaned out of the courtyard, I took my coffee and a pair of tweezers to the porch and sat on the steps and plucked my legs. It was the long, steamy holiday of Pat and boys and intrigue, and I was expecting a visit at two.

They were over an hour late back because Aunt Hope's train was an hour late. Jocelyn had hung around on the platform without so much as a cup of coffee, the station buffet being closed. I learned that, but not much more, from Jocelyn. Aunt Hope was silent and distracted. Before she'd even got her mac off she was at the whisky bottle, pouring a stiff one. Neither of them was hungry for the supper I'd made:

boiled potatoes, French beans, a salad of cos lettuce and sorrel, all of it out of the garden – all of it dug, cut or picked by me. I'd imagined I'd get praise for the trouble I'd taken. I'd put a clean cloth on the table, and candles. Despite the excitements of my afternoon, I'd remembered to feed Jemma. And I'd fed the hens and, an hour ago, when the sun vanished behind the ash trees, shut them up. Not a word of thanks for any of this.

'Aunt Hope, how did you hurt your face?' I'd just noticed it, two red lines like bramble scratches the length of her cheek, eye-socket to chin.

Aunt Hope left the table and began pacing the kitchen.

'Sit down, Hope,' Jocelyn said. 'Sit down and eat your food.'

Aunt Hope sat down.

But she didn't eat, or speak, she just sat there, staring at her plate. From her expression you'd think I'd offered her poison.

Eventually I said, 'If you'll excuse me, I'm going to have a bath.' And I left them to clear up.

Lying in the bath, watching the hard-water scum settle on my stomach and thighs, rinsing and squeezing it off with a sponge, I heard noises from below. Laughter, could it be? Or weeping? Oh, no. Oh, do me a favour, please.

On my way down the stairs, wrapped in Jocelyn's white silk kimono, which I'd had to fold over and over at the waist, it was so long, the word 'murder' – it might have been 'murderer' – floated up, and I stopped and sat down on the stairs.

'You know it's not true. You know we're not murderers. You know she's sick.'

I could not hear my aunt's reply.

'You mustn't, mustn't let it get to you. It's what she's after, but you mustn't let her. She's sick.'

'We are murderers.'

'No, we're not. Listen to me. How much whisky have you

had? Because I'm going to find you a sleeping bomb and knock you out. Stay here.'

I heard her get up and walk to the door, and I got up myself then and went down the stairs and into the kitchen, gliding like a ghost. I felt like a ghost. White and cold, like a ghost.

Jocelyn's back view was at the sink; she was filling a tumbler from the tap. I glided towards her, silently, I thought, but she must have heard something.

'Hope, will you go and sit down? I'm just coming.' She reached an arm to the saucepan shelf where a load of medicines had collected – cough syrup, vitamins, indigestion remedies, aspirin, ten-year-old prescriptions for God knows what. Sleeping pills.

'It's not Hope, it's me.'

'Oh. Hannah. Just looking for something to help your aunt sleep. She's had a very distressing day.' She unscrewed a bottle and shook two yellow pills into her palm. 'Did you have a nice bath?'

'That says "For Animal Use Only".'

'So it does.' She selected another bottle. 'You off to your wagon-lit now?'

I hesitated, but I had to ask. That's what I was there for. 'Is Aunt Hope a murderer?' I said. 'Are you? I heard you talking. I was coming down the stairs, and I heard her say you were murderers.'

Jocelyn laughed, heartily and convincingly – although later I thought, She's trained to do that. She's an actress, she's been trained to laugh or cry.

'No, of course not. Of course not.' And she raised her eyes to the ceiling and spread her arms wide, a gesture that implied: When will this nonsense end? or, How did I ever get mixed up with this bunch?

'Why did she say it, then?'

'Well, I don't – '

'She said it over and over. I heard her. She was weeping. She was – '

'We can't go on standing here, Han, I've got to get back to her. I want her to take these, now. Look, I can see you're upset, but I'm not sure what I can say that won't upset you even more. Well, all right then. Your mother's illness, her behaviour, has changed. From what I gather, she's become increasingly voluble lately, and violent too sometimes. Violent with the nurses, violent with the other patients. They've been having to keep her in her room. Hope told me in the car. She didn't want you to know – and now I've told you.'

She stopped as though she'd finished, as though the explanation was complete, which it wasn't. So I stood there.

'And then today, when Hope was with her – there was a nurse there too, they had a nurse in the room, I'm glad to say – your mother started on about the accident, and she screamed a lot of dreadful things, untrue things, and she accused your aunt and me of –'

'What accident?'

'The accident, the car accident, you know.' She sounded exasperated. 'When Ivo was killed.'

'But what's the accident got to do with Aunt Hope?' I was exasperated too. I, too, had had an exhausting day.

'Well, quite a lot, obviously, seeing as we were both in the car. Seeing as she was *driving* the car. As you very well know.'

I didn't know. No one had ever told me. Why should I know?

Jocelyn has made a boo-boo there. I remember thinking that. In the cold, deep silence her words fell into, the thought bubbled to the surface, She's made a real boo-boo there.

'Didn't you know?' she asked eventually, peering at me (willing me, I afterwards decided, to change my mind). 'Surely you knew? Why did I think you did? Oh, God!'

I shook my head. 'No.' I went on shaking my head, I couldn't stop shaking it. My head was a pendulum, slow and relentless, tick-tock, tick-tock.

'Han, I'll come and see you and tell you about it. I'll get Hope to bed and then I'll come and see you.' She stopped, and I saw that her eyes were brimming with tears. 'Don't go and say goodnight to her. It's better not. I'll come and talk to you. I promise. You go off now.' She took the torch off the worktop and put it in my hand.

Hot sunshine, blue sky, a car bowling merrily along a seaside road; the breeze through the open windows smelling of sea and tar; grown-ups in the front chatting and laughing; children in the back shouting and pointing. And then, out of a side road . . .

In the picture I had of the accident that killed my brother, I had always seen the grown-ups as my parents – my big, handsome father at the wheel, my delicate, pretty mother in the passenger seat. A family outing. It's what a child would see, isn't it? It's what she would assume, unless someone told her otherwise.

I was soberly awake when Jocelyn came to the railway carriage, and she smelled of whisky. I dare say she'd needed a drink to cope with my aunt and then with me. In the hour since I'd left the house I'd had time to consider her disclosure, to chew it and worry it and drop it and retrieve it the way Jemma, when she had teeth, had chewed and worried a succession of disgusting old bones.

'But you don't even know my mother, you've never met her, so why – ?' That was the first, unfinished question I tried on Jocelyn.

During the hour that separated us, Jocelyn, fortifying herself with whisky, must have decided her best chance was to make a clean breast of it. She must have worked out that it was the only course left to her, that she had said too much to avoid my inquisitor's stare. If she were to make a full and contrite confession and water my breast sufficiently with her tears, there was a chance she might be able to melt my heart. Who knows, if she managed to gain my sympathy, it could just be the start of something new and warm and wonderful between the three of us.

This is the story Jocelyn told me.

She did know my mother, or rather, she had known her.

My mother had been her best friend. They had met when they were eighteen. My mother was the assistant stage manager of the repertory company Jocelyn had then been a member of. (My mother had trained at RADA, was I aware of that? But they hadn't met then, although they were the same age, because Jocelyn had been at the Central School. My mother had given up her not entirely successful career to marry my father.)

Jocelyn had met Aunt Hope through my mother. She couldn't remember exactly when that was, or where the meeting had taken place, but it was a long time afterwards. Years afterwards. Aunt Hope was, of course, married to Uncle Ber at the time. Jocelyn couldn't be certain, she couldn't remember, but it was likely he'd been there too, at that first meeting with my aunt.

Jocelyn had known my father, naturally. They hadn't liked each other. She had tried to dissuade my mother from marrying him. She believed he was aware of this. He had not been pleased when my mother asked her to be godmother to her first-born, Ivo. 'She called him after me, you see,' Jocelyn said, 'my second name's Ivy. It was the nearest she could get to my name, to calling him after me. She didn't dare call him Jocelyn.

When the accident happened, my parents were away. They had gone to some business conference, some animal food-stuffs convention in Birmingham. My mother had not wanted to go, but my father insisted, saying it would be good for her to get away. She was an anxious mother, always in a flap about something, a surprise because she'd appeared so capable and carefree before she had children. Jocelyn put her anxiety down to the period of bad depression she'd suffered after the second birth. Aunt Hope had had to look after her then. She'd had to leave Uncle Ber and her own home and move into my parents' semi in Tunbridge Wells, and run the place – shopping, cooking, the lot. She'd stayed there over a month.

So it was natural Aunt Hope should be the one to take

charge for the five days my parents were to be away. (The conference was only two days, but my father wanted to make a little holiday of it, and he'd booked rooms in a hotel in the Lake District, a part of England my mother had never seen.) It was then that she, Jocelyn, came into the picture. She was living in London at the time and between boyfriends, and often asked herself down to my mother's at weekends, or even midweek if she was out of work. She liked to get out of London whenever possible in the summer, and she enjoyed being with her little godson Ivo, playing with him, watching him grow.

'I remember ringing your mother,' Jocelyn said, 'and asking her if I could come down for a couple of days, and her telling me she'd be away, and that we'd better make it another week. And then she said, "Unless you'd like to come anyway. I'm sure Hope would be glad of your company. And Ivo would." And she seemed relieved when I said yes. She knew it would please your father if she went, but at the same time she was anxious about leaving you two. She had never left you for more than a night in someone else's care. I think she felt that in the circumstances two heads would be better than one, and four hands better than two.'

Jocelyn and Aunt Hope had arrived, from opposite directions, the night before my parents left. My mother had written out a timetable and a list of instructions for them to follow – bedtimes and rest times, eating habits, how to sterilise the nappies, how to strap me safely in my pram – pages of stuff. She'd led them all round the house, a house they both knew well, pointing out hazards and danger zones. She'd taken them round the garden and showed them the gap in the fence Ivo had been known to squeeze through (already plugged by a piece of board) and the lily pond, whose netting cover must be immediately replaced each time they fed the goldfish. Were they aware that a toddler could drown in three inches of water?

It was while they were standing beside the pond that Jocelyn had made an 'Oo-er, how are we ever going to manage with all these hazards?' face, and Aunt Hope had caught her eye and made a face back. They hadn't really known each other then. They'd met a few times, but they couldn't be said to be more than acquaintances. But when they made those faces at each other, and then got the giggles, and had to cover their mouths with their hands in order to disguise their giggles, something happened. Some sort of bond developed between them.

'I'm telling you all of it,' Jocelyn said. 'I'm telling you all of it, Han, so you'll understand. I don't want to leave anything out or cover any of it up.'

The following morning, my parents had left. Before she got into the car, my mother had unhooked the child's chair from the back seat and carried it in and put it in the hall. She was leaving it there, she'd told them, in case of emergencies, in case one of the children had an accident and had to be driven to the hospital. (The hospital's address and telephone number, along with their GP's, was at the top of the list my mother had made.) My mother said she hoped they wouldn't mind, she hoped they wouldn't take offence, but except in the case of an emergency, she'd rather they didn't drive us anywhere. It didn't mean one of them couldn't get out to the shops while the other was looking after the children, it didn't mean they were imprisoned. Of course not. It didn't mean they couldn't go for walks with the pram. It was just that she'd be happier if they didn't drive us anywhere. She'd feel a lot easier and more relaxed if she knew for certain we wouldn't be taken anywhere in a car while she was away.

My father had been getting very impatient while this was going on, Jocelyn said. He'd been sitting in the driving seat, sighing and banging the palms of his hands on the steering wheel.

To begin with, everything had gone according to the timetable and instruction sheets. And then, that first afternoon, the washing machine had broken down and spewed dirty nappy water all over the kitchen floor. And then, at bath-time,

Ivo had refused to have a bath – he'd wanted his mummy to bath him. When they'd at last got him into his pyjamas, he'd had hysterics because his daddy wasn't there to read to him. No one else would do – only his daddy daddy daddy.

That first evening, when they were in the kitchen eating their omelettes, they'd heard a crying noise – me this time. They'd been warned I might cry, because I was teething. They'd been told what to do if I did, but the teething gel they rubbed on my gums, and the quarter aspirin they crushed into my rosehip syrup, hadn't stopped the crying – the screaming, rather. They'd taken turns to put me over their shoulders and walk me round the room, but each time they put me down, I started up again. Teething seemed to have a direct connection with my bowels; no sooner had they changed my nappy than there was another explosion. (Those were the days of terry towelling, Jocelyn explained. Disposable nappies were almost unknown.)

They were up half the night with me, and with Ivo – because of course my crying woke him in the next room. They had a bucketful of dirty nappies and no washing machine to put them into. They had two screaming children who refused to sleep or be consoled. They were nearly weeping themselves. 'But then, suddenly, one of us started laughing. It was Hope, I think. She prodded the top nappy in the bucket, holding her nose, and started laughing. She rolled around on the floor in her nightie, with the tears streaming down her face, and laughed and laughed. And then I started. You must remember we were young then. Hope was thirty-five at most, and so I must have been twenty-eight, same age as your mother. We'd both imagined we wanted children, we'd discussed it over supper. But when we'd stopped laughing we decided we didn't. We decided that children – and dirty nappies and sore bottoms and screams and sleepless nights – were the last thing on this earth we wanted.'

The following day had been hot, 'the sun at breakfast as strong as you get in Naples' – and they'd parked me in my pram in the shade of a laburnum. That is, until they'd remembered what my mother had said about laburnum pods being poisonous; then they'd moved me elsewhere. Then they'd got on with the housework, followed everywhere by Ivo, making truck noises and pushing a toy truck over the furniture, up and down the arms of chairs, along the back of the sofa. He'd got bored with that and trotted to the cupboard under the stairs and brought out a bucket and spade. 'We're going to the seaside today,' he'd informed them.

Aunt Hope had said no, they weren't, not today. She'd said they couldn't anyway, because they had to stay home for the man who was coming to mend the washing machine. She told Ivo that when she'd spoken to the washing-machine man on the telephone, he'd said he couldn't say when to expect him because he had a lot of calls to make and machines to mend; he might not get there before teatime.

When he'd taken in the bad news, Ivo had dashed himself to the ground and screamed for a while.

But the washing-machine man had come, after all – mid-morning, in the typical, dementing way of washing-machine men. Ivo had cheered up to help the man mend the washing machine. He'd handed up the wrong tools from the toolbag and knocked over the washing-machine man's full coffee mug into the toolbag. He'd told the washing-machine man they were going to the seaside as soon as the washing-machine was mended. 'Then I'd better hurry up, hadn't I?' the washing-machine man had said. 'It's a great day for the seaside. Wish I was going.' Ivo had asked the washing-machine man if he'd like to see his new bucket and spade his daddy had given him, which he was taking to the seaside; and the washing-machine man had said yes.

'No, Ivo, I've told you already, we are not going to the sea today,' Aunt Hope had said when the washing-machine man had gone. 'We are not going, so you had better get used to the idea. If you make no more fuss, Jocelyn will see if she can mend the paddling pool.' (They'd found the paddling pool in the cupboard, but when she'd tried to blow it up, Jocelyn had discovered several punctures and, more problematical, a sizeable tear.)

Ivo had immediately dashed himself to the floor again in a frenzy of rage and grief. He'd arched his back and drummed his heels. He'd rolled over on his stomach and pummelled the lino with his fists.

Aunt Hope and Jocelyn had got down on the floor and knelt, one on either side, and tried to reason with him and pacify him, but he would not be reasoned with or pacified. Each time they'd put out a tentative, conciliatory hand, he'd screamed and kicked, louder, louder, harder, harder. One kick had landed on Aunt Hope's face. The buckle of Ivo's sandal had caught her on the cheek and drawn blood.

Even the sight of his aunt's blood hadn't impressed Ivo. 'He'd gone too far by this time,' Jocelyn said. 'I remember that feeling from my own childhood, as I expect you do. That feeling of not being able to stop the tantrum or control it, of being taken over by its momentum. That's the stage he'd got to, of hardly being able to breathe, and wanting to stop, but not being able to stop. I looked at Hope over the top of that purple, screaming face, and I said, "Does this constitute an emergency, d'you reckon?" and she said, "It certainly does. In my book it does." She got to her feet then, and stood over him, and said, very loudly and clearly, "Ivo, if you stop this at once, we might, we just might, take you to the seaside this afternoon. If you don't stop, I'm going to get a bowl of cold water and pour it over your head. Now. And then I'm going to drive you to the hospital and leave you there.'

And after a minute or two, he had stopped. The screams had given way to shuddering, breathy sobs, and then he'd gone limp and quiet and put his thumb in his mouth. He'd laid his burning cheek on the lino, closed his swollen eyes and gone to sleep. He'd slept on the floor, quite peacefully, for over an hour, right till lunchtime.

'I'm not sure I can tell you any more,' Jocelyn said. 'I

mean, there isn't any more. We just got you both up after your rests – you were all happy and smiley that day, I remember, your teeth didn't seem to be bothering you at all, you were cuddly and smiley and adorable – and we put all the beach and picnic things in the boot of Hope's car. And then we hooked your little chair over the back seat and strapped you in, and we sat Ivo beside you. We took the eiderdown off his bed and wedged it between him and the door so he couldn't reach the handle. Then we locked both back doors. But we had to have the windows open – not right down, about halfway – because it was so hot in the car. It was like a furnace until we got going.'

'Where were you going to?' I asked her, the first question I had asked.

'Well, we'd imagined Bexhill must be nearest, but then we looked at the map and saw it was rather a complicated route, so we decided to go to Hastings instead – main road all the way on the A21. And then when we were nearly there, about five miles away, and Ivo was chanting seaside, seaside, seaside, and swaying his bucket about, I saw a sign on the right to St Leonards, and I said, "Why don't we go there? I've never been, and I hear it's ever so genteel and suitable for kiddies." So we turned off.

'I can't say any more,' Jocelyn said. 'I can't go any further with this, don't ask me to tell you any more.'

'He was my godson,' Jocelyn said, and she wept. 'And you know, Hannah, he was a dear little boy, affectionate and funny. He could be very funny. He'd stare at you, deadpan, and come out with something quite devastatingly funny. That tantrum I've told you about, it wasn't typical of him. He was just playing up, trying it on because his parents weren't there.

'He was only four,' Jocelyn said, and she wept. 'He'd had no life at all. He was only *four*.'

Throughout this story, Jocelyn had wept from time to time. It doesn't come across the way I've related it, but in fact she punctuated the story with her tears. Incoherent, she'd had to stop, and start again, more than once. And now she gave herself entirely over to grief. Lying across my narrow bed, she howled and howled, in that cathartic way people occasionally can. And I, famously dry-eyed, who never cried if I could help it, whose tears never flowed except over a movie or a dead bird on the path, howled with her.

But something happened to me that night, between Jocelyn's leaving my bed to return to her own, and the sun's rising. The cold light of the dawn, as first light is often described, happened. It was cold. And when I woke into it, I was cold and clear-eyed.

I saw that Aunt Hope and Jocelyn had ruined my life, had taken from me the life that should by rights have been mine. Through their foolishness and and disobedience, these two women had robbed me of a brother, a father, a mother, and the whole world of family feeling and experience those names described.

I saw that they had robbed my mother of everything, including her sanity.

I saw that they were not even friends. What I had always believed to be friendship, however bizarre and inexplicable sometimes, was not that. The only real thing they had in common was guilt and fear.

I saw that they were cowards and hypocrites and accomplished, brilliant deceivers; that this had been so all the years I'd known them. All the years I thought I'd known them.

I went over to the house later that morning. They were both in the kitchen. Jocelyn was mixing hen food in a bucket. Aunt Hope, at the stove, said, 'Sleep well, Hannah? Cup of coffee for you?' – but too brightly; so lightly and brightly, I knew she had been told.

Jocelyn wouldn't look at me. She swivelled her eyes in every direction but mine. In the cold light of her dawn, she must have realised the risk she'd taken, and perhaps regretted it. And now she was anxiously waiting for a sign from me, a gesture of compassion, or forgiveness, or love, to prove to herself, and my aunt, she had not made an irreparable mistake.

I despised her for this. I despised them both. In their different ways, they were terrified of me, I could see.

From that moment, I forgave them nothing. The moment I realised they were in my power, their punishment began. Knowing that they would not now dare to admonish or obstruct me, I embarked on a career of lavish delinquency and truancy; so that when the time came, the following year, for O levels and CSEs, I did not sit the exams let alone pass them, but instead ran off to London with a local boy made bad; and never saw Aunt Hope and Jocelyn for three years; and never once returned to Arizona until Finch was on the way.

The day after his first, snowy visit to Arizona, I related that story to Diarmid. Everything Jocelyn had told me about the accident; my initial, sad response to it; my cold-light-of-dawn rethink; my three-year punishment of Aunt Hope and Jocelyn – I told him it all. Finch had gone to bed, and Diarmid and I were sitting up late in the living rom of his flat, drinking whisky and smoking and talking.

'They're not alcoholics, you know, Hope and Jocelyn,' Diarmid said. (This was how the conversation had started.) 'You told me they were. They're heavy drinkers; that's not the same thing.'

'They were on their best behaviour,' I said. 'They wanted to make a good impression. They wanted you to like them. You've no idea how much they normally put away.'

'Why d'you think they wanted me to like them? Because I'm your boyfriend. That's what you do when you love someone – make an effort with the person *they* love. That's what I did with them. I worked my socks off at it – no, that's not true, I didn't have to work that hard because, as it turned out, I liked them anyway. Both of them.'

I said nothing to this.

'You're such a jealous person, Evie, aren't you?' He ruffled my hair. 'You know, you really behaved monstrously while we were down there. You behaved like a jealous child – and I don't mean like Finch, he was a little angel the whole visit.

All that sulking and hanging behind on the walk, refusing to join in. I couldn't believe it. And then not talking at supper – what did you think you were up to?'

I had no answer to that, no answer that I was prepared to give.

'But to get back to your aunt and Jocelyn being alcoholics. How dependent are they? Think about it. Do they, like, start on the booze after breakfast? Before breakfast, even? Do they as a rule need a hair of the dog before they can face their day?'

'No, but – '

'Did they ever lie to you about their drinking when you were living there? Did they ever hide their booze in strange places – in the washing machine or the airing cupboard – places they didn't think you'd find it? Did you ever come across bottles in places you wouldn't expect bottles to be?'

'Not exact – '

'You're not always right in your assessment of things and situations, are you, Evie? Or people. You're not always right about them. It strikes me you get things quite wrong sometimes. I think you're wrong when you say Hope and Jocelyn don't love each other, that there's no relationship there. Because I perceived that there is and that they do. I think you said it was guilt has kept them together all these years. Now how could that be? What sort of guilt could do that?'

So then I told him.

I'm not sure what I was expecting when I'd finished. Sympathy, I imagine. And some sort of climb-down from Diarmid – an admission that I'd been right all along. An apology, perhaps.

But when I came to the end, Diarmid said nothing. He put his elbows on the table and his thumbs on either side of his head just above the ears, and he rested his hands on the top of his head so that the tips of his fingers met in the middle of his coarse, springy hair, and he stared down at the table.

Eventually, addressing his words to the table, he said, 'Well, that is tragic. That is a tragic story.' And he went on sitting there in an absent way (as though he were absent, or I was, or we both were).

It was the following morning that he found questions to ask. Not questions; one question, variations of it, rephrasings of it, repeated over and over. How could I do that to them, my Aunt Hope and Jocelyn? How could I have done it? How could I have punished them the way I did and for so long? After all they'd suffered – all they must have suffered since the death of that little child. How was I able to be so cruel?

'I was fifteen,' I reminded him. 'That's why. People are cruel at fifteen. If they're hurt, they are. I wouldn't do that now.'

'You stayed away for nearly three years, Evie,' Diarmid said. 'Nearly three years. You didn't answer their letters. As far as they were concerned, you'd vanished into a big black hole. Just like Ivo.'

'I was in a big black hole,' I said.

'D'you realise, I hope you do realise, that there never was a right time to tell you how the accident happened? And it was an accident, make no mistake, it wasn't your aunt's fault. I mean, when would have been the right time? When you were five? When you were seven? When you were twelve? There never could have been a "right" time, could there? Not for that kind of bombshell.'

'*They* didn't tell me,' I said. 'Jocelyn did. Aunt Hope wouldn't have. I've thought about it, of course I have, and I'm sure now she must have made a decision very early on that it wouldn't be helpful to me to be told. And she was right. Knowing wasn't helpful. My knowing didn't help any of us. So I agree with you – there wasn't a right time. Jocelyn shouldn't have told me.'

'Didn't it ever occur to you, all that time you were punishing your aunt, that the childhood you didn't have was unlikely to have been any better, happier, than the one you did? That it might have been worse? Because your mother never was a stable person, was she? If she had been, her reaction to the death of her first-born wouldn't have been so extreme. Mothers normally do get over those sorts of terrible losses. Not get over them, but learn to cope with them or suppress or sublimate them, because they have to. My mother lost a child – Mary Ann, the one before me – but that didn't stop her having me, or loving me. As for your father, who did a runner at the first sign of trouble – what sort of dad do you imagine he'd have been to you if Ivo had survived? As it was, you had your uncle Ber all to yerself for what, eight years? He was as good as a dad to you, surely? Better than a lot of dads, for sure. A lot better than some.'

Diarmid's lecture made me ashamed, though I didn't tell him so. I just kept quiet for a while. I still feel shame, and sorrow, when I allow myself to consider all the things he said. Coming from him, though, who'd caused, who no doubt still causes, a deal of pain and messiness himself, the high moral tone was a bit rich. 'A bit rich, Diarmid,' I say out loud when I'm feeling bad and sad about the way I treated Aunt Hope and how much I must have hurt her. 'A bit fucking rich, coming from you.'

When I search for excuses for my cruelty – as I need to, as increasingly I find I need to – I think about my brother Ivo and his tantrum (the thing that caused his death if anything can be said to have done). He'd wanted to stop it, Jocelyn said, but he couldn't. He'd had enough of that screaming and kicking, he was exhausted, but he couldn't. He wanted someone else to stop it for him.

It was like that for me, I think. Yes, I'm sure it was. All that time I was in my black hole or well, I wanted to get out of it. I wanted to go home almost as soon as I'd left, I wanted to answer the letters, and I couldn't. I wanted Aunt Hope to come and rescue me.

Diarmid forgave me eventually. At least I thought so. After a week, perhaps, of awkwardness we eased back into the people we had been and into our old loving and arguing ways. We laughed a lot. Our sex life resumed its old tenderness and frequency, its old ferocity and inventiveness. My cooking improved, or Diarmid said it did.

Yet looking back now, I'm not so sure he did forgive me. Or perhaps it was that he lost all faith and trust. It doesn't take much to trigger doubts about the one you think you love. A chance insensitive remark of his or hers can do it. Or the discovery of some tiny, absurd meanness.

Sometimes, when he was working late – head down, writing fast, stopping, lighting another fag, inhaling, leaning back, stretching his arms above his head – I'd look across and catch Diarmid staring at me. Who are you? his stare seemed to say. I don't know you. What are you doing in my life?

Diarmid and I were still together, after a fashion, when Jocelyn died. It was he who answered the telephone. I had already left for work.

He came straight to the shop to tell me; that was kind of him. I've thought about it since, and I see that it was kind. He was doing some building work for a friend at that time, mixed in with the journalism jobs that had come his way as a result of the critical success he'd had with that book of stories, *Paradigms and Epiphanies*: everyone wanted his opinions for a while. (And he'd got very conceited with it, I thought; conceited and smart-arse. 'What d'you want to be remembered for?' one interviewer had enquired. 'The ubiquity of my by-line' had been his smart-arse reply.)

But he wasn't really conceited or smart-arse underneath. No. It suits me to say he was. It helps me to get over him to say to anyone who asks, and to myself: Diarmid's a shit, a right faecal smear, a skid mark on the underpants of life. But it isn't, and wasn't, true. 'The ubiquity of my by-line', for example, was a joke, he explained, a silly answer to an even sillier question. Earlier, he'd had to explain to me what a by-line was. I had it in my head it was something to do with football. The truth is, Diarmid and I didn't have enough going for each other for our entanglement to last one minute longer than it did.

The night before Jocelyn died, Diarmid had been working on a piece for a Sunday newspaper, for the magazine section of that paper. They were running a series under the general heading 'Roots', and they'd asked him to write about Donegal and his relationship with Ireland altogether, and why he'd chosen not to live there. He'd been up all night trying to write it, chain-smoking and tearing his hair out, and had got into bed only half an hour before I was due to get out. When Aunt Hope telephoned, he was asleep. He was woken, eventually, by that insistent, alarming bell.

'Is there somewhere we can go that's private?' He'd found me in Garden Tools, where I was doing a stock check of shears and secateurs.

I knew at once something was catastrophically wrong. I could see it from his face and hear it from his voice, and I went cold. Finch, I thought, something's happened to Finch. Diarmid followed me up the stairs to the back room. There was a Belfast sink in there, a microwave and an electric kettle. It was the place we went, where we still go, to make our elevenses coffee and heat up our pizzas at lunchtime. There were two beaten-up armchairs in that room, and Diarmid sat me down in one. He pushed the other chair up close, sat down, took both my hands in his and held them tight, and told me.

She'd gone into the garden to cut a cabbage leaf. I think of it like that – of it being a leaf only, because of that book she gave me, *The Great Panjandrum Himself*. It helps to think of it like that – it's the necessary banana skin, for me, that people slip on on the way to funerals, the ridiculous thing that makes you smile even when your heart's breaking, that reveals to you the whole absurdity of life and death. She had gone into the garden before breakfast to feed the hens, and on the way back she'd stopped off at the veg patch and cut a cabbage for lunch. And she had died there. Dropped dead, face down in the cabbages. She was fifty-eight.

When, after twenty minutes, she hadn't returned, Aunt

Hope had gone to look for her. She'd run through the garden calling her name. She'd stopped and shouted, 'Your egg's hard-boiled! It's stone cold already! Where the hell are you?'

Aunt Hope told the doctor that Jocelyn had seemed perfectly well the night before, was her usual self, but when she came down in the morning she'd complained of a headache. She'd gulped a couple of aspirins before going out to feed the hens.

The doctor said he couldn't be certain, but he thought it was her heart. Probably a heart attack. The autopsy would reveal the cause. There would have to be an autopsy and an inquest, as was the law in cases of sudden death.

It was a cerebral aneurysm that killed Jocelyn, the autopsy revealed. Death would have been virtually instantaneous; she wouldn't have suffered at all; it was just one of those things, it could happen to anyone, the doctor told Aunt Hope – though it had to be said that, as with heart attacks, the risk of aneurysm was always greater for heavy drinkers and smokers.

It was booze and fags that killed Jocelyn. That's what the doctor was saying, not unkindly, in so many words.

Jocelyn! Dead! She had always been so strong and energetic. So vital, so alive. I couldn't believe it. I couldn't accept it. It wasn't true.

Diarmid put his arms round me, and I laid my head on his shoulder. 'Poor Hope,' he kept repeating into my hair as we cried together, 'poor, poor Hope, what will she do?'

I wanted to go down to Arizona straight away and be with Aunt Hope, but she said no. Her voice on the phone was calm and flat, as calm and flat as the sea seems when you look at it from a distance. She said thank you, she was all right, there was a lot to do, there was the funeral to arrange, she was very busy, it was best for her to be busy.

'Diarmid says, is there anything he can do to help with the funeral, with the arrangements?' I said. 'He says he'll do anything, put the notice in the papers, deal with the undertakers, anything. You only have to say.'

Aunt Hope said to thank him, he was very kind, but there was nothing. She said she preferred to be on her own just then.

Jocelyn had told Aunt Hope she wanted to be cremated. ('I don't want it, exactly,' she'd said, 'because I don't want to die. But when I am dead, I think I'd rather burn than rot. Provided they're sure I'm dead. I've no wish to play St Joan at my age.') That meant the crematorium in the county town. Diarmid and Finch and I went down for the ceremony together. We went by train. When it was over, Diarmid and Finch planned to go back on the train, while I drove Aunt Hope back to Arizona in her car. We'd agreed she shouldn't be alone that first night, after the cremation. Whatever she said. We'd agreed I should try and persuade Aunt Hope to let me stay with her for a week at least.

I'd imagined there'd be no more than a handful of us to say goodbye to Jocelyn – a few local farmers, the greengrocer regulars who took our produce, Bernie Mann who supplied us with manure, and a few of Jocelyn's relations from the north. I'd imagined a few of those would come out of the woodwork, relations tend to for funerals.

But the chapel was packed. They had to fetch extra chairs from a side room, but even then there weren't enough seats. When the service started, late, because of the seating problem, there was a crowd of people in the lobby area, pressing against the glass doors, trying to get a view.

Who were all these people I didn't know? They were actors, male and female, old and young; theatre managers and directors; TV and radio producers; cameramen and technicians. They were people Jocelyn had worked with, recently or a long time ago. They were Jocelyn's colleagues and admirers. Her friends.

The people I'd imagined would be there, Bernie Mann and so on, were there. And a handful of relations with

Manchester accents. I talked to some of them afterwards, at the wake.

Sitting beside Aunt Hope in the front row, twisting my head to watch the stream of people flowing in, I thought, It's a theatre, not a chapel. These people are the audience, they've come for a performance.

Four famous, or nearly famous, faces read poems or speeches from plays during the service. One famous voice sang an unaccompanied solo, 'Blow the Wind Southerly'.

I thought, all those years Jocelyn lived with us, I never asked her about her life, her other life. I didn't ask her one question that I remember. And now I can't ask her anything.

I turned my head away when the coffin began its glide towards the curtain. I knew it was going to, I had my eyes fixed on it, but the moment Aunt Hope's bunch of garden flowers, the only flowers that adorned it, started to wobble, I looked away.

Anyway, Jocelyn wasn't in that closed pine long-box, heading for the furnace. Of course not. How could she be?

Aunt Hope, pale and composed, stood in the doorway, shaking hands. A lot of people kissed her, on both cheeks. People I didn't know. A few gripped her by the shoulders, without speaking, or clasped her hands and hung on to them, reluctant to let go. One man I saw, a big man, white-haired, who wore a pink bow tie with his black coat, bowed.

We walked in the sunshine to a pub – hotel, rather – the White Hart. A room upstairs had been set aside for us. At the far end was a table with a buffet laid out and, at one end, rows and rows of upside-down glasses. Two lily-white boys in green jackets went round with bottles of wine.

I remember suddenly feeling lost and out of it in that crush of cheerful mourners. Seeking out Diarmid to pinch a cigarette off him, I shouted in his ear, 'How did Aunt Hope manage to organise all this? Why is she coping so well? How?' (For through a gap in the heads we could see my unsociable aunt, with Finch by her side, at the centre of an animated group.)

Diarmid shrugged and smiled a search-me smile, and turned back to the actor he'd been talking to.

Three days after the funeral Aunt Hope swallowed the contents of a full bottle of sleeping pills, washing them down with the equivalent of two tall glasses of whisky and water. Then she went upstairs, got into bed, switched off her bedside light and closed her eyes.

She had coped with the funeral because she knew she wasn't going to have to cope with anything at all much longer. She had already made her decision. Having made it, she was then able to manage everything: the service, the people, the wake, the laughter. Having made it, she was able not just to act, but to be, serene.

It wasn't a messy suicide, as suicides go. It wasn't in the same class of cruelty as her father's, say. But then hatred must have been the spur for him. Triggered by disappointment, perhaps. But you'd have to hate a lot to blow your head off in your own front hall. When you know who's going to find you. I think about it sometimes, and I allow myself a picture of the scene. Look, here's my beautiful step-grandmother Irene, setting off for the shops with her basket on her arm. There she goes, into the butcher's for a piece of brisket. Out she comes, consulting her shopping list. A quick pop into the baker's – 'No, no buns today, thank you; I'll just take the one loaf, must watch the pennies!' On to the grocer's for a pound of lard. And so on, up and down the High Street, in and out the shops, till the basket's full. 'Good morning, Mrs Chillingworth, how are you today?' And now she's coming back, pleased with her purchases, humming a little tune – thinking, as she mounts the step and slips her latchkey in the lock, What I could do with now is *a nice cup of tea*.

How he must have hated her. That's not what I think, it's what I know. You're never going to forget this one, baby, so long as you live. I can hear him say it, as he loads the gun.

Aunt Hope didn't do that to us. It wasn't hatred that prompted her. She left notes. She left her affairs in order, paid all her bills. In the days between Jocelyn's funeral and her own death she cleaned and tidied the house from top to bottom, burned her letters, cleared out junk. And she arranged for Bernie Mann to take the hens, which he did the day before she died, and which suited him as he already kept a few on a scratch-what-you-can barnyard basis.

I'm not angry at her now. Four years on, I can see she tried to warn me, though I refused to understand her at the time. That evening of the funeral, when she and I went back to Arizona and sat at the kitchen table, pushing the whisky bottle back and forth, she said, 'About Finch. I worry about you and Finch. It's not good to see you two together. It's never been good to see you two together. But I have a feeling, a strong feeling' – she paused to sip her whisky – 'that it will be all right between you one day. I don't know when, it may take a long time. He may be grown-up before it happens, but I think, I believe, it will. And I think you should try to believe it will.'

We sat in silence, drinking for a while. Eventually she said, quite matter of factly, 'I've managed a whole week now – an achievement, surely. I can't live without her, you know, Hannah. I'm sure you realise that.'

And I, tanked up with whisky and emotion, got up and put my arms round her. 'Don't worry, Aunt Hope,' I said. 'I'll look after you. You won't have to be lonely. You can live with us, Diarmid and Finch and me – or we'll come down to Arizona and live with you. Whatever you prefer. Whatever you want. You won't have to be lonely, I promise. I won't let you be.' I loved her at that moment. I put all the love I felt into my arms that were holding her, in the way I imagine healers do, so she would really feel my love, really know. *I love you, Aunt Hope.* I held her tight. Then I released her.

Aunt Hope, who didn't smoke – I'd never seen her smoke in all those years – took a cigarette out of my packet, lying open on the table, flicked my lighter and lit up. 'I'm not lonely.' She inhaled deeply, tipping her head back, letting the smoke escape. 'I'm not lonely as such. I'm not lonely for just anyone – don't get me wrong, I'm not meaning to be unkind, I'm touched and grateful for your offer. I'm lonely for *her*.'

You're haunted after someone dies. Things about them – facial expressions, gestures, voice, laughter – come back like ghosts to tell you never again. Never again will you hear or see this. (Except in dreams, except in memory, never, never, never, never, never again.)

After Aunt Hope's death I became obsessed with her handwriting – strong and quirky, not at all the regular blackboard hand you'd expect – and I carried notes she'd written me, and even an old shopping list, around in my pocket or bag. I found myself prowling as she prowled when Uncle Ber died, and clapping my hand over my mouth in the way she did then (as though she'd just remembered, or forgotten, something). Whole conversations came back to me; whole detailed scenes were laid out for me to watch.

In one of these, we're in the Long Room, Aunt Hope, Jocelyn, Diarmid, Finch and I. It's a summer day, sunny but windy, and the curtains are blowing about and somewhere I can hear a door banging – the larder door, it could be. We've been working in the garden all morning, grass-cutting (Jocelyn), hedge-cutting (Diarmid), weeding (Aunt Hope and I), reading, on a lilo (Finch), and we're all flaked out in chairs, lying back, with our legs stretched out, our arms hanging down over the arms of our chairs. All except Diarmid who, in T-shirt and jeans, and with hedge-clippings in his hair, is examining the bookshelves with a mug of beer in his hand.

'You don't have much biography, do you?' Diarmid turns to Aunt Hope. 'I've only just noticed. Any reason?'

'There's never been much money to spare for new hardback books,' Aunt Hope says, 'and biographies tend to be expensive. When we lived in Green Copse Road we had an excellent public library a short bus ride away and anything I wanted to read I could get from there. But since you ask, I do have a problem with biographies – I don't like the curve they follow. You know, that semicircle, up, round and down. I don't like that.'

'But that's inevitable.' Diarmid sounds amazed. 'That's the birth-life-death curve. If you're writing a life I can't see how you can avoid it.'

'I don't like it,' Aunt Hope says. 'I don't care for that inevitability. Those awful endings – you know: "Only a straggle of bareheaded mourners braved the winter wind/summer rain to follow the coffin up the winding hill" or "On his headstone are engraved these words . . ." So depressing, don't you think? So defeating.'

'But logical,' Finch murmurs from his chair.

Diarmid stands by the bookshelves, incredulously shaking his head. 'I think you're being a bit sweeping there, Hope. Some biographies don't end as you describe. Some have a little life-after-death piece in the form of an envoi or a coda or what have you. A postscript, an epilogue. Organ music of a triumphal or affecting kind.'

'It's not just the ending I've a quarrel with,' Aunt Hope says. 'It's the whole curve, and that *shutter of time darkening ceaselessly*. They allow so little room for manoeuvre. You can be pretty sure most of the interest will be in the middle – that's always the place where the mountains are conquered or the oceans sailed, or the books written. Then, unless the subject dies suddenly in his or her prime, all you've got left to look forward to is the long descent, health failing, friends falling away . . .'

'Well, what would you do instead then?' Diarmid says. 'If you were writing a biography, how would you get round the problem?' To Jocelyn he says, 'What a difficult friend you have. Is she always so difficult?'

'Yes. Always,' Jocelyn says, and she smiles, revealing her little child's teeth, still perfect on the surface, after all these years.

'I don't know,' Aunt Hope says. 'I really don't have any idea. I suppose I could do the funeral scene on page one and get it over with. Or I could sandwich it in the middle somewhere, in a parenthesis, between feats of derring-do. Or – no, no. No, there probably isn't a way, a satisfactory way, an honest way, round this particular problem.'

'Aha,' Diarmid says, pleased with himself, 'Aha.' And he drains his beer mug. 'All you're really saying is, you don't want to die. And I'm with you there. Is there any lunch today? Would you like me to make it?'

I took no part in this scene, as you see. I was just an observer. But I had opinions. I found myself on Aunt Hope's side for once. Not about biography itself – I hadn't read any – but with her reservations, as she described them, about the shape, or do I mean course, biography takes. I understood her resistance to that relentless, inevitable curve.

So I'm sure that Aunt Hope did not have a death wish as such. It must have been that, when Jocelyn died, and without warning, with no opportunity for hand-holding and good-byes, she found she did not want to live, and had to choose between those two positions. It must have been something like that.

That friend of Diarmid's, Brian, whom he used to share with – I saw him on the tube the other day. I kept looking at this baldheaded man and thinking, Is it, or isn't it? He was on the opposite side, a very long way down, and there were strap-hangers blocking my view. If it was Brian, he was thinner than I remembered him.

I've felt badly about Brian, when I've allowed myself to, because I was responsible for his having to leave Diarmid's flat. Not at the time, of course. I felt nothing then. When you're in love you don't consider other people, in my experience. They simply don't exist. If my moving in meant Brian having to move out, well, tough. I didn't worry about it at the time.

But I'd liked Brian when I'd known him. He was a kind, funny man, and a brilliant cook. (When I took over, the cooking went downhill in a one-in-seven gradient.) I remember he wished me luck before he left.

The carriage emptied at Victoria, but Brian, or the Brian lookalike, was still there. I kept on staring and willing him to look in my direction, and suddenly he did. He blinked and shook his head. Then he came over and sat beside me.

'How are you?' we both said.

'What are you up to?' he said.

I told him I was going on a trip – to Arizona. I'd saved all these air miles, and I was going soon.

'Arizona?' he said. 'Arizona! Is that God's own country? Or is that somewhere else?'

And I thought of that first summer at Arizona, when Aunt Hope, Jocelyn and I were decorating the place. I remembered nipping out for a breather – 'skiving', Jocelyn said it was – and standing on the porch and looking out. And I remembered shading my eyes – the way women do in Westerns when they're expecting their loved one to ride in – and seeing in front of me, so clear it was like a memory, not the humpy, tussocky garden we hadn't got round to yet, but a pump and the metal vanes of some sort of windmill, and a stockyard fence; and beyond them a grassy plain, or plateau, dotted with pink flowers; and beyond that, far, far in the distance, so far I had to strain to see them, a line of hills, mauvish, that might turn out to be mountains; and above them a white, simply enormous sky.

Travellers aren't allowed to visit Eggshell Arch without a back-country permit from the Navajo Nation Parks and Recreation Department, but that's not a problem. According to the issue of *Arizona Highways* magazine I stole from a waiting room, the permit is obtainable on application, and costs five dollars.

The journey to Eggshell is a 'four-wheel-drive proposition', the article in this issue says. The route is lonely and rough and, after dark, hazardous – travellers should plan to be out of the area by nightfall.

To get there I shall drive through a section of the Navajo Indian Reservation, where I can view the purple Navajo Mountain across a desert of pinks and blues. I shall be following this exact, exacting route: from Tuba City, take US 160 east to State Route 98; go north on 98 for 11.5 miles; right at Navajo Route 16 (a paved, though unmarked, road); 5.2 miles to the Inscription House Full Gospel Church; left onto dirt road; left at first fork, left at second fork, right at third fork (I'll spot a fenced cornfield if I'm on the right dirt track); continue 3.5 miles till road vanishes on a sandstone slab; walk 0.4 of a mile south, then east 0.25 miles. That will take me to Toenleshushe Canyon and, spanning the 600-feet-deep chasm, arching over it, in flame-red sandstone, Eggshell Arch. Nothing like an eggshell, from the photograph. Seventy-five feet across. A geological miracle, the article says.

So I shall have to hire a Jeep to make this trip, which as described here does not sound like trailer country, the 'one big trailer park' Finch swears Arizona is. (That 'walk' to Eggshell, when the dirt road runs out, is a rocky, hilly hike and takes a good half-hour even if you're in shape.) Eggshell, as a black and white photograph, featured in Jack Bowdell's exhibition, which is why I want to go there. I'd like to see the monuments and places he saw. The Hopi Reservation in northeast Arizona, for example. The Haunted Wilderness, whatever Finch says. And Sedona, and Verde Valley, and the Pinaleno Mountains.

But Arizona is vast, the Navajo Reservation alone 26,000 square miles – about the size of Ireland, it says here. You couldn't expect to see much on a two-week visit. There may not be time to take in all the towns on my list – Phoenix, Bisbee, Tucson, Prescott, Tombstone.